P9-CLZ-852

UNDUE
INFLUENCE

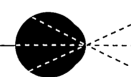

This Large Print Book carries the
Seal of Approval of N.A.V.H.

UNDUE
INFLUENCE

SHELBY YASTROW

Thorndike Press • Thorndike, Maine

Library of Congress Cataloging in Publication Data:

Yastrow, Shelby.
   Undue influence : a novel / Shelby Yastrow.
   p. cm.
   ISBN 1-56054-132-6 (alk. paper : lg. print)
   1. Large type books. I. Title.
[PS3575.A754U5   1991]   91-2413
813'.54—dc20   CIP

This book is a work of fiction. Names, characters, places, and incidents are used fictitiously. This work of fiction does not purport to be a factual record of real events or real people. The actions and motivations of the characters named after real people are entirely fictional and should not be considered real or factual.

Thorndike Press Large Print edition published in 1991 by arrangement with Contemporary Books, Inc.

Cover design by Sean Pringle.

The tree indicium is a trademark of Thorndike Press.

This book is printed on acid-free, high opacity paper.

For Sybil, whose own achievements prove
that she can do anything — except
teach me to use the PC — and
to Judge Glenn K. Seidenfeld,
who trusted me more than I would have

PART I
THURSDAY

1

STILLMAN
Benjamin Stillman, 83, resting at
Webster Funeral Home. Private
interment Saturday. No flowers.

"Mr. Ogden's office."

"Ogden the lawyer?"

"Yes, ma'am. Philip Ogden. Who's calling, please?"

"The name's Yolandis, Mrs. Martha Yolandis. Can I talk to Mr. Ogden?"

"One moment, please." Carol Stephenson put the caller on hold and pushed another button on the phone.

"Yeah, Carol?"

"Phil, there's a Mrs. Yolandis on line two. I don't recognize the name and she didn't say why she's calling."

"Okay, put her through." *Yolandis,* he thought, *I don't know any Yolandis.* He leaned back in his chair and automatically reached for a yellow notepad. His poplin topcoat, still damp from the cold rain so typical in

Chicago in the fall, was carelessly thrown over one of the other chairs. His office was cluttered — even for a lawyer — and the coat simply added to the disarray.

Philip Ogden was not the kind of lawyer who appears in slick television dramas. His modest practice, begun six years earlier, involved mostly wills, contracts, and routine real estate transfers. Little excitement — let alone adversity — enlivened his day-to-day work. And he liked it that way. Phil was fascinated with the words or, more specifically, the language of the law. It was the precision, the exact word for the intended expression, that intrigued him, and had since that first year in law school when he had learned how much could depend on precise wording. One phrase omitted and an entire trust could be thrown out for violating the Rule Against Perpetuities; an inadvertent misuse of a few words and an entire generation could be disinherited. Phil's documents were both technically correct and understandable — rare traits among lawyers. His practice produced enough income for his needs, but only because his needs were far from extravagant.

He had graduated from law school ten years earlier, spending the first four years of his practice in a twelve-lawyer firm that did mostly bankruptcy and collection work. He hated it. The work was depressing, and the office politics were worse. As soon as he developed a nucleus of clients he could count on to stay with him, he gave notice. He decided to go it alone; he knew it would be risky, but the risk of failure was preferable to the certainty of unhappiness.

He was above average in height. His modishly long black hair framed an angular face, the most remarkable features of which were dark, deep-set eyes and a square, firm jaw. While his overall appearance was nonthreatening to men, it was devilishly appealing to women. He wore inexpensive clothes and a Timex wristwatch.

"This is Phil Ogden." His voice was calm and professional.

"It's about Mr. Stillman. I have to see you about Mr. Stillman. He asked me to see you."

"Wait a minute, Mrs. — uh — Mrs. Yolandis, is it? I'm sorry, but I don't recall a Mr. Stillman. Do I know him?"

There was a slight pause, a beat just long enough for the caller to question whether she had the right Mr. Philip Ogden.

"Aren't you the Mr. Ogden who is a lawyer and does wills?"

"Well, yes. And other things."

"And didn't you do a will for Mr. Benjamin Stillman?"

"I may have. It'll only take a minute to check, but I'm not sure I should answer that without his consent."

"Then we have a problem, young man. Mr. Stillman died last night," Martha Yolandis stated imperiously.

"Oh. But I — "

"He gave me a letter that said to call you right after he died. And he gave me an envelope for you. That is, if you're the right Mr. Ogden."

"Excuse me, Mrs. Yolandis. Please hold on a minute." He pressed the hold button.

Not every lawyer grieves when he learns of a client's death — especially when he thinks there's a chance he could handle the estate. Probate work is a lawyer's dream. Simple, no pressure, and generally no opposition. And who's to complain about the quality of the work or the amount of the fee? The client's dead, the family's mourning, and the beneficiaries are getting a windfall.

With that in mind, and not bothering with the phone, Philip Ogden shouted toward his open office door: "Carol, quick, check to see if we have a will for a Benjamin Stillman."

Carol Stephenson poked her head in the door and showed one of her smug grins that said she was a step ahead of him. "Don't have to check, counselor. We did the will less than a year ago, and I remember Mr. Stillman. Nice old guy."

"How do you remember these things? His name doesn't even ring a bell with me."

Carol looked exactly like the kind of secretary a woman would hire for her husband: a little too short and a little too fat. But her secretarial skills were impeccable, and her efficiency and organization — to say nothing of her excellent memory — perfectly complemented Phil's shortcomings in these areas. Conciseness of speech, however, was not one of her attributes.

"Don't forget," she said, "that I sit out there in the reception area. While the clients are waiting for their audience with you, they're just about sitting in my lap. It's only natural that we have some conversation. I don't remember them all, but some stand out.

"I remember this Mr. Stillman real well," she continued. "He wanted you to do the will while he waited, and he wanted to sign it the same day and not have to come back. So while he was sitting there he must've realized I was typing it up. I probably asked him a question, like whether he used a middle initial. And he acted like he thought he should explain — "

"Just a second, Carol." Phil punched the

blinking button on his phone. "Mrs. Yolandis? Yes, we did the will for Mr. Stillman."

"I thought I had the right Mr. Ogden. Can I bring you the envelope? I have your address. I can be in the Loop in an hour."

"Please. I'll be here all day."

Phil turned to his secretary and explained that Mr. Stillman had died the night before and that this Mrs. Yolandis was bringing in some papers.

"I'm sorry to hear it. He seemed like such a nice old guy." Carol left the office and returned a minute later carrying a slim manila folder. "Not much here. Just our office copy of a simple one-page will — short even for you, Phil — and a few notes of yours. They say no relatives and — listen to this — 'client won't disclose assets.'"

"And we know what that means, don't we?"

"Yes, that there aren't any assets. Sorry, pal. Doesn't look like we'll get rich on this one."

"Damn!" The lawyer tossed his pencil on the desk. "Whenever I get a call from a stranger, I think of an old Paul Newman movie where he was a young lawyer — in Philadelphia, I think, in a big firm. Some old lady in a fur coat with a poodle under her arm picks his name off the building directory in the lobby, marches into his office, and asks him to write a will leaving some of her money to the mutt. He thinks the whole thing is a practical joke cooked up by his pals. The more Newman tries to laugh it off, the more she insists. Finally, he figures he better do the dumb will before the dog pees on his desk. You can guess the rest. She has millions, she keeps him as her lawyer, he becomes senior partner in the firm. Mansion, limousines, the whole scene."

Despite his disappointment, Philip Ogden smiled wryly at Carol Stephenson, his friend and secretary for the six years since he had opened his own law office. "Carol, by any chance did Ben Stillman have a poodle with him out there in the waiting room?"

2

Martha Yolandis was one of those ageless women who could have been five years on either side of fifty. She was tall and strongly built, and on this brisk fall day she wore a no-nonsense windbreaker, which Carol took as the woman walked into Phil's office. She wore slacks, a sweater, sensible walking shoes, and no makeup or jewelry. Her slight accent, Phil guessed, was Slavic.

She took a seat facing the lawyer across his desk. The single window behind him provided a limited view of a few office buildings, certainly not a broad panorama but sufficient to demonstrate Chicago's eclectic architecture. Directly across the street stood the Cook County courthouse, officially called the Daley Center in honor of the late mayor, standing tall and occupying an entire square city block. Both the courthouse and the incomprehensible Picasso sculpture standing on its plaza had been constructed in the 1960s, but their intentionally rusted surfaces suggested greater age. While Phil's building was near the courthouse and the major title companies and banks — all important conveniences to a lawyer — it was older and therefore offered lower rents than the glitzier glass and steel buildings springing up all over the Loop.

"Here's the envelope Mr. Stillman wanted you to have. Don't know what's in it, but I think it's important."

"How so?" The word *important* sharpened his interest.

"Well, he *acted* like it was important. Made me promise over and over again to bring it to you right away."

At the lawyer's gentle prodding, Martha Yolandis began to speak more freely.

"I cleaned house for Mr. Stillman for nearly fifteen years. It was an apartment, small but comfortable. Came in once a week. Only saw him a few times, like when I came in extra early. Mostly he'd already be at work. He'd leave my pay in the silverware drawer."

The lawyer was struck by the woman's ability to relate facts, even though she had spoken only a few sentences and often dropped the first word. Clear and concise; no frills. *She may be an unpolished cleaning lady,* he thought, *but she's no dummy.*

"Had the feeling," she continued, "he had no family, or even close friends. Guess I'm right, 'cause it was me he called from the hospital."

17

"When was that?"

"Almost three weeks ago. On a Tuesday. I'm at his place on Tuesdays, and that's when he called me. Told me he'd been ill and asked if I could leave early and come up to St. Francis Hospital. Then he'd give me my money. Asked me to bring a few things — personal things like socks and slippers. And I was to bring the metal strongbox he kept in a dresser drawer. 'Make sure you don't forget the box,' he said. Said that over and over again, maybe three or four times."

"Was the box locked?"

"Didn't try to open it, Mr. Ogden," she said with a touch of resentment. "But it had one of those things with the numbers on it. Dial the right numbers and you could open the box. Wouldn't need a key."

"I understand. Did he tell you what he kept in the box, or did he open it in front of you at the hospital?"

"Lord, no! Mr. Stillman was a very private man. And when I brought it to him he acted like it held important things. Kept making sure it was locked. Wanted me to make room for it right there on the nightstand next to him, not on the dresser across the room."

Phil reached for the yellow pad on which he had started making notes during their phone conversation. "Did Mr. Stillman tell

18

you why he was in the hospital?"

"He didn't, but I could tell it was serious as soon as I walked in. He was getting a lot of attention from the nurses, and there were those god-awful tubes everywhere. Could see he was scared, too. So when I left, I stopped by the place where the nurses sit. Explained that I was the only person he had, and asked them what was wrong with him and if I should be doing anything. They called for one of those young doctors — I think they're doctors, or will be when they grow — "

"You mean interns?"

"Whatever. Anyway, this young man told me that Mr. Stillman had cancer — called it something else at first — and that it didn't look so good for him. That's about all he said, but that was enough for me. I was already starting to think about losing my Tuesdays."

One tough lady, Phil thought. Tough, or just plain cold and self-centered. Here she was, describing a dying man in obvious fear and pain, and she was worried about losing her Tuesday work.

"How old was he?"

"Not sure, but I'd guess about eighty. Used to think he was younger, but he looked a lot older there in that hospital bed."

"And did he stay in the hospital until he died?"

"Yes, but that wasn't until last night."

"How did you find out he died?"

"They called me from the hospital. I left my name when I was there, and they knew I stopped by to see him two or three times. They also said that he put my name on the forms."

"As the person to be contacted?"

"I suppose."

Phil thought it was about time to get to the point.

"What about the envelope?"

Martha Yolandis chose her next words very carefully. "Well, there are really *two* envelopes. But only one of them is for you. The other one's for me. Told me to open it after he died."

Phil thought a moment, and then plunged ahead. "Do you want to tell me what was in yours?"

"If you tell me what's in yours."

Phil couldn't help admiring the lady. *She has brass,* he thought, *and now she has me playing I'll-show-you-mine-if-you-show-me-yours.*

"I can't promise to do that, Mrs. Yolandis, until I see what's in my envelope. Mr. Stillman might have intended it to be confidential, and as a lawyer I'd have to treat it that way."

"Fair enough," she replied. "You read it and then let me know if you want to tell

20

me what's in it. If you do, then I'll let you read mine."

"Somehow I have the feeling you're winning this game."

"Well, let's just say I had more time than you to think about it." She smiled for the first time. "Even practiced it last night."

Her smile prompted him to smile in return. He slit open "his" envelope and withdrew several documents clipped to a neatly handwritten letter on the stationery of St. Francis Hospital.

November 3, 1989

Dear Mr. Ogden,

If Martha is up to her usual efficiency, you will be reading this within a few hours of my death. I have notified the hospital staff to contact her, and I asked her to call you and deliver these papers to you in person. (I expect therefore that she is in your office as you're reading this, and that she is desperate to know what I am writing. I have no objection to your telling her.)

Phil was struck by Stillman's intuition about Mrs. Yolandis. He interrupted his reading to look up at her, his dark eyes twinkling. "Okay, my friend," he grinned, "you've got a deal. Show me what Mr. Stillman gave you in your envelope, and then I'll show you what he gave me."

Mrs. Yolandis would have preferred it the other way around, but she decided to go along. Mr. Stillman had told her he was putting his trust in this young man. She might as well do the same.

"Here." She handed the lawyer a small letter-size envelope that she had previously opened. Three sheets of hospital stationery were enclosed, and on them were the neatly printed words of Benjamin Stillman. Phil noticed that this block-printed letter used plainer language than the one addressed to him. He assumed Stillman had chosen this simpler style to insure that his cleaning lady would not misunderstand him.

November 3, 1989

Dear Martha,

Thank you for taking care of my apartment, and thank you for visiting me in the hospital and bringing my things.

I would like you to do some more things for me when I am gone. I know I can depend on you.

1. As soon as you learn of my death, call Webster Funeral Home (555-9288) and tell them. I already made burial arrangements with them and the cemetery and prepaid everything. I do not want a funeral service.

2. Call Mr. William Barnett at Barnett Brothers where I work (555-8180), and tell him that I died. Let him know that he should send whatever is due me to Mr. Philip Ogden. Mr. Ogden will be handling my affairs. You have his address on the other envelope I gave you.

3. Call Mr. Ogden (555-0419). Arrange to take him the envelope I gave you with his name on it.

4. Call my landlady, Mrs. Fortino (555-9754), and tell her I'm gone, but ask her not to rent my apartment until Mr. Ogden can arrange to have my furniture and other belongings packed up and disposed of.

5. I'm sure my apartment is tidy since you have been there to pick up, but please go back to unplug the appliances, strip the bed, and turn down the heat. While you are there, I would like you to take any of my things you would like for yourself. That would be better than selling them used or giving them to strangers.

I am enclosing something for you. I'm sorry I didn't have enough cash with me, and I didn't want to give you a check in case the bank freezes my account after my *death. I assure you that this bond is just as good as cash. Mr. Ogden or any broker or banker can help you turn it in for money.*

You have been very kind. The bond should take care of you for your troubles. Be very careful not to lose it!

Good luck in finding work on Tuesdays.

Benjamin Stillman

Phil was impressed by Stillman's attention to detail and his generosity toward Mrs. Yolandis. However, he still thought it strange that this dying man would find it necessary to place so much reliance on a cleaning lady he saw only rarely. Even if he didn't have close family, he must have had someone, perhaps a niece or nephew, or maybe one of the people he knew from work.

"Have you made the telephone calls yet?"

"Called the funeral home, but the hospital already reached 'em. Good thing I called, though. They want me to bring over a suit and some things to dress him in. Then I called that Mr. Barnett. Decided not to call the landlady until I saw you, in case you want me to tell her anything."

"Good thinking. Do you have the bond with you?"

"I do."

Philip Ogden smiled. "Since Mr. Stillman said I might help you redeem — uh — turn it in for cash, perhaps I should see it."

Martha Yolandis seemed hesitant. Nevertheless, she reached into her purse, withdrew a folded document, and handed it to the lawyer.

Phil unfolded the thick paper bordered with curlicues and found himself staring at a ten-thousand-dollar municipal bond with several interest coupons attached. The bond was payable to bearer.

Before he could speak, Martha Yolandis blurted the question that had haunted her since she first opened her envelope: "Does this mean what I think it means? Is this thing really worth ten thousand dollars?"

Phil checked the interest rate of eight percent printed on the face of the bond, mentally comparing it with what he knew of current bond rates. "Indeed it is. It might be worth a little more or a little less, depending on today's bond market, but it should be very close. In fact, one of the semi-annual interest coupons is mature, and you can snip it off and turn it in right now for an extra four hundred dollars. And please be careful with this thing. It's what we call a bearer bond, and losing it would be like losing cash. Either lock it up in a bank box, or — "

But she wasn't listening. "You mean one of those little things is worth four hundred dollars, and it doesn't even come off of the ten thousand?"

"That's right."

"That's a lot of day work!"

Martha Yolandis, who had shown herself to be so efficient, capable, and stoic up to this moment, broke down in tears. She had a tissue out before Phil could react.

Thinking she would prefer not to even speak for a few minutes, Phil returned to the letter Ben Stillman had written to him. "I'll finish reading this, Mrs. Yolandis, and then we can talk. In the meantime, you can think about how you want to spend that ten thousand dollars." He leaned back in his chair and resumed reading his letter.

First, I think I should tell you a little about me.

I'm 83 years old and live alone. For over 40 years I have worked at Barnett Brothers brokerage house on LaSalle Street. It's a successful firm, but not as warm and friendly a place to work as when the original Barnett Brothers were there. In more recent years, everything centered on the interests of the partners and their clients, and little consideration was given to the "hired help."

But that's not surprising these days.

I worked in the accounting department. It was my responsibility to post transactions and check and balance the accounts of the partners and their clients.

To get right to the point: You are the first to know that my holdings are worth approximately $8,000,000.

Phil suddenly sat up. *Eight million dollars! Christ!* He took a deep breath, shifted forward in his chair, and slowed down his reading to be sure he wouldn't miss anything. Martha Yolandis watched him like an eagle but resisted the temptation to break in with questions.

The size of my estate will surely send shock waves throughout the community in view of my modest employment and lifestyle. Few would believe that this was the result of prudent investment management and frugal living.

Many will attempt to lay claim to my holdings, either as "rightful owners" or as forgotten relatives. I also expect that my affairs will be questioned by Barnett Brothers and may even arouse the interest of law enforcement agencies. I beg that you vigorously defend against all such attacks!

27

Why did I select you to write my will and serve as executor of my estate? My reasons are simple and may sound superficial. I was never entirely satisfied with my previous will, and I finally decided to do something about it. My landlady, Mrs. Fortino, mentioned that you represented her in a real estate transaction. She said you answered her calls promptly, you were courteous to her, and your fees were reasonable. I have known Mrs. Fortino many years, and if you could treat her with courtesy and charge a fee that she considered fair, I felt that you deserved my trust and confidence. Also, as far as I could tell, you had no connections with Barnett Brothers or any of the firm's partners, and I'm sure you will understand — or come to understand — why this is important.

You will not be able to verify the size of my estate until you are permitted entry into my safe-deposit box (which is identified, along with all my other assets, on the attached pages). For temporary substantiation, I am enclosing the most recent statements of my accounts with several banks and brokerage houses. (I did not handle my personal investments through Barnett Brothers, for reasons that should be obvious.)

You will see that my estimate of

$8,000,000 is conservative.
I'm sure that I can count on you to handle everything in accordance with my wishes.

Benjamin Stillman

As Phil quickly examined the other papers included with the letter, his excitement started to mount. His hands and eyes moved constantly from sheet to sheet, as if he were having trouble concentrating on the material spread out in front of him.

There were account statements from several brokerage firms and banks, an identification of Stillman's bank safe-deposit box together with a meticulously prepared inventory of its contents (with the key taped to it), and an authorization to pick up the metal strongbox from the vault at St. Francis Hospital. There was also a note furnishing Phil the combination to the strongbox lock. This box, according to Stillman's notes, contained papers that had no value in themselves but would be helpful in tracing past transactions, filling out tax returns, and the like. The signed will was not included in the envelope, nor was it listed in the inventory of the bank safe-deposit box. Phil therefore assumed — and hoped — that he would find it in the strongbox.

Without speaking to Martha Yolandis,

whose patience was visibly fading, he reached for the manila folder Carol had brought him earlier. He read the unsigned office copy of Stillman's will, rapidly scanning the opening paragraphs and Article I, boilerplate clauses attesting to Stillman's soundness of mind and declaring this to be his last will and testament. He stopped abruptly when he had finished reading Article II.

"Jesus Christ!" he exclaimed.

ARTICLE II

I give, devise and bequeath all of the property which I may own at the time of my death, real or personal, tangible or intangible, wherever situated, to the Beth Zion Synagogue, located at 2100 Sherman Avenue, Chicago, Illinois, as follows:

(1) Twenty percent (20%) thereof shall be used as the governing board of said Synagogue may determine in its own discretion for its own purposes; and

(2) Eighty percent (80%) thereof shall be used to create a trust fund to be used as the governing board of said Synagogue may determine in its own discretion for the purpose of furthering other Jewish causes.

Now Phil had a glimmer of recollection.

The guy had come in without an appointment. He wanted to leave whatever he had to his place of worship. He wouldn't disclose his assets and didn't see why it was necessary to mention who his relatives were. Actually, it *wasn't* necessary as long as he didn't have a wife, and he said he didn't. Phil had simply drawn the will so that Stillman, who apparently didn't have any close relatives, could leave what he had to the place where he prayed and where he probably had his only friends and social life. *But damn! I can't place him; no face, no voice.*

Phil looked up and spoke quietly to Mrs. Yolandis, whose curiosity was by now clearly getting the best of her. She could see that the lawyer on the other side of the desk had been absorbed in more than routine papers.

"Before we talk about what's in here, Mrs. Yolandis, are you sure that Mr. Stillman didn't have any family at all? Any brothers or sisters, or anyone?"

"Don't know anything about no family," she replied. "He never said anything about relatives, not even when I saw him at the hospital, and I never saw anyone visit him there or at the apartment. Just thought all along that he never had anyone."

"You probably knew that Mr. Stillman was Jewish. Did he strike you as a deeply religious man?"

"Oh, I don't know. Never thought about it. Didn't even know he was a Jew. If he went to that Jewish church next door, I never knew about it."

"Next door?" Stillman had given his home address as 2104 Sherman Avenue. Phil knew the area. It was on Chicago's North Side, in the area known as West Rogers Park.

"Yes, next door to his apartment building."

"Is that the Beth Zion Synagogue?"

"Don't know the name. Could be."

"On Sherman Avenue?"

"Sure. Right next door."

"Now, Mrs. Yolandis — "

"Call me Martha," she interrupted, "Nobody calls me by my last name." She realized that being friendly and informal might produce more information from the lawyer, who so far was getting much more than he was giving. It was clear that the contents of the envelope she had delivered were of great interest, and she meant to learn as much as possible.

"You said you were going to tell me what was in there," she complained, nodding toward Benjamin Stillman's letter to Phil.

"You're right," said Phil. "We made a deal. And I was just about to do that." He then explained the contents of the letter —

he read most of it to her — and other papers he'd received from Benjamin Stillman. He thought it would somehow make the cleaning lady feel good to learn of the eight-million-dollar fortune her employer had accumulated and his generosity in leaving it to his synagogue.

However, by the time he finished speaking, Martha Yolandis's mood had visibly changed. Learning that Benjamin Stillman had so much more, and that he was giving it to others, destroyed the elation that had been growing within her since she had first opened her envelope the night before.

She was still only the cleaning lady and the errand runner! What he'd left her was nothing more than a tip. A goddamn *tip* for all her trouble.

"Here I thought he gave me everything he had. 'Take my things,' he said, 'and here's ten thousand dollars.' Then he goes and gives millions to a bunch of Jews who already have all the money they can ever spend. It's not fair. It's just not fair."

"Mrs. Yo — Martha, please — "

"And to hell with calling that dago landlady and going back to the apartment! Let them Jews do something for their goddamn money!"

With that, Martha Yolandis stormed out

3

"Carol, you better screen my calls for the rest of the day. And please call Sally. Tell her I might be a little late picking up the boys tonight."

Since the divorce, which Phil had resisted as long as his pride would permit, Thursday night had been his weeknight with Jeff and Charlie. Bowling and pizza had come to be the customary way of spending the evening; bowling because Mom couldn't, and pizza because Mom wouldn't. Bowling, of course, is the universal activity for divorced fathers and their sons. It was easy to do, Phil often explained, and the boys loved it. There were plenty of other dads around for conversation, and it was one of the few places where he could have a few beers without dragging the kids into a saloon.

Phil hated to let other things interfere with these Thursday outings, but he needed the time to assemble and study Benjamin Stillman's papers and he knew he should refamiliarize himself with the state statutes governing the administration of estates —

the Probate Act. His probate experience was limited to a handful of small estates involving no serious problems or adverse claims.

Other tasks to be done came to mind. He knew he should contact the administrative office at St. Francis Hospital and arrange to pick up Stillman's strongbox. And he should call the funeral home to learn of the arrangements and advise Mr. Webster that he, Phil, could pay the expenses from estate funds if necessary. The letter to Martha Yolandis said the arrangements had been prepaid, but perhaps there were some additional charges.

But was it too early to make these calls? After all, this could be nothing more than a snipe hunt. What if Stillman had revoked the will after he signed it? Or signed a subsequent will naming a different executor? Or what if Stillman was a fruitcake — a penniless fruitcake — who really left no substantial estate at all?

Phil quickly dismissed the idea of a subsequent will because only days before his death Stillman had written the letter explaining why he chose Phil as his lawyer and executor and urging him to defend against all attacks on the will. Why would he write such a letter if he had revoked this will or written a later one?

And as for the fear that Stillman really didn't

have any money to speak of, what about the ten-thousand-dollar bond for Mrs. Yolandis? Or the current statements of accounts enclosed in the envelope, which tended to substantiate the eight-million-dollar estimate?

And was there any cause to doubt Benjamin Stillman's sanity? His letters reflected an intelligent and careful mind, and he had been employed until his recent hospitalization in a position that required skill, concentration, and an eye for detail. A shaky mind could not have been hidden and would not have been tolerated. Phil knew the law didn't require that a man be brilliant to write a valid will; requisite mental capacity existed where the testator generally "knew the nature of his assets" and "the objects of his bounty." Stillman would seem to pass this test with flying colors.

No, as cautious as Philip Ogden thought he should be, all indications were that Benjamin Stillman had indeed been both rational and wealthy.

The first call to the hospital was quick. Yes, Mr. Stillman had left a metal strongbox in the hospital vault. Yes, he had signed an authorization for a Philip Ogden to pick up the box after Mr. Stillman "expired." And yes, Mr. Ogden could pick it up if he had proper identification. "Please come in Saturday," he was told. "Mr. Cox, the administrator, would be in then, and he's the only person authorized by Mr. Stillman to release it."

The call to Mr. Webster began as another routine conversation. Yes, Mr. Stillman had made all the burial arrangements, and yes, everything was prepaid. Responding to the lawyer's final question, Mr. Webster explained that the burial would take place at St. Mary's Cemetery on Saturday.

For an instant, the place and day of the interment made no impact on Phil. But then it registered.

"I beg your pardon, Mr. Webster. I wonder if there could be some mistake. Are you sure that Mr. Stillman is to be buried at St. Mary's — and on Saturday?"

"Certainly. I made the arrangements myself."

"Is that consistent with Mr. Stillman's instructions?"

"Precisely consistent, Mr. Ogden. Mr. Stillman explicitly directed his interment at St. Mary's. I admit he said nothing about Saturday, but I see nothing odd about the interment taking place at that time."

To fill the pause, Mr. Webster added: "Am I missing something, Mr. Ogden?"

"One of us is. Jews don't get buried on Saturday — which is their Sabbath — and they sure don't get buried in Catholic cemeteries."

Now it was Webster's turn to register surprise. "Jewish? Mr. Stillman Jewish?"

"Well, I assume as much. It may be premature to mention this, but he signed a will that leaves a substantial bequest to Beth — to Jewish charities. It was his principal bequest. There was nothing to indicate he *wasn't* Jewish, and the name Stillman could go either way."

"Mr. Ogden, would you mind waiting on the line a moment? I'll be right back."

For the next two or three minutes, Philip Ogden tried to recall the events of the past hour or so, searching for any clue he could have missed concerning Stillman's religion, family, or testamentary motives. Nothing came to mind while he doodled and waited for Mr. Webster to return to the line.

"Still there, Mr. Ogden?"

"Uh-huh."

"I may not be able to confirm absolutely that Mr. Stillman was a Catholic, although his instructions to us would indicate as much. But I assure you he wasn't a Jew."

"How do you know that?"

"I just checked the body. Need I say more?"

"I'll be damned," muttered the lawyer.

39

4

"N-42."

Throughout the large hall, hands were already reaching out to place plastic chips on small squares.

A moment later the nasal voice slowly repeated the number into the microphone. "N — 4 — 2."

"Marty! Wake up! You have an N-42 right there. What's the matter with you tonight?"

It was unlike Martha Yolandis to miss a number. She lived for the bingo games she attended two and sometimes three nights a week. They were her only real recreation. She enjoyed the excitement of the game, and she looked forward to these evenings with other bingo followers with whom she had become friendly over the past few years. Most of her closest friends attended these games and most of them, like Martha, worked days as cleaning ladies. Her group referred to themselves as the Bingo Buddies.

The Thursday night game was at the hall of the Veterans of Foreign Wars, and it was her favorite. The coffee was free and the sandwiches generous and reasonably priced. Also, the staff who worked the VFW games was expert at maximizing the excitement in the hall by cheering, giving spontaneous pep talks to losers, applauding winners, and racing around the hall to pat backs, deliver refreshments, and joke around with the regulars. The Bingo Buddies suspected that these workers had their own "refreshments" in the back room, which accounted for their happy attitude as well as the large number of volunteers among them.

It was a far cry from some of the church games where the callers almost whispered the numbers and the floor workers tiptoed around the room. And where the players had to get their own coffee — and pay a quarter at that!

But Martha Yolandis could not get herself in the mood to enjoy tonight's game. She missed numbers and abstained from her usual banter with the workers and her fellow players. She was grateful when the fifteen-minute intermission was announced, and she even considered going home.

"C'mon, Marty, what's eatin' you?" This from Rosemary York, also a cleaning lady and Martha's best friend on the bingo circuit. They nearly always came to the games together, played eight cards between them, and pooled their winnings and losses. Their

41

friendship had reached the point where there was little that Marty and Rosie didn't confide to one another.

"I'm all messed up, Rosie. I'm not even sure if I should be happy or sad."

Knowing she had an attentive and understanding listener, Martha Yolandis confessed the news of Benjamin Stillman's death, his letter and gift to her, his letter to Philip Ogden, and his will. As other Bingo Buddies came by, they too were filled in, and they in turn offered their ideas as to how Stillman had come by his money, why he left it to "a bunch of Jews," and why he gave "only" ten thousand dollars to Martha. Some thought she was lucky and some thought she'd been cheated, but all envied her gain and her place in the spotlight. The conversation lasted well beyond intermission, and none of the participants returned to the game.

And so the evening ended, with several ladies going their separate ways, each eager to recount Martha Yolandis's adventure to anyone who would listen. By mid-morning Friday many had heard and in turn had relayed the news to others.

Somewhere in the telling and retelling of the story the next day, it was not surprising that it reached the ear of Eloise Byrd.

PART II
SATURDAY

5

MYSTERY RECLUSE LEAVES MILLIONS TO SYNAGOGUE

BY ELOISE BYRD

Benjamin Stillman, 83, who worked for over 40 years as an accountant in a securities and commodities firm, left his entire estate, valued at an estimated $8 million, to the Beth Zion Synagogue on the North Side, according to Philip Ogden, the attorney who drew up the will. Ogden pointed out, however, that the will had not yet been approved for probate and that it would therefore be "inappropriate" to comment further at this time.

When pressed by this reporter, Ogden acknowledged that he had not yet verified the size of Stillman's estate and based the $8 million figure on other documents in his possession. He is presently trying to ascertain whether Stillman was survived by any immediate family or other relatives.

None was mentioned in the will.

Rabbi Jacob Weiss of Beth Zion and Samuel Altman, president of the synagogue, denied knowing of the bequest and declined further comment. They would not confirm whether Stillman was a member of their congregation.

Stillman, who resided at 2104 Sherman Ave. and was employed at Barnett Brothers, a Loop brokerage firm, died of cancer Wednesday night at St. Francis Hospital.

Rabbi Jacob Weiss finished reading the article and handed the *Chicago Tribune* back to Sam Altman, who had brought it to the rabbi's house only moments earlier. Rabbi Weiss had been Beth Zion's spiritual leader for nearly thirty years. It had been his first pulpit, and no one doubted that it would be his last. "We're stuck with each other," he would joke with his congregants, "so let's try to make the best of it." He was in his mid-fifties but still had a lean, hard body, thanks to tennis and jogging.

"There's an old Talmudic expression, Sam. Roughly translated, it says, 'Don't count your chickens until they're hatched.' "

Both men laughed as they worked their way back to the study to await the others invited to the meeting. After the calls from

Eloise Byrd the previous evening, Sam Altman and Rabbi Weiss had compared notes and made a few discreet inquiries in hopes of learning something about Benjamin Stillman. They had learned nothing except that Stillman had lived in the apartment building next door to the synagogue. They had decided that except for calling this meeting they would say and do nothing further until they had a chance to study Ms. Byrd's story and collect their thoughts. In fact, the three men they were expecting had not even been told why they were being summoned to the rabbi's house at seven-thirty in the morning.

"Do you really think it was necessary to have this pow-wow so early, Jake?" It was customary at Beth Zion for the older congregants to address the rabbi by his first name, and he preferred Jake to the more imposing Jacob. "Pete and Lee have to drive down from Glencoe."

"Serves 'em right for moving to the suburbs," Rabbi Weiss chuckled. "Actually, it'll take them only twenty minutes, Sam. I would've suggested an even *earlier* time if I'd known for sure the morning paper would be here. Our phones will be ringing off the hook as soon as people see that column, and it's important that we agree on what we should tell them. And we have to consider whether there is anything we should be doing."

"You embarrass me," said Sam. "I'm supposed to be the big shot who runs the business end of the synagogue, and you're here as our spiritual leader. But you always seem to be a step ahead of the rest of us, even when it comes to fiscal and secular affairs." Although modest and self-deprecating, Sam Altman had a reputation as a crafty and successful plastics manufacturer. He was short, fat, and bald, but he had a cherubic look that made him more physically attractive than his features, taken independently, would have suggested. His movements were quick, and he had the lightness of foot that, incongruously, is often seen in obese people.

"I'm here all day every day, Sam, while you and the others are in your plants and offices. I'm not trying to run a business, so I probably have less on my mind than the rest of you."

Entering the study, Rabbi Weiss motioned for Altman to take the well-worn leather chair near the door. It was the rabbi's favorite chair for reading, judging from the objects on the side table: pipe rack and tobacco, notepads, a mug filled with pens and pencils, and an adjustable reading lamp. It was here, Altman thought, and not at the small, tidy desk on the opposite wall, that the rabbi probably composed his enlightening sermons. The walls were lined with bookshelves containing a wide array of reading material, ranging from religious tomes to tennis magazines. Here and there Altman spotted a family photograph or knickknack. Several components of a high-tech stereo system were on one of the shelves near the leather chair, but no television set was in evidence. The entire room was as comfortable as the chair.

Within minutes after Rabbi Weiss and Sam Altman were served coffee and rolls by Mrs. Weiss, they were joined by Peter Golden, Howard Rhyne, and Leon Schlessinger. All three were veteran members of Beth Zion. Pete Golden ran a small but successful advertising agency, Howard Rhyne was a real estate developer, and Lee Schlessinger was the distinguished senior partner of the law firm of Schlessinger, Harris & Wade.

Since it was Rabbi Weiss who had called the meeting, the others waited for him to explain its purpose. As soon as they all took chairs and were served their coffee and rolls, he came directly to the point.

"Except for Sam, do any of you gentlemen have any idea why I would call you to my home at this ridiculous hour?"

Silence.

"First of all, I normally refuse to discuss business matters on the Sabbath. You all know that, so you can assume this is important. I think God will forgive my spending a few minutes to bring you gentlemen together. Now, have any of you read this morning's *Tribune?*"

Since none had, he looked over to Altman. "Sam, perhaps you could read Ms. Byrd's column aloud."

Altman read the column to the others, pausing dramatically throughout to watch the expressions of the three who hadn't known of the Stillman will. None interrupted to question or comment. When Altman finished he sat back, looked at the others, and waited.

"Holy shit!" It was Howard Rhyne who broke the ice. "Forgive me, Jake."

"No need, Howard, quite all right. Do you all agree that this was worth getting together for this morning?"

Pete Golden, seldom at a loss for words, simply nodded his head. Everyone looked to Leon Schlessinger as if to say, "Okay, you're the lawyer. Say something profound."

Schlessinger took the cue and, with the same solemnity with which he would address the United States Supreme Court, said: "If I may be permitted to quote the eloquent Howard Rhyne, 'Holy shit!'" No one laughed harder than Rabbi Weiss.

"Since I've been thinking about this since

last night and you gentlemen haven't had a chance to digest it and reflect on it, let me take a few minutes to give you my initial thoughts and explain why I took the liberty of inviting you to this meeting.

"First, I have not discussed this situation with anyone outside this room, except for Ms. Byrd, of course. And I think that is also true of Sam." He glanced at Sam Altman for confirmation.

"Well, I *did* talk to Carolyn," Altman confessed.

"Sure, and I discussed it with *my* wife." Rabbi Weiss returned to the business at hand. "My reason for asking Lee here should be obvious. This is legal business, and Lee's been Beth Zion's attorney for as long as I can remember." He turned to Golden. "Pete, you're in the advertising business. I presume that you can be helpful in guiding us with respect to the media and, for that matter, the community in general. For example, should we be thinking about issuing a press release? If so, what should it say? I'm very concerned with the public's reaction to this whole business."

To say Pete Golden was in the advertising business was like saying Itzhak Perlman was a fiddler. Many successful brands owed their popularity to the catchy jingles, slogans, and themes concocted in Pete Golden's fertile brain. He had few accounts of his own, relying instead on the larger, national agencies. They would seek his help when struggling to come up with the eleventh-hour idea needed to hold a wavering client.

"And, Howard," the rabbi said, "you are one of the most popular and influential men in Chicago, and one of the most respected — and your long involvement with Beth Zion is well known. Many people will naturally consider you to be a spokesperson for us, so they'll listen to you. Likewise, you can keep us advised as to how our good fortune is being perceived by others. In either case, it's critical that you be one of our insiders. I couldn't imagine this meeting without you."

Howard Rhyne's real estate developments, ranging from shopping malls to industrial parks to urban renewal projects, were improving many of Chicago's previously blighted neighborhoods. He was on a first-name basis with congressmen, senators, aldermen, assessors, bank presidents, and even whoever happened to be sitting behind the mayor's desk at City Hall.

These men were leaders, in and out of the congregation. Like most leaders, they stepped to the front in a crisis. And that was just what the tall, lanky, distinguished-looking Leon Schlessinger was about to do.

Originally a feisty trial lawyer, Schlessinger had become one of the most venerable advisors to and confidants of Chicago's rich and famous. Because of the legal aspects of the problem, he decided to take charge of the discussion.

"First of all," he said, "we should contact this Philip Ogden fellow as soon as possible. If this thing's for real, we'll want to have a good relationship with him. He's likely to be the lawyer who'll handle Stillman's estate, and we want him to have good feelings about us." The lawyer explained that if Ogden represented the estate — or were himself the executor — he would be controlling the money, participating in investment decisions, and otherwise taking actions that would affect the synagogue's ultimate bequest.

More important, Schlessinger knew others would inevitably be making opposing claims to the money, and in that case it couldn't hurt to cultivate Ogden's friendship. He probably already knew about Stillman's family and whether they would be heard from, and he might even know about major creditors looming on the horizon.

For his part, Pete Golden had already decided that his first call should be to Eloise Byrd. "For that," he complained, "I should personally be awarded half the Stillman estate.

Eloise Byrd is a giant pain in the ass!" His assessment was not based on the fact that she was a relentless reporter, for which Golden respected her, but mostly because she tried to find a scandal in every story.

Golden predicted how she would write about Ben Stillman. "He may have been a quiet man who lived alone, had one job for forty years, and never left his apartment except to go to work, but Eloise will have her readers believing he was a combination of Don Juan and Jesse James."

"Who in the hell is this Ben Stillman?" Howard Rhyne asked. "I don't think I know him, do I? I have an account at Barnett Brothers, but I don't think I ever met him. Maybe I can find something out over there."

"He's not a member of Beth Zion," Rabbi Weiss replied, "and neither Sam nor I know anything about him. How about you gentlemen?" he asked, looking to Schlessinger and Golden.

They both shook their heads.

"Okay, Jake," said Howard Rhyne. "I'll keep my ear to the ground and keep you guys posted on everything I hear. I'll try not to say much to people for the time being, but it will be hard to avoid saying *something* when the subject comes up. I'll simply explain that we're saddened by Stillman's death, we're grateful for his generosity, and we'll make every effort to use the money in a way that would have pleased him."

Sam Altman's silence did not conceal his excitement at the prospect of the Stillman legacy. Until twenty-four hours earlier he'd carried the burden of being president of a synagogue that operated at a deficit, had a building, furnishings, and equipment in disrepair, and found membership was decreasing because younger members were switching to the newer, Reform temples or, worse, no temple at all.

But that was before. A stroke of Benjamin Stillman's pen had put an end to problems that had seemed endless. Howard Rhyne's reference to uses of the bequest brought Altman back to the conversation.

"I think we should announce that we'll build a new building, or at least do a substantial remodeling and expansion, and that we'll name it in honor of Benjamin Stillman."

"Please, Sam, don't even *think* about making such an announcement!" It was Leon Schlessinger speaking, and in an uncharacteristically sharp voice. "Ben Stillman is not even cold yet, and you're already spending what it took him years to accumulate. It's not only indecent, it's unwise. For one thing, the community would look upon us as a bunch of money-grubbing Jews who are joyously dancing on Stillman's grave, and they'd be justified. For another, we can't be certain that we'll even get the money."

The tall, dignified lawyer, wearing khaki slacks and a maroon crewneck sweater on this Saturday morning, surveyed the room and saw the quizzical looks on the others' faces. "All we know at this point," he explained, "is that some reporter *said* Stillman wrote such a will. We haven't even seen it, and she probably hasn't either. And if there is such a will, how can we be sure it's valid? Was it properly signed and witnessed? Was Stillman mentally competent? Did he really have millions? Even his lawyer was quoted as saying he hadn't verified the size of the estate.

"And even if the will is perfectly legal and valid, and even if Ben Stillman left eight million dollars, how can we be sure that someone else doesn't have a better right than we do to the money? Maybe he stole it. Maybe he has a wife. She'd have a legal right to half, regardless of that will. That's the law. Or maybe he wrote another will leaving everything to the Knights of Columbus. Maybe, maybe, *maybe!* And Sam here is already spending the money."

"Easy, Lee," said Rabbi Weiss. "You must understand Sam's enthusiasm. I'm sure he won't embarrass the congregation or himself with an inappropriate public remark."

"I know that, Jake, and I apologize to you, Sam. It's just that I see problems here that you don't."

With that, they decided to adjourn the meeting. The rabbi would shortly be starting the Saturday morning Sabbath service, and in any event they could do nothing at the moment. The five men agreed to "think on it" and reconvene after sunset, when the Sabbath officially ended.

As Pete Golden was rising to leave, he suggested that the rabbi mention the bequest sometime during the morning service. "Many will have read the paper, Jake, and they'll expect you to say something."

Jacob Weiss nodded his head grimly. He sensed that there would be many questions — asked and unasked — in the days to come.

And somehow he knew that Benjamin Stillman's generous but mysterious bequest would not be handed to Beth Zion on a silver platter.

6

As one meeting was breaking up, another was beginning.

"This is incredible," Jim Masters was saying. "I knew Ben Stillman for over twenty-five years, and there's just no way this story could be true. We never paid him enough for him to save *anything*. He always brought his own lunch to work, and he dressed like a friggin' pauper."

William Barnett and Jim Masters were sitting at a corner table in the men's grill at Twin Oaks Country Club. Both men were fiftyish, both were partners in Barnett Brothers, the brokerage firm founded by Bill Barnett's father and uncle, and both were members of Twin Oaks, one of the more elegant and prestigious country clubs in the fashionable suburbs of Chicago's North Shore. They were having coffee and talking in hushed tones. The morning paper, opened to Eloise Byrd's column, was on the table between them.

"No," Masters was saying. "There is just no way. Eloise Byrd is full of shit, plain and simple."

"Maybe she is and maybe she's not," Barnett replied. "But the fact remains, she wrote the story and we have to be prepared for questions. Anyway, she's too good a newspaperwoman to make up a story like that out of whole cloth, and she wouldn't have quoted that lawyer, Ogden, if she hadn't talked to him. And he confirmed the existence of the will."

Barnett leaned forward in his chair. "And there's another problem — a bigger one. How many of our clients will now think that we have thieves working for us, and that millions can disappear from our office without our even knowing about it? Maybe it didn't occur to *you* that Ben Stillman stole that money, but you can bet your sweet ass other people are thinking just that."

Bill Barnett was right. It hadn't occurred to Masters that Ben Stillman could have stolen the money. But, Masters thought now, what other explanation could there be?

"What do you have in mind?" he asked.

"Not much, but for starters I asked Ed Hirsch to come out to the club and meet us for breakfast."

"What would Eddie have to do with any of this?" Ed Hirsch, still in his mid-twenties, had been with Barnett Brothers for only a few years and wasn't even a partner in the firm yet.

"Well, Ed's a member of Beth Zion," Barnett said. "He should be able to explain Ben's connection with the synagogue. Hell, I didn't even know the guy was Jewish. Maybe he and Eddie talked about it before Ben died. If Eddie doesn't already have the answers, I'll bet he can damn well get 'em in a hurry. He's our best source of information."

"Jesus, Bill, I think we ought to talk that through, out of fairness to Ed." Masters was by far the more deliberate of the two men. "You're putting him in a tough spot. He works for us and would be hard-pressed to refuse to help us if asked. On the other hand, he belongs to the synagogue and probably has for his whole life. His friends and family are there. If we get into a fight with the synagogue over the money, then using Ed, even just to get information for us, could put him in a bind. Let's not squeeze the kid, Bill."

It was while they were weighing his possible involvement that Ed Hirsch walked into the grill. He was easy to spot in his business suit; nearly everyone else in the room was dressed for golf, which at a club like Twin Oaks — even on a chilly fall day — meant colorful beltless trousers, white shoes, and a shirt, sweater, or windbreaker with an animal on the pocket. Hirsch simply had no idea how the country club set dressed on a

Saturday morning.

If he was curious about why he had been summoned to Twin Oaks on such short notice, he did his best to conceal it behind his customary banter. "Mornin'. Was it really necessary to get me up at dawn just to offer me a full partnership in the firm?" He pulled up a chair. "I was sound asleep when you called, Bill, and I got here as fast as I could." As he looked around the room, he added, "I guess I didn't take enough time choosing my clothes." Although not yet a partner in the firm, Ed Hirsch had already passed through that awkward period when an associate feels uncomfortable addressing a partner by his or her first name.

"Don't give it a thought, Ed," Barnett said. "You look just fine, a hell of a lot better than those fat asses in their yellow double knits." He indicated to a waitress to bring Hirsch a cup of coffee. "Jim and I were just having a discussion about you. He thinks I made a mistake asking you down here this morning."

"Nothing personal, Ed," Masters volunteered. "Then again, maybe it *is* personal. I was just saying to Bill that he might be unwittingly compromising you by calling you out here."

"Why not let me be the judge of that?"

Hirsch took a sip of his coffee. "You tell me what you're cooking up, and I'll decide if I feel compromised. But since I'm poor and single, I can't imagine much that would bother, embarrass, or scare me, especially if you two are in it."

"First," said Masters, "did you know that Ben Stillman died?"

"Oh, no, I had no idea. I mean, I knew he'd been ill, but I had no idea it was all that serious." Hirsch paused a moment to reflect on his memory of Ben Stillman. "I knew him for only a few years, but I really liked the guy. You both knew him forever. You must feel awful about this."

"We do," Barnett responded. "Ben was like family to us. My father hired him when I was still in grade school, and he used to keep Jim and me in line when we were new in the firm."

"Is there anything I can do?"

Jim Masters answered. "We didn't ask you here this morning, Ed, with the idea of really having you do anything. Here, read this," he said, sliding the newspaper across the table and pointing to Eloise Byrd's column.

Hirsch flinched when he saw the headline, but said nothing. A few seconds later his head snapped up. "Wow! This is crazy! It doesn't make any sense at all. No way was

Ben a millionaire, and why on earth would he leave anything to Beth Zion?" He looked inquisitively at the two older men and then once again lowered his eyes to the newspaper. "I'd better read the rest of this thing."

When he finished the article, Hirsch took another sip of his coffee. He then continued to stare at his cup while shaking his head from side to side. "You know, it never even occurred to me that Ben was Jewish, but I'm damn sure he wasn't a member of Beth Zion. I sit on our finance committee and I know all the members, or at least their names."

It was Bill Barnett who spoke next. "Not a member? That makes it all the crazier. We were hoping you'd be able to shed some light on this — that you'd know why Ben left everything to your synagogue."

Jim Masters straightened up in his chair. *Christ, I wish he wouldn't pump the kid for information.*

"After all," Barnett continued, "Ben must have had some connection with Beth Zion. A person simply doesn't give millions of dollars to a church or temple without *some* connection."

"I wouldn't think so," Ed replied. "But then again, I wouldn't think Ben would have eight million dollars either." He stirred his coffee as his mind raced to sort all this out.

63

"Maybe I should talk to Sam Altman — he's Beth Zion's president — or some of the other members. They might know something about this. In fact, I can go over to the synagogue this morning and probably catch some of them at the Sabbath service."

Well, it worked, Jim Masters said to himself. *In no time flat Bill has turned the kid into a confederate of ours, and in another few hours he'll be our source — our own mole — inside the walls of the synagogue itself.* "I think you should give this a little thought, Eddie," he said at the risk of irritating Bill Barnett, "before you run over to the temple and ask a lot of questions. This whole thing might be deeper than you realize, and we wouldn't want you to stub your toe without knowing why."

"I don't understand."

"Well, look at it this way," Masters pointed out. "We all thought the world of Ben, and he'll be sorely missed around the office, not only because he was a sweet guy but also because his experience and efficiency will be tough to replace. But the fact remains he somehow managed to accumulate millions of dollars, at least according to this newspaper, and he certainly didn't save that kind of money by brown bagging it. We have to face up to the possibility, no matter how farfetched it seems, that he came by the money improperly. Now, I'm not saying that he did. I'm only saying that he *might* have, and that's a possibility we must at least consider."

"Came by it improperly?" Ed Hirsch laughed. "What's your guess? Old Ben was running a chain of whorehouses? Or do you think he was just a bookie?"

"No." Bill Barnett said it flatly and without a trace of humor. "My guess is that he stole it from the firm."

"Shit," Ed whispered, "I hadn't even thought of *that*, but — " He stopped in midsentence, then shook his head. "It just can't be. I wouldn't believe it without seeing it with my own eyes. Not in a hundred years." Hirsch took another sip of his coffee, then looked over to Jim Masters. "Jim, it sounds like you're trying to warn me about something. I still don't understand why *I* should be careful or, for that matter, why this even concerns me."

"Look at it this way, Ed," Masters replied. "If Ben Stillman *did* take the money from the firm, and if it could be proven, then the synagogue — "

"Oh, my God!" Ed cried. "Now I see it. If the money really belonged to the firm and it was stolen, then Beth Zion would be shit out of luck."

"Exactly," Masters confirmed. "I don't

know if there will ever be a contest between Barnett Brothers and the synagogue. I hope there isn't. But if there is, it could turn out to be a pissing match, and you sure won't want to be in the middle of it. If we challenge Beth Zion's right to the money, they won't be very happy with us. And if you do or say anything to indicate that you're partial to the firm rather than the synagogue, they'd treat you like a Benedict Arnold."

"That's true, Ed." Barnett now saw that Masters had been right all along. Their meeting with Ed could put the young man in a terrible squeeze. "And it's even more delicate now that you tell us you're on the temple's finance committee. Hell, you've got no choice. You've got to do all you can to help Beth Zion get the money, even if that means fighting us. And we'd never hold that against you."

Hirsch saw the bind he was in. Barnett was absolutely correct. The congregation needed money badly, and he himself had spent countless hours with the finance committee trying to figure out ways to raise it. The deficit could not be covered with bake sales. In fact, the news of Stillman's will was probably already causing a celebration over there. If he so much as hinted that he thought the money might rightfully belong to Barnett Brothers, his family and friends at Beth Zion would disown him.

On the other hand, Ed thought, *if the firm does make a claim to the money, will my actions on behalf of the finance committee put me in a bad light at the firm?* He had a bright future there, he believed, and had been working very hard toward the day when he would be offered a partnership. Would he be risking that by showing allegiance to the synagogue? Sure, Bill Barnett said it wouldn't be held against him, but would they really be all that forgiving if he went to bat for the synagogue and fought the firm for the eight million dollars? They *had* to get the idea of theft out of their minds.

"I appreciate that," he said, "I really do, but I hope it'll never come to that. I just can't believe that Ben Stillman was capable of theft. He seemed so darned straight. And even if he did have larceny in his blood, how could he possibly get away with millions of bucks without you knowing about it? In fact," he said, pulling a ballpoint pen from his shirt pocket, "let's do some quick arithmetic."

Barnett and Masters watched as Hirsch began to scribble numbers across a paper napkin. In less than a minute he looked up at them.

"Since Ben worked for the firm for about forty years, he would have to have taken an average of about two hundred thousand bucks each year, forgetting interest and all that. And since we don't work weekends or holidays, that would come to nearly a thousand dollars a day. Now, c'mon, it just isn't possible. He'd be so damn busy stealing that he couldn't get anything else done. And you guys haven't been asleep for forty years; you would have smelled something rotten years ago."

Jim Masters nodded. "No question about it, Ed. We can't argue with your arithmetic *or* your logic, and that's precisely why we aren't making any accusations. We're simply considering possibilities. Christ, we'd be crazy not to."

Ed Hirsch wadded up the napkin he had used for his calculations. "It was an understatement, Jim, when you said the congregation would treat me like Benedict Arnold if I sided with the firm." He gave a sickly smile and added, "More like Adolf Hitler."

7

Philip Ogden spent the first few hours of Saturday morning on personal chores: doing the laundry, dropping off the dry cleaning, and stopping by the grocery store to replenish what Phil considered to be staples in his bachelor apartment — peanuts, chips, chili, frozen pizza, beer, and coffee. He hated these jobs and wished he could do them as effortlessly as his ex-wife had. Even his recent habit of making lists didn't help; it still seemed he was always backtracking to pick up something he'd forgotten or couldn't find, especially in the grocery store, where he would chase up and down the same aisle over and over again.

He didn't often get started this early, but he was eager to get over to the hospital to get his hands on Ben Stillman's strongbox as soon as Mr. Cox, the elusive administrator, reported in. He wasn't sure what he'd find in the box, but whatever it was should shed some light on this whole mysterious business. After all, hadn't Martha Yolandis said that Stillman wouldn't let the box out of his sight in the hospital? If he could get all these things taken care of by noon, he'd still have time for his regular Saturday afternoon with Jeff and Charlie; that would help assuage his guilt for missing his Thursday night outing with them.

The laundromat, cleaner, and grocery were all within a couple of blocks of Phil's apartment. That was one of the conveniences of living in the neighborhood known as DePaul, that and being able to get downtown by public transportation or car in fifteen minutes, even during rush hour. Located about two miles north of the Loop — the heart of downtown Chicago, so named because it is within the circle of elevated railroad tracks uniting the city's transit system — DePaul had recently become a favorite neighborhood of yuppies, who bought up and rehabilitated its many older homes and townhouses as fast as they came on the market.

By mid-morning, Phil was in his three-year-old Saab heading east toward Lake Shore Drive. From there he'd be less than fifteen minutes south of St. Francis Hospital (all Chicagoans measure distance in minutes, not miles). As he swung onto Lake Shore Drive, he could see the waves of Lake Michigan crashing over its stone breakwater. Two months earlier the scene would have been dotted with bathers and boats, but not in November.

At the hospital, Phil went directly to the bookkeeping office to verify that all of Stillman's bills had been paid or were covered by insurance. He left his name in case any additional payment was needed. Then one of the staff whispered into an intercom and ushered him into a small office where a young man was working at a desk made of imitation wood. The man stood and extended his hand as soon as Phil appeared in the doorway.

"Mr. Ogden! I've been expecting you. I'm Don Cox."

Phil had expected the hospital administrator to be older. "Good morning. Then you know why I'm here?"

"Oh, sure. My secretary told me you called Thursday. I didn't think much of it until I saw Eloise Byrd's column this morning. Then I made the connection. You're here for Mr. Stillman's strongbox."

Phil smiled and helped himself to the only other chair in the office. "Actually, I would've been here yesterday, but they told me you were the only one who could give it to me. Is that customary?"

"Not at all. As a rule, anyone in the office can turn over a patient's belongings. But Mr. Stillman left specific instructions that only I could do it in this case, and then only if I was satisfied that you're you."

"Well, I'm me." Phil reached into his back pocket and pulled out his wallet. "Here's my driver's license and, let's see, my lawyer's ID from the state. That do?"

"Sure will." Cox swiveled around in his chair and removed a gray metal box from a cabinet behind him. "Here you are, Mr. Ogden. Just sign this release and it's yours."

Like most lawyers, Phil signed the release without reading it. "I'd love to know what's in there," Cox said as Phil stood up to leave.

"Me too," said the lawyer, already heading for the door.

Phil couldn't wait to get home to peek into the box. He drove two blocks to a shopping center and pulled into a corner of the parking lot. After satisfying himself that no one was around to interrupt him, he checked his notes for the combination and then carefully opened the box. Sitting on top of the other papers was a white envelope embossed with the words "LAST WILL AND TESTAMENT OF" and typed below that was the name "Benjamin Stillman." Phil recognized the envelope as the kind he used in his office.

He hurriedly slit the end of the envelope and removed the one-page document. Thank

God! It was the original of the one in his office, signed by Stillman and witnessed by himself and Carol. Although Phil hadn't seriously doubted that he'd find the will in the strongbox or in Stillman's safe-deposit box at the bank, he was still relieved to get his hands on it. Wills sometimes had a way of getting lost or misplaced, or even stolen or destroyed by disinherited relatives, and that could have put an end to everything before it even got started.

The strongbox contained numerous other documents substantiating the size of Stillman's estate, although final verification would have to wait until bank accounts could be checked and securities inspected. The strongbox papers included neat stacks of brokers' transaction confirmations and account balances, together with lists of stocks and bonds prepared in Stillman's careful hand. As Stillman's letter mentioned, it looked as if he'd done business with at least a dozen different brokerage firms until the very end. And since none of the brokers' statements showed that they'd held securities for him, it was probable that the certificates would be in the safe-deposit box.

The strongbox contained no information whatsoever about Stillman's family. That was a mystery that had to be solved soon. No estate can be probated without the decedent's lawful heirs being given an opportunity to challenge a will that leaves to others money or property that, but for the will, would pass to them. This is a protection the courts strenuously enforce. Otherwise, relatives might be deprived of their rightful inheritance by a will that was forged or signed by a decedent while mentally incompetent or drugged or under the control of someone exercising threats, coercion, or undue influence. Since decedents can't testify as to their wishes or even confirm that they did in fact sign the will, the law gives broad rights to their heirs to inspect the will, cross-examine the witnesses, and otherwise probe the validity of the document.

As he pulled out of the parking lot and headed back toward his apartment, Phil began to reflect (as he had several times during the last forty-eight hours) on what this could mean to him financially. If Stillman really had left eight million dollars, then Phil's executor and attorney fees could easily come to a couple of hundred thousand bucks — more if there were complications requiring extra work. *Hell,* he thought, *even if I charged a lousy two percent, it would come to a hundred and sixty thou.* And he had never even *grossed* that for a whole year.

Turning south on Sheridan Road, Phil let

his imagination run with ideas of what he could do with such a large fee. His first thought was that now he could be sure of giving Jeff and Charlie a good college education. And maybe he'd buy one of the rehabs in the neighborhood and get out from under the monthly burden of rent. Sure, the monthly mortgage payment would be more, but at least he'd be building up equity — and he wouldn't have to worry about that tight-ass landlord raising the rent every year.

Then a picture of Sally came racing across his mind, and he realized that sure as hell she'd be at his door before he could deposit the check. "I want half," she'd say, "and if I don't get it, I'll tell the boys what a cheap bastard you are. And they have a right to know, since they're the ones you'd be depriving." Damn, she probably already had Eloise Byrd's column taped to the refrigerator door.

All in all, he concluded as he swung onto Sheffield Avenue and began looking for a parking place, it was still a pretty good deal, considering that it took only about fifteen minutes to draw up the will and have it signed. He smiled to himself when he realized that he'd probably charged Stillman all of fifty bucks and — *oh, shit!*

Phil suddenly abandoned any thought of

parking his car. Instead he speeded up and set his course for his office in the Loop. For the first time in a long time, he felt fear. Real, honest-to-God, sweaty-palm, tingly fear. Like many lawyers who practice alone or with only one or two partners, Phil would occasionally "forget" to enter a fee on his books, particularly a small one that was paid in cash. What if he had no record of Stillman's fee on his books and that fact came out — as it surely would when the family challenged the will? *Tax cheat!* That could invite problems he didn't even want to think about, but he had to know, and he couldn't wait until Monday morning. *Shit!* As he sped south, he realized that it would be impossible to fake an entry on his books if the fee wasn't already recorded; it would be out of sequence and stick out like white socks at a wedding. *Double shit!*

In less than twenty minutes he was tearing through Carol's file cabinets searching for his journals and ledgers. When he found them he sat down at her desk and opened the ledger to S. Damn, there was no account set up for Stillman. But wait! Hadn't Carol once told him she seldom opened separate ledger accounts for one-time office calls, bunching them instead into a miscellaneous account? But where was it? He didn't see it in the Ms. *Damn!*

He grabbed the journal in which the daily receipts were posted. *When was Stillman here?* He ran over to the strongbox, which he'd brought with him to the office. He pulled out the will and checked the date. January 10! That meant the fee should have been entered either on that date or during the next month or so, depending on whether Stillman had paid on the spot or after a bill was sent.

Phil flipped the journal pages back to January 10 and — *praise the Lord!* — there it was, big as life: "$65.00, B. Stillman."

He sat back in his secretary's chair, threw his feet on the desk, and then, for what seemed the first time in the last half hour, exhaled.

Phil would not have felt so relieved had he known that the will in his hand was not the last one bearing the signature of Benjamin Stillman.

8

"Kam? Bill Barnett here. . . . Listen, Kam, I'm sorry as hell to bother you on a Saturday morning. . . . Know why I'm calling? No? Well, I'm out here at Twin Oaks with Jim Masters. Any chance you could come out and see us? . . . You bet it is, or I wouldn't be calling you on a Saturday. . . . Great, we'll be here in the grill. Oh, and Kam, take a look at Eloise Byrd's column in this morning's *Trib*. That'll give you a hint of what this is all about." Then, recalling Ed Hirsch's embarrassment at being overdressed, he added, "By the way, remember this is a country club. Casual clothes will be fine."

Bill Barnett beckoned to the waitress to take the portable phone he'd used to call Kamley Schultz, a partner in the accounting firm primarily in charge of the Barnett Brothers account. For as long as anyone cared to remember, the account had been under the tight control of A. J. Dickenson, one of the senior CPAs of the firm, who was careful not to let anyone get very close to his preferred clients. Only Kam Schultz, one of his personally unattractive, nonthreatening associates, was allowed near their books. Then, less than two years ago, A.J. had walked into a massive coronary that ended his life and launched Kam Schultz's career as the partner in charge of several of A.J.'s former clients.

At first Bill Barnett had been reluctant to accept this young, overweight, pigeon-toed nerd. "Just look at him," Barnett would whisper to his partners. "He looks like an unmade bed. How's he gonna keep the books in order when he can't even keep his hair combed or his shirt tucked in?" But Barnett knew good tax advice when he heard it, and he heard it often from Kam Schultz. For that he could put up with baggy pants, cheap ties, and scuffed shoes.

Jim Masters returned from walking Ed Hirsch to his car. "What are you trying to accomplish?" he asked.

"I want to tell him to get an audit started right away. No later than Monday morning. I gotta find out how the son of a bitch stole all that money, and then I want Schultz to tell me how he and those blind-as-batshit partners of his let it happen. Christ, when I think of what I pay those bastards to watch the books."

Kamley Schultz's arrival at the Twin Oaks grill caused Bill Barnett instantly to regret his admonition about casual attire. Although Ed Hirsch's clothes might have been somewhat out of place, they were pressed and fit well. But Schultz illustrated how impossible it is for a poor dresser to dress casually. No one that fat should wear jeans, particularly jeans with a narrow belt and an extra set of unnecessary pockets just above the knees. And cowboy boots! Even the shirt, which might have looked okay on a thin flamenco dancer, was a travesty on Kamley Schultz.

Uncomfortable with social niceties, the accountant wasted no time getting into the subject at hand. "I read the paper and I know what must be on your mind. You want to know if Stillman took the money and, if so, *how*. Right?"

"And why you didn't stop him," Barnett added.

"Now, wait a minute," the accountant replied, spreading his arms with his palms facing up. "Most of the checks and balances — the controls — were put in by A.J. long before I came along. Frankly, I never thought they were all that foolproof, but — "

"Let's not lay it off on old A.J., shall we?" Barnett interjected.

"I didn't mean it that way, Bill, like I was covering my ass. But your office has a lot of sophisticated new electronic equipment, and new controls haven't been added fast enough to keep pace. In fact, that may be just what this is all about."

"Meaning what?" Jim Masters asked.

"Well, I worked closely with Ben Stillman on your account, and the guy knew every piece of that equipment like the back of his hand. I think he understood it better than the people who installed it — certainly better than anyone else who works for you. You knew how valuable he was. Hell, that's why you guys were so relieved when the old man didn't want to retire."

Schultz seemed to reflect for a moment, then smiled and shook his head. "Geez! He was a genius when it came to runnin' numbers through those friggin' computers."

"The point being?" Masters prodded.

"The point being that Ben — if he wanted to — would've been able to hide and change data, to move things in and out and back and forth so neatly that he could slip in between the checks and balances. He could've made entries to balance an account the day before it was audited and then reversed them the day after. And he could've done it from any terminal in the office, maybe even from his home."

"You're saying," Barnett repeated slowly, "that he could have actually taken money out of an account, parked it somewhere, put it back when someone was going to look at the account, and then taken it out again?"

"Piece of cake, except that he wouldn't really put it in or take it out. He'd just make entries to make it look that way."

"Christ!"

"I'm not saying he did it, Bill. I'm saying he could have."

Barnett and Masters looked at each other, realizing that the calculations Eddie Hirsch had made on a napkin an hour earlier were meaningless. Whatever Stillman did, he didn't do it by slipping dollar bills into his pocket one at a time.

Masters looked back to Schultz. "Could he have made off with eight million like that, Kam?"

Kam Schultz leaned back and pursed his lips in thought for several moments. "That's the tough part," he finally said, "but when you think of the total number of dollars traded through your firm, including pension plans and trust funds, well — anything's possible. A lot could be hidden without anyone missing it. And ol' Ben could've pulled it off if anyone could. Geez! He sure knew his way around computers!"

While Bill Barnett sat quietly drawing imaginary patterns on the tablecloth with his spoon, Jim Masters posed the nagging question: "Kam, before today, did you ever see anything about Stillman that gave you pause — that gave you any reason to think he could be a thief?"

"I gave that a lot of thought driving out here. I honestly never had any suspicions about Ben. Hell, I'd have reported it if I did. But as I look back on some of the things he did, well, I'm not so sure."

"What kind of things?"

"Like the way he'd question every suggestion I'd make — like he didn't want me changing things. Or else he'd want to know every detail of what I was planning. I always wrote it off to the fact that Ben knew his job very well and didn't want me changing it on him."

"But now?" Masters asked.

"But now I'm thinking that maybe he was just trying to stay one step ahead of us."

Jim Masters slumped in his chair, shaking his head. His gesture could have indicated that he still didn't believe Ben Stillman was a thief — or that it had finally sunk in that he was.

But there was no equivocation with Bill Barnett. He leaned forward and spoke slowly and deliberately. "All right, Kam, you've convinced me that I was right all along.

Stillman had the ability, he had the opportunity, and then the bastard had the fuckin' money. Now get your goddamn bean counters out there Monday morning and find me the proof I can take to court."

"We'll try, Bill, but it could take months."

"Months!" Barnett exploded. "With all your hotshots? Chrissakes! One little eighty-year-old man and you guys can't figure out what he did?"

"I didn't say we *can't;* I said it'll take time. Remember, we do a certified audit every year and we've never seen anything irregular. So it's gotta be well hidden. I tell ya, Bill, the guy was a magician with those computers."

"I'll give you one month. But don't come up empty. I don't need auditors who can't find an embezzler right under their fuckin' noses."

"Okay," Schultz sighed, "but there's one other thing I gotta mention." The two brokers just sat there listening, so he plunged ahead. "It just might be that Stillman was a crook, all right, but not a thief, and maybe you won't want to find that out."

"What the hell's that supposed to mean?" Barnett asked.

"Well, maybe he didn't *steal* the money; maybe he just earned huge profits on trades using insider information. God knows he had access to it around your place. That would be a federal crime, Bill. And the firm could be in big trouble — for employing him and letting it happen. Fines, civil liability, your licenses, the whole shootin' match."

Bill Barnett looked as if he'd just heard that the world was about to come to an end.

PART III
MONDAY

9

Philip Ogden was not one of the better-known lawyers around the courthouse. He did show up in court from time to time, mostly on routine matters, but he was still a desk jockey to the courthouse regulars.

It was easy to recognize the regulars — the full-time litigators. They were the ones who addressed the clerks, bailiffs, and court reporters by their first names, somehow managed to have their cases called first, and wore a look of insouciance as they approached the bench. They were, in a word, cockier.

The litigators aren't rude or condescending toward the nonlitigators, Phil thought, *they just don't take us seriously.* The relationship is frequently — and accurately — likened to the way surgeons regard dermatologists and allergists. Trial lawyers don't consider themselves better or brighter, just more "real" in terms of what a lawyer is supposed to be: a gladiator who goes head to head against an equally daring opponent in an open and public courtroom. Ironically, litigators' success is born of more hard work, discipline, creativity, and intelligence than they like to admit; they prefer to give the impression that their success is due solely to guile, personality, and good instincts.

Early on that Monday morning following Ben Stillman's death, when Phil stopped at his regular haunt for coffee and Danish, he was taken aback by his new notoriety. It seemed that everyone knew of the Stillman will — and that Phil Ogden had drafted it and would be handling the estate. By then the local radio and television stations had picked up the story initiated by Eloise Byrd. But owing to the fact that a weekend had elapsed and most people had been unavailable for comment, few additional details were disclosed. It was unusual for a desk jockey to be the subject of a news story; it was generally the litigators' performances that attracted the media.

Now, as Phil entered the courthouse, he wondered whether the spotlight would cause problems in his handling the probate of the estate. Somehow he knew it would.

The reason for his trip to the courthouse this Monday morning was to "open" the *Estate of Benjamin Stillman, Deceased.* Riding up the elevator, he reviewed what he had to do that morning: go to the probate clerk's office, file the signed will, pay a filing fee, and be given a case number for the estate;

have the clerk enter the case on the daily docket so it would be called in open court that morning; appear in court to file his appearance as attorney; and request that the probate judge appoint a lawyer to serve as guardian to protect the interests of Stillman's unknown heirs.

The clerk stamped the papers with a case number; appearing just below it was the name of the judge to whom the case had been randomly assigned. *Verne Lloyd!* Phil shuddered. Lloyd had a deserved reputation for being both fair and smart, which was good, and overly strict — in fact, exasperatingly hypertechnical — when it came to following even the most obscure rules of procedure. This was bad for Phil, since his probate experience was limited. Judge Lloyd's penchant for chiding lawyers in open court was legendary, and even the toughest lawyer dreaded the prospect of being dressed down by him while opposing counsel smirked with sadistic pleasure.

As he left the clerk's office and headed for the courtroom, Phil saw as if for the first time the imposing courtroom doors, stout enough to contain the battles within. And now he knew he would be tested as one of the battlers. "Money attracts claimants like shit attracts flies," one of his early mentors had counseled.

In the past ten years Phil had seen no reason to question the point (other than to suspect that it was the lawyers, not the claimants, who were aroused by the scent).

He expected to hear from relatives and from others as well. There would be parties claiming to have been Stillman's partners in his investments, others — Barnett Brothers, for example — claiming that he had stolen the money from them, and still others who would claim that they had given Stillman the information he used to amass his fortune and were therefore entitled to a piece of the pie.

Phil remembered Ben Stillman's admonition: *Vigorously defend against all such attacks!*

Philip Ogden entered the windowless courtroom of the honorable Verne Lloyd a few minutes before the morning call was scheduled to begin. As in most courtrooms, there were two counsel tables placed between the judge's bench and the pews that made up the spectator section. When Phil saw there were no empty seats at the counsel tables, he glanced toward the jury box, where Judge Lloyd permitted attorneys to sit during his motion call. Since that area was also filled, Phil slid into one of the rear pews beside Henry Patterson, a law school classmate who specialized in trusts and estates.

"Mornin', Hank."

"Hi, Phil. See you hit the jackpot."

"You, too? C'mon, give me a break. I've been getting that crap all morning. It's not a real good feeling to know that if I screw this thing up, the entire world will know it."

"The price of success. Is that what you're here for?"

"Yeah," Phil answered. "To open it up and get the show on the road. I suppose Lloyd will — "

"Shh!" Patterson interrupted. "Here goes Rudy."

10

"Oyez oyez everyone will please rise this court is now in session the honorable Verne Lloyd presiding."

Rudy Wysocki, Judge Lloyd's bailiff, droned these words — with neither inflection nor punctuation — whenever court convened, which was every morning and every afternoon of every weekday. The judge seemed always to have a crowded calendar, and he needed all ten sessions a week just to keep from falling further behind.

As always, Rudy's announcement began *precisely* as Judge Lloyd opened the door behind the bench. The lawyers continued to speculate on how Rudy and the judge carried this routine off so flawlessly twice a day. Rudy's first word and the judge's entry were so perfectly simultaneous that one could not possibly have cued the other. Guesses ranged from near-silent buzzers to hidden mirrors.

Although there was no forced retirement age for state court judges, Verne Lloyd was nearing the age when most judges either retired or took "senior status," which entitled them to reduced caseloads. There was, however, nothing to indicate that his energy or ability was waning. On the contrary, he worked longer hours and disposed of more petitions and cases than any other judge in the county. His strong voice seemed out of sync with his small body, and even the body seemed taller when he presided because of his elevated chair behind his imposing bench. His white hair had by now retreated to small semicircles above his ears.

"Be seated," Rudy Wysocki ordered, banging his gavel at his small desk below and to the left of the judge. The court stenographer sat at an identical desk on the opposite side; the clerk sat between them, directly in front of the judge.

After shifting into a more comfortable position and rearranging a few papers, Judge Lloyd looked up for the first time and allowed his eyes to scan all those in his courtroom.

"Good morning, gentlemen, Ms. Griffin, Ms. Kroll, and Ms. Silversmith."

The three female lawyers in the courtroom that morning smiled at each other briefly to acknowledge once again how the judge always made a point to greet each woman individually, regardless of how many appeared for the session. Since he never had to grope for their names, he clearly knew who was present. That meant he somehow identified the lawyers for every item on his docket before he came into the courtroom.

Thus, within seconds of his initial entry, Judge Lloyd had demonstrated his punctuality, his good manners — even if they smacked of male chauvinism — and his precourt preparation. It was now reasonable for him to demand the same from the attorneys.

As if on cue (and it may have been), the judge's clerk called the first case for the day: "In the matter of the *Estate of Benjamin Stillman, Deceased,* number 89-P-21349."

Christ, Phil thought as he stood and assembled his papers, *last in, first up.* Cases were normally called in the order they were docketed for the session. Since Phil had placed his new, highly publicized estate on the docket only minutes before the session started, his being called first meant only one thing: Judge Lloyd must have reviewed the morning docket right before his grand entry into the courtroom and somehow managed to have his clerk call the Stillman case first and out of turn. *I was right about you, you old bastard, you wanted to get to this beauty first so you'd have an audience to watch how you handle Act I.*

"Good morning, Your Honor," Phil said

as he approached the bench.

"Mr. Ogden. To what do we owe the pleasure?"

As if you didn't know!

"I'm appearing as counsel for the estate of Benjamin Stillman, a decedent's estate," he replied. "I am herewith submitting a conformed copy of a document that purports to be the decedent's last will, the original of which I have placed on file in the clerk's office. I move the court to set a date certain for a hearing to prove the will, and to appoint a representative or representatives for the unknown heirs."

Even as he was saying these words, Phil's mind was telling him how ridiculous they sounded. *Why do we have to talk like silly goddamn kids playing grown-up when we're in a courtroom? Why can't we talk like real people and not like ham actors?*

"Does counsel have a sworn table of heirship, or at least a list of the known heirs?"

"I'm sorry, Your Honor, but as far as I've been able to ascertain thus far, the deceased had no heirs." The words had no sooner crossed Phil's lips when he realized he had misspoken, and he silently cursed himself for the error. Judge Lloyd, of course, caught it, and he wouldn't miss the opportunity to use it for one of his classic mini-lectures to Phil and everyone else in the courtroom.

He looked as if he had just caught Phil playing with himself. "Shame on you, Mr. Ogden! *Nemo est heires viventes!* Even a green law student knows that. *Nobody* dies without leaving heirs — at least a long-lost aunt or a seventh cousin or, if you're a Darwinian, Mr. Ogden, perhaps a monkey."

"My mistake, sir. I only meant to say that I haven't yet located any relatives, but of course I intend to pursue that."

"As you know," said the judge, continuing his lecture, "you must turn over every stone to find them. They are the ones who would inherit Mr. Stillman's money if the will were invalid, and therefore they must be given every chance to contest it. They can't do that if they don't know about it or if they don't know Mr. Stillman is deceased."

"I understand, sir, but — "

"Perhaps I should appoint a guardian ad litem right away to assist you."

"Your Honor, what I'm trying to say is that I just haven't had a chance yet to start looking for Mr. Stillman's relatives. I didn't learn of his death until Thursday."

Ignoring the explanation, Judge Lloyd looked directly into Phil's eyes. "In the meantime, the media have already informed us of this unusual and sizable estate." Then looking around the courtroom to indicate that his next words were for the benefit of everyone within earshot, he added in a slightly slower but louder voice: "I generally like to know about my cases *before* I read of them in the paper."

Phil flinched. "I understand, Your Honor."

He decided not to be defensive in the full courtroom by explaining that he had not contacted Eloise Byrd, but she him, and that he had told her and the other reporters who called very little. *Deep down, you're probably thrilled at getting a highly publicized case for a change, you pompous prick.*

Satisfied that he had made his points in open court, Judge Lloyd cut the discussion short. "Would you be good enough to wait until the end of my call, Mr. Ogden," he said as he redirected his attention to the other papers before him, "and then we can discuss this further in my chambers? Next case, please."

Cute, Phil said to himself as he turned to leave the bench. *Make a fool out of me in front of the whole world and remind everyone what a stickler you are for legal technicalities and high ethics, and then get me in private to play buddy-buddy and get the down and dirty on Stillman.*

★ ★ ★

"Coffee, Phil?"

"Thanks, Judge. Black."

"I swear, that call seems to get longer as I get older. Over thirty this morning, and there are even more set for this afternoon. Sorry you had to sit through it."

"It was interesting. I wasn't aware of the sticky issues a probate judge wrestles with."

"You're like the rest of them," Lloyd said, "surprised to see that a probate judge actually has to think and make decisions. Wealth accumulated over lifetimes passes through this court, young man, and it's my job to see that it ends up where it *should* end up. It gets tricky when we get conflicting claims, complicated tax and accounting questions, indivisible or unsalable assets, and so forth. And all the while there are impatient families and creditors eager to get their hands on the cash. If I sat back and trusted the lawyers to do it right, you would hear the dearly beloveds rolling around in their graves from here. Fact is, I'm frightened over the mistakes I miss that may never come to light."

"Which, I suppose, is why you wanted me in here," Phil responded. "You believe I shouldn't dabble in probate and should call in help from one of the probate regulars who are in your court every day."

100

If Judge Lloyd was taken aback by Phil's boldness, he didn't show it. Instead, he poured more coffee into the lawyer's cup, looked up, and smiled.

"Not really, Phil. I can't tolerate poor lawyering, but I'm not convinced there's a correlation between experience and proficiency. The regulars, as you call them, tend to get over-confident and even complacent. They coast and rely on their instincts too much, practice law by the seat of their pants. Then they come up against some youngster who's scared to death and researches the hell out of a problem. He reads and rereads the cases and statutes ten times, edits and re-edits his papers, and then proceeds to kick the shit out of the so-called regular. You take experience and I'll take preparation, and I'll beat your ass every time."

Phil appreciated these comments. It was Lloyd's way of telling him that he need only do his homework to get a fair shake from the court and that he shouldn't be intimidated by the lawyers who had more courtroom experience than he.

And Judge Lloyd's use of a few four-letter words did not go unnoticed. It was a signal to Phil that behind his robes he was one of the boys. The role of the judges necessarily keeps them at a distance from the lawyers who appear before them. Judicial propriety prevents them from socializing with lawyers very often. But during the few conversations off the record, lawyers and judges can feel each other out. A few "shits" and "damns" go a long way to convince lawyers that the judge is a straight shooter. And judges know that when a ruling goes against a lawyer, it will be easier to take if the lawyer knows the judge is an okay guy.

"I'll be prepared, Judge, you can bet on it. I don't want to get caught short in any case, let alone one where the newspapers and television reporters are there watching like hawks. I'm not sure what I'm preparing *for*, though, since no one has yet challenged the will or made a claim for the money — assuming Stillman really had the money."

"I'm afraid you won't have to wait long."

"Have you heard anything?"

"No, not at all, but I can't imagine that eight million dollars won't attract a good many creditors and relatives. You mentioned in court that you haven't yet begun to search for the relatives. I don't think you'll have to. They'll find you!"

Since Judge Lloyd's comment didn't require a response, Phil said nothing, thinking his silence would prompt the judge to get more specific. It worked.

"I see where you attested the will."

"Right."

"And I presume the other witness is one of your office staff?"

"My secretary, Carol Stephenson."

"Although the state law requires only two witnesses to attest a will," Judge Lloyd recited as if reviewing a beginning course in probate law, "the better practice is to have three. That way, if one of the witnesses is ineligible or unavailable, we have a backup."

"I know that, Judge, and that's usually what I do. But in this case Stillman wanted to sign the will immediately, and only my secretary and I were around. Even then I would've chased someone up, but I honestly didn't think it'd be worth the effort. I mean, the guy didn't give me a clue about his finances. So I wrote a simple one-pager. Who knew we'd be dealing with millions?"

Phil knew his explanation was lame. One doesn't practice law carelessly just because there is less at stake. And a lawyer shouldn't draw a will without knowing what — or how much — is involved.

Judge Lloyd evidently decided not to rub his nose in it any longer. He stirred what must have been his third cup of coffee and got to the point. "As one of the witnesses," he said, "you realize you must testify that your Mr.

Stillman was of sound mind when he signed, that he signed of his own free will, and that he was not under any undue influence."

Phil nodded, remembering Carol's mention of a conversation she'd had with Stillman in the reception room while he was drafting the will. Phil had had Martha Yolandis holding on the phone; Carol was relating the conversation, and he put her off in order to get back to Mrs. Yolandis. He made a mental note to ask Carol about that chat with Stillman. It could be important.

"I'm aware of that," Phil said aloud, wondering why the judge was bothering to explain such basics.

"Please consider bringing in cocounsel, at least during the hearing on the validity of the will. You shouldn't be a lawyer and a witness at the same time. You may be subjected to heavy cross-examination and it would be improper, as well as awkward, for you to raise objections, argue evidence, and conduct a redirect examination of yourself."

"Good point, Judge." *Damn! I should've thought of that!* "I'll have standby counsel ready to step in if there is any challenge during the prove-up of the will."

Judge Lloyd winked, smiled, and added, "That should not disqualify you from handling all other aspects of the estate, so you will not be sacrificing that outrageous fee you will doubtless be submitting for my approval."

There it is! Phil had been waiting for the judge to make some remark about the fee. Most judges, he had learned, were jealous of the fees lawyers earned. They seldom missed an opportunity for a snide comment on the subject.

"One final point, Phil. I noticed that you permitted the press to interview you. Indeed, I assume you were the one who called the press in the first place to tell them you had a will leaving millions to a local synagogue."

"Yes to the first, no to the second. I answered reporters' questions, but they came to me. I didn't call them."

Judge Lloyd peered over his Ben Franklin glasses directly into Phil's eyes, not sure whether to believe him.

"I'll reconstruct it as best I can," said Phil. "Mr. Stillman had a cleaning lady with whom he left instructions requesting her to take certain steps when he died."

"Was his death sudden?"

"No. As a matter of fact, Stillman died in the hospital, where he had been for nearly three weeks. He knew he was on his way out. Cancer, and the doctors didn't pull any punches, at least not with the cleaning lady. He was a meticulous man, as I've now learned, and it was characteristic that his affairs would be in order. This included instructing Mrs. Yolandis — that's the cleaning lady — to notify me of his death and to bring me a letter and other papers I'd need."

"So how do you think the press learned of the will and the money and that you were involved?"

Phil told of his meeting with Martha Yolandis and how she reacted to learning of the size and disposition of the estate. "She loved getting the ten-thousand-dollar bond until she realized it was only a drop from Stillman's bucket. Then she became furious — thought she should have been given more."

"How did she learn the estate was so large?" the judge interrupted.

"Stillman said it himself in a letter she brought me, which he authorized me to read to her."

"I see. Go on."

"My guess is that she complained to friends or to her other employers. Since it's the kind of news that would travel fast, it's easy to see how it would quickly come to some reporter's attention. But I do know this much: I didn't spread the word, and I'm quite sure my secretary didn't either. Hell, I haven't even called the Beth Zion Synagogue yet, although I suppose I should've. It's not right that they find out from a reporter."

Phil went on to tell the judge of the strong-box and how its contents tended to confirm the size of the estate. "The only mystery is that he dealt with several brokers — none with great frequency — but didn't appear to make any buys or sells through Barnett Brothers, the place where he worked."

"That *would* be a mystery," Judge Lloyd said, "if he came by his money legitimately. But if he acquired it illegally, one might suspect that his employer was the victim, in which event he would hardly want to wave the evidence of his guilt in front of their noses."

"The thought did cross my mind, Judge, but I don't think I should be the one to raise that issue. If I represent the estate, then I indirectly represent Ben Stillman. It's my job to see that his wishes get carried out. If someone accuses him of embezzlement, I'll defend him."

"As you should," observed the judge.

"And I'll maintain that Stillman's use of different brokers is not evidence that he stole the money from Barnett Brothers," Phil continued. "More likely, he didn't want his employers to know what he had. I think that's understandable, especially for the private person that he seemed to be."

Verne Lloyd stood up, walked across his

chambers, and looked out his twelfth-floor window southeast toward Shedd Aquarium, the Field Museum, and Lake Michigan beyond. With his back to Phil, he made his point: "I can't prevent you from talking to reporters, but I can — and *will* — ask you not to comment on evidence or on facts that may be in dispute. I don't think you should discuss, for example, Mr. Stillman's mental condition or his motives for leaving his estate to his synagogue. And, for God's sake, don't speculate as to how you think he acquired his fortune."

"Anything else?" Phil inquired.

"Yes, as a matter of fact. In looking over the papers you filed, I didn't see a request for me to appoint an administrator de bonis non, or what we sometimes call an administrator to collect."

"I'm sorry, Your Honor, I'm not familiar with that."

"I thought that might be the case."

Judge Lloyd stepped out of his chambers for two or three minutes and returned with a signed court order. "This will let you get started with your job of administering the estate. It's your authority to gather the assets, clip coupons, pay bills, and do other such things until the will can be proven and an executor is officially appointed. Also, it will let you into the safe-deposit box."

"I appreciate the help, Judge, and I hope my red face doesn't show. Any other advice?"

The judge sat down. "As a matter of fact, there is. I'd like to make another suggestion, Phil, if you don't mind."

"Not at all."

"When you go to the safe-deposit box, consider taking a witness with you, someone disinterested. Who knows what you'll find — or won't find? It may be useful to have someone to corroborate your word later on. I suggest someone from the attorney general's office. They used to do that anyway, before Illinois repealed the state inheritance tax."

"Good idea, Your Honor. Anything else?"

"Not for now. I'll notify you of my decision to appoint a guardian for the unknown heirs."

"Thanks, Judge."

"Good day, counselor, and be prepared for some surprises. This one has all the makings of it."

"Maybe even more than you realize, Your Honor."

"How so?"

"A minute ago you said that I shouldn't discuss the reasons for Stillman's leaving his money to *his* synagogue?"

"So?"

"Beth Zion was not his synagogue. Benjamin Stillman was a Roman Catholic."

11

As Philip Ogden left the courthouse for his office directly across Washington Street, he was thinking about all the things he had to do on the Stillman estate. But first he had to get some routine office work out of the way. A couple of appointments, some phone calls, a lease, and a set of corporate minutes. He'd still have ample time to take care of three more tasks that had to be done that day on the Stillman case.

His top priority was to call Beth Zion Synagogue, something he probably should have done on Friday. As Phil had admitted to Judge Lloyd, the beneficiary of an eight-million-dollar bequest shouldn't have to learn of it from the newspaper. He wasn't sure who at Beth Zion he should call, but Eloise Byrd's article in Saturday's paper had mentioned a Sam Altman as president of the congregation. He'd have Carol try to find a phone number for Altman.

Also, Phil had to get over to the bank and check out the safe-deposit box. Until then he couldn't be sure this wasn't all a wild-goose chase. Before the repeal of Illinois's inheritance tax, opening a decedent's safe-deposit box had been an involved procedure. When a bank learned that the owner of a box had died, it was required to seal the box against entry by *anyone* until the state authorized entry, at which time a representative from the attorney general's office would be present to observe the opening and inventory of the box. This was the state's safeguard for the collection of its inheritance taxes. Without such a law, the family or business associates of a decedent could have entered his or her box and removed cash, securities, and jewelry. Then they could claim at a later date that the box contained nothing on which inheritance and estate taxes could be levied.

Phil mentally ticked off the different maneuvers by which the contents of many safe-deposit boxes had escaped the watchful eye of the tax collector in Illinois — and probably still did in those states still imposing inheritance taxes. Sometimes the box was cleaned out immediately *before* someone's impending death, or a family member with a right of entry got to the box after the death but before the bank learned of it and sealed the lock.

Another gimmick was for the depositor to put the box in the name of a corporation;

since corporations don't die, anyone listed with the bank as a signator would have free access to the box. In fact, Phil knew of cases in which people applied for safe-deposit boxes in fictitious names that would never appear in obituary notices, thus insuring that the box would never be sealed. W. C. Fields had supposedly done just that with banks all over the country, using the outrageous names of the characters he portrayed.

But even with the change in Illinois law, Phil decided to follow Judge Lloyd's advice and request that a deputy be at the box opening as a witness.

And then there was his secretary. *I've got to ask Carol about the conversation she had with Stillman the day he signed the will. Probably idle chitchat, but he may have said something that could shed some light on all this.*

When he left the elevator, Phil felt a slight twinge of embarrassment, as he did whenever he saw the nameplate his father had personally mounted on the door when Phil's office was first opened:

PHILIP OGDEN
ATTORNEY AND COUNSELOR

The identification seemed arrogant to Phil. He considered himself a *lawyer*. He had studied *law* in *law* school, and he practiced *law*. If the description *attorney* seemed a little frilly, then *counselor* was downright phony. The lawyers who refer to themselves as counselors are the same ones who add esq. to their names. To Phil, that was horseshit. Also, "Attorney and Counselor" was probably redundant and certainly ambiguous. Technically, an attorney need not be a lawyer or have a law degree; the term merely describes one who represents another, even in a nonlegal capacity. And a counselor could be anyone who counsels. There are marriage counselors, teen counselors, camp counselors, and sex counselors.

But, confessing to a certain amount of hypocrisy, Phil had reluctantly left the nameplate on his door. He hadn't wanted to offend his father. And what the hell, "Philip Ogden, Lawyer" might have discouraged potential clients who would assume that a lawyer wouldn't be as brilliant as an attorney and counselor.

More important, the nameplate was a daily reminder of his father's long campaign to persuade him to seek a law degree. "A profession, kid, is something they can't ever take away from you." Phil figured the same was true for birthmarks, but he never challenged the point. He knew his father had grown up during the Great Depression and had seen his own father's business and fortune go down the drain. "Only the lawyers made out, kid. Lawyers and undertakers. There'll always be trouble around, so be something people need when they're in trouble."

The senior Mr. Ogden had been a successful sales rep — hardware supplies at wholesale — but hated every day of it. "Shit work, kid, pure shit work. First off, you gotta play kiss-ass your whole life. Second, get too successful and you get pink-slipped so the company can take over your territory and save the commissions. Same if you're an outside rep. Know why? 'Cause the big shots have smart hotshot lawyers who tell 'em not to give us contracts. So I'll schlepp garden hoses and toilet plungers till I'm too old to walk straight, then I'll get the fuckin' pink slip. Uh-uh, kid, better you be one of the smart hotshot lawyers."

When Philip Ogden's father said, "be a lawyer," it was less a suggestion than an announcement. He was a good sales rep, and his son never seriously questioned the decision.

On the very day Phil received his law degree, his father presented him with the embarrassing nameplate — even before there was an office door on which to hang it. From that day on his father, who still hadn't been given the dreaded pink slip, never called him "kid." He called him "counselor."

Carol Stephenson's typewriter was clacking away as Phil entered his small suite, consisting of his own office and a larger room, the latter divided by a waist-high partition to separate a client waiting area from Carol's desk and filing cabinets.

"Hi, Carol. Any messages?"

"A few. I think you'll want to get to this top one right away."

The top slip indicated a phone call from Leon Schlessinger, who identified himself as the attorney for Beth Zion Synagogue.

"Oh, hell," Phil muttered, half to himself. "They beat me to it." He handed the message slip back to his secretary. "Try to get Mr. Schlessinger on the phone for me, would you?"

"Like me to bring you some coffee first?"

"No thanks. Judge Lloyd had me in his chambers after the call. Filled me full of the stuff. Must have been his peace offering after reaming me out in open court."

As Carol was picking up the phone, Phil walked back to his office and tried to remember what he knew of Leon Schlessinger. He knew him to be a senior partner in the prominent firm of Schlessinger, Harris & Wade, but beyond that he knew nothing of the man he was about to speak with. He quickly scanned his other messages, none of which was important, and was just glancing at the morning mail when his phone rang. Carol had reached Schlessinger, who was already on the line.

"Hello, Mr. Schlessinger, this is Phil Ogden."

"We're going to have problems if you call me by my last name, and we'll have bigger ones if you call me Leon. Call me Lee. Everyone does."

"I'll do that — Lee."

"Sounds better. The reason for my — "

"Before you go any further, please accept my apologies for not contacting you or the people at the synagogue before now. Frankly, since I learned of Ben Stillman's death on Thursday, I've been so preoccupied with this whole thing that I just didn't get around to picking up the phone."

"No problem. In fact, I thought about tracking you down on Saturday when we first learned of the bequest, but I didn't see anything that couldn't wait until this morning."

"I guess we should get together," Phil said. "After all, it's your client who's getting the money."

"I'd like that," said Schlessinger, hoping Phil was right. "Are you free for lunch today?"

116

Phil wasn't eager to have a leisurely lunch. He'd planned to use that time to get over to the bank to inventory the safe-deposit box. He also remembered his promise to himself that he wouldn't have lunch on Mondays as punishment for over-eating on the weekends. But he felt he had already slighted Schlessinger and the synagogue by not calling them earlier, and he wanted to rectify that.

"Sure am. Where would you like to eat?"

"How about the Standard Club? Easy for us to chat there. Know it? It's on Plymouth Court near Jackson."

"I'll be there around twelve-thirty."

It was already after eleven, and Phil had to hurry to make his arrangements with the attorney general's office if he wanted to get into the box that afternoon. He was expecting to get the usual runaround for which governmental offices are famous. He didn't. Evidently Eloise Byrd was widely read at the State of Illinois Building, and the people in the A.G.'s office were as eager as anyone to find out if there was really eight million dollars in that box.

The appointment was made for two-thirty that afternoon. Phil smiled as he hung up the phone. He could get used to fame in no time at all.

12

The Standard Club occupied all ten stories of an older building at the south end of the Loop. Ever since its founding in the mid-1800s, the club had been *the* exclusive private Jewish club in Chicago. The most prominent Jewish business and professional men and women in the city belonged — some for the excellent food, some for the extensive athletic facilities, and some just to belong.

When Phil arrived, Leon Schlessinger was already waiting in the well-appointed lobby. The receptionist pointed him out.

"If it's all right with you, Phil," the older man said as they shook hands, "I think we'll be more comfortable in the grill than in the main dining room."

As Phil walked through the majestic hallways and glanced in all directions, he couldn't help but note the opulence all around him. *How many Ben Stillmans would have to combine their fortunes to create a place like this?*

Entering the grill, they were ushered to a table in the far corner. Judging from the nods exchanged between Schlessinger and the headwaiter, the table selection was prear-ranged. Phil ordered a chef's salad (chopped); his host chose the whitefish (tail section).

Despite the elegance of the surroundings and the food, lunch was a disappointment to both of the lawyers. Each came with the idea that the other would provide an explanation for Ben Stillman's leaving his money to Beth Zion, but neither had even a clue. Schlessinger had the added disappointment of learning that Beth Zion was not to be given all Stillman's money outright. Eloise Byrd's column had said nothing about eighty percent being held in trust for "other Jewish causes." But still, twenty percent of eight million wasn't hard to swallow, and in a way it made the synagogue's position easier to defend. They wouldn't be fighting only for themselves but also for countless others who would ultimately benefit from the bequest.

The two men did, however, take a liking to each other, and both left the meal with a feeling of a shared interest. Phil had reported Stillman's plea that he vigorously defend against all attacks, and said that he meant to do just that, not sit back and watch the vultures fight for the money. Schlessinger was relieved at the younger lawyer's dedication. Phil, likewise, was pleased with their alliance. To have Schlessinger's probate ex-

13

The First Illinois State Bank & Trust was one of the Loop's oldest and most conservative banks — exactly the kind of institution, Phil thought as he walked past the uniformed guard at the main entrance, that Ben Stillman would have selected to hold his stocks and bonds. It would have been out of character for this mysterious old man to have trusted a newer or smaller bank.

The attorney general's man was already waiting at the safe-deposit vault in the bank's lower level. Middle-aged and fat, he was puffing on a huge cigar that clouded the entire waiting room in a blue, acrid haze. Judging from the familiar conversation he was having with the vault clerk, he'd been here many times before.

As soon as Phil told the clerk why he was there, the fat man turned to him and extended a large hand.

"Good afternoon, counselor. I'm Casey from the A.G.'s office."

"Hi. Phil Ogden."

"I've already filled out the forms. All you

have to do is sign. Got the court order and key?"

"Right here."

The clerk led the two men through the large circular portal, which at closing time would be sealed with a thick, round steel door. He moved toward Stillman's box on one of the lower shelves. Phil was much relieved to see the size of the box's door; it was among the largest in the entire vault. *No reason to have a large box,* he thought, *unless there was a lot to put in it. So far, so good.*

As the vault clerk squatted to open the door, he said over his shoulder to Casey: "Not as many seals around here as there used to be, huh, Case?"

Seeing Phil's blank look, Casey pointed to a small red seal on the lock of a nearby door. "A seal like that used to mean one of two things, counselor. Either the rental was past due and they wouldn't let the son of a bitch in till he ponied up, or the son of a bitch was dead. Now that the state threw out the tax, they don't give a shit if he's dead."

"How did the bank know when a person died?" Phil asked.

"From the obituary notices," the fat man replied. "Every bank had someone read the obits each day and compare the names against the list of box owners. Good job for dummies, which is why they missed half of 'em. Hell, I been to banks a hundred times to inventory boxes when they weren't even sealed. Can you imagine the idiot lawyer trying to explain to the family that he had me there to keep them honest when it wasn't necessary? Then they'd open the box and find cash and jewelry that they could've taken away without paying taxes — except there's good ol' Casey standing there with a shit-eatin' grin and a notebook. No offense intended, counselor, but most of you guys are schmucks."

Phil couldn't help but smile. "Well," he said, "no one needed to read the obits to know about this one. It was all over the papers and TV this weekend."

By now the bank clerk had opened the door, using Phil's key and one of his own. With a grunt, he removed Benjamin Stillman's box.

Phil saw that it was large indeed. And heavy. It was fully thirty inches across, eighteen inches deep, and ten inches high. And judging from the clerk's effort in carrying it, it was packed full.

The clerk carried the box to a small room, adjacent to the vault, that was furnished with a table and four chairs. He placed the box on the table and stood back to turn the show over to Casey.

But Casey didn't make a move toward the box. Instead, he stared at the vault clerk until the latter cleared his throat and, as if remembering an urgent appointment, quickly left the room. The A.G.'s deputy then turned to Phil. "Well, counselor, whaddya think we'll find in here?"

"Beats the hell out of me, Mr. Casey, but unless Ben Stillman had a morbid sense of humor, I know what we *should* find in there. He left me enough clues."

"Then let's get to it and end the suspense. And just call me Casey."

"Who has the honor?"

"Go ahead," said Casey, nodding toward the box.

Phil pulled the box closer to him, flipped the manual latch, and lifted the lid to expose the contents.

And there it was. All of it. Just as Benjamin Stillman had said.

A long, low whistle came from somewhere within Casey.

And the two men just sat there staring.

At five o'clock there was a rap on the door.

The two men inside the room had their jackets off and neckties loosened. Between them were stacks of stocks, bonds, certificates of deposit, and other securities. The large table was fully covered, the piles were high, and the metal box was still nowhere near empty.

The rap was repeated.

"Yeah, whaddya want?" shouted Casey.

A voice announced it was nearly closing time. The room would have to be cleared and the box returned to the vault.

"My ass," Casey said to Phil, loud enough for the intruder to hear. He removed his large frame from his chair for the first time in over two hours, lumbered over to the door, and pulled away the chair he had earlier jammed under the doorknob. He turned the lock and opened the door just wide enough to speak around it.

"Send the president of the bank down here. If he's not around, send a vice president or manager or somebody else important."

"But it's nearly — "

"Do it! And while you're at it, find out how we can get some sandwiches sent down here. And some beer," he added, turning his head to wink at his good friend Phil.

There was another rap at the door a few minutes later. This time both Casey and Phil stepped out into the hall. They were met by two men, one in a well-tailored three-piece suit and the other in the uniform of a security guard.

"I'm Avery Austin, president of the bank. I understand you gentlemen have decided to make camp here."

Phil introduced himself and Casey and was starting to explain the situation when Austin cut in.

"I think we can accommodate you. I know why you're here; in fact, the whole bank is buzzing. We can let you stay as long as you like, and Sergeant Wilson here will stand guard outside the door. We'll keep a few people here to lock up when you're done."

The banker started to turn away, but stopped short and added: "Oh yes, we'll be *happy* to have some sandwiches and beer sent down. Would you like to take a break to call your homes, or shall we do that for you?"

It was after ten when the sorting, counting, and stacking of the securities was completed. The two men had been at it for over seven hours, and the intensity of their labors added to their fatigue.

"Amazing," said Casey as he leaned back for the first time. "I ain't seen this much dough at one time since I was a kid and my old man took me to the mint — and I don't think *they* had this much. If anyone ever told me I'd be listing piles worth fifty thousand dollars in a miscellaneous column, I'd tell 'em they was full of shit. But damn, that's what we been doin', huh?"

"I know. When I come back I'm bringing a camera. People just won't believe this."

"I guess that does it for now, whaddya think?"

"Looks like it," Phil responded. "There are still a few envelopes left in the box, but they're only for personal papers. No monetary value."

"Then leave 'em till you come back. Right now let's get everything back into the box so Dick Tracy and his buddies can put it back in the vault and we can go home."

Philip Ogden's high spirits would have been dampened if he'd known what had happened a few months earlier, when Benjamin Stillman crossed paths with Darlene DuPres.

14

"You idiot! You stupid goddamn *idiot!*"

Strong language, but not for Darlene Du-Pres. Willard DuPres, of course, was not an idiot; he was just a little too honorable and a little too straight — attributes that Darlene saw as naive and that interfered with her goals.

Attractive, with a sardonic sense of humor, Darlene Newman could have been among the most popular girls back in her high school in Peoria. Good grades came easily, and her self-confidence gave her a maturity beyond her years. But Darlene had a chip on her shoulder. Maybe it could be traced to her parents, who fought bitterly before and after their divorce when she was twelve, or maybe to the constant shortage of money that forced her to work at the five-and-dime while her classmates were cheerleading or gossiping endlessly on the phone. For whatever reason, she resented her classmates, especially those from happier or more affluent homes, and she didn't try in the least to conceal it. She was biding her time until she could turn her heels to that godforsaken hick town.

Her time came two months after graduation, and not a moment too soon. That entire spring and summer had been insufferable, with all the excited talk about who was going to which college. She couldn't imagine four more years of school with rich preppies, even if her family could have afforded it. She enrolled instead in a nursing school affiliated with a hospital on Chicago's Near North Side.

She was an excellent nursing student. She found camaraderie with her classmates, whose backgrounds were more in line with her own, and for the first time in her life she enjoyed warm friendships. After discovering her popularity with the young residents and interns at the hospital, she set her priorities in life.

"Asleep yet, Betsy?" she asked her roommate a few minutes after they turned off their lights one night.

"Uh-uh. What's up?"

"What're you planning on doing after you get your R.N.?"

There was only the briefest pause before the answer came. "I think I'd like the O.R."

"I mean, do you intend to do nursing your whole life?"

"Suppose so," Betsy yawned. "At least until some Prince Charming finds me and takes

129

me away from all this."

"Well," Darlene Newman said with determination, "I'm not waiting for any Prince Charming to find me. I'm gonna do the finding myself. But it's gonna be a *Doctor* Charming."

Darlene and Willard DuPres were married three years later, shortly after Willard finished his residency in internal medicine. In the early years of his practice, which he began in Evanston just a few blocks north of Chicago's border, Willard was described as ambitious and sincere, with the accent on sincere.

It didn't take Darlene long to change the accent.

At first, she was content — even delighted — to be the young, beautiful wife of the bright, handsome Dr. Willard DuPres. But she soon realized that young and beautiful and bright and handsome didn't add up to furs, jewelry, private clubs, luxurious vacations, and the right invitations. Doctors were supposed to do better than Willard was doing.

"What the hell's going on, Willard? Where's all the money? We're barely making ends meet." Willard never answered, of course, because there was no answer that would satisfy his discontented wife.

Eventually Darlene put her finger on the problem. "It's Vicki," she concluded, referring to the woman who had been Willard's receptionist/office manager/bookkeeper since he first opened his office. "She doesn't know shit about scheduling, billings, and collections, and on top of that she probably has the books all screwed up. She's costing you a fortune, and you're too goddamn trusting to know it."

Darlene moved quickly to correct the problem in the fastest, most direct way: she replaced Vicki, moved into Willard's office, and took over.

It was both a surprise and a disappointment for Darlene to learn that the office and bookkeeping procedures were perfectly efficient. The real problem, as she came to see it, was that as an internist her husband simply could not command the fees charged by other specialists. A dermatologist can charge two hundred dollars to remove a wart during a ten-minute office appointment, and the patient will rush out to recommend the doctor to others whose lives need saving. Proctologists and gynecologists, who find healthy fees where others fear to tread, are applauded for the miracles they perform with the flick of a finger. But the internist, whose job it is to *discover* the tumor, murmur, defect, or deficiency after an hour of thumping, pressing, listening, squeezing, and analyzing, would be run out of town for charging half the dermatologist's wart fee.

Darlene DuPres knew the answer was not for Willard to go back to school and then serve a residency in another field of medicine. "I don't have time for that," she would confide to her closest friends, "and I'll be damned if I'll go back to nursing to pay the bills. I put that shit behind me when I married a doctor."

She tried a more expedient solution. Although it turned out to be less than the whole answer, it set her and Willard on a course that eventually led to the rewards she sought. "Willard," she announced one morning, "we're increasing our fees by ten percent."

With overhead steady, the higher fees produced a noticeably greater cash flow. It wasn't enough for Darlene, of course, but the exercise taught her something much more important: *the patients didn't seem to mind.* "They keep coming back for more," she would tell her husband triumphantly whenever a patient returned. In fact, the office patient count actually increased.

Then she tried something they don't teach at Harvard Business School: she persuaded

Willard to up the fees again several months later, this time by twenty percent. It worked even better than the first time. Even Willard became excited by his higher income and popularity. The patients evidently believed higher fees meant better treatment. And what the hell, their insurance paid for most of it anyway. Soon the office was booked weeks in advance, so the fees went up again.

Dr. and Mrs. DuPres were shrewd enough to know that this formula wouldn't work forever. Indeed, the last increase met with some slight resistance. Something else was needed. That something else arrived one day in the form of Helen Stanton.

Mrs. Stanton, the wife of a local Methodist minister, was convinced that the lump under her left armpit was a malignant tumor. Her mother and her mother's mother had both succumbed to cancer in their early sixties, and here she was at sixty-five. She had discovered the dreaded lump, which wasn't much larger than a grape, several weeks earlier. Too frightened to hear the pronouncement of her death sentence, she had put off coming to the doctor. When she finally told her husband, he immediately called Dr. DuPres's office for the appointment. His plea and his position persuaded Darlene DuPres, who booked the appointments, to squeeze

Mrs. Stanton in between two other patients.

Willard DuPres was satisfied that the suspected tumor was nothing more than a subcutaneous cyst — fatty tissue that formed a harmless mass just beneath the skin. No treatment was necessary, other than to watch and perhaps periodically measure it. But it was obvious to Willard that Helen Stanton was nervous almost to the point of hysteria and that he must do something to convince her he wasn't letting her die without a fight. It was an ideal time to prescribe a placebo, an innocuous pill that would have no physiological effect whatever but would satisfy Mrs. Stanton's craving for treatment. He threw in a mild sedative to calm her down.

Of course, one does not prescribe "medication" for a totally harmless condition, so Willard DuPres soberly explained to his patient that while the lump might well be nothing serious, they could not be too cautious.

"I'll write out a prescription for you, Mrs. Stanton. Take these pills four times a day, after meals and before you go to bed. Come back in two weeks and we'll have another look. I'm sure we'll be able to control this thing."

As soon as Helen Stanton heard the doctor say she had "this thing," she panicked. *I have it! And he confirmed it!* She burst into tears and pleaded for Dr. DuPres to call her husband in from the waiting room. As soon as Rev. Stanton entered the examination room, his wife explained between sobs that her condition was everything she had feared. The reverend also went to pieces, and together they begged the doctor to do everything within his power to save Helen Stanton.

Willard DuPres called Darlene in to help calm the Stantons while he excused himself momentarily to release a patient waiting in the other examination room.

"Please explain to the doctor that I'll do anything, pay anything, to get cured," Mrs. Stanton cried. "I don't want to die like my mother and grandmother. Please! Make him do something for me!"

Darlene stepped out of the room to find out the nature of Mrs. Stanton's complaint. Willard explained it was only a harmless cyst.

"So why in the hell does she think she's dying?"

"She's convinced she has cancer," Willard answered, "and nothing I say will cause her to believe differently. She and her husband are begging for a cure, but she has nothing to cure. I prescribed a placebo and a sedative, but they're hollering for something more."

"Why not aspirate the damn thing?" Darlene assumed the insertion of a needle into the fatty mass would satisfy the Stantons' desire for an aggressive attack on the imagined illness. Moreover, this would produce a small tissue sample that could be tested. Not only would the procedure add another fifty dollars to the fee, but when the test proved negative the Stantons would be delirious with relief. Then, Darlene told her husband, everyone would be happy.

"Why not?" Willard DuPres replied.

The terrible burden on Helen Stanton's mind was only slightly eased when Willard came back into the room and announced that he had reconsidered and decided, after all, to have the "mass" analyzed at the lab. "I still feel this is nothing we can't control, but why take any chances? Some of these things can fool you."

At least, Mrs. Stanton thought, the doctor would be doing something to that thing that was alive and growing under her arm. The Stantons left the office with the pill prescriptions and with Willard DuPres's assurance that he would call the minute the lab report on the tissue sample came back.

"She'll have only two days to agonize before we get the lab report," Willard told Darlene. "But I'm so damn positive the thing is harmless that I really don't have to wait for the report; I could give her the good news tomorrow and spare her one more day of misery."

"Then why bother to send the sample to the lab in the first place? We may as well save the lab fee."

Willard looked at his wife and slowly shook his head. "But I'll bet you want to keep the lab fee on the Stantons' bill. You never miss a trick, do you?"

"Don't get sanctimonious with me, Willard DuPres!" Darlene took a step closer to her husband. "If it weren't for me never missing a trick, as you put it, you'd still be driving that fuckin' Chevy. You don't seem to mind my tricks when you go to your fancy country club or your tailor or your Mercedes dealer. So stop your goddamn whining and let *me* run the business end of this place."

Willard DuPres quickly retreated, as he usually did when his wife got her back up. The rest of the afternoon passed without their speaking to each other; she was irate and he was afraid he might set off another of her explosive tirades.

Their dinner, too, began in silence. However, as if by magic, Darlene's mood changed during the meal. She made friendly conversation, refilled his plate, and poured his coffee. By the end of the meal she was actually pleasant. Willard, who was no match for his wife's ability to manipulate him, responded as she willed. He became amiable and chatty. And he slipped into a mood that would make him receptive to the idea that had been taking form in her mind for the past few hours. She decided to spring it on him at the proper time and place.

"Honey, I've been thinking about Mrs. Stanton," she said later that night as she slipped slightly over to his side of the bed.

"So have I. I can't wait to tell her she's okay." He shifted an inch or two closer to her.

"Well, that's what I've been thinking about." Her toe touched his foot.

"What, babe?" He moved another inch closer.

"What if the lab report were positive? What if you had to tell her she had cancer?" She moved against him and put her head on his shoulder.

"Christ, I don't even want to *think* of that. Thank God it won't happen." He put his arm around her.

"But if it were positive, and if she had cancer, wouldn't you have to tell her? And if you had to, wouldn't you?" She put her arm over his chest and her knee between his legs.

"Well, sure. If I *had* to I would, but so what?" He was losing interest in the conversation.

"Then why don't you?" Her knee was making circles.

"I don't understand. Why the hell — "

"Why *don't* you?" she whispered in his ear.

"Why would I? How could I possibly do such a thing?"

"Because," she said as her hand replaced her knee, "if she thought she had the big C she'd keep coming back for more treatment — expensive treatment. She said she'd pay *anything* to fight it. So let's do what she wants and then tell her later that she's cured. And that *you* cured her."

Willard DuPres sat up and buried his head in his hands. It wasn't anger or frustration as much as resignation and defeat. He could not reject Darlene's suggestion without making it sound as if he were more noble or honorable than she. She would respond violently. Only a few hours earlier she had called him sanctimonious, as if it were an indictment. He couldn't handle another outburst like that, not today, and certainly not when he'd had his mind on better things less than a minute earlier. But some remnant of honor kept him from readily agreeing to Darlene's scheme.

"Please, Darlene, I don't want to upset you and I don't want us to argue about this. But give me a chance to sort this out in my head. This is not a casual thing we're talking about. We're talking about playing games, dangerous games, with someone's life. I can't just say yes or no and let it go at that."

Darlene gently pulled him down onto his back and unfastened his pajama buttons. "Sure, honey, we can talk about it in the morning. I wouldn't want you to do anything you didn't want to do."

But in the dark bedroom Darlene DuPres was smiling. *I've got him!* In the morning she would bring the subject up as if Willard had already committed himself to the plan. If he balked, she'd go into a calculated rage and accuse him of breaking his promise to her. He was a patsy and she knew she could control him, if not by doling out morsels of love, then with fury. Darlene DuPres could already see Willard treating — and then miraculously curing — Helen Stanton's cancer. *I've got him!*

Willard hedged when he called Mrs. Stanton two days later. He couldn't bring himself to tell this woman she had a deadly disease when in fact she didn't. But he lacked the courage to go back on his word to Darlene. When he'd tried to talk her out of her idea the day before, she'd become furious. He was a wimp, she said, and he cared more about the feelings of his goddamn patients than he did about his wife — the same wife, she reminded him, who worked her ass off running his office while other doctors' wives played golf and went shopping. And those same other doctors, she said, didn't bat an eye at overdiagnosing and overtreating *their* patients so *their* wives could lead respectable lives. Fifteen minutes later, as her harangue approached a peak of histrionic fury, Willard capitulated.

What he chose to tell Helen Stanton was that the tissue test was "inconclusive." This was not quite a lie: the lab test didn't conclude a thing because Darlene had called the lab to cancel it. But of course the lab fee remained on Mrs. Stanton's bill.

"*Inconclusive?*" Helen Stanton was beside herself. Waiting for the lab report the past two days had been next to impossible. By now her nerves were completely frayed. She had talked herself into accepting the worst, but she didn't know how to deal with "inconclusive."

"Doctor, are you trying to spare me the bad news? Are you being considerate of an old lady's feelings, and you want to break the news gently?"

"Not at all, Mrs. Stanton. I mean exactly

what I said. It's not at all unusual for a test to produce inconclusive results, especially a test such as this where a small sample of tissue has to be analyzed. Some tissue is obviously malignant and some is obviously benign, but there is a large gray area in the middle where the answer isn't so obvious. You wouldn't want me to give you an answer if I weren't absolutely sure, would you?"

"No, of course not. Please, forgive me for questioning you, but the reverend and I are so nervous about this whole thing. We've been on pins and needles waiting for your call."

Willard DuPres winced when she referred to her husband. He had forgotten that Mr. Stanton was a minister, and now his guilt was compounded. It was one thing to mislead a patient for a few weeks, but it was quite another to lie to a man of the cloth, particularly when the motive was to charge him unnecessary fees. He would have loved to back off the scheme right then and there, but the memory of Darlene's wrath was too vivid in his mind.

"I fully understand, Mrs. Stanton."

"Where do we go from here, Doctor?"

"I'd like you back in the office tomorrow morning at ten. I think we should repeat the test, even though it may well be inconclusive again. Also, I want to run some other

142

tests — blood, urine, lymph, and so forth. We'll need to check out your resistance to certain drugs and chemicals, and I want to prescribe additional medication and vitamins. I've also got to schedule a lymphography for you."

"A *what?*" Helen Stanton's terror doubled when she heard the strange medical term.

"Now, Mrs. Stanton, these are all routine procedures that I'm doing as a precaution. This doesn't mean that you have what you think you have. Just come in tomorrow at ten."

Darlene DuPres's plan eventually produced results beyond her wildest expectations. Although Willard never actually confirmed to Helen Stanton that she had cancer, his serious manner, repetition of tests, prescriptions for a multitude of medications, and solicitous attention to her — coupled with his refusal to *deny* that she had it — were enough for her. *She* knew she had it, and when she finally saw the negative lab report with her own eyes several weeks later, she was convinced beyond a doubt that Dr. Willard DuPres had cured her.

Helen Stanton was ecstatic. The few thousand dollars she and Rev. Stanton had spent for the "cure" was nothing in comparison to her life. She told anyone who would listen about her marvelous doctor. Her husband even devoted a sermon to Willard DuPres.

In the years that followed, Darlene and Willard DuPres repeated the scam, with embellishments and refinements that led to even greater recognition. Their methods were simple: diagnose cancer or, at the very least, a "suspicious condition"; order a battery of tests, both in the office and at the hospital; and prescribe massive doses of vitamins C and E and an array of placebos that could fill a shopping bag. Over time, other treatments such as exotic diets and regulated exercise, were added to the regimen. For the more gullible patients, ultrasound, salt baths, or coffee enemas might be required. Willard was even reading up on acupuncture.

Soon the office of Willard DuPres, M.D., became the DuPres Oncology Clinic. It provided a haven for the multitudes who had, or suspected they had, the dreaded disease of cancer. It was seldom necessary for Willard to lead his patients to the belief that they had it; they did that for themselves.

The only patients who weren't cured by the miraculous Dr. Willard DuPres were the unfortunate ones who actually had the disease.

15

It was to the DuPres Oncology Clinic that
Benjamin Stillman went after his own physician advised him that the agonizing pains
throughout his midsection were not merely
stomach disorders. They were in fact the
symptoms of a progressive malignancy that
had advanced to the point where a cure
was, at best, remote. However, Stillman was
told, his life could be prolonged and made
more comfortable if certain radical procedures
were tried at once. Some were surgical and
some involved radiation and chemotherapy.

Even with surgery, however, nothing could
be guaranteed except that Stillman would
leave parts of his body on the operating
room floor, the treatment would be prolonged
and painful, and he would forever have to
wear the plastic bags that disgusted him. He
thanked his doctor but said he would have
to give the matter more thought before submitting to the recommended treatment.

Ben Stillman had heard of the DuPres
Clinic and of the many patients cured by
the amazing Dr. DuPres. Why not give it

a try? What did he have to lose?

He made his appointment and was interviewed in depth by Darlene DuPres, the clinic administrator. It was customary at the initial interview to inquire about the patient's family. Stillman said he had none. Darlene asked about other relatives or friends, but still no names were given. When she told him she would need *someone* for her records, she was given the name of Martha Yolandis, who Stillman said was his cleaning lady.

The interview then moved to more important areas as far as Darlene was concerned. "Do you have insurance, Mr. Stillman?"

"I do." He handed her a summary of the group policy from Barnett Brothers. "It's an extra copy. You may keep it."

She then asked about his income and assets, information she knew would determine the treatment and procedures Willard would prescribe. The more money the patient had, the more elaborate and strung out the treatment would be.

"Why is that necessary? You can see I have insurance."

"That's right, but insurance doesn't always take care of everything. For example, there may be questions about the deductible or the extent of coverage." She also knew quite well that the clinic's charges for many procedures were higher than most insurance carriers would allow, but she didn't volunteer that as a reason for her inquiry. "Moreover, your treatments could go on for a long time, but your coverage may have a time limit. I simply have to have some information about your ability to meet any expenses not covered by the insurance."

But Ben Stillman refused to furnish her with any information bearing on his ability to pay. Darlene insisted, but he was adamant. The interview would have ended right there, with the clinic refusing him admission, but Darlene knew that people who wouldn't disclose their money or assets to doctors were generally the ones who had plenty. Poor people talked about money freely (though they might lie). She decided to take a chance and press the point. She had nothing to lose.

"Mr. Stillman," she asked, "if you don't answer these questions, how will we know whether you can pay the clinic's charges? There may not be enough insurance."

"Don't worry, I can pay."

"But how will we *know* that? Just because you *tell* us?"

Benjamin Stillman thought for a moment, and then posed a question that surprisingly few people asked at the clinic. "How much would you estimate the charges to be?"

"Well, of course that would depend on the precise diagnosis, what treatment would be needed, your ability or willingness to undergo some of the treatment, and so forth. We can't really say in advance."

"But surely you could give me a reasonable guess, based on what you've already seen. I gave you my records from the other doctor and I assure you of my willingness, as you put it, to be cured. I won't hold you to it. In fact, guess on the high side."

Darlene DuPres looked at the old man very carefully for a few seconds before she spoke. "Thirty-five hundred to four thousand dollars."

"No problem at all. I'll bring you a cashier's check this afternoon."

"At a minimum," Darlene quickly added.

"Then I'll bring in five thousand dollars to be on the safe side and you can refund the difference if it turns out to be too much. And you won't have to worry about insurance; I'll apply directly to the carrier for reimbursement. Is that fair enough, Mrs. DuPres?"

"Quite fair, Mr. Stillman. I'll be here till six." Darlene DuPres was very proud of herself. She had not only kept a patient from walking out the door; she had managed to set him up for an excessive fee — payable in advance. This was further confirmation, she thought, of how capable she was at her work and how the success of the clinic rode on her shoulders.

Ben Stillman brought in the money, and the tests and treatments began.

A few days later Darlene was ready to execute a plan that had been percolating in her mind since her first meeting with Stillman. At first it was purely fanciful, outrageous even to her. But each time she thought about it, poked holes in it, and refined it, the idea seemed less crazy. The execution began with a phone call to Eric Stone, the lawyer she had retained a few years earlier to handle the clinic's legal affairs.

"Eric, it's important that I see you tonight. I have something to talk over with you. Can you get out?"

"Yeah. She plays bridge tonight. Sure we can't do more than talk?"

"Well, that too," she replied, sighing to herself. The relationship Darlene and Eric Stone had gradually worked out was one of accommodation. Eric would now and then cut a few corners and bend a few rules when processing insurance claims for the clinic, and Darlene would now and then suspend her marriage vows to keep Eric under control. She rationalized her behavior by telling herself that Willard, too, benefited from the increased insurance receipts this arrangement produced. "But we have to leave time to talk. It's important."

"Gonna give me a hint?"

"Only that I'd like you to do something, uh, unusual," she said with a trace of contrived sensuality.

"Marvelous. Usual place?"

"Sure, make it eight o'clock."

She knew she'd have to be good that night, better than she'd ever been. And she was.

Although Darlene DuPres's hunch about Ben Stillman's money was correct, her assessment of him as a naive and gullible old man was dead wrong. After only a few sessions at the clinic, Stillman saw it for the sham that it was. It wasn't so much the extensive tests and medications, since these were expected. Nor was it the mountains of papers he was asked to sign; he knew that the recent surge of medical malpractice suits forced doctors to practice defensively, and one of their best defenses was to have patients sign forms consenting to various procedures and to acknowledge that the procedures and risks had been explained to them.

What bothered Stillman was the lack of organization. The staff consisted only of Dr.

and Mrs. DuPres and a few nurses. That was inadequate for the number of patients and resulted in long delays followed by a hurried few minutes of attention. None of the staff seemed to know what the others were doing, and each gave different answers to his questions.

He was also bothered by the fake air of optimism, by all the patronizing bullshit. He knew he had cancer and he knew he would very probably die from it. Going to the clinic was a last-ditch effort, a grasp at a straw, and he allowed no false hopes. But with cancer there was always a chance — that's why he was there in the first place. The cheery pep talks from the staff, however, were more than he could take. "You're looking better every day, Mr. Stillman." "You'll be cured before you know it, Mr. Stillman." "You're responding beautifully, Mr. Stillman." Even if they were somehow arresting the ugliness growing in his body, which he doubted more with each visit, they were playing him for a stupid, senile old man, and that was unbearable.

The end of his reliance on the DuPres Oncology Clinic came unexpectedly to everyone but him. He had just been prepped for an enema — he didn't even know it was a *coffee* enema — when the nurse was called out of the room. When ten minutes passed and she still hadn't returned, Ben Stillman decided he had had enough. No one was going to keep him waiting while he was crouched on his knees and elbows with his bare ass sticking straight up, not after he had prepaid five thousand dollars. Especially not this gang of bullshit artists. So he dressed and walked out of the clinic. He never returned, never explained, and never asked for a refund.

When Darlene DuPres was told of Stillman's disappearance, she went into a frenzy. First she berated the nurse for leaving him alone while he was waiting for his enema. Then she made a dash for the papers that Stillman had signed that day. As soon as she found the one she was looking for, she became enraged. She ran directly into Willard's office, where he was consulting with a patient. Seeing the fury in his wife's eyes, he quickly excused himself and stepped into the hallway with her.

"What's up?" he asked innocently.

"You idiot! You stupid goddamn *idiot!*"

Willard was stunned. He was also frightened. Darlene seemed angrier than he had ever seen her, and he could remember some furious scenes.

"Darlene, what's the matter? What's wrong?"

"What's wrong? What's *wrong?* Here's what's wrong." She thrust a sheet of paper at him.

"What is this?"

"Look at it, you idiot! Don't you recognize it?"

"Well, here's my signature, along with Alice's and Mr. Stillman's. But I can't tell much else because the other pages are missing. What the hell is this all about, anyway?"

"This, Willard DuPres, is the signature page for Stillman's will. I had it all set up. Everything was perfect. And then you blew it by witnessing the goddamn thing yourself, you and that bitch of a nurse of yours." She was half screaming and half crying, and her fists were clenched and shaking.

Willard DuPres grabbed his hysterical wife by the shoulders and steered her farther down the corridor. "Pull yourself together, Darlene. Let's not discuss this where the entire staff can hear. We'll go back to your office and you can tell me what this is all about, slowly and from the beginning."

Darlene then told her husband about the plan she had devised for Benjamin Stillman. She explained how she had suspected that Stillman had some money and no family. In

153

fact, the only name he could come up with for their records was a cleaning lady's. As long as he'd soon be dead from the cancer, she said, and he had no family depending on him, why not let him leave whatever he had to the clinic?

"Did you discuss that with him?" Willard DuPres asked.

"Are you out of your mind?" She was incredulous at his stupidity. "How could I discuss it with him? He would have laughed in my face. He thought we were a bunch of quacks, and his walking out proves it."

"Then you're crazy to think he'd sign a will leaving anything to us."

"First of all, Mr. Smartass, it so happens he *did* sign it. There, right there, see it? 'Benjamin Stillman,' and it's in his own handwriting. I *knew* he would."

"But how — ?"

"Never mind how. He did it, and that's all that counts."

"Well then," Willard asked, "what's the problem? It looks like everything worked out okay."

"It *would* have worked," she answered, "except that you and that dumbshit nurse of yours, Alice, went ahead and witnessed the damn thing after he signed it."

"Hell, we witness patients' signatures all

day long. Nearly every form we give them has a place for one or two witnesses to sign. I just assumed it was another routine medical form. But what's the big deal? What's the matter with our witnessing it?"

Darlene sighed and shook her head. "This is a *will*, stupid. No one connected with the clinic should witness it — especially not you, since the place is in your name."

"I'm not sure I — "

"Eric says a will's no good when it leaves money to someone who's a witness. Got that? So if you're named in the will, you can't also be a witness. Got *that*? Since this will leaves everything to the clinic, and the clinic's in your name, the court'll probably throw the whole thing out. Can you get that through your thick skull? I just wanted *Stillman* to sign it for now, and then I'd get someone else to do the witnessing."

"Why did you say the court will *probably* throw the whole thing out? It's either good or it isn't."

"Christ, how do I know? I'm no lawyer. Maybe you can be a witness, since the clinic is a corporation and the will leaves everything to *it*, not to you. But I doubt it. The shares are in your name. A good lawyer would cut through that in a minute."

She leaned against the wall and buried her

155

head in her hands. "Damn," her muffled voice said. "It almost worked."

She started to walk away in disgust, but then turned back and stared into her husband's eyes. "You better pray that the old fart didn't have any money."

On the Monday evening following Benjamin Stillman's death, Willard and Darlene DuPres had just returned from a long weekend at their lakefront cottage in Wisconsin. Because of the ever-increasing work load at the clinic, they never took regular vacations, and it was rare for them to tear themselves away even for a weekend. That was quite all right as far as Willard was concerned. Darlene was getting testier, especially after the Stillman episode, and being alone with her for an entire weekend was a trial.

Happily, this past weekend had been far better than most. It was Indian summer, and they had spent hours walking through the woods and along the lake. They had sipped brandy by the fire. They had even talked. For three days they had been like married couples were supposed to be. As Willard pulled the car into the driveway of their Winnetka home, he thought things might be getting better between them.

The thought was short-lived.

While he was unloading the car, Darlene picked up the weekend's mail and newspapers, which their neighbor had put behind the storm door, and went into the house. Just as he was closing the garage door, Willard heard the shriek. He ran into the house to find Darlene at the kitchen table with the Saturday *Tribune* spread out before her. It was open to Eloise Byrd's column. Darlene was almost incoherent.

"Oh, Christ! Oh, shit! Look what you — oh, you *asshole!* We could have — oh, my God, what a — aw, son of a bitch! You stupid son of a goddamn *bitch!* I hate you! I *hate* — "

"What the hell's the matter with you?" Willard shouted.

"You! You are what the hell's the matter with me, you asshole! Read this! Read it and weep, you bastard!"

Willard peered at the article on which she was drumming a forefinger. He got no further than the headline, "Mystery Recluse Leaves Millions to Synagogue," and a glimpse of Benjamin Stillman's name. He collapsed into a chair, realizing that he would never again know peace unless he committed suicide or murder.

Not another word was spoken between them that entire night. When Willard was preparing to leave for the clinic the next morning, he asked Darlene if she was coming along.

"To hell with you and your goddamn clinic. I'm going to see a lawyer, the best damn lawyer I can find in Chicago. If I can't find one who'll — "

"You won't have to go through all that. If you want a divorce, you can have one. I won't fight it. You can have whatever you want."

"What divorce? You're not getting off that cheap. I figure you owe me eight million bucks, and I'm gonna stick around until you earn that and more."

"But you just said you were going to hire a lawyer."

"Not for any two-bit divorce. I'm gonna make Stillman's will — *our* Stillman will — stick, and I'm gonna need the sharpest lawyer I can find to help me. I'm not about to lose that money without a fight."

"But you said the will's no good because I witnessed it and the clinic's in my name."

"Well, what if the clinic *isn't* in your name?"

"But it *is*."

"Don't be too sure about that. Remember that we incorporated the place a few years ago for tax purposes. It was the stock, not the clinic, that was put in your name."

"But — "

"And I distinctly remember that you transferred that stock to me more than a year ago." Now Darlene, who was developing her plan as she spoke, was building up a head of steam. "And you endorsed the stock certificates and gave them to me, and that means they're mine and I own the place. Remember that! And you only work there. Remember *that!*"

"But Darlene, I didn't give you the — "

"*Remember!*" she screamed. "You blew it the first time. Now don't blow it this time. *Remember!*"

Within fifteen minutes Darlene DuPres telephoned a lawyer she knew in another state, an old friend. She had no intention of retaining him or even telling him about the Stillman situation. She was merely asking a simple legal question "for a friend." Would he mind? No? Great, here was the question: If a will left something to a corporation, was it okay if an employee of that corporation was also a witness to the will?

The lawyer said he thought there would be nothing wrong with that, but he'd double-check Illinois law and call her back. Within twenty minutes he phoned to give Darlene the answer she wanted: Yes, it was just as he thought. It was all right for a corporate em-

159

ployee to witness a will leaving something to that corporation, though it wasn't recommended practice and might raise some questions.

Questions I can live with, Darlene DuPres said to herself as she hung up the phone. *But I can't live without that eight million bucks.*

Her lawyer friend had given her the right answer. But she had asked the wrong question.

16

Monday was a rough day for Ed Hirsch.

He had thought of little other than Ben Stillman and his money since the Saturday morning meeting with Bill Barnett and Jim Masters. However, he still couldn't focus on the potential conflict between Barnett Brothers and the synagogue. It was simply impossible that Stillman had stolen the money and he was certain that time would prove him correct. He was equally sure his co-workers would agree that Stillman was not a crook.

But on Monday morning the office was buzzing with enmity toward Stillman. One would have thought he'd already been indicted and convicted. Although everyone had his or her own idea *how* Stillman did it, no one seemed to doubt that he had indeed stolen the money from the firm. The partners cursed him and called him a thief; the rank and file made morbid jokes. By now the word was out that he wasn't Jewish, and this only heightened the intrigue.

Ed Hirsch was one of the very few who

still believed that Ben Stillman had been honest, but the more he said it the less sincere he sounded. After all, wasn't it only natural that a member of Beth Zion should defend its benefactor? How could he agree that Stillman was a thief when that would mean the money would go back to the rightful owners — Barnett Brothers — and not to the synagogue? Hirsch sensed that the others, behind his back, were ridiculing his defense of Stillman. He wondered what other jokes were being told about the money going to the Jews.

Despite his Saturday conversation with Barnett and Masters, Ed decided not to bring the subject up with the synagogue officials or members. If asked, he planned to say only that he had always liked Ben Stillman and had no reason to suspect he had done anything wrong. He chose not even to go near Beth Zion over the weekend.

But by Monday afternoon Hirsch felt isolated, and he sensed a polarization developing between the firm and Beth Zion. Only two days earlier Jim Masters had cautioned him against being caught in the middle of a "pissing match," and now it was beginning to happen even though Ed hadn't done a damn thing to provoke it. He was certainly not working with the congregation. Hell, he was *avoiding* them. Yet he still felt alienated from his colleagues at the firm. It just wasn't fair, he decided as he reached for his phone.

"Hi, Sam, it's Eddie Hirsch."

"Eddie! How are you?" Sam Altman had known the younger man since he was a baby, and he had always been fond of the only son of Mort and Ida Hirsch, his dear friends since childhood. In fact, one of Altman's first acts on becoming president of Beth Zion had been to appoint Eddie Hirsch to the synagogue's finance committee. Ed was only twenty-four at the time, and the appointment raised questions among the older congregants. The work of the finance committee was critical, particularly now, when they were fighting to save the place. Could a young man barely out of college be trusted with such responsibility? Altman had stuck to his guns and he had never had reason to regret it. Ed Hirsch worked hard and contributed many innovative ideas to increase income and cut expenses.

"I'd like to say I'm just fine, but this damn Stillman business is driving me nuts," Hirsch answered.

Altman paused for a moment. He too had been thinking about the "Stillman business" for the last few days. And he had thought of Eddie Hirsch the second he'd learned that

Stillman had also worked at Barnett Brothers. But he was reluctant to call Eddie for almost the same reasons Jim Masters didn't want to involve him. Masters didn't want the young man getting in trouble with the congregation, and Altman didn't want him in trouble with his employers.

"I can understand your feelings, Eddie. I hope this whole thing doesn't put you in an awkward situation at the firm."

"It shouldn't. I was assured by the senior guys over here that they understood my position. In fact, they said they fully expected that as a finance committee member I'd probably be helping Beth Zion all I could, and they actually thought I *should*. They couldn't have been nicer about the whole thing."

"Then what's the problem?" Sam Altman asked.

"Well," said Hirsch, "I'm not sure the others over here got the message. Not that anyone's said anything to my face, but I'm starting to get paranoid about what they're thinking or saying behind my back."

"C'mon, Eddie, you're not the paranoid type. You must have heard *something* that caused this concern."

"Yeah, I did. Actually, I've been hearing plenty, though none of it was aimed at Beth Zion or at me. It's just that everyone over here takes it for granted that Stillman stole the money from the firm. I can't believe it, but don't ask me to tell you how else he could have come into such a fortune."

"So?" prodded Altman.

"So, if that's what the people at Barnett really believe, they're not about to say good-bye to all that cash without a fight. I thought about it over the weekend and concluded that Stillman just wasn't a thief. There must be another explanation for the money. I guess I assumed that everyone else who knew Ben would come to the same conclusion. But I tell you, Sam, I'm a minority of one over here. If we put it to a vote, these people would march right out to the cemetery and dig the old bastard up just so they could beat the shit out of him and then hang him. They're convinced the money's theirs, and they want it back, period."

"Well, Eddie, it looks like we'll have a fight on our hands then, doesn't it?"

"I'm afraid so."

"And where do you stand? Are you with us or agin us, or would you prefer to remain neutral?"

"I wish I could stay out of it, but I can't. I take my commitment to Beth Zion very seriously, and I've worked too damn hard on the finance committee to see our chance to survive go out the window. And even if it sounds corny, I feel a sort of duty to Stillman's honor. He has no one at the office defending him, and I think he needs *somebody* on his side. Since I'm one of his beneficiaries it may as well be me."

Then Hirsch added with a grin Sam couldn't see: "Anyway, Bill Barnett himself told me that as a finance committee member I should fight for the money. Those were his exact words. I guess I'll put them to the test."

Sam Altman was touched. He'd always liked the boy; now he loved the man.

"Tell me, Eddie," he said, "would you be willing to come to an informal meeting tonight at my house? We've put together a small group — you might call it an ad hoc committee — to represent the congregation's interest in this thing. There's Lee Schlessinger, Pete Golden, Howard Rhyne, and me. The rabbi really organized us, but he thinks it's inappropriate for him to participate except on a now-and-then basis." With a laugh, Sam added: "Jake doesn't think he should be involved at the warfare stage, but if we get the money you can be sure he'll be there at the spending stage."

"I'll be happy to come, Sam."

"Terrific! I think it's only right that we

have someone from the finance committee on board. Eight o'clock."

And just twelve hours later Alan Fiori would be convening his own ad hoc committee of two to stake its claim to the Stillman fortune.

17

Leon Schlessinger was the last to arrive at Sam Altman's home in one of the few still-fashionable neighborhoods on Chicago's Northwest Side. He didn't arrive alone.

"Gentlemen, may I present Margaret Flynn. Maggie is an associate of mine at the firm. I've asked her to help us on the Stillman case. She does a good deal of the firm's probate work and can answer some of our questions."

Maggie Flynn was an extremely attractive young woman who appeared both pleasant and professional. Her golden hair was pulled tightly into a bun, with just a few wisps drifting around the back of her long, graceful neck. She wore natural tortoiseshell glasses with large round frames, a no-frills white blouse, and a gray wool skirt. Although the skirt was full and hung to mid-calf, it did little to conceal her slender but shapely figure.

All the men stood to welcome her and introduce themselves. None was so ill-mannered as to comment on her good looks, but none was so blind as not to notice. Especially the young bachelor, Ed Hirsch, who was probably the only man there to observe that she wasn't wearing a wedding or engagement ring. (And he made certain the bare third finger of *his* left hand was conspicuous all evening.)

After introductions were made and Sam Altman took orders for coffee and cocktails, Leon Schlessinger opened the discussion. His dark business suit suggested that he had driven to the meeting directly from his downtown office instead of first going out to his home in Glencoe. Even though it had been at least twelve hours since he'd dressed for work that morning, there wasn't a wrinkle to be seen. He appeared fresh and perfectly groomed.

"I'd like to report that I had lunch today with Philip Ogden. He's the lawyer who drew Stillman's will and he'll be handling the estate once the will is admitted to probate."

He described the lunch as uneventful. He said he liked and trusted Phil Ogden and he believed that the young lawyer would sincerely work to see that Stillman's will was carried out to the benefit of Beth Zion. "He doesn't strike me as the type of lawyer who will just sit back and collect his fee while we fight off creditors and other claimants. He admitted to a lack of experience in probate law and invited my assistance. I'm making Maggie here available to him."

Each man silently assessed the value of Maggie Flynn's good looks for the task of keeping Philip Ogden in their camp. Each concluded that it wasn't only her probate experience that qualified her for this assignment.

"Lee, you said on the phone this afternoon that the will was different than we thought." This from Howard Rhyne. "Why don't you tell us about it?"

"Of course. That was the first thing on my list." And that was Maggie Flynn's cue to hand out copies of Stillman's will. Schlessinger continued: "Until my lunch with Ogden, I — we all — assumed that Ben Stillman left his entire estate to us outright; that is, no conditions or restrictions. Well, that's true up to a point. He left twenty percent, something over a million and a half, to us to do with as we please. No strings attached. But the rest he gave to us to hold in trust for other Jewish charities."

"*What* other Jewish charities?" asked Pete Golden.

"That would be up to us," the lawyer replied. "The will was very clear about that. We could pick them ourselves."

Golden looked confused. "You mean we decide which Jewish causes we like and then we just turn over all that dough?"

"No, Pete, it doesn't work that way. We would set up a trust fund — a foundation — to invest that eighty percent. That would be about six and a half million dollars. So we'd invest it and earn about five hundred thousand a year, and that's what we'd give away. But we'd retain control over the principal, the six and a half million, and keep investing it and doling out the income."

"You know, I like it better that way," said Howard Rhyne. "The twenty percent for us is just fine, thank you. Hell, I don't know what we'd do with more than that. We could fix up the building, pay off the debt, and still have plenty left over. And we could do so much for our people all over the world — that's right, isn't it, Lee? We could use it anywhere?"

"Right. It's not restricted to Chicago or even the United States."

"Okay, then." Rhyne continued. "We might use some of it to help resettle the Jews coming out of Russia. Or the starving Jews in Ethiopia. We could even set up scholarship programs. Hell, we could involve so many of our congregants in this thing — it would be fantastic!"

"I agree," echoed Leon Schlessinger, "and it improves our legal position."

"How so?" Ed Hirsch inquired. He was so obsessed by the inevitable showdown between Beth Zion and Barnett Brothers that any mention of the legal angle piqued his interest.

"Because now we're on the side of the angels, don't you see? We're not fighting for eight million dollars to roll around in and spend on ourselves. We'll be representing every poor, hungry, sick, and persecuted Jew in the world. Now who's going to take that money away from them? A bunch of rich brokers who sell tax shelters and drive around in Jaguars? No way! And what about the judge? If he takes that money away, he'll go down in history as the worst anti-Semite since Herod."

Leon Schlessinger looked around the room. "Get the picture?" Everyone nodded and smiled.

"Now, before we get into the meeting any further," he continued, "I think it would be helpful to review the bidding up to here. Let's see if we can agree on what has happened so far, what problems we're likely to face, and how we can best avoid or overcome them. We can't afford any mistakes."

"Good idea, Lee," said Sam Altman before anyone else could speak. "Suppose you lead off." Altman hadn't been pleased with the first meeting when, it seemed, he was all but ignored. The one suggestion he had made — using part of Stillman's money to construct a new building — had evoked sharp criticism and a personal attack from Schlessinger. Well, damn it, he was president of the congregation, and he was the one who would ultimately be held accountable if they didn't get the money. Even if he wasn't a lawyer like that know-it-all Schlessinger, he could at least exercise his authority by having the meetings at his home and acting as moderator.

"Happy to." Schlessinger opened his briefcase and pulled out a yellow legal pad full of notes.

"First off, let's agree on what we know so far. We know that Ben Stillman died last Wednesday night, that about a year ago he signed a will leaving all his property to us, and that a few days before his death he still intended for us to get it."

"How do you know that — that last part?" Howard Rhyne asked.

"Ogden told me at lunch today that the old man wrote him a letter from the hospital. He referred to the will Ogden drafted for him and urged Ogden to defend both the will and his honor if either were attacked. He even sent Ogden a list of his securities and the key to his safe-deposit box. These are hardly the actions of a man who had changed his mind."

"Good point," Sam Altman volunteered, eager to be heard from whenever possible.

Schlessinger went on. "What we *don't* know, however, is more important than what we *do* know." He looked around the room to give that comment a chance to sink in. "First, we don't know *why* he left us his money, and the answer to that could be crucial if we have to defend the will. It's tough to defend something you can't even explain. Second, we don't know for sure if the will is valid, although I don't have any reason to doubt it."

Now it was Pete Golden who had a question. "That should be easy to find out, shouldn't it? I mean, I'm not an attorney, but can't you just look at the damn thing and tell if it's valid?"

"Yes and no." Although Schlessinger relished having the floor, he thought Maggie Flynn should participate as much as possible. Since she'd be working on the case and giving advice to the others, it was important that she gain their confidence. Schlessinger remembered when he was just beginning his career. How he hated it when a senior partner took him along only to take notes and keep the papers straight! If his boss didn't ask

174

for his advice, why should the client? "Maggie, would you answer Pete's question?"

Maggie Flynn, who was sitting on the sofa, leaned forward to set her coffee cup down and began to answer Pete Golden's question while letting her eyes move from person to person. She spoke clearly and confidently.

"It's easy to tell if the *form* of a will is valid. As long as it's signed by the testator — that is, the person whose will it is — and his or her signature is attested by two witnesses, the form is perfectly valid. No magic legal words are necessary, it can be on any kind of paper, and it can be signed with pen, pencil, or crayon. It doesn't have to describe the property being transferred — except when specific articles, like jewelry, are given to specific people. Even if there is something unclear or ambiguous about the will, it's still valid; in those cases we just have a judge construe it."

Maggie Flynn looked at Pete Golden. "So yes, Mr. Golden, it's easy to look at a will and tell if it is valid *as to form*." She took a sip of her coffee, leaned back, and continued. "But we have to look at more than the *form* of a will before we can determine its validity."

"What else is there to look at?" This question was from Ed Hirsch, who was fascinated with Maggie's explanation of a subject that, he was sure, must be more complicated than she was making it sound.

"We have to look behind the document itself — at the testator and the witnesses — and ask some hard questions. Was the testator mentally competent to sign the will *at the time* he signed it? Was he sane? Was he under the influence of drugs or alcohol? Was he being coerced or unduly influenced by someone? Did the witnesses actually *see* him sign it, as they must unless he later acknowledged the signature as his in their presence? Could either of the witnesses benefit from the will?"

She paused long enough to make sure she still had everyone's attention. "Some of these questions are very hard to answer. What is 'sane'? An intelligent person could, at a given moment, be legally incompetent due to a temporary lapse or delusion. What quantity of drugs or alcohol would be needed to destroy competence? And what about coercion or undue influence? There have been many cases where a parent leaves money to a child, which seems quite normal, and then we find out the child had threatened to put the parent in a nursing home or even a mental institution unless such a will was written. Coercion? Undue influence?"

"Whoa," Sam Altman interrupted. "Slow down a minute. Does any of this really apply here? Do we even know who the witnesses were? Do we have any reason to suspect that Mr. Stillman was anything but sane? And who says he was subjected to — what did you call it — undue influence?"

Maggie started to speak, but Leon Schlessinger held up his hand to stop her. Everything Maggie had said up to that point was accurate, but Schlessinger saw that she was making a mistake common to younger lawyers eager to impress their clients. They not only answer the question at hand; they tell all they know about the subject. Ask a young lawyer what time it is and he'll tell you how to make a watch. It's sophomoric, and worse, it tends to deflect attention away from the central point. Why the hell waste time, Schlessinger thought, talking about drugs, alcohol, and ineligible witnesses? He'd already told Maggie what he'd learned about the will from Philip Ogden. None of this rhetoric was pertinent.

"You're right, Sam," he said, "most of these things aren't directly applicable, but Maggie thinks — and I agree with her — that it's important for you to understand the broad guidelines on the subject. Even if some of them don't apply, it will provide a background for a better understanding of the rules that do." In fact, Schlessinger didn't agree with Maggie's conducting a seminar on the entire subject of wills, but it was important to support her in front of the others.

"Based on what Ogden told me at lunch, I'm satisfied that the form of the will is valid. He and his secretary witnessed it, and that should be that. They're adults, they're not beneficiaries, and they know the rules about signing. And I don't think we have to worry about Stillman's state of mind. The fact that he appeared perfectly normal when he was in the lawyer's office for about an hour on the day he signed the will dispels the idea that he was drugged or drunk or under anyone's influence — especially since he reaffirmed the will in his letter from the hospital just before he died.

"Finally, how can anyone question Stillman's sanity or competence considering the nature of his job right up until the end?" He looked to Ed Hirsch, who was nodding his head to confirm the point.

"So you're telling us we have nothing to worry about?" Sam Altman asked.

"No, I'm not, Sam." Schlessinger repeated some of the questions he'd raised at the earlier meeting, any one of which could defeat

178

Beth Zion's right to the money. They still didn't know if a Mrs. Stillman would show up, and they still didn't know if the money was stolen.

"By and large," he added, "we're pretty much in the dark, but I feel better about this thing than I did Saturday, when all we had to go on was that story in the paper. At least now we know the will exists. Ogden said he'd already filed it with the probate court. It now seems clearer that Stillman wasn't a loony and it seems more likely that he really had money. Hell, on Saturday I suspected that this whole thing could be a practical joke. I don't think so now."

Ed Hirsch had been biting his tongue listening to everyone speculate about Stillman's sanity and his money. He thought it was about time to throw in his own two cents' worth.

"I think maybe I should say something."

All eyes turned toward him.

"It's nothing really important, but I'd like to clarify a couple of things. Things about Ben Stillman, Barnett Brothers, and me."

"Go ahead, Eddie," Sam urged.

"Well, I'm the only one here who knew Ben, and I think you should know something about him." The others were clearly interested in learning about the mysterious man who was trying to give them everything he owned. "Ben was not a partner in the firm. He wasn't even a broker. He was an accountant; he posted transactions and balanced accounts.

"And he was a sweet guy. I never saw him lose his temper and never saw him be rude or mistreat anyone. In fact, he was one of the most polite men I've ever seen. This is not to say that Ben was one of those old-timers who is always taking you under his wing or telling you stories. It was nothing like that. But he always had a smile and a thank-you and was always willing to give you a hand. If he saw that I was working through lunch, he'd offer to bring me a sandwich; if he saw I was having trouble balancing an account, he'd ask if he could do it for me. I know people can fool you, and every once in a while we read about a little old lady who turns out to be the ax murderer who's been doing everyone in for the past twenty years, but I just can't imagine Ben Stillman stealing a cent, let alone millions."

"Who said he did?" The question came from Pete Golden.

"For starters, just about everyone who works at Barnett Brothers."

"I'm confused," Leon Schlessinger said. "From the way you describe him — quiet, polite, helpful, diligent — I wouldn't think his fellow workers would be so quick to call him a crook. Was he less polite or less helpful toward them? Did they have reason to see him differently from you?"

"No, not at all," Ed answered. "No one at the office ever said an unkind word about him — until he died."

The room fell silent as the listeners asked themselves whether the "sweet old guy" Ed Hirsch portrayed could possibly have stolen millions of dollars.

Howard Rhyne broke the silence by changing the subject. "A minute ago, Ed, you said you wanted to clarify something about Barnett Brothers. What's that?"

"Only this. Even though I'm irritated by what the people there are saying about Ben right now, they're good folks and I like them. And I like my job. I want to keep it, so I'm not going to be a fink or a double agent and keep telling you guys tales out of school. I'll only tell you this much: I think the firm is going to fight you for the money. Nobody actually said that to me, but they're sure the money was taken from them and they'll want it back."

"If they can prove the money was theirs," Rhyne asked, "would that mean they can challenge the will?" He looked toward Maggie Flynn.

"They wouldn't have to," she replied. "A will disposes of only the money or property left after the creditors have been paid. They come first. If Barnett Brothers could show that the money was illegally taken from them, they would come into court as a creditor of Mr. Stillman and demand repayment. They wouldn't have to attack the will. But I see at least three major obstacles they'd have to overcome in order to prevail." She'd evidently gotten the earlier message from Schlessinger, since she asked, "Would you like me to go into that now?"

"Yes, please do," Sam Altman suggested. "That's important for us to understand."

"First, it would be very difficult to prove that the money was stolen, even if it really was. If Mr. Stillman took it, he must have been very careful in leaving no evidence or he would have been found out long ago. Brokerage firms deal with other people's money and hold large amounts of cash and securities for their customers. They are therefore subject to very strict accounting and auditing procedures. If the theft didn't show up before, I don't know why it would show up now. The best argument they have, as I see it, is that if Stillman does have millions it would be a good guess that he stole it from the firm. But that's not enough. Guesses aren't proof.

"Second, even if they could show a theft, they would still have a problem of mathematics. For example, what if they can prove a theft of, say, three million dollars and Stillman had eight million when he died. Would proof that he stole three be sufficient to prove that he must have stolen the other five? Or what if the other five million was the result of Stillman's prudent investments? Would Barnett Brothers be entitled to recover the interest or investment growth of money taken from them?

"Finally, there is the statute of limitations. A person who has a right to bring a lawsuit must do it within a certain length of time or lose the right. The length of time depends on the type of case, but it's seldom more than five years."

"Well, that's encouraging," Howard Rhyne said. "Stillman worked at the firm for forty years, and he couldn't have stolen it all at once — even if we assume that he stole it in the first place. So the firm would lose the right to get back the amounts that were stolen except for the last few years. Right?"

"Not really," Maggie explained. "In cases like this, the time for filing suit might not start to run until the plaintiff — that is, the person bringing suit — knew or should have known that the theft took place. Since Barnett

Brothers didn't know about the theft, if there was a theft, until Stillman died, they may still have time to file their claim for anything stolen more than five years ago."

Pete Golden asked, "Do you agree, Lee, that it would be hard to prove the money was stolen? Or would we have to prove the money *wasn't* stolen?"

Schlessinger paused to organize his thoughts. "No," he said after a moment or two, "we don't have to prove a thing. Since Barnett Brothers would be making the claim, they would have to prove the theft; if they couldn't, we'd keep the money. They have what the law calls the burden of proof.

"As to whether they *could* prove theft, I agree with Maggie that it would be hard to do. It would take teams of accountants who would have to examine Stillman's investments and then work backward."

"Backward?" This from Sam Altman.

"Yes. Let's assume, for example, that Stillman had one hundred thousand dollars' worth of General Motors stock. The accountants would then go back and determine what he paid for that stock. Not hard to do; there are records of that. If it turned out that he paid eighty thousand, his gain was twenty. That would account for twenty thousand that wasn't stolen. That process would have to be repeated over and over again until, we hope, they could account for the whole eight million."

"And if they couldn't?" Golden asked.

"Then things start to get a little dicey. That would be proof that some of the money, the part they couldn't account for, came from somewhere else. But does it prove that it was stolen from Barnett Brothers? I don't think so, even though it might be *evidence* that it was stolen from them. Maybe he got a gift or an inheritance. Hell, maybe the son of a bitch won a lottery." Schlessinger smiled and added, "Or maybe the old coot robbed a bank or snatched purses or peddled drugs. But if those guys at Barnett Brothers can't prove that he stole the money *from them,* they lose and we win."

Now it was Maggie Flynn's turn. She asked Ed Hirsch if he or anyone at his firm had had a chance to review Stillman's securities transactions. She knew that Stillman's estate consisted almost entirely of stocks and bonds; Philip Ogden had said as much to Schlessinger at lunch. Maggie naturally assumed that Stillman would have run his transactions through Barnett Brothers.

"I meant to bring that up earlier," Ed Hirsch said. "There was no record whatsoever at the firm that Stillman ever bought so much as one share of stock."

The silence that engulfed the room was finally broken by Sam Altman.

"Jesus, then maybe he did steal the . . ." He couldn't finish the sentence.

Alan Fiori would have had no trouble finishing it for him.

18

Benjamin Stillman would have been amused to see all that was taking place that Monday evening. No one connected with the "Stillman thing," as it had come to be called, was idle.

Philip Ogden was in a small room in the basement of a bank busily adding up Stillman's net worth. Darlene DuPres was similarly occupied in her kitchen with her newspapers, berating her husband and trying to find new adjectives to describe his stupidity. At the same time she was beginning to formulate a plan to salvage something from the wreckage. And Stillman's beneficiaries at Beth Zion, who were still pinching themselves to make sure that their legacy wasn't a dream, were busy debating for the umpteenth time whether their benefactor was really rich, rational, and honest.

Bill Barnett suppressed a smile as he looked about the room and saw the faces of his partners. How things had changed since his father and uncle had started the firm at that same South LaSalle Street address nearly fifty years earlier. Whereas Bill, Sr., and Uncle Joe hadn't added a third partner until after the war in 1945, Barnett Brothers now had thirty-one full partners, half a dozen juniors, and an equal number of salaried, or staff, brokers. The original support staff for the firm had been one person, Bill and Joe's older sister Claudia, who acted as secretary, bookkeeper, notary, and cleaning woman. Now, with programmers, processors, filers, supervisors, managers, researchers, and secretaries, the support staff far outnumbered those actually selling securities.

And the equipment! What had once been a couple of mechanical Smith Corona typewriters and a single ticker-tape receiver was now an endless array of computer terminals. Bill Barnett's father and uncle had once resisted using a mechanical adding machine. By the time they'd learned to trust "those gadgets," the adding machines had been replaced by calculators, which were in turn replaced by computers.

And the partners themselves had changed. They had once been called stockbrokers; now they were securities dealers. They had traditionally been the men in the gray flannel suits; now they wore plaids and checks, sport coats and Gucci loafers. More significantly, they were no longer homogeneous. The partnership roster now included a black, three women, and two Jews. (The three women and two Jews added up to only four people — Dorothy Fine was both.) Neither of the two Jewish partners belonged to Beth Zion, so their presence at tonight's meeting would not be a problem. Ed Hirsch, who was a member of the synagogue, was not yet a partner in the firm and therefore was not at the meeting.

Generally partnership meetings took place outside the firm's offices. They would sometimes be dinner meetings but, more often than not, mid-afternoon "cocktail hour" meetings, which were convenient because the market closed early.

But tonight's meeting had been called for after dinner, at eight o'clock, in the firm's large conference room. Bill Barnett, who as the managing partner had called the meeting, knew the hour would be inconvenient for some of his partners, but he had his reasons. The time and the privacy of their own offices would insure the confidentiality of the evening's discussions. With luck, neither the public nor any of the office staff would even know that the meeting was taking place. The safest place for thirty people to meet in Chicago without being seen is right in the heart of the financial district — after

7:00 P.M. After that the street sees only a few late-working, tired lawyers and secretaries racing for their commuter trains.

As Barnett's eyes passed over the room one last time before he called the meeting to order, he noticed the clothes his partners were wearing. Because the partners' meetings usually convened immediately after office hours, he was accustomed to seeing his colleagues in the clothes they wore to work. But tonight many of those who lived in the city had gone home first and changed to more comfortable attire. He saw blue jeans, jogging suits, sneakers, cowboy boots, turtlenecks, and leather windbreakers. It seemed to him that the more successful people were between nine and five, the less they wanted to dress like it between five and nine.

When the attendance was as complete as it was likely to get, Bill Barnett called the meeting to order. "I think you all know why we're here. We have several items to discuss about this Stillman thing. How can we find out for sure whether the money was stolen from us? If it looks like it was stolen, what, if anything, are we going to do about it? And most of all — "

"What do you mean 'if anything?' " The interruption came in a loud voice — almost a shout — from one of the newer partners. "Do you really think we would forget about going after the money? Not me. I want my share back, and I damn well mean to get it!"

Bill Barnett knew that feelings were running high, but he hadn't thought anyone would be getting so emotional this early in the meeting. He immediately rearranged his mental outline of the agenda; he had to defuse the bombs that were ticking in this room.

He looked directly at the young partner who had interrupted him and spoke slowly and quietly. "I know exactly how you feel, George. Hell, if he stole from you, then he stole from me too. In fact," Barnett added with a shrug, "he would have taken more from me. My share of each buck around here is larger than yours. And I've been a partner for over thirty years, while you've been one for — what, less than two? How much could Ben Stillman have taken from you? Compare that with what he could have taken from me.

"I'd be very upset, much more than any of you, if it turned out that Ben Stillman embezzled from us. I'd be disappointed; he was like an uncle to me. But I'd also be pissed off — excuse me, ladies — angry, angry and irate that a person in whom my own father and uncle, and all of us here, put so much trust could do such a thing.

"No, George, I'm not suggesting that any of us 'forget about' the money if it was stolen."

Changing character, Bill Barnett leaned forward and slammed his fist onto the conference table. "But goddamnit, I'm not going to run around calling someone a thief until I see pretty good evidence that that's the case. And the same thing applies to all of you. If you have proof that Ben embezzled, bring it forward. Otherwise, keep your opinions to yourself."

Jim Masters, the number two man at the firm, broke in. He knew that Bill wanted to keep things cool, but even he was getting caught up in the emotions of the thing. And Masters was well aware of Barnett's frustration at having to appear as if he were waiting for proof before believing Stillman stole the money. Hell, Bill Barnett was already convinced that it had been stolen, but he was doing his best — at Masters's insistence — to keep his feelings to himself.

"Bill's absolutely correct," Masters interjected. "It's imperative that none of us says anything about a theft or embezzlement unless we have clear proof. It's not only unfair to Ben; it makes us look like a bunch of idiots. Just think about it for a second. We ask people to hand us their money and trust us to take good care of it and invest it wisely. But in the meantime, they hear that one of our own employees — someone we've trusted for over forty years — is helping himself to eight million bucks of our own money."

Masters paused just long enough to recall the calculation Ed Hirsch had made on the napkin Saturday morning. "And that comes out to one thousand smackers a day. Is that what you want people to think of when they think of Barnett Brothers? That we hire thieves? That we're so careless we don't even know when someone is taking our *own* money in bushel baskets? That our security is so lax we can't prevent it before it happens and our auditing procedures so poor we can't even find it after it happens? Is that what you want people to think? It'd be bad enough if it were true, but we don't *know* that it's true. So why spread it around as if it were?"

By the time one or two others had spoken about the need for secrecy, there seemed to be general assent that the partners should keep the lid on any suspicions they might have concerning Ben Stillman's honesty. Nearly all of them still believed Stillman had stolen the money, but they understood the need for keeping it quiet — at least for the time being.

One of the more senior partners, Adam

Carmichael, made a related point. "Seems to me," he said, "that it's essential we be consistent among ourselves in talking with people on the outside. A lot of my friends are asking me about this thing. You all must be getting it, too. I think we should be telling them all the same thing. Actually, I wish to God we didn't have to say anything, but that's unrealistic. You can't *not* talk to your friends and, if you did, it would raise even more questions. But let's be consistent, and let's agree on what we should tell them."

Bill Barnett spoke. "Good point, Adam. I agree that we should speak with one voice. I suggest we first try to make some decisions among ourselves and then see if we can agree on whether and how to communicate them to outsiders." He held up a scrap of paper. "I took the liberty of making a short list of a few questions I think we should address right away. If you have no objection, I'll share them with you." Without waiting for an answer, he walked over to an easel that held large white sheets of paper and with a marking pen printed on the top sheet:

1. Outside Audit? Should we order? Who use? How much cost?

2. Spokesman for us? Who? One of us?

Outside PR firm? Public statement?

3. Lawyer? Too early now? Who?

4. Beth Zion Syn? Do we contact? When?

5. Ed Hirsch?

6. Risks of fighting (assuming Ben stole the $):
   A. Expense of litigation?
   B. Advertise our carelessness?
   C. Alienate Jewish clients?
   D. Reaction of other clients?

Bill Barnett turned and saw that everyone in the room was studying his list, each already formulating his or her own answers to the questions.

"Okay," he said. "Let's take these one at a time. I encourage anyone and everyone to participate, but I want some ground rules so we're not here all night. Raise your hand if you have something to say or ask. Don't speak until you're recognized. Don't hesitate to speak your mind. Finally, and most important, we must treat what is said here tonight as strictly confidential. I'll have no patience with anyone who gossips about this meeting."

It went without saying that Bill Barnett would act as moderator of the discussion.

Three hours later, the only thing on which everyone agreed was that very little had been accomplished. Whatever topic was discussed, someone inevitably asked a question only a lawyer could answer. Would an auditor's report be good evidence in court? If Barnett Brothers used its own regular auditors as opposed to independent auditors, would their partiality taint their findings? If there might be litigation, wouldn't it be inappropriate to make a public statement or contact the people at the synagogue? How much would a lawsuit cost? How long would this whole thing take? What were their chances?

One point that hadn't been anticipated by Bill Barnett turned out to be of serious concern to everyone. Since a lawsuit would necessarily involve an examination of the firm's books, would the earnings and holdings of the respective partners be open to the public? If so, wasn't there some way their right of privacy could be protected? These, too, were questions that could be answered only by a lawyer. Although there was general agreement that the firm should retain an attorney, there was no agreement on who this attorney should be.

To lighten the tension, one of the younger

partners violated the rule about not speaking without being recognized: "Christ, Bill, how can you expect us to agree on these things? We can't even agree on which stocks to buy, and *that's* something we're supposed to know about." Barnett joined in the laughter.

One of the partners offered a suggestion that was readily agreed to by everyone: have a committee make an informal study and recommend two or three lawyers for the entire firm to consider at a later meeting.

Seeing that the idea was acceptable to the others, Barnett embraced it. "Good idea. I'll head up the committee myself, and I'll appoint two others. But we won't formally retain anyone until we're all sure he's the one we want."

"Or *she's* the one we want," interjected Bea Clemmins, one of the three women partners in the firm, from her seat in the front row. One of the most successful women in finance in Chicago, Bea Clemmins was the self-appointed spokesperson for all other women in those professions traditionally dominated by men. She and Bill Barnett had been close friends since their junior high days at the Francis Parker School. But she was never hesitant to take him on, especially in the presence of the other partners.

"Of course, Bea. That goes without saying.

Everyone here knows full well how liberal I am in these matters."

Barnett's statement evoked the guffaws he intended. It was a joke around the office that Bill Barnett thought women should be home and pregnant, and he himself got a kick out of saying things that added credence to the story. In fact, he was a strong supporter of women's rights in the office, as Bea Clemmins could attest. It had been his decision to change the firm's annual golf outing to a place and time when the women could play, just as it had been his decision to cancel the firm's membership at a men's club after Bea was admitted to partnership.

Pat Singleton, the second woman to become a partner at the firm, was definitely not a feminist. In fact, she was always embarrassed by Bea Clemmins's objections to the way clerical women were treated around the office by men who expected them to get coffee, sew on buttons, or run personal errands for them. Pat Singleton preferred staying out of both limelight and controversy, content to remain in the background and collect the substantial commissions from investing her wealthy family's portfolio. During this meeting she was sitting at the back of the room.

The third female partner at Barnett Brothers, Dorothy Fine, quietly suffered through the meeting. As she had reached partnership status only a year earlier, she was reluctant to voice her concern about a possible battle with Beth Zion. Dorothy Fine was Jewish and, even though she was not a member of Beth Zion, she felt seriously threatened by this whole business. Many of her clients were Jewish, and she was certain the entire Jewish community — regardless of synagogue or temple affiliation — would be outraged if Barnett Brothers challenged Beth Zion's claim to Stillman's estate. Many people might register their anger by refusing to invest through the firm.

When the meeting reached the item on Bill Barnett's agenda marked "Alienate Jewish clients?" Dorothy Fine felt everyone's eyes on her. She said nothing until one partner put the question to her point-blank.

"I think Dorothy should be heard from on this one."

"Yeah, whaddya think, Dot? Will the Jewish folks in town hold it against us if we go after the money?"

Oh, how she wished that Charlie Wolf were at the meeting. Charlie was the other Jewish partner in the firm, and he wouldn't hesitate one second to raise hell about anything that might jeopardize his relationships with clients. But he was on vacation this week, and she would have to handle this on her own.

Dorothy measured her words carefully before speaking. "Yes, I think there would be a big backlash from the entire Jewish community. Jewish people support one another on these issues, even those not directly affected. It's almost a genetic thing. For example, Jews who are anti-Zionists — that is, who don't believe Israel should be the official homeland for the Jewish people — nevertheless contribute generously to help Israel fend off the Arabs. Nonreligious Jews fight like hell to defend the rights of the religious ones. And Jews who love to tell Jewish jokes resent it when the same jokes are told by non-Jews."

She looked toward the partner who asked the question. "So yes, if you — we — decide to fight for the money, we'll be fighting more than just the Jews at Beth Zion."

Although Dorothy decided she had answered adequately for present purposes, she knew the point about alienating Jews in general would have to be made more forcefully later on, or she and the firm would risk losing all their Jewish clients.

She resolved to contact Charlie Wolf first thing in the morning to let him know what was going on. She also entertained the thought of talking this over with Ed Hirsch, but she remembered Bill Barnett's warning about not discussing the meeting with outsiders. Since this was a partners' meeting, Ed was an outsider.

The meeting ended with no comment at all on that item on Bill Barnett's agenda labeled "Ed Hirsch." Nothing had to be said; the agenda itself said it all. *Ed Hirsch is one of "them." Be careful what you say around him.*

PART IV
TUESDAY

19

MYSTERY DEEPENS IN STILLMAN LEGACY — CONTEST HINTED

BY ELOISE BYRD

The mystery surrounding the will of Benjamin Stillman, first reported in this column Saturday, deepens. Courthouse observers are already placing bets on the eventual outcome.

The questions that are sure to keep the lawyers guessing are multiplying. How did a salaried office worker manage to acquire $8 million? Why did he leave it all to a synagogue when, this reporter has learned, he was not even Jewish? Where are the relatives he has disinherited? Will his employers claim he embezzled the money from them?

Stillman's safe-deposit box was opened yesterday under the watchful eye of an attorney general's staffer. Reliable sources have verified that the box contained securities valued in excess of $8 million.

Officials of Beth Zion Synagogue, Stillman's beneficiary, have confirmed that he was not a member of the congregation. More curious is the fact that Stillman was buried in a Catholic cemetery, St. Mary's, where he had purchased a plot several months before his death.

Stillman's relatives have yet to surface. It is not known whether he was survived by any family members. But, according to lawyers we have questioned, everyone has some relatives who would stand to inherit in the absence of a will. Who are they? Where are they? Is anyone looking for them?

But the biggest question — the $8 million question — lies with Barnett Brothers, the brokerage house where Stillman worked for forty years preceding his death last week. Sources within that firm confirmed that the Barnett partners met last night for several hours to consider whether to sue for the money they believe Stillman stole from them. The results of that meeting were unknown at the time this column went to press.

Philip Ogden, the attorney who drafted the will and who is named as executor, refused to comment. The only comment from Beth Zion was that the synagogue was taking a wait-and-see attitude.

The will itself, which was filed yesterday in probate court, made no additional bequests and furnished no clues as to Stillman's family or motive. It simply left everything to Beth Zion, 20 percent to be used for the synagogue's own purposes and 80 percent for other Jewish causes.

The case has been assigned to Judge Verne Lloyd, a senior member of the Cook County bench.

It was nearly eight o'clock Tuesday morning. The newspaper, open to Eloise Byrd's column, was spread out on the table of the corner booth. By now the tabletop also held two empty plates, two coffee cups that had been refilled four or five times, and an ashtray that had been emptied twice and was again half-full of cigarette butts. The tabletop in front of one of the occupants was a mess.

The two lawyers sitting in the booth had been the sole partners in their firm since leaving the state's attorney's staff three years earlier. They met most weekday mornings at the Courthouse Square Café for a quick breakfast and, generally by eight-thirty, left the cafe for their Randolph Street office around the corner. This particular morning, however, they were engrossed in a subject much more interesting — and potentially much more profitable — than the mundane evictions and divorces awaiting their attention at the office.

"I guess you're right, Al. If we don't, someone else sure as hell will."

"Bet your life. And we'd be kicking our asses the rest of our lives for bein' chickenshit." Al Fiori snuffed out another cigarette. "I've been thinking about this since Saturday, when I first read about it, and I say we do it — and fast."

Carl Sandquist was the dull, unimaginative half of the firm of Fiori & Sandquist. His partner, Al Fiori, was the risk taker, the one who preferred the all-or-nothing, contingent fee cases to safer hourly rate work. Although each spent most of his time on court disputes, Carl's cases were usually of the less dramatic kind — foreclosures, evictions, and collections. Al, on the other hand, found contested divorce, personal injury, and criminal cases better suited to his flamboyance and thirst for excitement. Carl handled his cases by the book, seldom trying a new approach or taking a chance that might backfire. Al, however, always searched for the unexpected angle, whether a novel legal theory, a mystery witness, or a surprise document.

Their different approaches were the result of different styles. Carl always took the straight line, relying on tested methods; Al played the angles, relying more on intuition. Al's methods had always been ethical and aboveboard — but barely. He walked very close to the edge.

This improbable partnership had struggled along for three years. Carl, a born follower, needed the leadership Al Fiori provided. And Al, who couldn't yet attract the clientele necessary to maintain his lifestyle, needed the fees generated by Carl's father, a master slumlord who operated anonymously behind secret land trusts and dummy corporations. This union, doomed by incompatibility, would last no longer than it took Al Fiori to bring in some fees — real fees — on his own. The circumstances of Ben Stillman's fortune, he believed, just might be his way out.

"But we've never handled a class action," Carl Sandquist was saying. "That bother you?" The tabletop in front of him was liberally punctuated with crumbs and small puddles of juice and coffee. Carl's eating habits left much to be desired.

"Hell no, not a bit," Al replied, trying to ignore the slop on the table. "I sure as hell don't want to chase alimony checks the rest of my life. This thing could mean a big payday for us and some healthy publicity along the way."

"But a class action . . ." Carl shook his head. "Christ, Al, you'd be taking on a Jewish synagogue and the biggest brokerage house in town. Do you realize how much money they'd have to fight us with? Between 'em they'd hire the whole fuckin' bar association."

"Good," Fiori said, laughing. "They'll have all the lawyers and we'll have all the clients. Let me explain how I see this thing unfolding."

Fiori's plan was simple in concept. He and Carl would identify someone who had been a client of Barnett Brothers while Ben Stillman worked there. They would convince that person to let Fiori & Sandquist file suit on his behalf against the Stillman estate on the theory that Stillman stole the money from the *clients* of Barnett Brothers, not from the firm itself. Since this person had been a client of Barnett Brothers, he would be entitled to reimbursement from the estate for the amount stolen. The money would come off the top before anything passed under the will to Beth Zion.

If the claim could be proven, all of Barnett Brothers' clients would be entitled to reimbursement. To avoid a multiplicity of suits over the same issue, the law permits the filing of a class action, that is, a suit by one person "on behalf of all persons similarly situated." Once the judge is persuaded that a class action is appropriate, he or she allows the attorneys representing the single person filing the case (the plaintiff) to represent all the other persons in a similar position. These others are collectively known as the "class."

Once an individual's suit is converted to a class action, his or her lawyer will probably be the lawyer for the entire class. Instead of one client, the lawyer could, overnight, have hundreds or even thousands of clients, and a relatively modest claim could become a claim for millions. More important, legal fees in class actions, normally set by the judge, are based on the amount of money involved and are paid out of the funds in dispute.

"First thing we do," said Al, "is find someone to be our plaintiff. That ought to be a cinch. All we need is someone who had an account at Barnett Brothers while this Stillman guy worked there. There're probably thousands of people in town who fit that description."

"You're lookin' at one," said Carl. "Peggy and I bought and sold a few stocks over the last couple of years, and we used Barnett."

Al shook his head. "You're too close, and it just wouldn't seem legit. Anyway, I'd rather use someone who had a running account there with a cash balance. I'm not sure what you call it, but one of those deals where the broker sells stock for a customer and then uses the money to buy other stock, and so on. There would always be some cash left over for the broker to use for commissions or toward the next purchase. If Stillman did any filching, it probably came from those cash accounts, so I think our plaintiff should be someone who had one of them."

"Let me handle that," Carl volunteered. "I'll find us a plaintiff. I know a guy at Barnett Brothers, and I can ask him to give me some of their customers' names."

As well as Al Fiori knew his partner, he was always annoyed with Carl's poor instincts when it came to litigation strategy. They were even worse than his eating habits. Here they were, planning a case that they had to file quickly before some other lawyer got the same idea, a case that would pit them against Barnett Brothers — who, in all probability, would also be making a claim for the Stillman money. In fact, they might even sue Barnett Brothers while they were at it, since the brokerage house was obviously negligent in hiring an embezzler and then allowing him to continue to steal for forty years.

Yet here was Carl suggesting something that could tip off their plan to the firm. Worse yet, he apparently believed someone at Barnett Brothers would cooperate. Al told himself once again that if it weren't for the fees produced through Carl's old man, he'd flush this jerk in no time flat.

"I have a more important contribution for you, pard. I'm depending on you to run the office while I go after that eight million bucks. If you just hustle your files and take care of some of my overflow, it'll pay the rent and the secretaries. Then I'll be free to work full time on this one.

"Another thing," Al added. "I have to get my ass in gear. It's crucial that *no one* knows what the hell we're up to until I get this thing filed, and I hope to do that by the end of the day."

Carl Sandquist looked at his partner in disbelief. "By the end of the *day?* Jesus, Al, can you really do it that fast? You've never done one of these."

"No problem. All we have to do to get the case started is file a simple petition in the probate court. That's enough to preempt anyone else from doing the same thing. Then the case is ours. After that I can amend the petition by adding all the fancy legal bullshit.

"But," he went on, "first things first. We must get on file before we do anything else."

"What about a plaintiff?"

"Easy. My old man has plenty of friends who trade in stocks and bonds. It's all they ever talk about. He'll know which of them use Barnett Brothers. I know most of those guys. In fact, we've done a little legal work for some of them. I'll pick one who I can trust and who isn't afraid of a little publicity, and that'll be that. It'll take two phone calls, tops.

"Then, once the judge rules that a class action is okay, he'll order Barnett Brothers to give us the names and last known addresses of all their customers for the last forty years. We'll send each of them a notice giving them three options. One, if they do nothing, absolutely nothing, they stay in as our clients and split the recovery. Two, any of 'em could ask to have his own lawyer represent him. Or three, any of 'em could drop out of the thing altogether.

"But," Fiori added with authority, "two and three never happen. That's because those choices require people to *do* something. What happens is they do nothing, either because they don't understand all the legal gobbledygook or because they moved away and didn't get the notice. And those who know what's goin' on figure it's easier just to do nothing and come along for the ride. It costs nothing and, who knows, maybe they'll get a payday out of it."

Fiori's analysis was accurate. It was likely that the firm of Fiori & Sandquist — if they could get their one case on file first — could end up representing almost every single person who had traded with Barnett Brothers over the last forty years.

"I remember hearing about a case right here in Chicago," Fiori continued. "The public transportation people raised all the bus, subway, and el fares by a nickel or so. This was maybe twenty or thirty years ago. The law provided that fares couldn't be increased until notice of the increase was published in the newspapers. There were several technical requirements; the notice had to be published for a certain number of days in a certain number of papers, and specific information had to be included. Anyway, they did all this and then raised the fares.

"Months went by, and then some lawyer filed a suit against the city. He claimed that the notice was defective for some nit-pickin' reason, like maybe a t wasn't crossed or something wasn't notarized, and that the fare increase was therefore void. His named plaintiff was one person — probably some little old lady — who could prove she had paid the new fare. According to the lawyer, she wanted her damn nickel back. But he went further, of course, and asked the court to convert the case to a class action on behalf of *all* riders who'd paid the extra nickel. It added up to millions! I can't remember whether he won or the case was settled, but I understand that he got enormous fees and they were paid right out of the refund pot."

"How are fees figured in these class actions?" Carl asked.

"The court sets them after the trial. If the case is settled, then that would be part of the settlement agreement approved by the court."

"With all those people," Carl said, "it must be next to impossible to settle."

"Nope. Makes it easier. Judges always want to see cases settled, especially these big complicated mothers where it's easy for them to make mistakes and their mistakes make the newspapers. In fact, most lawyers who file class actions do so in the hope they *can* settle, but only after they make enough noise to justify a big fee. The game plan is to drive the defendants crazy with publicity, subpoenas, inspections of books and records, depositions, everything, and then say, 'Okay, guys, it's only gonna get tougher, so why not buy me off and I'll get out of your hair?' And the lawyer gets a hefty fee in the process."

"But," Carl asked, "how do the class members get their money?"

"Maybe they don't. They'd have to show up and prove how much they lost because of whatever it was that the defendant did wrong."

"Jesus Christ! Do you mean that all those people would have to *prove* how many times they rode a bus? Who the hell keeps bus receipts?"

"Big deal," said Al. "Do you think anyone would even bother to show up to ask for a goddamn nickel? Even if someone could prove he rode the bus a hundred times, he'd only be entitled to five bucks. The end result of the whole case, probably, was that nobody got anything — except the lawyers — and the defendant didn't even have to make a refund after all. Great for the profession, huh?"

"But that could never happen with this Stillman thing," Carl Sandquist pointed out. "The Barnett Brothers' customers could be identified from the firm's files. It's not like a bus company that doesn't keep records of its passengers. Also, the customers would have enough at stake to make it worth their while to show up and demand some cash."

"But," Fiori countered, "they'd still have a hell of a time proving exactly how much they lost. Showing that Stillman stole millions

217

is one thing; showing how much he stole from any given customer is another." He lit another cigarette. "A lot will depend on what the auditors find. And I don't think Barnett will want their books audited for the last forty years, especially in the public limelight. That's why I think they'll want to settle with us — and fast!"

"So who do we sue?" Carl asked, still in the dark on some procedural points. "Do we go after Barnett Brothers, or do we file our claim against the Stillman estate?"

Al Fiori grinned. "I haven't figured that out yet. Maybe we'll sue 'em both; Barnett because they allowed the embezzlement to take place and the estate because that's where the money ended up."

Carl shook his head as he reached for the check and stood up to leave. "So you don't have a plaintiff yet and you're not sure who the defendant is going to be. Sounds like you have one hell of a case, partner."

20

Judge Verne Lloyd's Tuesday morning call was nearly over. The last item before the judge was the presentation of an executor's final accounting, and the lawyer representing the estate was already standing before the bench handing papers to the judge.

Philip Ogden, sitting near the back of the courtroom, looked around and saw only one other person except for court personnel. The man in question was sitting in the same pew as Phil and didn't appear to have any files or even a briefcase with him. Phil remembered having seen him around the courthouse and figured he was a lawyer, but he'd never met him. He was very tall, maybe six-foot-three, thin as a rail, and black. Even though he was seated, Phil could see that his dark, narrow-cut suit fit perfectly. Yet, on closer inspection, Phil saw the telltale signs that the suit was well worn — a slightly frayed cuff, a hint of shine on the knees.

Phil was still trying to figure out why Judge Lloyd had had Rudy Wysocki call and ask him to come to the judge's chambers when Verne Lloyd's voice thundered throughout the room.

"You know better than that, counselor! Now take these *things* back, and don't bring them back to me until you have the proper receipts and vouchers to substantiate these expenses. Did you really think I would approve expenditures without verification? And I expect an explanation of why these expenses were necessary in the first place."

As the shell-shocked lawyer gathered his papers and prepared to leave, Judge Lloyd gave him a parting shot. "And when you come back, please bring me an itemization and explanation of the hours you've devoted to this estate. Frankly, your fees seem excessive. I won't approve them until I'm satisfied they're fair and reasonable."

With that, Judge Lloyd whispered a few words to Rudy and stormed out the door behind his bench.

The bailiff looked over toward Phil and the man sitting near him. "The judge will see you both now in his chambers. You can use this door."

Phil assumed that Judge Lloyd wanted to see him about the Stillman estate and that this other person was somehow involved. His curiosity was getting the better of him.

"Hi," he said as they approached the door

to the judge's chambers. "Looks like we're invited to the same party. I'm Phil Ogden."

"I thought so. I'm Tom Andrews."

"You thought so?"

The black man smiled. It was a warm, friendly smile. "When the bailiff called, he said this had something to do with the Stillman estate — the one that's been all over the papers. I didn't think the judge would talk to me about the case without the estate's attorney being present, and I'd read that someone named Phil Ogden represented the estate. When I saw you here, I put two and two together."

"Do you have any idea why he wants to see you — uh — us?" Phil asked.

"Yes, but it's only a guess." Tom Andrews winked as he knocked once on the door to the chambers. "And I'd rather not guess. Suppose we wait to hear what the judge has to say."

Judge Lloyd's secretary, who doubled as his court reporter, opened the door and invited Ogden and Andrews in. She offered them chairs facing the judge's desk, explained that the judge would be with them in a moment, and asked if they would care for coffee.

As they took the chairs, Phil was feeling a bit defensive. He had a hunch that Andrews knew more about what was going on than he let on. Also, he knew who Phil was, but

Phil had no idea who *he* was. He wasn't even sure if Andrews was a lawyer. *May as well find out,* he thought.

"You know, Tom, you look familiar, but I don't think we've met. I would've remembered."

"Remembered what?" he snapped. "Me or my color?"

"Aw, come off it. I only meant — "

Just then they heard a toilet flush. A side door swung open and Verne Lloyd walked over to shake hands with his guests.

"Morning, gentlemen. I presume you two know each other?"

"We just met," Phil said, adding as he glanced at Andrews, "for the first time."

"Well," Judge Lloyd remarked as he sat down behind his imposing desk, "I'm sure you'll get to know each other quite well during the months to come. I'm thinking about Mr. Andrews — Tom — as guardian ad litem for the unknown heirs in the Stillman estate. But before I make it official, I thought we should have this little chat off the record. Okay with you, Phil?"

"Certainly, Judge. I'm never opposed to conversations off the record — as long as I can be there." All three smiled at the quip, since it's highly improper for a lawyer and a judge to have *any* conversation about a

222

case, even a casual comment, unless all the lawyers in the case are present. Yet some lawyers do violate the rule by seizing any chance to make an off-the-cuff remark that might give them an edge over their absent opponent.

"What I meant," Judge Lloyd said, "was whether it's okay with you that I appoint Tom G.A.L. Do you have any objections or questions?"

"No, of course not," Phil replied, keeping his misgivings to himself. He would be working closely with — or against — Andrews, and he was wary of beginning a relationship with someone as sensitive and sarcastic as Andrews appeared to be. However, he glanced toward the black lawyer and smiled. "Welcome aboard."

"Thanks," said Andrews, giving no hint at all of his earlier hostility. Looking at the judge, he added, "I'm sure Phil and I can work well together. I don't see our positions as being opposing, or am I missing something?"

"I think maybe you are," Phil answered. "It seems to me you have two primary jobs here. First, you'll have to try to identify and find Ben Stillman's heirs. I have no problem there, and I hope you can do that as soon as possible. But your second job is going to involve one hell of a fight with me. Those heirs will be your clients — unless they hire their own lawyer — and the only way you'll be able to get them any of Stillman's money is to show that his will, which leaves the money to Beth Zion Synagogue, is invalid. That's when we'll do battle. *My* job is to defend that will, not only because I'm executor but also because I drafted the damn thing. I'll consider your attack on that will as a personal attack against me and my ability to draw a proper document."

"Well said," the judge interjected, "and that's precisely why I decided to appoint Tom here to represent the heirs. Evidently your paths haven't crossed before, but as I understand it Tom has done a good deal of pro bono legal work and is accustomed to representing, shall I say, the downtrodden and the underdog. He has a reputation for fighting hard for his clients and doesn't bow down to his more affluent opponents and their high-priced attorneys. This case will get a lot of publicity — it already has — and I don't want anyone to get the impression that the 'forgotten' heirs were not adequately protected. I think Tom will fill the bill in that regard."

Maybe so, Phil said to himself, *but it's also a lot of bullshit.* Tom Andrews was being appointed guardian because he was black, not because he was used to representing the "downtrodden." It was a politically slick move on Judge Lloyd's part. For one thing, it was a plum appointment and would mean a big fee to Andrews for easy work. Lloyd would be seen as the judge who threw a nice big bone to a black guy who donated much of his valuable time to charity cases. It would make the judge popular with liberals and the various minority groups and at the same time keep him from being accused of playing favorites — as he would be if he appointed one of the probate regulars or a lawyer from one of the silk-stocking firms.

Moreover, appointing a black lawyer had another advantage from Judge Lloyd's point of view, the advantage of apparent impartiality. A Jewish guardian, for example, could hardly be expected to be impartial when it came to fighting a synagogue for Stillman's money. And the appointment of a WASP lawyer would inevitably give rise to the suggestion of anti-Semitism. A black guardian would avoid both of these pitfalls, either of which could cast a cloud on the integrity of the proceedings. *Yep,* thought Phil, *he's one slick son of a bitch.*

Judge Lloyd leaned back in his chair and looked Tom Andrews straight in the eyes. "Well, Tom, how about it?"

"I'd be very happy to serve as guardian for the heirs, Your Honor. And I'm pleased that it's me instead of one of the guys who usually get these appointments."

The judge bristled. "Now, see here, young man," he said, leaning forward over his desk, "just what do you mean by that? Are you insinuating that I'm in the habit of doling out these appointments to only a handful of my pet lawyers?"

Philip Ogden immediately looked down to avoid eye contact with either Andrews or the judge. He couldn't understand the judge's explosive reaction to Andrews's remark, which Phil had not perceived as sarcastic. He felt sorry for Tom Andrews and wondered how the black lawyer would apologize for his unfortunate choice of words.

Phil was amazed when Andrews, after waiting a moment to choose his words, replied to Lloyd's challenge. It was anything but an apology.

"It's a well-known fact, sir. And not only when it comes to appointing guardians, either. You're frequently called upon to appoint appraisers and brokers and sometimes even receivers. Your list of appointees is rather short — and white. I'm not saying that your choices aren't qualified, but I *am* saying there are plenty of qualified people who never get on your 'lucky list.' "

Verne Lloyd was taken aback. He wasn't accustomed to attorneys speaking to him like this, and he wasn't sure how to respond. But he *did* know that he didn't want the conversation to linger on his so-called lucky list.

"When I mentioned your reputation for defending the downtrodden, I didn't add that you also have a reputation for being an angry young man. I'll tell you this much, right here and now. You say or think what you want to about me. I'm a big boy and I can handle it. But the minute I think you're using this case — or my courtroom — as a soapbox for spouting your personal views on civil rights, you'll wish you'd never heard of me. You may question my judgment and you may not like my legal decisions, but if you make any comments critical of my or my court's integrity, you'd better be prepared to back 'em up or you'll pay dearly."

Tom Andrews could turn it off as fast as he turned it on.

"As I said, Your Honor, I'd be pleased to accept the appointment to serve as guardian for the unknown heirs. I promise you I'll do the best I can and that they'll be adequately represented. And I won't use the case to grandstand for any of my personal causes or beliefs. Neither you nor Mr. Ogden

227

nor his clients at Beth Zion have anything to fear from me on that score. In fact," Andrews added with a grin and a wink at Phil, "some of my best friends are Jewish."

The guy's both a snake and a charmer, Phil thought. *I've already hated him twice and liked him twice, and I've only known him ten minutes.*

"Done," Judge Lloyd announced. "I'll sign the appointment order and file it today. In the meantime, I suggest you two get together so that Mr. Andrews can get familiar with the case." He addressed his next words to Phil. "He has a right to see whatever you've got. No sense in messing around with subpoenas and formal production orders when you can handle it in the comfort of your own offices. In fact, I'd like that to be a guiding principle throughout this case. I have little patience with lawyers who insist on compliance with unnecessary or obscure technicalities, or with those who hide what the other guy has a right to see."

He removed his glasses and began to clean them meticulously. "I regard probate as being different from other civil litigation in that respect. Most cases are nothing more than shoot-outs between two litigants and their handpicked lawyers. But in probate cases the rights of others are involved. Unknown and minor heirs, creditors, even the wishes of the decedent himself. Some of these people aren't here to speak for themselves or to consult with the attorney representing them. I'm here to make sure they all get a fair shake. In most other cases, the craftiest lawyer wins. But in this court I want the side that's *right* to win, regardless of who the lawyer is."

"We won't disappoint you, Judge," said Andrews. "Right, Phil?"

"Absolutely. I'd be the last guy to insist on compliance with technicalities," Phil added with a smile, "since I'm not all that familiar with them anyway."

"That doesn't mean, of course — "

Phil interrupted the judge in mid-sentence. "I understand, Your Honor. I was just making a poor attempt at humor. Naturally, I — and I'm sure I'm speaking for Tom as well — we will comply with all the court's procedural rules, and we won't use your admonition about cooperation as an excuse for sloppy work or cutting corners."

"I was in your court a few minutes ago," Andrews added, "and I heard what you said to the lawyer who didn't have his receipts and vouchers in order. I don't ever want to eat what you dished out to him. I have a hair trigger and may spout off here and there, and you may jump on me for that, but I won't give you any reason to get me for poor legal work."

"Enough said," Judge Lloyd commented. "I'm sure we understand each other on that score. By the way, Tom, I've only seen you in my court once or twice. Have you had any probate experience?"

"No, sir."

Verne Lloyd leaned back in his chair, covered his eyes in mock prayer, and shook his head. "Lord, here I am with the biggest estate this court has had in years. The press will be watching us like hawks. And I've got two lawyers who don't know shit. Please guide me in guiding them."

He looked back at the two lawyers. "Now get the hell out of here. I have work to do."

As they rose to leave, Phil barely heard Tom Andrews mutter, under his breath, what the judge could not have heard: "Yassuh, boss!"

21

The building looked more like a factory than an office building.

In fact, it had been a factory for more than fifty years when it was converted into an office building in the mid-1980s. It still had the high ceilings and large, square windows, and much of the piping and duct work — though now painted or wrapped in muted pastels — was still exposed. It was not the only such building conversion in or near downtown Chicago. These conversions were a natural result of the decreased need for industrial space and the increased demand for office space. Even many of the new yuppie apartment buildings had once been manufacturing plants.

Darlene DuPres pulled her car into the parking lot across the street from this factory turned office building at one o'clock that Tuesday afternoon.

Christ, she thought to herself as she double-checked the address, *what kind of lawyer would have an office in a place like this?* The question was strictly rhetorical, since Darlene had made enough inquiries that morning before making the appointment to know exactly what kind of lawyer Sarah Jenkins was. She was clever, aggressive, and experienced, and she had never been tainted by any professional indiscretion — a fact that would surely help a case based on a will that was, to say the least, suspicious.

However, Darlene's hurried research had uncovered one little-known blemish on Sarah Jenkins's record that had, as it happened, ended her career in the U.S. Attorney's office. And it was that blemish, which Eric Stone had learned from a friend and passed on to Darlene, that rendered her uniquely qualified to represent the DuPres Oncology Clinic.

It was only a half hour earlier that Darlene had finally decided on the story she'd tell Sarah Jenkins. As much as she would have preferred to give her the facts, she knew Jenkins would refuse to take the case if she knew how Ben Stillman had come to sign the will she was carrying in her purse. More important, wouldn't she be expected to report these facts to the authorities, notwithstanding that bullshit about lawyers not breaching confidences?

No, Darlene DuPres thought as she entered the front door to the law offices of "S. JENKINS, ATTORNEY AT LAW," *I'll tell her the same story. I'll tell the judge and jury. May as well find out right now if I can sell it.*

Sarah Jenkins had practiced law for over twenty years, the first six as a promising young prosecutor in the criminal division of the U.S. Attorney's office in Chicago.

"Enjoyable and instructive" was how she described the years she'd spent prosecuting criminals. (She had considered the defendants in all her cases to be criminals, even if they were eventually acquitted. Acquittal had nothing to do with innocence, she believed; it only proved that the liberal rules of criminal procedure had once again allowed a crook to walk the streets — and even if he hadn't committed *this* crime, he sure as hell had committed others.) Sarah Jenkins might gladly have spent the rest of her career trying to put people behind bars, especially since her parents' wealth and generosity lessened her need to seek the substantial fees a private practice affords. But one indiscretion had brought a premature end to her days as a public prosecutor. All concerned agreed it would be called a resignation.

At first she had been bitter that it was she and not that deputy D.A. with the hard prick who had to take the fall. But in retrospect she felt it was well worth it. It had been the only case they'd prosecuted together as a team, and it had been fabulous, a dream come true — working closely all day and then every night gliding into an undisciplined session of lovemaking. No need to manufacture phony alibis; everyone *expected* them to be together throughout the trial. Even his wife had agreed that he should stay in the city, at a hotel, until the case was over.

He had needed that conviction and Sarah had meant to see him get it. He was bucking for the first assistant slot, but his last two cases had gone sour. And then this one had started to fall apart too, right in the middle of the trial. The medical examiner had had second thoughts about his forensic report; now he wasn't so sure about the time of death, and that single shift toward indecision would permeate all of his other findings.

Well, screw it, Sarah had thought, *no one knows about his change of heart but me.* The M.E. would be only too happy to stay off the stand and keep his mouth shut. And as long as the defense didn't know about the change, they wouldn't call him in a hundred years. So Sarah had kept to herself the fact that the M.E.'s original report was no longer reliable.

But the M.E. had fooled her. He had stepped forward when the prosecutor rested the case without disclosing his reconsidered opinion on the time of death. This was followed by a quick plea bargain to a lesser offense, a suspended sentence, and the quiet exile of Sarah Jenkins from the D.A.'s office forever. And loverboy had been no help; in fact, he had actually turned on her. Instead of thanking her, he had told her she was an unprincipled bitch.

It wasn't long thereafter, however, that she realized the bastard had done her a favor. For she loved private practice from the moment her first client came through the door, not so much because of the fees but because, for the first time in her life, she answered to no one. She could turn down a case if it (or the client) was unappealing. She could employ a strategy without needing a supervisor's approval. Best of all, she could knock off for an hour or two of tennis whenever the opportunity arose (or a day or two of catering to her eroticism if *that* opportunity arose).

The success of her practice had been an unexpected bonus to Sarah. Though she seldom made a conscious effort to hustle for clients, new ones kept showing up. They were frequently referred to her by other satisfied clients. Even more frequently during the past few years, the referrals had come from other lawyers who shied away from the trial work she preferred. She made it a point to take even the rinky-dink cases from lawyers who sent her some good ones, for which the referring lawyers were grateful, and she never, *ever* tried to solicit other legal work from the client, for which the referring lawyers were even more grateful. And it didn't hurt that she would send referring counsel one-third of her fee (for *assisting* in the case, of course, since a referral fee is unethical).

After bringing in associate lawyers and additional secretaries to help with the growing work load of an increasingly successful practice, Sarah had found herself in need of more office space than she could create merely by moving another wall or occupying another hallway. When she spotted the "office space for rent" sign in front of the newly converted factory only a few blocks from the north end of the Loop, she had made a beeline for the real estate agent. Within the hour she had inspected the interior, made a deposit, signed a lease, and begun to think about furnishings.

As soon as she met Sarah Jenkins, Darlene was convinced that this was the lawyer for her. Sarah was warm and attentive and gave the impression that the client facing her was the only client she had. They didn't sit at opposite sides of a desk, but rather in comfortable chairs by a coffee table.

"May I call you Darlene?"

"Please."

"I'm Sarah. How can I help you?"

"Well, I suppose you've heard about Benjamin Stillman, the man who just died and left millions to a synagogue."

"I sure have. It's the talk of the courthouse, and Eloise Byrd has already devoted a couple of columns to it. But I don't have any special or inside information." Sarah Jenkins leaned forward and smiled. "Are you about to tell me you're Mr. Stillman's daughter and all that money should be yours?"

"You're closer than you think, my dear," Darlene replied, staring the lawyer right in the eyes. She opened her purse and removed an enveloped which she handed to Sarah as she announced: "I am the sole owner of the DuPres Oncology Clinic."

The lawyer didn't react, except to take the envelope and remove from it a document entitled "LAST WILL AND TESTAMENT OF BENJAMIN STILLMAN." If the title surprised her, it didn't show. She looked over the will quickly, as if to scan it.

"Before I read this more closely," she said matter-of-factly, "I'd like to ask you a couple of questions. I'm sure I'll have more after I study it further."

Darlene was ready for the first defense of the will that she had gotten Benjamin Stillman to sign and that she prayed was her passport to utopia. She nodded her readiness to answer Sarah Jenkins's questions.

"First, I presume this is really Mr. Stillman's signature, but I'd like to hear you verify that."

"It is." Well, Darlene thought to herself, that much is true.

"Did you see him sign it?"

"No." She had decided earlier to give short answers to the lawyer's questions — yes or no whenever possible. Embellishing her answers would make her sound too eager and, perhaps, less sincere. Later, if Sarah Jenkins took the case, Darlene's enthusiasm could show. In fact, she would then demand like enthusiasm from her attorney. She'd be damned if she'd be represented by a lawyer who took this case casually.

"How do you know it's his signature?"

"Mr. Stillman told me in advance that he wanted to make a will leaving something to the clinic, which is something grateful patients do from time to time, and later he told me he had done it. Also, you'll see that his signature was witnessed by Dr. DuPres, my husband, and by Alice Doakes, one of our most reliable employees."

"I'll get to the witnesses in a moment. What about the date here under his signature? It says August 22 of this year, but it appears to be written with a different pen."

"I think August 22 is correct. It looks to me as if my husband inserted the date on that blank, probably when he signed his name as a witness. Same felt-tip pen, and it looks like the way he makes numbers."

Darlene was not unhappy with the lawyer's questions. They had been expected, and she wouldn't have felt comfortable with a lawyer who *didn't* ask these basic questions. Sarah Jenkins didn't seem *too* suspicious, and that was good.

Sarah looked up toward the ceiling, as if searching for a fact that was eluding her. "I can't recall the date of the will that's been filed already, the one leaving everything to the synagogue. I'm not even sure if the date was mentioned in the newspaper, but of course I can look it up at the courthouse."

"I already checked. It was signed earlier than this one. January 10 of this year."

"How did you check?" Sarah Jenkins asked. She was worried that if Darlene had gone to the probate clerk's office or called Philip Ogden's office it could betray her interest.

Timing, Sarah had learned from experience, can be everything when it comes to asserting claims.

"I had an attorney look it up. He didn't mention my name, and no one in the clerk's office asked why he was interested."

"May I ask why you're here, since you evidently have another attorney?"

This was an area Darlene wished she could avoid but knew she couldn't. It would have to come out sooner or later that Eric Stone had drawn the will that bore Ben Stillman's signature. In fact, when she'd called Stone that very morning to check the date of the other will and to ask what he knew about Sarah Jenkins, he'd said he had already read about Stillman's death and remembered the will he had prepared at Darlene's request. He couldn't be trusted to keep quiet about that, especially if she hired another lawyer to press her claim — something she would surely do rather than rely on that jerk, whose talents were limited to shuffling papers.

"It was Eric Stone who checked the date of the other will for me. He's done routine legal work for the clinic for some time. Corporate resolutions, insurance claims, health department reports, tax returns, that kind of thing. Believe me, there are plenty of forms to be filled out and filed for a health clinic, and Eric does a good job with that stuff. But, between us girls, he's not the guy I want to represent the clinic in this case. He's not a fighter. But I hear you are."

"And where did you hear that?" Sarah asked.

"Actually, from Eric Stone."

This wasn't one hundred percent true, for Darlene had heard good things about Sarah Jenkins from various sources. But when Stone had confirmed Sarah's abilities and then realized Darlene wasn't going to retain him to press her claim, he had made a desperate attempt to salvage something for himself. He had suggested that *he* contact Jenkins on Darlene's behalf, thereby inserting himself as the referring attorney and assuring a hefty referral fee if the case were successful. Darlene had figured this out herself and really had no problem with Stone's getting a referral fee — as long as it didn't come out of her share. But she wanted to meet Sarah Jenkins before entrusting the case to her. So she'd told Stone that she would interview Jenkins but she would make clear, if Jenkins was retained, that the referral had come from him.

Darlene was playing another angle as well, one that afforded an opportunity to influence events. If Stone anticipated a referral fee, he would surely be more cooperative if called on to testify as to how he came to draw the will. He'd have an incentive to say it was Stillman's, not Darlene's, idea. He might even be persuaded to say he had discussed it with Stillman.

"Do you know who prepared the will for Mr. Stillman?"

"Yes. It was Eric Stone."

Sarah Jenkins's eyebrows rose. She said nothing, but her expression clearly sought an explanation as to how it was that the beneficiary's attorney happened to draw the will.

"I suppose that sounds strange, but it isn't, really. Mr. Stillman mentioned several times that he was very grateful for the attention and treatment he was receiving at the clinic. He said he wanted to express this gratitude by donating some money to the clinic so we could help others as we were helping him.

"None of this struck me as extraordinary. Other patients have made donations, either while they were alive or through bequests. Please understand that I had no idea Mr. Stillman was a wealthy man. On the contrary, I assumed he was of modest means. And since his records didn't indicate any family, I considered his intentions to be quite understandable.

"The last time the subject came up, he

asked me to suggest an attorney to prepare such a will. Naturally, I balked because I realized how it might appear if *I* selected the lawyer. But Mr. Stillman said he didn't know any, other than that Philip Ogden. He said he'd prefer to use ours, who'd more likely know the right language to make sure that the money got to the clinic with the least amount of hassle."

"I see," Sarah Jenkins said. "Did you then ask Mr. Stone to draw the will, or did Mr. Stillman ask him himself?"

"I'm sure I mentioned Eric's name to Mr. Stillman, and I suppose I also brought up the subject to Eric during one of our meetings on clinic business. I assume they talked, but I wouldn't know who called who."

"Do you know if Mr. Stone, after he drew the will, gave it directly to Mr. Stillman? Or mailed it to him? Or did he give it to you to take to Mr. Stillman? It's really important for me to know just how much connection you had with the will."

Darlene DuPres appeared to give this deep thought before answering. However, she had expected this line of questioning, and she had determined her answers even before she met Jenkins.

"As I recall, I picked up the finished will along with several other papers that Eric had ready for me during one of our sessions. I could be wrong about that, but I'll check with him. I'm sure he'll remember."

In fact, Darlene remembered exactly how the will had gotten from Eric Stone to her. He'd handed it to her himself, but only after some gentle persuasion. He'd come to the clinic while Willard DuPres was away at the hospital making rounds. "I've got the will you asked me to do for this Ben Stillman," he said, "but, shit, Darlene, I've never even talked to the guy. I could really get burned on this thing."

Once again Darlene had resorted to her standard ploy whenever she had to convince Eric to cut a corner or bend a regulation. She lured him into her private office, sank onto the leather couch, and patted the cushion beside her. She knew she couldn't go all the way right there in the clinic, but she sure as hell could go however far she had to to get him back in line. By the time Eric Stone was ready to give her the will, Darlene had him in the palm of her hand — literally.

"Before I ask a few questions about your husband and the other witness," Sarah Jenkins was saying, "I'd like to ask one more question about Mr. Stone." She leaned forward and, using the same voice that she found so effective when cross-examining a

244

hostile witness in the courtroom, aimed a question right between Darlene's eyes: *"Who paid Eric Stone's fee for preparing that will? And I want you to think very carefully before answering that question."*

Darlene silently cursed herself. She hadn't anticipated *that* one. She knew she appeared flustered, and she did her best to make it seem that her confusion was only because she didn't know the answer, not because the answer might fuck up her case.

"Well, I — I *assume* Mr. Stillman paid Eric's fee. That is, if Eric sent him a bill. How would I know that? I certainly wouldn't be expected to pay the fee to prepare someone else's will, would I? Of course, Eric may have mistakenly billed the clinic while billing us for other work, and I guess we could have accidentally paid it without checking the bill. But if that happened, it could surely be cleared up in a minute. I'll check today."

She's a lying bitch, Sarah Jenkins thought. But it wasn't clear whether Darlene was lying only about the payment of Stone's fee or about a great deal more. "Well," she said, "we can look into that later. Do you know whether your husband and the other witness, Alice Doakes, signed in the presence of Mr. Stillman and at the same time that he signed the will? That would be important."

"Yes, I understand that was the case." Darlene made a mental note to "remind" Alice and Willard of those points. "However," she added, "*I* was not present when Mr. Stillman signed the will."

"All right, Darlene," Sarah Jenkins said in an effort to help the other woman relax, "just a few other questions at this point. Can I safely assume that Mr. Stillman was mentally alert and in control of all his faculties when he signed this will?"

"Oh, absolutely!"

"And others could verify that?"

"I'm certain of it."

"And we could prove he wasn't under any medication or drugs that may have impeded his mental capacity at the time?"

"Of course. Nothing like that at all was given him, not then. Our records will show that."

I'm sure they will, Jenkins thought.

"You said earlier that you were the sole owner of the clinic. Is it incorporated?"

"Yes. I own all the shares myself. They're in my name. Willard transferred them to me a year or so ago. He only draws a salary as an employee, and we take out withholding on it."

To substantiate her ownership of the stock (which Eric Stone was seeing to at that very moment), Darlene elaborated. "It wasn't so much a matter of love and affection on Willard's part," she said with a coy smile, "as it was economic necessity. With all the crazy malpractice suits filed these days, especially by desperate patients and their families who think we can cure cancer in every case, we figured it made sense to keep the principal assets in my name. It's my husband who diagnoses and treats the patients; I'm the owner and I run the business end. By the way," she added as a final embellishment, "Eric Stone thought it was also a good move taxwise, but I don't understand those things."

Those things? She's supposed to run the business end of the clinic, Sarah thought, *but she doesn't understand taxes? And she refers to them as "those things"?* Sarah didn't think Darlene's explanation made much sense for still another reason. A patient harmed by Dr. DuPres wouldn't be limited to a suit against him. If he worked for the clinic, the clinic itself could be sued. So what good was it to put the stock in her name?

She stood up and walked over to look out the window, but she wasn't paying attention to the view. Her mind was racing over all she had heard from Darlene DuPres, trying to decide how badly she wanted to take on this potentially very lucrative case. She saw several serious problems. First, there were the natural suspicions surrounding a will signed by an ill person and leaving money to those in attendance. Those suspicions were compounded many times over when, as here, no family members were around, the only witnesses were people who had their own reasons for wanting to see the will stand up, and validation of the will would mean a tremendous loss to a religious institution.

This was a case, Jenkins knew, that wouldn't win much sympathy. And it wouldn't be helped much by Darlene DuPres, who struck Sarah as a little too cool and whose story was a little too pat, even if she did stub her toe when questioned about who paid Eric Stone's fee.

However, Sarah had already decided that if she took the case she would charge a contingent fee, and she wasn't about to let one-third of eight million bucks walk out the door. Even if further probing showed this to be a weak (if not altogether bogus) case, and the DuPreses' stories wouldn't hold water, she still might find some settlement value in it. And if the stench got too strong, she could always withdraw. In either event she'd get plenty of publicity. And that, to say nothing of her curiosity, persuaded her to try to keep the case in her office.

Having made that decision, she now had

to set about convincing Darlene that Sarah Jenkins was the lawyer for her.

"I've really been asking you a lot of questions," Sarah said as she turned back from the window, "and I'll have a lot more later. But for now you probably want to hear my initial reaction."

"I'm all ears."

"First, I can tell you right now that I'd be interested in pursuing this further, assuming you'd like me to. For all I know, *you* may not be interested in *me*, now that we've met, or perhaps you'd planned to interview other lawyers before making a decision."

Darlene, feeling that she and her case had just passed their first test, gave an inward sigh of relief. "No, not at all. I like what I see, and I'm all set to talk business if you are."

"Fine. What about your husband? Will you want to talk to him first or have him meet me?"

A conspiratorial smile crossed Darlene's face.

"Sarah, you may as well know right now. Willard is a lovely man, a true gentleman, and a damn good doctor. But when it comes to business decisions, or *anything* to do with money or finances, he's a loser. He has no feel for it and he has no interest in it. He's happy to leave those things to me; in fact, he *pleads* with me to make the business and money decisions myself. You can deal with me, and Willard will stay out of it."

"Okay, but I will have to talk to him. And also Alice Doakes and Eric Stone. Our case depends on their testimony." Sarah Jenkins always talked to her clients about "our" case, never "your" case. It helped create the feeling that they were allies, soldiers in the same trench.

"Before we get to them," Darlene said, "could we talk about expenses? I wouldn't want you to think we're loaded just because we have a medical clinic, and I know these things can get expensive."

Sarah knew she'd have to handle this just right. Like most lawyers, she had trouble discussing fees face to face with prospective clients. She was aware that her services were expensive but equally aware that to appear embarrassed or defensive invited negotiations or, worse, distrust. Quote a fee that sounds too high and your clients disappear; quote one too low and your profits disappear. When a case involves litigation, with all its uncertainties, as this one did, the difficulty is compounded. Simply quoting an hourly rate would not avoid the problem; a smart client like Darlene DuPres would ask her to estimate the number of hours involved. Sarah had no intention of charging Darlene DuPres an hourly rate or, for that matter, a fixed fee. She wanted a piece of the action!

"Darlene," she said as she leaned back in her chair, "what if I were to tell you this case won't cost you or your clinic a dime?"

"My dear, forgive me for saying so, but I'd say you were full of it."

Sarah Jenkins laughed aloud. "No, really, I'm serious. Interested?"

"I'd be a fool not to be. But you'd better explain."

Sarah knew better than to sound too optimistic about the case. That could later be interpreted as a guarantee. She preferred to have clients believe they had weak cases. It helped cover her ass if she should lose and made her look like a hero, worthy of a substantial fee, if she won.

"Look, Darlene, you're obviously a savvy woman, and you must be aware of all the pitfalls in this thing. It will be an uphill battle all the way, demanding one hell of a lot of my time. You could end up paying me a fortune and come away with nothing. You wouldn't want that, and neither would I. So I'd like to suggest a different arrangement."

"Go ahead."

"Leave me a check for one thousand dollars. That should cover out-of-pocket expenses, at least for the time being. As for my fee, I'd work on a contingency basis. If we lose and get nothing, then I get nothing. But if we win, then I receive a percentage of the recovery. If we end up settling the case, my fee would be a percentage of the settlement. Of course, you'd have the final say as to whether we settle and for how much; I'd do nothing more than make a recommendation."

"And what percentage would you take?" Darlene already knew the standard contingency fee was one-third, but she thought it might serve her purpose to appear naive.

"I'd receive a third of the recovery. I needn't remind you that this would create a hell of an incentive for me to do *everything* I could to win." Sarah Jenkins purposely stressed the word "everything." If Darlene DuPres was totally honest, which she doubted, she would simply interpret it to mean that Sarah would work very hard. But if Darlene had a crooked streak, she would take it to mean that Sarah might be willing to cut a few legal corners to get the desired result.

Sarah wouldn't do anything clearly improper, which was to say anything that, if she were caught, couldn't be explained away by carelessness or honest oversight. "Oh, I guess I just forgot to mention that. Sorry, Your Honor," or, "I suppose my secretary

forgot to include that; it won't happen again."
But for the purpose of establishing the fee,
she was willing to be whatever kind of lawyer
Darlene DuPres wanted her to be.

"I'm sure you would do your very best,"
Darlene answered, "but still, one-third
sounds like so much. It could come out to
be millions."

"Right. And it could come out to be *noth-ing*. And may I point out something else:
whatever I get, it will only be half of your
two-thirds, and," she added as she leaned
forward, "I'll have worked a damn sight
harder for that one-third than you and your
husband did for your two-thirds."

The lawyer waved her pen, remembering
a question she'd meant to ask earlier. "Which
reminds me, did Mr. Stillman pay for your
services at the clinic?"

"Uh, yes. Yes, he did."

Jenkins picked up the hesitancy in
Darlene's response, so she followed it up
with another question. "You gave him a bill,
and he paid it? Your books will show that?"

"Well, not exactly. You see, Mr. Stillman
gave me — uh, us — an advance payment.
As it happened, it covered all the treatment
we administered."

"And how much was that, if you remem-ber?"

"Five thousand dollars."

"Cash or check?"

"It was a check. A cashier's check, as I recall."

Sarah's suspicions were once again aroused. Darlene had said earlier that she had had no reason to assume Stillman had money. In fact, she'd said she assumed him to be of modest means. How many people of modest means have access to five grand and would be willing to pay it out *before* receiving treatment? She didn't want any surprises later on, so she decided to button this one point up then and there.

"Darlene, our opponents will surely pursue this, so I'd better make sure exactly what happened. We'll get into the details later, but for now I must know whether your books will reflect the five-thousand-dollar payment, and further, whether your records will show precisely what treatment was given to Mr. Stillman."

"Our records are accurate and complete. They will show the payment, as well as the diagnosis, treatment, medication, and so forth. If you're worried that we put the money in our pocket without reporting it for taxes, you can relax." *Of course,* Darlene thought, *if Stillman had paid in cash instead of check, an entry in the books might have slipped my mind.*

"So much for that, for now," Sarah said. "Are we agreed on the fee?"

Darlene knew that if she were ever going to get the fee reduced, this was the time to do it. After Sarah Jenkins was officially retained, it would be too late to play cat and mouse. "Well, I hadn't really expected a lawyer to charge a third. Maybe I'd better sleep on it for a day or two."

"Look, Darlene," Sarah said with a seriousness reserved for this moment, "you can sleep on it all you like. But you're not going to find a better deal from any lawyer in this town. At least not from any *decent* lawyer. Sure, you may find someone who will take your case for, say, twenty-five percent. But will they give it the attention — and the talent — it needs? Or will they try to talk you into a cheap settlement as soon as that synagogue's attorneys begin to snoop around the clinic's books and records? Will they run for cover when those Jewish lawyers start to interview your entire staff, not just Alice Doakes and your husband, to try to show you're all a bunch of quacks? Will they hang in there and defend you even after the entire town is convinced that you tricked or defrauded that poor old man and that you're trying to get rich at the expense of a *synagogue?*

"And I'll tell you something else. The longer you sleep on it, the colder your case is going to get. There's a lot of work to be done, and I mean right now! Before you let anyone know about your will, you'd better be damn sure what Alice Doakes and Willard and the rest of your staff will say when the questions start coming. And what about Eric Stone? He's probably already telling everyone in town about the will he drew for Ben Stillman, and yet you aren't even sure what he's telling people about his conversations with you and Stillman. If I'm going to handle this for you, I'll want to talk to all these people now — right now, before their friends hear fifty different stories from them.

"If you want to sleep on it, fine, that's your privilege. But if you don't call me by six tonight, don't call at all. It's a tough enough case as it is, and you know that as well as I do — maybe better than I do. In short, Darlene, I won't want your case if it gets any worse than it is right now."

Darlene DuPres was thrilled. She was already resigned to giving up a third. And she saw in Sarah Jenkins more than she could possibly have hoped for: a lawyer who was both bright and fierce, who could put together convincing arguments on the spot, and who would take charge of the entire case and fight tooth and nail for her, even to the extent of rehearsing the witnesses.

"Fair enough, Ms. Sarah Jenkins. One-third it is. I only hope you can sell that jury as well as you sold me. When do we get started?"

Sarah leaned back and smiled. "Ms. Du-Pres, you ain't seen nothin' yet. For openers, I'll want to interview your husband and Eric Stone immediately. Then the nurse. We'll start tomorrow, but I want to see them separately and without you present. Have them call me today, but *don't* try to tell them what to say to me. And, for God's sake, don't let them talk to anyone else! That goes for you, too!"

"What can I do to help?"

"I have only two instructions for you: Do nothing and say nothing. And I mean that. I'm your partner in this case, and if you fuck it up, you'll be fuckin' me up. You may find me to be a tough partner, but you'd find me an absolutely *miserable* enemy.

"And by the way," she added, "stop in tomorrow to sign the fee agreement, and don't forget the thousand dollars for expenses."

After Darlene left, Sarah immediately sent her secretary to the courthouse to file her appearance as the attorney for the DuPres On-

257

cology Clinic. Then she started making notes on a yellow pad. One of her first tasks was to verify that the clinic's stock was really in Darlene's name, as she claimed, and that Willard was employed on salary. That would be easy enough; all she had to do was look at the stock certificates and the payroll records.

She would also review the law to make sure that Willard DuPres, as a corporate employee, was an eligible witness to the will.

That was her first mistake; it was the wrong point to research.

He better be an eligible witness, she said to herself. *Every first-year law student knows that a will's invalid if it's witnessed by a beneficiary.*

She didn't even have to look that one up in the books.

And that was her second mistake.

22

Philip Ogden was starting to get accustomed to being the "star" of the Stillman show. He had drafted the will, he had seen and felt the money — all of it — and he would be at center stage as the stakeholder, the protector of Stillman's estate. Anyone challenging the will would have to deal with him. And purported creditors, whose claims wouldn't depend on the validity of the will, would likewise have to satisfy him that their claims were bona fide. If he wasn't satisfied, he'd fight the claim with the same intensity as if he were protecting his own money.

Yeah, Phil thought, *everyone will want to get into the vault, and I hold the keys.* He had to admit that he looked forward to the role he'd be playing. It would be fun for a change to be the recipient of some of the ass kissing that was sure to come.

But he had been feeling uneasy since leaving Judge Lloyd's chambers with Tom Andrews an hour ago.

First, it was clear that the judge would try to upstage him at every turn. This wasn't completely surprising, considering that Judge Lloyd rarely took a passive role in his cases, especially when the media were sure to have more than a fleeting interest in the proceedings. But wasn't he going a bit far in harping about keeping papers in perfect order, bitching about talking to the press, and complaining that he'd have to do the lawyers' work for them?

Second, Tom Andrews appeared to have both the role and the personality to become a star in his own right. *The oppressed black lawyer representing the abandoned heirs; the spokesperson for the voiceless.* Phil knew that Andrews, like Judge Lloyd, was better press than he. When the action heated up, Phil could be forgotten or, worse, ridiculed. Nothing could make a lawyer look sillier than a flashy, popular adversary who knew his stuff.

Phil decided to do all he could to stay on the best possible terms with Tom Andrews. *Be friendly and cooperative,* he told himself as he picked up the phone to suggest lunch.

"Love to, Phil. You buyin'?"

"Hell, no, Stillman is."

"Crazy. This mean we have to talk about the case?"

Lunch went well, putting Phil in a much better frame of mind about working with Andrews. He particularly enjoyed the good-humored repartee that came naturally to both of them.

When they left the restaurant, they agreed to stop at Phil's office, where Andrews could pick up copies of the will, safe-deposit box inventory, and other papers that would help familiarize him with the case.

While Carol Stephenson was making photocopies, the two lawyers talked about how Andrews might try to locate Stillman's heirs.

"It's been four or five days now, Phil. Hasn't *anyone* come forward claiming to be a son or a wife or even a long-lost nephew?"

"Not a soul. I know that's hard to believe, but I'd be the one they'd contact. It was my name in the papers," Phil replied.

"Shit, man, I would have tried myself if I was the right color. Always wanted to be a rich somebody's heir. If Stillman has heirs, they're not around here or we'd have heard from them by now."

"I suppose you're right," Phil sighed, "but we have to make enough of a search to convince Lloyd there are none to be found."

"I appreciate your concern, Phil, but why in the hell should you worry about whether I locate any family? That's *my* job. In fact, you're better off if I fall on my ass; if I find 'em, we'll have to try to knock out

261

your will so they can get the money instead of the synagogue. You don't want *that!*"

"That's not the way it works," Phil replied. "I *want* you to find some of Stillman's relatives."

"But why?"

Phil leaned back in his chair. "First," he said, "the probate procedures prevent me from really doing much until after the heirs are found, if they can be found, since they'd have a right to holler if, say, I wanted to sell any of Stillman's securities and reinvest some of the money. In fact, the judge wouldn't even let me prove the validity of the will until the heirs could be present. They have to be given the opportunity to challenge it, since they're the ones who'd be hurt if the money went to Beth Zion. So until we find them, or satisfy Lloyd that further search would be futile, my hands are pretty much tied and everything's at a standstill.

"Second, you have a duty to contest the will even if you can't find any heirs. You're their lawyer, even if you can't find them and don't know who they are. The only difference is that if you somehow prove the will is no good, the money will be held in trust until they eventually turn up. And if they don't, after seven years the money would be turned over to the state. Frankly, if the will turns out to be no good, I'd rather see the money go to someone in Stillman's family than to the state of Illinois. That's why I want to help you find them," he added. "Anyway, since everyone has *some* heirs, our coming up dry would only look like we never tried."

"All right, you've convinced me. How should we start?"

"Not sure. I suppose we could retain one of those outfits that specialize in looking for missing persons. You know any good tracers?"

Tom Andrews shook his head. "Tracers are thieves. If you hired one and he actually located an heir, he probably wouldn't tell him anything until he could shake the poor guy down for a piece of the action. I think we have to try, at least at first, to do some looking ourselves. Hell, we're not exactly idiots. Let's see if we can come up with a logical starting point. It might be easier than we think."

"Go ahead," Phil said. "I'm listening."

"Okay, what have we got so far? An old man who had the same job for forty years and who lived alone. As far as we know today, the only people he had contact with were his cleaning lady and his coworkers." Andrews paused for a moment and then slapped his forehead. "Wait a second!" he exclaimed. "Letters! He must have some letters lying around his apartment. They could be from relatives. Or how about an address book? Everybody has an address book! He probably has one in the top drawer of his desk, and it has the name, address, and phone number of every friend and relative he ever had. Find it and we could wrap this thing up this afternoon!"

Phil swore at himself for not having thought of looking through the apartment himself. It was so obvious.

"Sure worth a try," he said. "I'll call the landlady right now. Stillman left me a letter with her name and phone number."

Mrs. Fortino, Stillman's landlady, was accommodating, and her manner belied the curiosity she must have felt as the two lawyers carefully went through the drawers, closets, and papers in Benjamin Stillman's small, sparsely furnished apartment. After letting them in, she simply sat quietly at the kitchen table and waited for them to find whatever it was they were looking for.

But they found nothing that would help in the hunt for Stillman's relatives. In fact, all they learned about the dead man was that he was fastidiously neat and had no personal effects that he didn't absolutely need — a starter set of plates and kitchen utensils, a few out-dated appliances, a radio, and a small television set. The drawers and closet held only a few pairs of undershorts, two pairs of shoes and one of slippers, one winter coat, four suits, a handful of shirts, and so on.

"Christ," Tom muttered, "I stay with my folks for a weekend and I *pack* more shit than he *owned*."

The only incongruity they observed was the collection of books in the two unfinished do-it-yourself bookcases in the living room. About half were the classics and the rest were about computer programming.

As for Martha Yolandis, she lived up to her parting threat. "To hell with going back to the apartment," she had declared. "Let them Jews do something for their money." Mrs. Fortino, who lived downstairs and always knew when the cleaning lady was around, said she hadn't seen her since Stillman's death.

"Doesn't figure," said Tom Andrews as he and Phil were driving back downtown. "Nobody could live for over eighty years and not have a single piece of paper lying around to reveal *something* about his past. Not even a birth certificate, bank statement, or insurance policy. Goddamn! It just doesn't figure."

"Well, it isn't quite that bad," Phil said. "Stillman kept a strongbox full of papers at his apartment. He asked the cleaning lady to bring it to him at the hospital, and I picked it up. There *were* bank statements and plenty of other things. You know, the usual stuff — tax returns, a copy of his lease, some receipts, stuff from brokers, that kind of thing. But there wasn't a thing in there to give a hint about family or relatives. I went through it pretty carefully that first — *oh, shit!*"

"What's the matter?"

"The bank box!" cried Philip Ogden. "The fucking bank box!"

"What about it?"

"There was an envelope in there. I think it contained personal papers, but I didn't pay any attention to it at the time. We were so damn busy adding up all the securities and accounts that we didn't bother with that other stuff."

"Who's 'we'?" asked Andrews.

"Me and a guy from the attorney general's office. Name's Casey. I had him there as a witness. It was already late at night when we finished with the money, and I figured I'd look through the other papers later. Shit, I should've stayed there a few minutes longer and been more thorough."

"Can't we go back there? Now?"

"Yeah," Phil answered, "I have a court order. But I'd feel better if Casey went in there with us. As long as there are some papers we haven't examined yet, I'd still like a witness around. All we need is for someone to accuse us of removing a list of relatives."

"To say nothing of a few hundred thousand bucks," Tom Andrews said with a grin. "Let's go find a phone so you can call this Casey guy."

"Whaddya say, counselor?" Deputy attorney general Casey had a mouthful of peanuts as he entered the waiting room near the bank vault. "Sounded on the phone like you had a real case of hot pants. What's up?"

"No big deal," Phil replied. "Just that I'd like to get back into the box and look at a few papers I didn't get a chance to read last time."

"Whaddya need me for? We already made the inventory."

"Until we see those last pieces of paper, I'd just feel better if you were there. What's in there may be important, and what's *not* in there may be more important. It would be nice to have a witness just in case somebody gets the idea that I took something they wanted."

"Who's your friend?"

"I'm sorry. This is Tom Andrews. Judge Lloyd appointed Tom to represent the heirs. Tom, this is Mr. Casey."

"Glad to meet you, Mr. Casey."

"Just Casey. Let's go." He ignored Andrews's outstretched hand.

A few minutes later the three men were alone in the examining room with the safe-deposit box. As Phil fumbled with the clasp on the lid, Andrews reached out to assist him. In a flash, Casey's huge hand shot out and grabbed his wrist in a viselike grip.

"Hey!" exclaimed Andrews.

"Just sit back, fella! You can look but don't touch."

Andrews, who probably weighed a hundred pounds less than Casey, jumped to his feet and shouted right in the deputy's face: "Just who the fuck do you think you're talkin' to, you fat-ass son of a — ?"

"Cool it, pal," Casey interrupted without raising his voice or blinking an eye. "Or I'll throw you and that big mouth of yours outta here on your ass."

Phil jumped up and extended both arms as if he were a referee at a boxing bout. "Jesus Christ! What the hell is with you guys? Now calm down, both of you, or I'll yell for a security guard." Although he addressed both combatants, he was looking directly at Casey.

Casey replied: "I don't want no shine calling me a fat ass."

"And I," said Tom Andrews, jutting his chin out defiantly, "don't want any fat ass calling me a shine."

"And I don't want *either* of you fucking up the job I'm here to do," said Phil, his voice rising. "Now let's behave or I'll put the box back and we can all go home!"

He put both his hands on the table, leaned over it, and addressed the attorney general's representative. "*Mister* Casey, you're *way* out of line. This *gentleman* with me is not only an attorney appointed by the court for this case, but he's a friend of mine — a *close* friend. If you continue to insult him, you'll have to deal with both of us, right here and right now. Then you'll have to deal with the attorney general — *himself,* because I'll report this to him. And then, *Mister* Casey, you can take that fancy badge of yours and shove it up your ass — your *fat* ass, as my friend here described it — along with the pension you won't be getting. Now, do we understand each other, *Mister* Casey?"

Casey sighed in reluctant capitulation.

Tom Andrews was dumbstruck! Phil had leaped to his defense, called him a friend — a close friend — actually offered to fight the

269

deputy, and threatened to take the whole thing upstairs. No one had ever done anything like that for him before. No one white, anyway.

When peace had been restored, Phil opened the box. He silently breathed a sigh of relief when he saw that everything was as he'd left it: neat bundles of stocks, bonds, and certificates of deposit wrapped in rubber bands, each identified with a small slip of paper bearing the face value of the contents and the scrawled initials of Phil and Casey. Being careful not to disturb these bundles, Phil slowly reached toward the rear of the box, where he recalled placing the envelope containing Stillman's personal papers.

When it was removed, the three men were looking at a worn manila envelope about nine by eleven inches. Though not sealed, it was secured by a string connecting the outer flap to a tab around which the string was looped several times. Phil pulled a pad of yellow lined paper from his briefcase, preparing to list and identify each item he would take from the envelope.

The first item Phil removed was a social security card issued in Stillman's name. There followed a tenant's insurance policy to which was clipped a handwritten list of furniture, clothing, and appliances, which Phil recognized from his visit to Stillman's apartment.

"He probably kept this here in case of fire or theft, so he'd have a list for his insurance company."

A few other inconsequential papers were removed before Phil felt a smaller envelope within the large manila one. This too revealed nothing about Ben Stillman's family.

But it revealed something about Ben Stillman.

Phil quickly looked up, hoping to find that Casey and Tom were too preoccupied with everything else to see what he was reading. *Good! They didn't seem to notice.* Trying to be casual, he replaced the smaller envelope in the large one, but not before slipping its contents between the pages of his yellow pad.

"Doesn't look like we'll find anything in here that'll help us," Phil announced. "Let's pack it up." He tossed the large envelope back into the box and slid the yellow pad into his attaché case.

"Up to you," said Casey as he stood up and made for the door to call the guard.

They were surprised to find three security guards awaiting them instead of the one who had fetched the box and escorted them to the small room. "Are we under arrest?" Tom Andrews quipped, raising his arms in the air.

The senior security officer couldn't hold back a smile.

271

"Nothing to be concerned about, fellas. It's just that quite a few people in this town know what's in that box. They read the papers. We think it'd be a good idea to have a couple of extra guards with you whenever you take the box out of the vault. Two of us are armed, and we can wait right outside the door while you're going through it, like we were doing right now."

"Good thinking," said Casey as he slapped the older guard on the back. "Should've thought of it myself. I can just see some nut following Ogden to the bank and then pulling a gun or knife. Especially," he added, glancing at Tom Andrews, "if someone tipped him off as to when the counselor here was coming."

Andrews didn't want to rekindle the earlier altercation, but he couldn't totally let Casey's remark pass. He rolled his eyes in feigned frustration: "Shee-it! There goes my plan, sho' nuff."

"C'mon, you guys," Phil laughed. "I'll need those extra security guards just to keep you two apart."

23

After the two lawyers said their good-byes to Casey outside the bank, Tom put his arm around Phil's shoulder. "Tell you what, ol' buddy, suppose we go over to that bar across the street. I'll buy you a beer, and you'll tell me what it was you slipped out of that envelope and hid in your briefcase. Maybe that fat-ass redneck didn't see you, but I sure as hell did."

Phil was embarrassed. "I was going to tell you, Tom. No shit. I just didn't want Casey to know what I found, not until we had a chance to study it. It might be nothing."

"*What* might be nothing?"

"Let's get those beers. We'll talk there."

"What do you make of it?" Tom Andrews sensed the papers Phil had just shown him were significant, but he wasn't sure why.

"Well, I can't even guess about the letter. It's handwritten in a foreign language — maybe German — but I can't read it. Can you?"

Tom shook his head.

"We'll have to get it translated. But I'll tell you this much: even though it's undated, it's old. And it must be important. Why else would Stillman keep it inside a separate envelope, then put that envelope in a larger one, and then put both envelopes in a safe-deposit box?"

"To hell with the letter. What about the other stuff?"

Philip Ogden took another long swallow of beer, set his glass down, and leaned forward. "I think it adds a whole new dimension to the case," he said. "Up to now, everyone has assumed that Mr. Benjamin Stillman was an old man who was either a thief or a shrewd investor. Nothing else, just one or the other. As if he had no life apart from Barnett Brothers." He paused. "But now for the first time we're getting a glimpse of his past — a past that he evidently did his best to conceal but that just might throw some light on why he left all his money to a synagogue."

"How do you get all that from just a few pieces of paper?" Tom asked.

Phil picked up a blue-backed typewritten sheet of paper. "This is a certified copy of a court order officially changing the name 'Bergen Schtillermann' to 'Benjamin Stillman.' It was issued by the circuit court, right here in Chicago, in 1947. And this," he continued, pointing to an aged printed form, "is an immigration certificate issued to Bergen Schtillermann. It shows that he came to the United States from *Mexico*. In *1946!* Now, how many Bergen Schtillermanns do you think lived in Mexico before 1946?"

"Go ahead," Andrews urged.

Phil dropped the immigration document and picked up what appeared to be an even older paper. "Now let's look at this one. Granted, I can't read it because of the language. But it's dated 1906 and you can make out the name Bergen Schtillermann on this line right here. Looks like a birth certificate — a *German* birth certificate — for Bergen Schtillermann, alias Benjamin Stillman. And that would fit with the date and place of birth shown on the immigration certificate. The rest of the information on a birth certificate could help us find his family, if he has one."

Tom Andrews signaled the waitress for two more beers and a refill of their popcorn bowl.

"Tom, you know that one of the big questions in this case is why Stillman would leave all his money to a synagogue. He didn't belong to it, we don't think he knew any of the members, and he wasn't even Jewish. On the contrary, he made arrangements to

275

be buried in a Catholic cemetery. So what was his motive?"

Phil pointed to the documents spread out on the table. "These papers tell us that Stillman was born in Germany in 1906. That puts him at the right age to be part of the Third Reich and old enough to have been a fairly prominent figure by the time World War II rolled around."

"If you're right about Stillman being part of Hitler's gang, he'd be the *last* guy to leave his money to Jews. Nazis didn't exactly love the Jews. They murdered 'em."

"Maybe Stillman's bequest to the synagogue was motivated by guilt," Phil answered. "An atonement. Or maybe he wasn't involved but felt guilty because of his Nazi associations. Or maybe he just felt sorry about the whole thing. Shit, Tom, we just don't know, but I'll bet there's some connection between his coming from Germany and the bequest to Beth Zion."

"And maybe it's even simpler than that." Now Andrews was getting into the mystery and the endless possibilities it offered. "Like maybe he wasn't a Nazi at all. What if he was a *Jew!* A Jew in Nazi Germany who escaped with his life? Wouldn't that make it more logical for him to leave his money to a synagogue?"

Phil was shaking his head even before Andrews finished the question. "No, that couldn't be it. Like I said before, he was Catholic — at least he claimed to be when he made his burial arrangements."

"Phil, maybe he just said he was Catholic. Or maybe he converted after he came here. I can't understand why a Catholic would leave all that money to a synagogue, but I *can* understand why a Jew would. No, sir, you'd have to tell me more to convince me he wasn't Jewish."

"What if he wasn't circumcised?"

Andrews burst out laughing. "Now how the hell would you find that out? Dig up his grave and look at the guy's dick?"

"I don't have to. I already checked with the undertaker."

Tom Andrews made no comment for several seconds. Then: "Asshole! You could have told me that twenty minutes ago."

The two men sat in silence for a few minutes. Finally Andrews brought up a different subject. "You gonna get in trouble for taking those papers out of the box?"

"No. I have court authorization to get in the box and remove things."

"Then why in the hell were you so sneaky back there?"

"I just didn't want Casey to know about

Stillman's background until we had a chance to think about it. It's none of his business, and I don't want it all over town before we know what it means. All we need is for Judge Lloyd to read about it before we tell him."

"I'm with you," Tom said. After a few seconds of silence, he added softly, "I really am, Phil. I want you to know that."

"Know what?"

"That I'm with you."

"Just what the hell are you talking about?"

"Back there. At the bank. It meant a lot to me, what you said to that prick."

Phil smiled and shrugged his shoulders. "Forget it. He's just a fat ass."

Nothing more was said on the subject, and nothing had to be said. A friendship was cemented, the kind of friendship that doesn't need words.

"Well, what next?" Andrews finally asked.

"Let's find someone who can read German. Maybe we can learn something from this," Phil said, tapping his finger on the old, wrinkled letter.

24

When Darlene DuPres left Sarah Jenkins's office, she stopped at a little coffee shop on Clark Street. She needed a little time to plan her next move.

Her meeting with Sarah had made it painfully clear that more would ride on Eric Stone's testimony than she had originally thought. Last night she'd figured Eric's involvement at the trial would be perfunctory. *Yes, I drew the will. Yes, I discussed it with Mr. Stillman. No, neither Dr. nor Mrs. DuPres discussed the specifics of the will with me.*

But after hearing Sarah's probing questions, Darlene realized she might have to put a little more pressure on Eric. He'd have to be very convincing about who said what to whom, a meeting with Stillman that never took place, and Stillman's payment of his fee. They'd even have to go over the clinic stock transfer to make sure Eric would stand up under cross-examination.

Within an hour she was riding up the elevator in Stone's building.

"But, Darlene, I just can't lie about that," he said over and over again.

At first Darlene tried to persuade him with sweetness. "It's not *really* a lie, Eric, because Stillman *wanted* to come to your office. I merely saved him the trouble and went *for* him. Isn't that just like him coming himself? So it's not really a lie to say he came over to see you about the will. And it would be so helpful to the clinic."

Stone was not that easily persuaded. "For all I know," he protested, "the man was too sick to come to my office or so damn senile that he was in no position to discuss or sign anything. If I testified that we met and talked about a will, and then it came out that he was in a coma at the time, I'd lose my license and probably go to jail."

"Christ, Eric, I told you he was in good shape when the will was drafted and signed. Sure, he had cancer, but he was well enough to come to the clinic two or three times a week. And I promise you he knew what the hell was going on. He sure knew enough to leave when he wasn't getting any better."

A stronger lawyer would have reported Darlene to the local prosecutors by then, or at the very least would have thrown her out of his office. But Eric Stone wasn't strong.

He also wasn't stupid. Darlene still held a few aces, and he knew it.

"God, Darlene, do you know what you're asking me to do?"

The lady decided it was time to play one of her aces.

"Eric," she said, looking him straight in the eye, "don't pull that holier-than-thou shit on me. It was *your* idea that we backdate all the stock transfers to show that the clinic was in my name. And a few minutes ago it was *your* idea to destroy all copies of your bill to the clinic for the will and instead backdate a bill to Stillman. Where were your goddamn morals then? Or was it only that you thought you could — "

"Wait a minute! Those were not *my* ideas. You're the one who — "

"Bullshit! I distinctly remember that the whole damn thing was *your* idea. And that's just what I'll testify to, goddamn it! And they'll believe me, too, because that's just the kind of stuff that a conniving lawyer would think of."

Darlene knew she was getting to him and decided to play her second ace. "Now listen, Eric, and you listen good! You owe me! You've been sniffin' around me like a horny toad for years, and you can't get near me without gettin' a boner. Okay, so I let you cop a few feels and play a little kissy-face when no one's around, and I even let you climb in the sack with me a few times. And all the while I've had to listen to those sad stories about your sex life at home. Now, are you gonna help *me* when I need it, or do I have a little talk with that squirrelly wife of yours?"

Eric Stone was trapped, and he knew it. Worse, there were other things Darlene could pull out if she were desperate enough. In a flash he recalled all the tax returns, health reports, and insurance and Medicare claims he'd prepared for the clinic. He'd always suspected that they contained phony information, but he'd never said anything. If someone dug around and turned up fraud — and that could happen during this damn lawsuit — she could lay the whole thing in his lap. *What do I know about all these forms,* she would say. *I trusted Mr. Stone and put it all in his hands; he told me he does it that way for all his clients.* Christ! They could yank his license and throw him in the big house before he knew what hit him. He slouched back into his seat, defeated.

Darlene knew it was time to ease off. "Look, Eric, I know this is tough for you, but it's really the right thing to do. I swear Ben Stillman wanted to leave his money to the clinic. He said it a thousand times. Willard heard him and so did Alice Doakes.

"And just think of what it would mean if we got it," she added. "We could begin to grow into a full-service hospital. There would be plenty of opportunity there for you, Eric, and not only as our lawyer. Why, Willard and I were thinking of putting you on the board and maybe transferring some of the stock to you after the inheritance is paid."

She leaned forward and took his hand. "You'll never be sorry for helping me, Eric. I pay my debts, and I've got a very long memory."

PART V
WEDNESDAY

25

"Ladies. Gentlemen. Thank you for accommodating me on such short — and irregular — notice. You are probably wondering why I had my secretary summon you here. Frankly . . ." Verne Lloyd looked from person to person, "your curiosity is no greater than mine."

It was Wednesday morning, and Phil and Tom had been speculating on why Judge Lloyd wanted to see them ever since they'd gotten the call. They had been in his chambers only yesterday. What could have happened in the last twenty-four hours?

Near one corner of the judge's massive desk, facing him, sat Leon Schlessinger. His expression reflected only his rapt attention; his eyes never left the judge's. Schlessinger's young associate, Maggie Flynn, sat beside him, her pen poised to take notes on the small tablet she had just removed from her purse.

Sarah Jenkins had chosen to sit at the center of the sofa on the far wall facing the judge's desk, leaving the space on either side for the two remaining lawyers, who came in moments later. To her left was Al Fiori, sporting a wild plaid sport jacket with a red handkerchief sprouting from the pocket. Maxwell Kane, a tall, distinguished attorney with steel-gray hair and steel-blue eyes, took the seat on Sarah's right. Kane's countenance revealed nothing, not even his interest in Sarah Jenkins's stunningly long legs.

Sarah Jenkins and Al Fiori were each ignorant as to why the other was there, but both felt a bit smug about playing the role of spoiler. Fiori was sure he'd stun the others by his announcement that he would be representing the betrayed clients of Barnett Brothers, pressing a class action to prove that Ben Stillman had stolen the money out of their accounts. And Sarah was certain that she would shock the hell out of everyone with the news that she had a later will that left Stillman's fortune to her client, the DuPres Oncology Clinic.

All the attorneys had briefly introduced themselves to one another when they had entered the chambers, but none had said anything to suggest an interest in the Stillman estate.

The judge resumed. "As of two days ago, I knew Mr. Ogden represented the estate of Benjamin Stillman, deceased." Judge Lloyd glanced toward Phil to identify him to the others. "He appeared in my court on Monday to file the decedent's will and open the estate." The judge moved his eyes to Tom Andrews. "And yesterday morning I appointed Mr. Andrews as guardian ad litem for the as-yet-unascertained heirs.

"But then I learned from my clerk that two additional attorneys had filed appearances later in the day. I refer to Mr. Alan Fiori, of the firm of Fiori & Sandquist, and Ms. Sarah Jenkins. It seems that Mr. Fiori represents one Ellen Gowe, while Ms. Jenkins represents the DuPres Oncology Clinic. I am not familiar with either party. Perhaps I could be enlightened?"

Sarah rose immediately. "I would be happy to explain my interest, Your Honor, but would I be out of place to ask first who the others in this room are?"

Verne Lloyd smiled. "Of course. I apologize for the oversight. When I learned of those two appearances, I thought it would be a good idea to call a conference of the interested parties. I knew someone from the Beth Zion Synagogue should be here, so I had my secretary call the president of the synagogue and ask who would be representing them. We were given Leon Schlessinger's name. Mr. Schlessinger is here today with Ms. Flynn from his office." Judge Lloyd nodded his head to identify the senior partner of Schlessinger, Harris & Wade and his attractive associate.

"I then had my secretary call Barnett Brothers brokerage firm. Incidentally, lest you be concerned, I don't believe I know any members of that firm and I've never had an account there. We suggested that if the firm had an interest in the Stillman estate, it might be a good idea to have someone here this morning." Judge Lloyd looked to the tall, middle-aged lawyer on the couch. "I take it, Max, that you are here on behalf of Barnett Brothers?"

Maxwell Kane nodded. Two nights earlier the Barnett firm had agreed, at a full partnership meeting, that a committee should decide who to retain as counsel. But when the office manager received the call from the judge's secretary and went to Bill Barnett for instructions, Barnett immediately phoned Max Kane. Max had been his friend and lawyer for years and was needed now more than ever. He'd worry about the damn committee later.

"You made it clear for the others, Judge," Maxwell Kane was saying, "that you had no relationship with Barnett Brothers. Apparently you're not bothered by the fact that you and I go back a long way."

The judge grinned. "Not at all, Max, but

perhaps we should get that out in the open." Looking around the room, he added: "Max Kane and I are both active alumni of Northwestern University School of Law, and we have enough mutual friends that we see each other from time to time at social engagements. I might also add that I've known Lee Schlessinger for over thirty years and we've served on a couple of bar association committees together." His eyes surveyed the other lawyers. "Do any of you young barristers have a problem with my relationships with these two old buzzards?"

His question was answered with shaking heads and smiles. "Good enough. Would you please proceed, Ms. Jenkins?"

"Yes, Your Honor." Sarah Jenkins removed her Ben Franklin glasses, letting them hang from a thin chain around her neck. She stood up and stepped forward. "As you indicated, I represent the DuPres Oncology Clinic. Also Darlene DuPres." She paused for effect, then dropped her bomb: "Mrs. DuPres is the executrix and the clinic is the sole beneficiary of the *last* will and testament of Mr. Benjamin Stillman — a will, I should point out, that was executed subsequent to the will Mr. Ogden has filed."

It's possible that her audience would have been more stunned if Sarah Jenkins had tossed out a live cobra or hand grenade. While they were collectively trying to digest her announcement, Sarah casually opened her briefcase and extracted a two-page, typed document.

"I have here a copy of Mr. Stillman's last will — his *final* will — the original of which I intend to file within the next few days. It was prepared by another lawyer, Eric Stone, a few months before Mr. Stillman died." She walked over to Judge Lloyd's desk and handed him the document. "I brought only this one copy with me, Your Honor, but you may have it."

As Verne Lloyd accepted the document, his eyes continued to focus on Sarah Jenkins. At the moment, she was the only person in the room who seemed comfortable. "Ms. Jenkins, are you satisfied that this is authentic?"

"The case didn't come to my office until yesterday afternoon, Judge, so I haven't really had a chance to do much. But I have no reason to doubt that this will is valid. I did compare Mr. Stillman's signature with that on other papers he signed at the clinic and it certainly appears genuine to me."

While the judge studied the document, Sarah returned to her seat on the sofa to observe the faces of the other lawyers in the room.

Leon Schlessinger was chewing his lower lip, apparently trying to figure out how he would announce the news of this bombshell to his clients at Beth Zion. His associate, Maggie Flynn, was staring at him as if waiting for a signal as to how she should react. A bystander would have sympathized with them, but Sarah Jenkins was a trial lawyer and sympathy was an emotion she could ill afford. To her, Leon Schlessinger was the enemy, and he and that cute little bitch next to him were nothing more than obstacles in her path.

But Schlessinger wasn't feeling sorry for himself; his mind was preoccupied with something that didn't fit. Why in the hell would Stillman write a deathbed letter to Philip Ogden about the will he signed last January if in the meantime he'd signed a *different* will? *It makes no sense.*

Sarah next looked at Philip Ogden and found his eyes looking right back at her. Phil was also thinking about Stillman's letter to him. Sarah didn't show it, but she was shaken by the thought that he somehow *knew* both she and her will were phonies. She returned Phil's gaze with a smirk that seemed to say: "Screw you, buddy, my will's gonna stand up. I'll walk away with the jackpot and you'll walk away with shit."

Something about Tom Andrews bothered

Sarah. She'd figured on shocking the hell out of everyone in the room, but here was that black dude nonchalantly leaning back as if he couldn't care less about the news of the DuPres will. She'd seen Andrews in the courts from time to time, and though she'd never litigated against him she knew he could handle himself in a courtroom. Since he was to represent the heirs, it was his job to contest *any* will that was offered for probate. That one could be a problem; she made a mental note to learn more about him.

Sarah didn't look at the two lawyers beside her on the sofa. It would have been too obvious, and it was too early to give a damn about them anyway.

The feeling was mutual. Neither Maxwell Kane nor Al Fiori gave a damn about Sarah Jenkins and the DuPres will. The validity of their clients' claims was not affected by her little surprise. Creditors with proven claims take first; beneficiaries under a will take only after the creditors have been paid. It was of no consequence to Kane or Fiori which will prevailed or, for that matter, whether either of them stood up. If they could prove Benjamin Stillman was a thief, then the victims of that theft would get their money back right off the top.

Judge Lloyd, elbows on his desk, finished

reading the DuPres will. He slid his glasses up on his forehead and peered at Sarah Jenkins with eyes that reflected both scrutiny and suspicion, but he spoke to the entire room: "I have no comment to make at this time about the validity of this document. That will come at a later time, after a full hearing when the witnesses can be examined and — "

"And cross-examined," Philip Ogden interjected, staring angrily at Sarah Jenkins, who simply returned his stare with her special "screw you" smirk.

"Please, Mr. Ogden. There's a time and a place. Now, as I was saying, it's premature to address the validity of this will, except that it appears valid *on its face*. It has the requisite signatures and is drawn with the customary language. What we can't know yet, of course, is whether the testator was of sound mind and mentally competent when he signed it, if indeed he did sign it, or whether he was defrauded or under coercion or undue influence." He again looked at Sarah. "Please understand, Ms. Jenkins, that my words are not an accusation against your clients or yourself; I'm only outlining the points we will consider."

"I understand, Your Honor."

"There is, however, a curiosity you will have to address sooner or later. One of the witnesses appears to be a Willard DuPres."

"Yes, sir." Sarah didn't want to be evasive on *that* issue. It would signal a problem she didn't have. Better to handle it as an insignificant point of concern. "Naturally, I myself raised that question when I first saw the will. But after looking into it I'm satisfied that Dr. Willard DuPres is a legitimate witness. He is *not* a beneficiary under the will. The beneficiary is a corporation, a medical clinic. Dr. DuPres doesn't even have an ownership interest in the clinic. He is merely an employee."

"*Merely* an employee, Ms. Jenkins? The clinic bears his name."

"Which is also the name of Darlene Du-Pres, who actually runs the place and, more importantly, owns all its corporate stock."

"And who, I suppose, is related to Dr. DuPres?"

"His wife."

"I would say, madam, that you have your work cut out for you."

Sarah Jenkins nodded, accepting the challenge.

Judge Lloyd replaced his glasses. "I'll have more copies made. In the meantime, I'll summarize it for all of you now."

Clearing his throat, he pointed out that the document appeared to be dated August 22 of that year, more than two months before Mr. Stillman died. "The preamble is standard," he said. "It simply states what the document is. I'll read it:

I, Benjamin Stillman, being of sound and disposing mind and memory, do hereby make, publish, and declare this as my last will and testament, and I do hereby revoke any prior wills or codicils heretofore made, published, or declared by me."

A valid will automatically revokes all prior wills, even if it doesn't explicitly say so. Revocation language is nevertheless standard. Useless words and redundancies are not foreign to legal documents, especially wills, which (except for contemporary tax considerations) have followed the same general format for centuries. The earlier will drawn by Philip Ogden, and the rights it bestowed upon Beth Zion Synagogue, would vanish if the DuPres will stood up.

Judge Lloyd continued: "Article I is likewise standard boilerplate language. It simply directs the executor to pay all Mr. Stillman's debts, expenses, and taxes and then gather and distribute the remaining assets in accordance with the provisions that follow. This article also appoints Darlene DuPres as executor."

The judge again slid his glasses to his forehead and directed a point to Sarah. "Incidentally, Ms. Jenkins, a few minutes ago you used the expression executrix. We don't use that term in this state and haven't for some years. Our Probate Act specifically provides that the terms 'executor' and 'administrator' should apply to females as well as males. I should think that our modern women would prefer that over 'executrix' and 'administratrix.' "

"I stand corrected, Your Honor. I'm afraid I just used the words I remembered from law school."

"It's not serious, but I urge that you familiarize yourself with the Probate Act and the rules of this court. This error was harmless; another one could cost your client eight million dollars. I assume a substantial part of that would be yours."

You fucking martinet! Sarah thought. A few minutes ago he had all but accused her of knowingly offering a fraudulent will. Then he'd taken a swipe at her being a woman with that "executrix" crap and chided her in front of everyone for not memorizing the goddamn Probate Act. And now he was gratuitously offering the assumption that she was in this for a "substantial part" of the eight million. *I'll show you, you son of a bitch,* she thought, knowing that when it came time to actually try the case she would be better prepared on the law, the facts, and the procedures than anyone else, including this cocky little bastard.

Meanwhile, the cocky little bastard had resumed his reading from the DuPres will. "Article II," he was saying, "is the part that warrants our closest attention. It's short, and I'll read it verbatim:

In recognition of the care, treatment, and attention which I have received and am receiving from the DuPres Oncology Clinic of Evanston, Illinois, I hereby give, devise, and bequeath all of the property which I may own at the time of my death, real or personal, and whatever nature and kind, including any property over which I may have a power of appointment or other right to designate distribution thereof at the time of my death, to the said DuPres Oncology Clinic, to be used by said Clinic for its own purposes in any way or ways which the directors thereof from time to time deem appropriate. This provision shall not be conditioned or affected in any way by the success, or lack of success, of the treatment rendered me by said Clinic, it being my express intention that this provision shall be binding and enforceable even if said treatment is unsuccessful and I expire as a result of my present medical condition."

When he had finished reading, Judge Lloyd looked around the room. Although no one uttered a word, he had little trouble reading their expressions and body language. Sarah Jenkins would not have won a popularity contest. She, of course, did her best to appear calm and confident of her position, but at the moment she must have felt like a hooker who'd crashed a debutantes' ball.

"Any questions?" the judge asked.

No one spoke. "The balance of the will," he continued, "consists of routine language. You can each study it at your leisure when you leave here with your copies. I'll point out only one thing: it appears the date was inserted by one of the witnesses — I'd say Dr. DuPres, judging from the pen. But I don't find that critical. There is no law that requires the testator himself to date the will, and a witness may do it without jeopardizing the validity of the instrument."

Everyone in the room had been so preoccupied with the DuPres will as to forget about Al Fiori. Tom Andrews took care of that. "Your Honor," he said, "I wonder if Mr. Fiori would tell us about *his* client."

300

All heads turned toward Fiori.

The judge spoke. "Yes, of course, we still have Mr. Fiori and his — what was her name again? — oh, yes, Ellen Gowe. Do you likewise have a surprise for us, Mr. Fiori? If so, and it's anything like the one Ms. Jenkins gave us, I'd ask you to break it slowly. This old heart of mine can't take two of those in one day."

"At least I don't have another will, Your Honor," Fiori said, "and I don't represent any relatives of the deceased. My client, Mrs. Ellen Gowe, has for many years been a customer, or perhaps I should say client, of Barnett Brothers brokerage firm. Before her husband's death, they had a joint account there."

Maxwell Kane stiffened. He wasn't sure what was coming, but he somehow knew he wouldn't like it.

"And what is the nature of Ms. Gowe's interest in this estate?" Judge Lloyd asked.

"As a creditor, Judge."

"Would you explain?"

"I'd be happy to. It's our contention that Benjamin Stillman did not come by his eight million dollars honestly. I would suppose that Mr. Kane would agree with me in that regard." Fiori glanced over toward Maxwell Kane, and was met with a stare that looked anything but agreeable. "If Mr. Stillman took — stole — money while at Barnett Brothers, and we contend that he did, then we submit that he took it not from the firm itself but from the *customers* of the firm. Our point is that Barnett Brothers had an enormous amount of money and securities in its possession and control at any given time, but none of this really belonged to the firm. The firm merely held these assets for its customers. If Stillman did any dipping, we submit that it was into the assets of these unsuspecting and somewhat removed customers."

"You can't be serious!" stated Maxwell Kane. "Barnett Brothers maintains very accurate records and controls on all of its accounts. In addition, its annual audits are conducted by outside independent auditors to verify the accuracy of all accounts."

Al Fiori smiled at the senior lawyer. "It would seem to me, Mr. Kane, that you have a dilemma. If it is in fact your position that Barnett's records are accurate and are annually verified by outside audits, then you must contend that Ben Stillman did not steal a dime. Otherwise, it would surely have been discovered through your internal controls or independent audits, and your clients would have fired him and gone after their money long ago. But they didn't! And you wouldn't be here today if you didn't think Stillman stole the money.

"In other words," Fiori continued, "you have to either admit that Barnett Brothers' records and controls are just plain lousy or else admit that Ben Stillman was an honest man and forget your claim. You can't have it both ways. So what do your clients want, Mr. Kane? Do they want a claim for eight million dollars, or will they walk away with the feeble assertion that their records are flawless?"

Maxwell Kane recognized that Fiori's point was all too logical, but that didn't prevent him from responding. "I am not necessarily here, Mr. Fiori, for the purpose of presenting a claim on behalf of Barnett Brothers. I'm here because Judge Lloyd invited me here. I'm not at this point saying that Ben Stillman stole anything from Barnett Brothers or anyone else. Maybe he did and maybe he didn't. It's too early to tell. *I* don't make unfounded accusations before I have the time to assemble the facts.

"And I'll wager," Kane's voice was rising and his finger pointing, "that you and your Mrs. Gowe don't have one single fact — one shred of evidence — to show that your client had anything stolen from her. She probably never even questioned her account until you put her up to this. You have a nerve coming in here and — "

"Gentlemen! Gentlemen!" It was now Judge Lloyd whose voice had risen. "This is neither the time nor the place to make accusations or argue your cases. I asked you here today hoping we could have an informal session where each of you could identify your interests and get to know who else would be in the case. We'll have plenty of time to do battle later. I'll have no more of this today."

The judge looked around the room to punctuate his last admonition. "I take it, Mr. Fiori, that you've completed your description of Ms. Gowe's interest."

"Not quite, Your Honor. It is my intention to represent not only Ellen Gowe but also all persons similarly situated."

"A class action? In the probate division?"

"Yes, sir. The Civil Practice Act and the local rules allow it. In any event," Fiori continued, grateful for the research he had already done, "even if you barred me from filing a class action claim in your court, I'd have every right to file it as a separate suit in the general division of the circuit court."

"Your theory, I presume," the judge asked, "is that if Mr. Stillman stole money from Ms. Gowe, then he must likewise have stolen from other customers of Barnett Brothers? And that presenting the matter as a class action in my court would avoid a multiplicity of suits involving the same issues? Am I reading you correctly?"

"Yes, sir. In fact, I intend to file a petition later today asking you to certify the class representation."

"Isn't that a bit premature, Mr. Fiori? You've had hardly any time to investigate whether Mr. Stillman could have stolen the money. Why the rush to make this a bigger case than it already is?"

"I'm not necessarily asking that you rule right away, Your Honor. I simply want to get my request on file." Al Fiori added lamely: "I figure that if *I* came up with the idea of a class action, other lawyers may also come up with the idea. I just want to be first in line."

"Thinking, I suppose, that it would be illogical for me to permit two class actions and that I would naturally give priority to the first one on file?"

"Correct."

Verne Lloyd removed his glasses and very deliberately began to clean them with a tissue. He slowly shook his head from side to side. "You know," he said to no one in particular, "I had this wonderful idea to call this little meeting in the hope that we might get to know one another and perhaps simplify what could be a complicated case. And look how much it's been simplified: we now have *two* conflicting wills and perhaps *thousands* of claimants. And Mr. Stillman has been dead for scarcely a week. I shudder to think what may be presented in the weeks to come."

He carefully replaced his glasses and looked around the room. "Does anyone else have anything to add, by way of either questions or suggestions?"

"Yes, Your Honor, I do." It was Tom Andrews.

"Go ahead."

"It's clear that Your Honor will be called upon to make many important rulings, not only on the merits of the case — such as which of the two wills, if any, should prevail — but also on procedural issues. For example, you will have to decide whether there will be a class action. But more important, you will have to establish a workable schedule of hearings." Andrews paused before making his point. "Thus, you may decide that you should hear the claims of the creditors *before* you rule on the validity of the wills, and that — "

"Why would I want to do that, Mr. Andrews?"

"Because if the creditors, whether Barnett Brothers or Mr. Fiori's clients, prove that all the money was stolen by Mr. Stillman,

306

then there won't be anything left to pass under a will. In that case, it wouldn't make any difference which will prevailed. The creditors would have all — or nearly all — the money."

Judge Lloyd nodded his head but countered with a point of his own. "On the other hand, in order for the creditors to present their claims, someone would have to defend *against* them. That would be the executor of the will. But who would be the executor? Mr. Ogden under the first will or Ms. DuPres under the second? We won't know that until I decide which will prevails.

"Therefore," he went on, playing the role of a law school professor fencing with his students, "wouldn't it stand to reason that we consider the wills first, and the claims of the creditors second?"

"I've given that some thought, Judge," Tom Andrews was quick to reply. "Even without ruling on the wills, you could appoint someone to represent the rights of the eventual beneficiaries — whoever they might turn out to be — and defend against the creditors' claims."

"And who did you have in mind?"

"Two attorneys, Judge. Mr. Ogden, who you've already given temporary authority to represent the estate, and me."

"You?"

"Why not? I think it's proper. I represent the unknown heirs, and their interest is certainly adversary to the creditors'. Between Phil Ogden and me, we could — "

"Excuse me!" Sarah Jenkins was already on her feet. "May I be heard on this, Your Honor?"

"Judging from the intensity of your voice, Ms. Jenkins, I doubt that I could stop you. Please proceed."

"It's very generous of Mr. Andrews to offer to fend off the claims of Barnett Brothers and their customers and to share the burden with Mr. Ogden, but to appoint either or both of them would be highly improper." Sarah looked directly at Tom Andrews. "Mr. Andrews represents heirs, and heirs would have no interest whatsoever until — and unless — *both* wills are ruled invalid. That, we must admit, is a very remote possibility. Accordingly, Mr. Andrews and the heirs — assuming he can find them — have no more than a theoretical interest in seeing that the creditors are defeated."

She then turned her eyes toward Philip Ogden. "Mr. Ogden presents a different problem. His only standing is that he has filed a will of the decedent. But so have I! And I must remind your honor that my will was executed *after* Mr. Ogden's. Prima facie, therefore, my will is superior to his, and that gives me a superior right to defend on behalf of my clients."

She sat down but never took her eyes off the judge. "More important, Your Honor, the successful defense of the creditors' claims will require the skill and experience of an able trial lawyer. I have specialized in trial work throughout my entire legal career, over twenty years. I have served on litigation committees for the American Bar Association and for the state and local bar associations and served as chair for the committee appointed by our own circuit court to revise its rules of procedure."

She looked directly at Philip Ogden to make her hardest-hitting point. "Mr. Ogden, on the other hand — and I say this with all respect — Mr. Ogden can hardly be regarded as a trial lawyer. He may have participated in a few hearings, but I can't recall his ever having tried a complicated or contested case. Frankly, Your Honor, Mr. Ogden is a neophyte when it comes to serious litigation. It would be a mistake to entrust him with the responsibilities of this case."

Out of deference to Phil, none of the other lawyers in the room looked at him. They didn't have to; they knew he was boiling.

Sarah Jenkins then delivered her clincher.

"With your permission, Judge Lloyd, I'd like to address a question to you."

"By all means." Like all judges, Verne Lloyd enjoyed hearing well-organized and well-articulated arguments, even when the remarks were, as here, unnecessarily vitriolic. Clear thinking was a sign of thorough preparation, and there was nothing he liked better than thorough preparation. More to the point, nothing displeased him more than a lawyer's being inadequately prepared. It was not only a disservice to the client; it was an insult to the court.

"It's a hypothetical question. Assuming you had eight million dollars, and — "

"Regrettably, Ms. Jenkins, it *is* a hypothetical question."

Sarah smiled, then proceeded. "Assuming you had eight million dollars, and assuming that many people sought to take it away from you by legal process — by a contested trial — would you hire a lawyer with little or no trial experience to represent you? More to the point, would you hire Mr. Ogden to protect your eight million dollars, particularly if the opposition were represented by Maxwell Kane and Al Fiori, both of whom are seasoned trial lawyers? Or would you hire a lawyer with over twenty years of trial experience, one who has proven she can win?"

A half smile crossed Verne Lloyd's face. "I must say, madam, you haven't allowed modesty or shyness to cloud your thinking."

But Sarah Jenkins wasn't done yet. She had the floor and wouldn't give it up until she'd made her final point. "This is not a mere issue of vanity with me, Judge. When I get around to proving the validity of Benjamin Stillman's *last* will, I'll want to know that there's still eight million dollars available for the DuPres Clinic. I don't want my client to be deprived of a just inheritance simply because the so-called creditors were able to prevail over an untested trial lawyer. If my client loses the inheritance, it should be on *my* head and no one else's. It wouldn't be right for the clinic to lose out because of the inexperience of a lawyer it didn't even select. That responsibility is mine."

"But," Lloyd countered, "the same would hold true for Beth Zion and the heirs. Like your clinic, they'd each want *their* attorney defending them against creditors. That's why I'm leaning in favor of ruling on the wills first, the creditors' claims later."

He stood up and arched his back, both to relieve the stiffness he felt and to signify that he was wrapping up the meeting. "Does anyone else have anything to say?"

It was Leon Schlessinger who spoke. "I'd

like to offer a suggestion, Judge."

"Please do, Lee. I could use one."

"The developments — or should I say revelations — this morning have been significant and unexpected. So much so that I think all of us should retreat to our respective lairs and give the whole matter some hard thinking. I for one would like to confer with my partners and, of course, my client. I suggest that we adjourn for now but regroup in a few days for another informal session." Schlessinger looked to the others. "Judge Lloyd has been good enough to make his chambers available to us, and I think we should take advantage of it."

Murmurs of assent were followed by the shutting of notebooks and briefcases.

As Verne Lloyd walked over to open the doors, he announced: "I'll get back to you folks as soon as I'm ready to talk further about the procedure we'll follow. In the meantime, let me know if you should stumble across any more wills."

Walking down the corridor toward the elevator, Tom Andrews sidled up to Philip Ogden. "Christ, Phil, that Jenkins broad has some hard-on for you. What'd you ever do to her?"

"Never met her in my life."

"Shit, the way she treated you, I'd have figured her for an ex-wife."

Phil offered no comment. He knew the woman didn't have to know him to attack him. She was of that breed of lawyers who regard every adversary, real or potential, as a dog-eat-dog, fight-to-the-death, take-no-prisoners enemy. Most lawyers, he had learned, are able to separate personal and professional attitudes; they can battle an opponent with every cell of their bodies and still treat him or her with respect. In his own experience, he had sometimes fought it out all day with the same lawyer who would join him for a friendly drink in the evening.

But some attorneys don't have, or even desire, that sense of balance. To them a lawsuit is a life-or-death proposition where no quarter is given or sought. They can't get their juices flowing unless they conjure up hate for the opponent, an all-consuming hate that makes civility all but impossible. That described Sarah Jenkins.

Phil took a deep breath. *Okay, bitch. I got mine today, but you'll get yours tomorrow.*

26

Leon Schlessinger began barking out orders as soon as he and Maggie left the courthouse for their Sears Tower office a few blocks to the south. He knew he had to get word of the DuPres will to the officials of Beth Zion immediately; this was the kind of news they shouldn't hear from someone else. But first he wanted to get a couple of other balls rolling.

"Maggie, we've got to learn all we can about that DuPres Clinic. Check with the secretary of state's office and get certified copies of everything they've filed. That Jenkins woman said they're incorporated. The annual report forms will show who the officers and directors are. Make sure you get those for the past five years. And check with the Department of Education and Registration. I want to find out who the hell really runs the place. I'll bet Willard DuPres is a lot more involved with the ownership and management than Jenkins let on."

He paused for a moment before adding a final point: "It's strange, but the one thing you won't be able to learn from the public records is who owns the stock. Each year every corporation has to file lists of everything — except its shareholders."

Maggie was doing her best to take notes and still keep pace with his long strides.

"Then ask one of the clerks to run a litigation search through the state and federal courts. I want to know of every lawsuit that the DuPreses or their so-called clinic have ever been in."

The staccato instructions continued as they entered the firm's reception area, which, despite being in the world's tallest building, was furnished in the style of nineteenth-century England. "Once you get these things started, I want you to find the best young researcher on our staff. Both of you should put your other work aside and dig into the books."

Schlessinger stopped to face his assistant and placed a fatherly hand on her elbow. "I know you think you're beyond the research stage, Maggie, but this is too important to leave in the hands of our younger folks. You'll be a vital part of our team on this case, and you or I will be supervising every move we make."

Leon Schlessinger did not have to explain to his young associate how important it would be to cull the law books for legal precedent.

Tomorrow's judge would be guided by what yesterday's judge had said, and finding that precedent often meant the difference between victory and defeat.

He was issuing his final instructions. "First off, your attention should be directed to the eligibility of a witness who stands to inherit under a will. We all know a beneficiary can't be a witness unless there are enough witnesses without him, but there aren't any spares in this case.

"And remember, we have a more subtle problem here. Would Willard DuPres be an ineligible witness — even though *he's* not a direct beneficiary — because the *clinic* is the beneficiary? There must be some cases where a will left money to a corporation or a partnership in which one of the witnesses had an ownership interest. And also where a will left money to a witness's *employer*. Sarah Jenkins said it's okay for a beneficiary's employee to be a witness, but I wouldn't take her word for *anything.*" He stopped to think for a moment, then nodded to confirm a silent thought. "And that would go for the other witness — Alice Doakes — too."

"What makes you think Alice Doakes was employed by the clinic?" Maggie asked.

"Stands to reason. The will must have been signed and witnessed right there at the clinic.

That would account for Dr. DuPres being a witness. They wouldn't have taken it somewhere else just to get *one* of the signatures, and if both signed at the clinic it just figures that both signers worked there." He grinned as he finished the point. "It's not likely that the Doakes woman is a patient. It wouldn't be in very good taste. Can you imagine saying to a patient: 'Mr. Stillman here has the same illness you do, we're giving him the same treatment we're giving you, and, by the way, we're helping him sign a will?' "

"It just seems so *stupid* for them to sign the will," Maggie said. "Surely they could have found someone else."

"Good point. But in the grip of greed people often do stupid things. And remember, what's obvious to a lawyer may not be so obvious to a layperson. DuPres probably didn't know that it might be improper for him to be a witness."

"But it's still stupid. Even if it were legal, it just *looks* so damn bad."

Leon Schlessinger laughed. "We won't win this case on looks, Maggie." He winked at her. "But if that's what it takes, I'm glad you're on our side. Now get to work."

As he went into his own office he asked his secretary to get Sam Altman from the synagogue on the phone. Oh, how he dreaded making that call.

While Leon Schlessinger and Maggie Flynn were half-trotting back to their office, Maxwell Kane was strolling slowly back to his. He knew he had to contact his clients at Barnett Brothers, but he wanted to sort out his thoughts before making the call. The issue troubling him wasn't whether the brokerage firm should file a claim and charge Benjamin Stillman with theft. That decision could wait.

The bigger problem was Al Fiori and his threatened class action. Goddamn money-grubbing shyster. Greed like that caused so many terrible problems for so many innocent people. Fiori had found this naive woman, Ellen Gowe, and was using her name — ostensibly in the interest of justice — to stir up a hornet's nest. The partners of Barnett Brothers would now have to open their books up to a bunch of hostile, nosy auditors who would swoop in to scrutinize forty years of complicated transactions. In addition to the inconvenience and publicity, there would be the inevitable accusations of sloppy record keeping. And if the public and the clients believed only ten percent of it, the business of the firm could be irretrievably damaged. *Bastard!* thought Kane. Fiori had no interest at all in his so-called clients' losses; none of them could have enough at stake to worry about. His only interest was in building up a fee to do work that didn't have to be done on behalf of clients who didn't even care if it was done, and probably wouldn't ever know if it was done.

From the moment Bill Barnett had first mentioned the Stillman business to him, Max Kane's thoughts had been directed toward a quiet settlement with Beth Zion. He had even learned that one of the firm's young associates, Ed Hirsch, was an active member of the synagogue; in fact, he was on the finance committee. Hirsch would have been a natural link for settlement talks.

Now all that was down the drain. With the surfacing of the DuPres will, how in the hell could he talk settlement with the synagogue? Worse yet, why would *they* want to talk settlement with Barnett Brothers when they'd still have to deal with Al Fiori and his bunch?

What a can of worms! Here there were two groups fighting to be beneficiaries of Ben Stillman's will, and there were two other groups fighting for the honor of being the victims of his theft — a theft that might never have taken place and that no one had even begun to figure out how to prove.

Well, Maxwell Kane thought as he neared the entrance to his building, *I'll go up and call Bill Barnett to break the news.*

Sarah Jenkins couldn't have been happier about the meeting.

She'd confronted the enemy — all the enemies — and wasn't impressed. As she left the courthouse and hailed a cab for the short ride to her office, she reviewed her opposition.

In her mind, Maxwell Kane and Leon Schlessinger were a couple of stodgy old farts who would give away the farm, under the name of compromise, before going through a contested public trial. The fight against Al Fiori would be a cinch; her strategy would be to make him out to be a charlatan. That should be easy. He looked, acted, and sounded like a charlatan.

Philip Ogden just might present a problem. He had very little trial experience, but that could be dangerous. Inexperience could be more than offset by careful preparation and determination. *I'll have to keep an eye on that one.*

And then there was Tom Andrews. If he should dig up any of Stillman's close relatives — especially a wife or kids — they would have sympathy on their side. And Andrews might have both talent *and* experience. Moreover, hadn't Judge Lloyd himself appointed him for this case? And wouldn't that make the judge just a little partial toward him? She underscored the mental note she had made earlier in chambers: *Learn more about Tom Andrews.*

Reflecting on the other lawyers in the case was one thing, but Sarah didn't forget for a moment that she had bigger problems. As she stepped into the cab she was already focusing on all four of them: Darlene DuPres, Willard DuPres, Alice Doakes, and Eric Stone. Her case would stand or fall entirely on the testimony of these four people. One wrong word from *any* of them and the whole thing would collapse. She had already asked Darlene to have them call her to set up appointments, but she still had to decide *how* to talk to them.

Interviewing witnesses is an art. The ability to interview a witness effectively separates successful trial lawyers from the also-rans. "Interview," of course, is a misnomer. "Prepare" is more accurate when the witness is already in your camp. In fact, when lawyers talk among themselves (and trust each other) they often match stories about prepping witnesses. This sounds wrong to the layperson, who naturally assumes that a witness casually takes the stand and spontaneously recounts the facts just as he or she recalls them. It might even appear to an onlooker that the lawyer conducting the examination is hearing the witness for the very first time.

In reality, a material witness will spend countless hours with a lawyer. The facts will be gone over endlessly. Those facts that help the most will be developed and expanded, and the well-prepped witness will manage to repeat them several times during the eventual testimony, even if they're not sought by a particular question. But that part of the witness's memory that recalls a damaging fact will be challenged and questioned by the "interviewing" lawyer so often and so effectively that the witness somehow comes to believe that the "fact" never occurred at all; it must have been an aberration, a figment of his imagination.

"That couldn't be," the lawyer will say. "Are you *absolutely* certain? Isn't it possible — just possible — that you were there, even though you don't recall it at the moment?" If the witness says yes, it's *possible,* the helpful attorney will then follow up: "And who else was there?" Or better yet, "And that's the meeting where so-and-so stood up and said thus and so, isn't it?" By the time the witness takes the stand, he will know things he couldn't recall earlier and will contradict things he earlier recalled with clarity. And he'll believe it all. His answers wouldn't even cause a blip on a polygraph.

Sarah Jenkins was a master at interviewing witnesses. She first had to decide whether to see her four witnesses together or separately. That was easy; she had learned long ago that it was best to talk to witnesses in a case individually. A witness was generally reluctant to change his or her story in the presence of others, and it was difficult for the lawyer to remind the witness of the "facts" when others, who might have a clearer memory, were present. But who should she see first? Her rule was to see the most reliable witness first — that is, the one most willing to help. Then, when his or her story was solidified, it could be used to "refresh the memories" of the others. Even though Sarah hadn't yet met Willard DuPres, Alice Doakes, or Eric Stone, she was satisfied that Darlene DuPres should be number one on her list.

Jaywalking across Randolph Street on the way back to his office, Al Fiori felt great. And, unlike Leon Schlessinger, Maxwell Kane, and Sarah Jenkins, he was not concerned about what he would tell *his* client.

Ellen Gowe was nothing more than a figurehead, a Barnett Brothers customer who merely lent her name to Fiori — a name on which he could hang his class action. There was no need to consult with her; she had no knowledge of any facts he would need for his case, and it was unlikely that she would even be a witness at the trial. At most she would be called upon to confirm that she and her late husband had long-standing accounts at Barnett Brothers. This was a mere formality and would probably be one of those stipulated facts that don't even require testimony or documentary proof.

True, neither Ellen Gowe nor any of the other customers in Fiori's class could actually walk away from the courtroom with money unless they could produce some evidence of the number and extent of their past trans-actions with the firm, but even this wasn't much of a problem. For one thing, the firm itself should have those records; if it didn't, it would actually help Fiori in his accusation that its books were sloppy and incomplete. For another, why the hell should Al Fiori give a damn if some of the customers didn't eventually share in the recovery? Once he could show — or persuade a judge or jury to believe — that Ben Stillman had stolen the money, he'd have won the case and his right to a fee. At that stage, the money would be held in a trust or escrow; if there were no records to verify the losses of a particular customer, his or her share would be forfeited and turned over to the state or county treasury.

That was not Fiori's problem; on the contrary, the harder it was to prove individual losses, the more time he would spend on the case and the higher his fee would be. From every aspect, it was a win-win situation for him, provided he could prove that Benjamin Stillman was a thief.

Ellen Gowe. Al Fiori smiled to himself as he thought about his client, the perfect nominal plaintiff for the class action. She was old, small, shy, and widowed. She had that special look that Fiori wanted: vulnerability. If one thought of a poor, defrauded widow, the image of Ellen Gowe would come to mind. Regardless of whether he needed her as a witness, Fiori decided, he'd be sure to have her sitting next to him in court whenever possible. Christ, it would be hard for *anyone* — even a hard-ass like Verne Lloyd — to think she *hadn't* been defrauded.

Finding Ellen Gowe had been a stroke of luck. Only yesterday he and his partner had first discussed the possibility of getting into the case. After their morning coffee they had gone to their office, where they'd found his secretary engrossed in Eloise Byrd's Tuesday column. Al had kidded her about reading the paper on firm time and, by way of apology, she'd said that she was more than passingly curious since her great-aunt Ellen had always kept her money at Barnett Brothers. She'd asked if he thought it was safe for Auntie Ellie to continue with the firm. Fiori's antennae had immediately started to hum and, with an uncharacteristic show of attention to his secretary's personal life, he'd generously offered to talk to Aunt Ellen. He smiled as he recalled the conversation.

"Oh, no, Al, I wouldn't want to — "

"Nonsense. I insist. I don't do enough for you or your family. In fact, let's all three of us have lunch. Call her and ask her to meet us at noon. You pick the place."

The rest had been duck soup. The moment he'd met Ellen Gowe, he'd known she was the ideal front for his class action. Not only did she look right, but she and her late husband had maintained accounts at Barnett Brothers for nearly forty years, just about the entire time Ben Stillman had worked at the firm. He'd brought along a single page for her to sign to confirm that Fiori & Sandquist would represent her in any claims she might have against Barnett Brothers or the estate of Benjamin Stillman.

And, from Mrs. Gowe's point of view,

Fiori had been so kind and willing to help, how could she say no? *Why* should she say no? He'd said it wouldn't cost her any money, and she certainly didn't want to risk offending her niece's boss.

By two o'clock that afternoon Fiori had been in the probate clerk's office to file the form to represent Ellen Gowe in the Stillman estate proceedings. And by this afternoon, only one day later, he would be back at the clerk's office to file his petition requesting that the claim of Ellen Gowe be certified as a class action "for all claimants similarly situated."

Al Fiori was congratulating himself as he climbed the two flights of stairs to his office. He might not be the smartest lawyer in town, he thought, but he sure as hell was the fastest. Those other bastards would eat their hearts out when they saw what he'd come up with, and he'd beaten every one of 'em to the courthouse.

But now that I got the case, I gotta figure out how to win it!

27

Phil and Tom had decided to have the mysterious letter and the other document found in Stillman's safe-deposit box translated by a professor of German instead of a commercial translation service. The case was becoming the talk of the town, and a professor would be more likely to keep the contents of the letter to himself.

Located near the southeast corner of the Loop, Roosevelt University was either a long walk or a short ride from the courthouse. Since it was a beautiful November day for Chicago, and since Phil needed to cool down from his morning's bout with Sarah Jenkins, he suggested to Tom that they cover the distance by foot.

"It'll be good to see the ol' school again," Tom said as they quickened their pace to cross State Street in front of oncoming traffic. "Haven't been back since graduation day in '73."

"Seventy-three?" Phil asked incredulously. "You're kidding! You couldn't be out of college that long. You're not that old."

"Shit, man, I'm thirty-seven."

"Well," Phil chuckled as they started south on Wabash, "I never could tell how old you guys are."

"Yeah, I know, and we all look alike."

"Naw, you're uglier than most of 'em."

"Honky bastard."

Waiting for a green light, Phil turned to look at the other lawyer. "Okay, you're thirty-seven years old. And I'm thirty-five. What else?"

"What else?"

"Well, here we are sharing the biggest case of our lives, but we don't know anything *about* each other. I don't even know if you have a wife and kids."

"Neither. Never married. Lived with a great lady for nearly a year, until she gave me the ultimatum. I didn't think I was ready for marriage and kids. Neither one of us would budge, so we split. Now the family scene doesn't seem like such a bad idea, but she's long gone. How 'bout you?"

"Divorced. Two sons." Phil proudly described his boys and tried to say a few kind words about his ex-wife. "Nice gal, really, but never thought I was exciting enough. Her idea of excitement was out of my reach. Bigger house, fancier vacations, that sort of

329

thing. Shit, I was fighting to make the car payments. Doesn't sound like a very good reason to toss it in, but it created enough tension that neither one of us was happy. Finally, we both admitted that it was probably a mistake from the beginning."

Working backward, Phil mentioned that he'd gone to law school at the University of Illinois, that his hometown was in downstate Galesburg, and that he'd studied law at his father's prodding. "Never a big jock in high school, but I was able to make the tennis team since I played a lot as a kid at my folks' club."

"Club, huh?"

"No big deal. Back home everyone belonged, if you weren't on welfare."

"Then I guess we couldn't belong. My ol' man was proud and cussed like hell every time he had to take those friggin' checks. But he took 'em — and he cashed 'em — so my sisters and I could eat."

"Couldn't find work?"

"Couldn't work, period. Got in the way of some asshole who was hotdoggin' on a forklift at the plant. Never walked again."

"Christ," Phil sympathized, looking down and shaking his head.

"At least he got a good settlement that helped me get through school. Still had to do odd jobs. Worked in the student cafeteria, that kind of shit. Even tended bar after I got out of Roosevelt and went to law school."

"Where'd you go?"

"Kent. Right here in the city."

They walked in silence for a few minutes. "Funny thing is," Tom said, "my ol' man pushed me to be a lawyer, too, just like yours. He couldn't do much but watch TV all day long when I was in high school. He saw what was going on in the country. 'Tommy,' he'd say, 'with all the stuff them hippies and liberals are doin', things are sure as hell gonna change. You'll be able to get further than any Andrews ever has. But you ain't gonna get there sellin' hair cream or insurance,' he'd say. 'You gotta be a lawyer. Lyndon Johnson is passin' all them laws for our people. You can't use 'em if you don't know 'em.' "

Phil laughed. "Pretty good advice."

"Good, bad, what's the difference? I did what he said or he'd start swingin' that fuckin' crutch. So now I'm a lawyer and get to break my ass racing between eviction court and police lockups. Judge Lloyd says I represent the 'downtrodden.' That must be judge talk for 'poor black motherfuckers who can't pay shit.' "

"Dr. Wechsler's class will be over in about

ten minutes. He'll be coming down that hall-way. You can wait here and catch him as he comes past," the receptionist said.

"Thanks, ma'am," Phil said. "Would you be good enough to point him out to us? We haven't met."

During their brief phone conversation the previous afternoon, Otto Wechsler had told Phil he'd be at the school today and, except for two classes, would be available to see him and Tom anytime. They'd taken a chance that now would be a good time.

Roosevelt University shared an old, large building with the majestic Auditorium Theater. The reception area was indistinguishable from similar areas in universities throughout the country. There were the pictures and busts of founders, benefactors, and famous alumni. The cork bulletin boards displayed the ubiquitous messages of colleges and universities: passengers or drivers were sought for the next vacation trip to Florida; typists were solicited for term papers; tutors were in demand for final exams; and descriptions of used books, computers, typewriters, and stereos were posted by would-be buyers and sellers.

As Phil and Tom waited, their conversation turned once again to the other lawyers in the case. They were in agreement in their respect for Leon Schlessinger and Max Kane and their distrust and contempt for Sarah Jenkins. Both thought Al Fiori was ridiculous, a joke, but must nonetheless be taken seriously; after all, he might end up representing nearly every person in town who had had any money to invest over the past forty years. That left only Maggie Flynn.

"Foxy chick," Tom observed.

"Didn't notice," Phil replied, not very convincingly.

"Oh, hell, no. Not much. Then how come she walks in the room and you start jumpin' around like a goat with two dicks?"

Mercifully, Phil was spared further conversation on the subject by a sudden rumble coming down the corridor: hurried footsteps, shouts, and laughter. It was the familiar sound of all stampeding students, whether third-graders or college seniors, leaving class — always rushing, always loud and, except for exam days, always happy.

"There's Dr. Wechsler now."

"Thanks again, ma'am." Phil approached the short, barrel-chested man in the bow tie. "Dr. Wechsler, I'm Phil Ogden. We spoke yesterday on the phone."

"Oh, yes, of course, Mr. Ogden. I hope you haven't been waiting long." His speech was tinged with a cultured German accent.

"Not at all. This is Tom Andrews."

After hands were shaken, Wechsler invited the lawyers to his office two floors up. They followed him up the stairs.

Just as the reception area was like the reception areas of all universities, so was Dr. Otto Wechsler's office like the offices of most university professors. Books and papers were everywhere — on the desk, chairs, sofa, windowsills, and floor. Phone messages and handwritten notes abounded. The professor was panting as he cleared away just enough debris to allow his guests to sit down. "Those stairs seem to get longer and steeper each year."

"Don't they have elevators?" Tom asked.

"Certainly they have elevators. I take the stairs because I need the exercise. You'll have to ask my wife to explain that."

After everyone was comfortable, Otto Wechsler asked what he could do to help his two visitors.

They had already decided that Phil would take the lead. "As I said on the phone, Dr. Wechsler, Tom and I are lawyers working on a case together. We contacted you because we have a couple of documents that appear to be written in German. They may be important for our case, and we thought you might be able to help us."

"I should think that would present no problem."

"Naturally, we would insist on paying for your time."

"Whatever, but if you have only a couple of documents, as you say, it shouldn't take but a few minutes."

"Perhaps," Phil replied, "but we may want you to furnish a written translation. And, depending on what's in those papers, it may be necessary for us to ask you to testify in court."

"I'm intrigued. May I ask what the case is about?"

"Have you heard about the Benjamin Stillman case? He's the man who just left a lot of money to a Jewish synagogue on the North Side."

"No."

"It's been in the papers. Eloise Byrd has been writing about the case."

"Eloise Byrd?"

"She writes kind of a gossip column," Tom Andrews offered.

"With all I have to read, gentlemen," the professor said, waving his arm around the room, "you'll excuse me if I don't read Ms. Byrd's gossip column." He grinned and added: "I trust that will not disqualify me from helping."

The two lawyers laughed and then set about

explaining the essential aspects of the case. Phil did most of the talking, Tom filling in details here and there for clarification. As the story unfolded, Wechsler's attention became more and more fixed, and that prompted the two lawyers to go into even more detail.

"Fascinating!" Otto Wechsler exclaimed when the lawyers had finished. "I know nothing of the law, but the drama of the entire conflict! Only in America," he sighed. "But where do I fit in? Where are the papers you want me to translate, and where do *they* fit in?"

Phil removed copies of the papers from his briefcase. "We don't know where these fit in, Dr. Wechsler. We don't even know *if* they fit in. They may not change the outcome of the case, but they may explain away some of the mystery."

"Mystery?"

"Why would Ben Stillman leave his fortune to this synagogue? He wasn't even a member. And where are his relatives? They don't seem to exist."

Phil handed copies of all the papers — even the documents in English — to the professor. Otto Wechsler adjusted his glasses and studied them in the order Phil had given them to him. The handwritten letter was last. He said nothing aloud while he read, but his lips moved silently as his eyes passed across the words. Every few moments he would pause and then nod his head as if he had discovered and then solved a minor ambiguity. Occasionally the professor stopped to make notes on a separate sheet of paper. His interest in the letter seemed quite intense. And his eyes, though riveted to the sheet, reflected deep emotion. By the time he'd finished he was visibly shaken. Then he looked up at the two lawyers.

These young men dabble in a superficial lawsuit over money. Who among the living will share in the booty? Nothing else matters to them. Will any of the lawyers or judges or litigants care about the past — about the people whose tragic lives and deaths set the stage for today's mercenaries? I do, yet here I am on the stage with the rest of the jackals.

Finally he spoke. "You're both too young to know — *really* know — what went on in Germany, and in Poland and Rumania and many other European countries, in the 1930s and early '40s. I was there, and I don't like the memories the letter brings back."

"I'm sorry about that, Dr. Wechsler. If you'd rather not get — "

"No, of course not. I didn't mean that. I *am* involved. I *must* be involved. I've been involved my whole life."

"I take it that you're Jewish?"

"Indeed I am, and I'm alive only because as a teenager I was strong enough to break rocks and build fences and dig graves and haul corpses. The rest of my family was not so lucky, if 'lucky' is the right word. I was the only Wechsler to leave the death camps on my feet."

The silence that followed was broken by Tom Andrews. "Dr. Wechsler, may I ask if you're a member of Beth Zion Synagogue?"

"I am not. I am a Jew by culture and heritage, and a proud one, but I am no longer a Jew by religion. I have not set foot in a synagogue or temple since I left the death camp. I will not pray to a God who let my entire family — and six million other innocent people — perish at the hands of murderers."

"I understand, sir. I only asked because your helping us may affect Beth Zion's chances of getting Stillman's money. If you belonged to the synagogue — "

"I know," the professor interrupted. "If I were a member I would be considered biased and therefore disqualified as a witness."

"Well not exactly *disqualified*, just suspect. Everyone would assume that you were partial to the synagogue."

"But of course I'm partial to the synagogue!

338

And it's not because I'm a Jew. It's because that's what your Mr. Stillman wanted, wasn't it? And why would anyone want to see all that money split up by quack doctors and shyster lawyers who — forgive me, I meant the *other* lawyers." He sat back in his chair. "I'm sorry. You didn't come here to hear me make a speech on morality."

"Quite all right, sir," said Phil. "I myself am pulling for the synagogue, and I hope the judge and jury feel the way you do. But my friend here has other plans. His job is to track down Mr. Stillman's heirs, if he can find any, to give them an opportunity to contest the will if they so choose."

"That's right," Tom said, "but if it doesn't go to the heirs, then I'm all for Beth Zion, and for the same reasons you are, Dr. Wechsler."

"So," the professor asked, "why all this concern about my impartiality? All you are asking from me is to translate a couple of pieces of paper. Words are words, they speak for themselves."

"Could you tell us what you make of them?" Phil asked.

"The document printed in German is a birth certificate, and it tells us your Benjamin Stillman was born in 1906 as Bergen Schtillermann, which you already knew from the

immigration certificate. His birth was registered in Dresden, but he was actually born
in the small city of Pirna, which is on the
Elbe River near the Czechoslovakian border.
The other two official documents you showed
me were written in English. As you could
see for yourselves, they tell us that Schtillermann came here in 1946, by way of Mexico,
and Americanized his name to Benjamin Stillman the following year."

Tom Andrews had a question for Dr.
Wechsler. "Does the birth certificate reveal
anything that could help me locate his family
or living relatives?"

"It gives only the names of his parents.
I expect you would have to go to Germany
— *East* Germany — or hire someone there
to examine the public records."

"Do you think that would produce names
for us?" Phil asked.

"I don't know why not. The German people
are well known for keeping meticulous records. It's interesting," Wechsler continued,
"that your search will start in East Germany."

"How so?" asked Andrews.

"It may actually make your search much
easier. Although the East German restrictions
on emigration have loosened, most of the
surviving Schtillermanns — if there are any
— are probably still there. It's the young

who leave. It's too difficult for older people to uproot themselves."

"Dr. Wechsler," Phil said, "could you tell us about the handwritten letter now?"

Dr. Wechsler nodded. He swallowed hard before speaking. "I will have an accurate translation typed up for you, but for now I'll read it aloud in English. You will forgive my emotion, gentlemen, but I am reading a letter — a final letter — that could have been written by my mother or sister.

My dearest Bergen,

I pray this short note finds you. One of the guards says he knows where you are. He promised to deliver it. Compared to the others he seems kind. I don't believe he approves or understands what he is doing at this unspeakable place.

It is good you can't see me. I am so thin (not so bad as others), but I am beyond being hungry. And my long black hair that you said was so beautiful is no more. It was shaved the day I was brought here.

Hans is also shaved. He is in the same compound with me. He talks about you all day long. I can't find Mama or Papa or my brothers. They separated us the first day.

Dearest Bergen, I know why we were

341

brought here. It is not a relocation camp like they said. I am so frightened — especially for Hans.

I can't hate you for this. How can I hate who I love? And what could you have done? Don't carry guilt. I forgive you and my God will forgive you.

I fear we will not see each other again. I wish you a good life.

I must stop now. The guard who is helping me is waiting.

I love you forever,
Your Frieda"

Even though the letter did not have the same impact on Phil and Tom as it had on Otto Wechsler, they knew they were dealing with something infinitely sad. Whether or not it was relevant to the lawsuit did not seem important at the moment. Out of respect for the professor, or perhaps for Frieda, they said nothing.

"Please, gentlemen," Wechsler said after a few moments, "don't feel uncomfortable. If you'd like to talk about this further, please do. I'm quite all right."

"Well," Phil said, "the letter was written to Stillman by a woman named Frieda, from one of the concentration camps. That much is obvious. We also know the letter was delivered to Stillman, and he kept it for close to fifty years with his most valuable papers. What else? Who was Frieda?"

"Stillman's wife or girlfriend," Tom Andrews volunteered. "She was obviously someone who loved him deeply. She said so, and if she took the risk to sneak a letter out — a *big* risk, since she would have to try to compromise a guard — it wouldn't have been to a mere friend. And she wasn't his sister because she mentioned "my" brothers; she wouldn't have said it that way if Stillman were her brother."

"But could a non-Jewish man marry a Jewish woman in Germany at that time?" Phil's question was directed to Dr. Wechsler.

"Well, we don't *know* they were married. But yes, that's a possibility. It wasn't common, but such marriages did indeed take place. Remember, people married younger in those days, especially in Europe. It's a good bet that Stillman was married by the time he was twenty-four, which would have been in — let's see — 1930. And in 1930 anti-Semitism wasn't *quite* as rampant as it became a few years later. So, yes, it wouldn't surprise me if Stillman, a non-Jew, and this Frieda, a Jew, were husband and wife. But," he shook his head sadly, "that wouldn't have saved poor Frieda. To Hitler, Jews were Jews."

Tom Andrews's mind was racing a mile a minute as he and Phil left Dr. Wechsler's office. If the German records were as complete as Wechsler indicated, there was still a chance that Stillman's heirs could be found.

Phil, on the other hand, wasn't nearly as concerned with Stillman's heirs as he was with Stillman's motives. He knew that if he could establish a logical reason for Stillman to leave his entire estate to a Jewish synagogue, it would help him in his coming battle against Sarah Jenkins, Max Kane, and Al Fiori. Judges and juries like to do the *right* thing, and Phil had to show them that it was only right that the money go to Beth Zion. For that he needed Stillman's motive. And Frieda and her family, he felt certain, were part of the motive.

Each of the two lawyers was now consumed with finding answers. Each had crossed the invisible line that exists in so many lawsuits, the line where the lawyer ceases to be the professional technician and instead becomes a crusader, where fees are less important than winning and where other clients and other responsibilities, including family, start to be ignored. Whoever says lawyers should not get emotionally involved in their cases has never seen a good lawyer at work.

"What's your next move, Phil?"

"I'm not really sure. I better start hitting the books. I have a lot of probate law to learn, and I want to prepare — and I mean *really* prepare — for my fight with Sarah Jenkins. I have a score to settle with that bitch. If those DuPreses get Stillman's money, it'll be over my dead body. I'll find out every fuckin' thing that went on at that clinic when he was there and how Eric Stone happened to draw that bullshit will. I'm sure I'll get some help from Schlessinger on that."

Phil's lips tightened as he thought about Sarah Jenkins and her clients. After a moment or two, he turned to face Tom. "What do *you* think we should do?"

"I don't know about you, but I'm goin' to Germany and try to find me some Schtillermanns."

28

"Please tell Mr. Barnett that Max Kane's calling."

Kane doodled on a scratch pad as he waited, weighing his mixed feelings about the decisions he and Bill Barnett, a longtime friend and client, would have to make in the days to come. Barnett was convinced beyond a doubt that Ben Stillman had stolen the money from him — not from the firm, from *him*. He could never accept the fact that his partners were really part of the firm his family had founded, and he would damn well want the money back. *How do I tell such a man,* Kane thought, *that he may have to give up any idea of a claim against Stillman's estate?*

More frustrating was the realization that he might be the wrong attorney to be advising Barnett in the first place. Sure, he had the talent and judgment to give counsel in even the most difficult cases, but a flaw had somehow crept into the psyche of Maxwell Kane, a flaw that finds its way into the psyches of many lawyers in their middle years. After thirty-five years of practice, Max Kane was getting gun-shy.

Or was it something else that lately had been leading him more and more to advise clients to stay away from the courtroom and head toward the settlement table? All lawyers hate losing; the good ones hate it more than their clients do. And the best ones hate losing more than they love winning, which probably accounts for their incredible resolve; you run faster when the bear is chasing you than when you're chasing the bear. *But do they fear losing?* he wondered. *Are trials as frightening to them as they now are to me? What causes this fear in a well-established, successful attorney? And how the hell do I deal with it?*

Max Kane had asked Max Kane that last question a thousand times, and the answer was always a mishmash of rationalizations for avoiding the courtroom: this trial would be too expensive or take too long. This judge is not the right judge for our case; he's a "plaintiff's judge," or he's a friend of the other guy, or he's not smart enough, or I think he was reached. Take the settlement on the "bird in the hand" theory.

And there was the unpredictability of the litigation. "I know what the law is," many litigators have told their clients, "but I don't know if the *judge* knows."

And the economics. Lawyers' time is expensive, and they now spend more of it than ever before on any given case because of pretrial maneuvering and broader discovery rules. Litigation has become a war in which paper is used instead of bullets and bombs, and every sheet of it has to be researched, drafted, edited, challenged, and then responded to by still other papers. It takes years to sort it all out and get on with the business of trying the case. The sad reality is that many people simply cannot afford to litigate, or they are forced to do so without adequate representation or preparation.

And here I am again, Max Kane was thinking as he heard Bill Barnett's phone click into action, *about to come up with reasons why still another client should veer away from the courthouse.*

"Mornin', Max. How'd it go?"

"We had a few surprises, Bill."

"Oh?"

"Can we get together? Lunch?" Kane knew that Bill Barnett rarely went out for lunch while the stock market was open for trading, and Barnett knew that Kane knew it.

"That important, huh?"

"I'd say so. Two new developments. One of them doesn't really concern us, at least not in a technical sense, but the other does — a whole lot."

Kane didn't want to go into details on the phone. That much was obvious, and Barnett didn't press him. "Okay if I bring Jim along?"

"Sure. Make it the Union League Club. Twelve-thirty."

When Bill Barnett and his partner, Jim Masters, arrived at the Union League Club dining room, Max Kane was already seated at a corner table. Before him was the same notepad he had used in Judge Lloyd's chambers an hour earlier. In defiance of the unwritten rule against openly displaying business papers in the sacred precincts of the club, he was now making some additional notes in preparation for this session.

"You beat us," Barnett said with a smile as the men shook hands.

"I wanted to get a table off the beaten track. Easier to talk. Sit down and order a drink. You'll need it."

"Hmm," Barnett muttered as he pulled out a chair. "Doesn't sound so good."

"What the hell's goin' on?" Jim Masters asked. "You scared the shit out of Bill with your phone call."

"Well, you know, Judge Lloyd called a powwow on the Stillman thing. He wanted a sit-down with all the lawyers in the case. I guess he — "

"You said there were a couple of surprises?" Bill Barnett interrupted, impatient to get to the point.

"Yes, two. Let me mention the minor one first — at least, minor as far as we're concerned. It seems that your friend Stillman signed another will, a later one that didn't mention the synagogue."

"Jesus," Masters blurted out. "Who'd he leave the dough to this time, the Hare Krishnas?"

"Not quite," Kane replied. "He left it to . . . ," he consulted his notes. "To the DuPres Oncology Clinic."

Masters and Barnett looked at each other and shrugged, then looked back at Kane.

"It's a cancer clinic in Evanston. Evidently Stillman was treated there shortly before he died — of cancer."

"Doesn't sound like they earned the money," Masters said with a grin.

Bill Barnett had a question. "You said this was a minor surprise, Max. It doesn't sound very minor to me."

"I said it was minor as far as *we're* concerned. It obviously isn't minor to Beth Zion. But from our point of view, it doesn't make any difference where Stillman's will leaves his money, or even whether he had a will. If we can show that he stole the money from Barnett

350

Brothers, we're entitled to get it back."

"So," Barnett asked, trying to clarify Kane's point, "we don't give a damn which will stands up? We don't care whether the synagogue or the clinic wins?"

"That's right, but only as a technical matter."

"I just love when you guys refer to something as only a technical matter," Jim Masters said. "You lawyers make your goddamned living on technical matters. And the SEC has sent securities dealers to prison on technical matters."

Max Kane smiled, remembering how many times he'd counseled the partners at Barnett Brothers on the importance of following all the intricate regulations of the Securities and Exchange Commission. "What I meant," he said, "was that our *rights* to Stillman's money are unaffected by whether the clinic or the synagogue wins. From a practical point of view, however, we're much better off if the clinic's will stands up and the synagogue's gets thrown out."

"How so?" Barnett asked.

"Because I'd rather be trying to take the money away from a bunch of rich doctors — probably more like *witch* doctors in this case — than from a respectable Jewish synagogue and the charities they'd hold the

351

money for. I think we'd have more public support. Moreover, there are some pretty kinky things about this will."

Kane went on to describe that the DuPres will had been drafted by the DuPreses' lawyer and witnessed by Willard DuPres and a woman who was probably a DuPres employee. "Even Judge Lloyd, who's normally poker-faced, raised his eyebrows when he heard."

"How about the clinic's lawyer?" Masters inquired. "He any good?"

"She."

"*She?*"

"Yes, and she's damn good."

"It figures," Barnett said, waving for the waitress to bring him another vodka. "What's the other surprise, the one that *does* concern us?"

"You won't like this one," Max Kane said as he folded and unfolded his napkin. He went on to tell his clients about Al Fiori and his proposed class action, carefully detailing how such a claim would inevitably involve an army of auditors crawling all over Barnett Brothers' books to dissect and scrutinize transactions over the past forty years. Even the confidential records of the partners themselves, he explained, would be subjected to review.

Bill Barnett, forgetting that on Saturday

he himself had thought an audit would be a good idea, exploded as the enormity of it sank in. "Fucking shyster!" A few heads turned at the outburst, but that didn't stop the irate senior partner of Barnett Brothers. "I'll never understand how you sonsabitches can make these phony claims and hurt innocent people. You talk about justice but act out of greed — sheer greed."

"Hey, wait a minute, Bill." Now it was Max Kane's voice that was stern, but not loud enough to be heard at other tables. "I knew you would be upset by the news, but that's no reason to kill the messenger. I'm as pissed off at Fiori as you are, maybe more so; it's guys like that who give all lawyers a bad name. But here you are climbing all over me because of what that prick's doing, and we've been friends our whole lives."

"I didn't mean you, Max, I really didn't. You know I don't consider *you* that kind of lawyer. It just seems there're so many of these bullshit cases these days. It's offensive, and not only because I'm the target of this one. I'd be just as angry if I were a bystander reading about it in the paper."

"No, you wouldn't," Kane replied. "You'd read about it, cluck your tongue once or twice, and then forget it. Just like everyone else."

Jim Masters felt uncomfortable during this

exchange and wanted to get back to the business at hand. "Okay, you guys," he said, "we all know you love each other. But the point is, what the hell are we going to do about this Fiori character?"

"What do you mean, what are we going to do about him?" Barnett exclaimed. "We're going to fight him with everything we've got. If I have to ruin the son of a bitch, I'll damn well do it. You can take *that* to the bank."

Max Kane was shaking his head. "Calm down, Bill. The bastard's not worth a coronary. Now I've had a little more time to think about this than you have, so let me make a couple of points. First, and most important, we don't have to do a thing about the case yet. We have six months before we even have to *file* a claim, and nothing's going to happen to Stillman's money during that time. There's no reason to take a position or make a stand until we have to, and by then we'll know a lot more than we do today. Maybe we'll find out more about Stillman and whether he was really stealing."

"Of course he was stealing — from me!" Bill Barnett was clearly not in a reasonable mood. However, Kane knew he had to make his points now before Barnett took a stand from which there could be no retreat.

"Bill, now sit back, pretend to enjoy your

drink, and listen to me. You pay me too much to ignore what I have to say."

"Go ahead," Barnett said reluctantly.

"All right, there are two things we have to consider immediately. First, what do you tell your partners, and second, what do you tell the press or others who ask questions. Let's take the second issue first: what is our public position? What do we say about Stillman and about our intentions? Once we decide on that, it'll be easier to know what to say to the others at the firm. The whole firm has to be consistent on this; it would be a big mistake for everyone to run around saying different things."

"I hear you, but I'm not sure I understand the significance." This came from Jim Masters.

"Look at it this way, Jim. How would it look if half the partners said Stillman was a thief while the others said he was as honest as the day is long? If that happens, then whatever position we take, half the firm will be on record as disagreeing with us. That alone would kill us at a trial. How do we convince a judge or jury when we can't even convince our own partners — and they're the ones whose money was supposedly stolen?"

"That's clear enough," said Bill Barnett, "but you make it sound like there's some doubt as to what we'll say. Of course Stillman was a thief, and of course that's what we'll tell everyone. That's what *all* of us will tell everyone. Any one of our partners says that money's not ours, I'll throw the son of a bitch right out of the office."

Maxwell Kane unwrapped a cracker, took a small bite, and pointed the remainder at Barnett. "Bill, you'll holler like hell at this, but there's an avenue we have to consider before we make a final decision. These cases are like giant chess games, and we can't make a move without looking ahead to anticipate what will happen later."

"I'm listening," Barnett growled.

"At this stage, I think our public statement still ought to be totally noncommittal. We should just say that we're looking into the whole thing but Ben Stillman was a good employee for forty-some years and so far we have no reason to doubt his integrity. That way we're free to go either way later on, and in the meantime we won't be helping Fiori. But if we announce now that Stillman was a crook, we'll be playing right into Fiori's hand; that's just what he wants everyone to believe. Why should we make his job easier?"

"But," Masters pointed out, "if we're going to say later that Ben stole the money, why not say it now? If it helps Fiori, then so be it. It's no worse helping him now than later."

"I disagree. Al Fiori is a lightweight. He may get discouraged if he sees that no one agrees that Stillman was a thief and that he's the only one trying to prove it. It could cost him one hell of a lot of money to prove his case — money he probably doesn't have. Let's let him hang out there alone, at least for now. Maybe he'll get discouraged, fold up camp, and go home. But if we join him in claiming Stillman was on the take, then *we'll* have to start laying out the money for auditors. That'll only make his job easier. Hell, we'd be spending money to help him prove *his* case.

"There's another consideration," Kane added. "Let's say we remain neutral for now, and then, after some evidence against Stillman is uncovered, we say we're forced to conclude he was a thief. Wouldn't we look a hell of a lot more reasonable and sincere than if we accused him now?"

Bill Barnett had a resigned look on his face. "Okay, counselor, I'll go along with you for now. Our public position will be that we're still looking into the thing, but as of now we don't have any reason to doubt Ben Stillman's integrity." A wry smile crossed his lips. "Of course that's bullshit. I have eight million reasons to doubt his fucking integrity."

357

29

Sarah Jenkins decided, after all, to violate her rule against interviewing more than one witness at a time. In fact, she decided to violate it twice.

As the testimony of Willard DuPres and Alice Doakes would be crucial as to the signing of the will, their stories should be worked out together. Nevertheless, the circumstances leading up to its preparation could not be overlooked. It was there one would look to question whether Stillman really wanted to leave his estate to the clinic. What had he said to Eric Stone, the drafter of the will? What had he asked him to do? So Sarah decided to talk to Stone before she met with Alice Doakes and Dr. DuPres.

However, the prospect of interviewing Stone presented special problems. He might be angry because Darlene hadn't retained him to enforce the DuPres will and possibly jealous of Sarah for having the case. Add to that the fact that lawyers are notoriously bad witnesses, and Sarah had all the ingredients for a dangerous situation.

The solution, she decided, was to have Darlene DuPres present when she met with Stone. As long as he represented the clinic on an ongoing basis — and would like to keep it that way — he would be at least semicooperative. Of course, Sarah knew she could help insure his cooperation if she let him know he could expect a piece of the action, but that would be unethical; a witness cannot have an interest in the outcome of a case, as it would taint his or her testimony. Sarah's plan was to leave the *impression* with Stone that after he testified and the DuPres will was approved she might call upon him to "assist" in return for a percentage of her fee. She wouldn't have to say anything definite; he'd get the hint.

That just might pass the ethics test and, better yet, they could ask for court approval in advance. If Judge Lloyd allowed it, fine; if not, finer still. Sarah could then keep the whole ball of wax herself, and by then she wouldn't need Stone's cooperation any longer. There was another reason for Sarah's not wanting to commit herself to rewarding Stone just yet: if the son of a bitch *hadn't* recommended her to Darlene, or if he didn't come through on the witness stand, she'd be damned if she'd let him share in the booty.

"Hello, Eric, it's Sarah Jenkins," she started

the conversation when she called him that Wednesday afternoon. She didn't want to mention the DuPres will until he said something to indicate he knew that was why she was calling. If he didn't, it would mean Darlene hadn't discussed Sarah with him, so he couldn't have referred the case to her.

"Hi. I understand you met the dragon lady."

Well, so much for that. If Darlene hadn't talked to Stone about Sarah before yesterday's meeting, she sure as hell had afterward.

"Yeah, I did. A tough cookie."

"Tell me about it. I've represented her for a few years now, and she keeps me on my toes. Asks all the right questions and insists on knowing why I'm doing what. By the way, I was the one who suggested she call you."

"That's what she said, and I appreciate it. Could we get together today, Eric? Around five?"

"Be happy to. Your place or mine?"

"Would you mind coming here?"

"No problem. See you around five."

"Mind if I have Mrs. DuPres here?"

"Not at all."

That brief conversation told Sarah a lot. First, Stone had spoken of having represented *Darlene,* not Dr. DuPres or the clinic. That seemed to confirm that Darlene did in fact run the show, as she'd said; it was therefore probable, in view of her personality, that she'd had the clinic stock put in her name. Also, Stone had been quick to disclose that he was responsible for her getting the case. He was laying the groundwork for a referral fee, and that led to something else Sarah had learned during their one-minute conversation: *Eric Stone would be cooperative.*

Stone's quick agreement to come to Sarah's office was another plus. There is considerable gamesmanship in the law business, and nowhere is it more apparent than when it comes to deciding which lawyer's office will be the site of a meeting. When the lawyers are adversaries, the host will be the one whose client controls the purse strings (that is, has the economic advantage in the matter at hand); where the economies are in balance, it will usually be the older of the two. Absent these factors, the meeting will be in the office of the lawyer who is to have the lead position. These are silent understandings that seem petty but nevertheless nearly always hold true. So when Eric Stone unhesitatingly agreed to come to Sarah's office, he showed a willingness to be on the team and, more important, to acknowledge that Sarah was in charge.

When Darlene DuPres and Eric Stone arrived, Sarah wasted little time in getting down to business. "Here's the retainer agreement, Darlene. Please look it over and let me know if you have any questions before signing it. If not, sign both copies where you see the Xs. By the way, did you remember the check for expenses? I've already advanced the appearance fee."

"I'll write it out right now."

"Fine. Now, I'd like to lay out some ground rules for this meeting. Ordinarily, Darlene, anything you and I say to each other — if it's related to my giving, or your seeking, legal advice — is privileged. That means that neither of us can ever be called to testify to what was said. It's called the attorney-client privilege. But we don't have that when our conversation is in the presence of a third person. Therefore, while I interview Eric, I'd like you to remain silent. Otherwise, Eric and I could be forced to testify to what you said."

"But Eric's also my lawyer."

"Not in this case he isn't." Remembering her intention to keep Stone warm by implying he might get a piece of the eventual fee, she added: "At least not yet. That's something we can't even talk about until after he's testified, and you can be sure that he *will* be called to testify. Eric may be your lawyer on regular clinic business, and for that your conversations with him are privileged. But he was not acting as *your* attorney when he prepared Mr. Stillman's will; he was acting as *Stillman's* attorney." Sarah uttered those words very slowly. "You must understand that, and you must not ever forget it."

After pausing to let the point sink in, she turned to face Stone. "Now, Eric, I'd like you to tell me all you can recall about preparing Mr. Stillman's will. Who first asked you to do it? What was said? What discussions, if any, did you have with Stillman? Who paid you?"

This was the moment of truth for Eric Stone, the moment he had been dreading since yesterday afternoon when Darlene had threatened him with everything from loss of his law license to loss of his wife and children, not to mention the loss of her favors.

To testify falsely under oath was something that Eric Stone could not contemplate. It was unthinkable. But how much worse would it be, he wondered, than the misrepresentations he normally made in his day-to-day practice? Most legal negotiations involve some misstatements of fact, or at least editorial license. For example, "My client doesn't really *need* the property, but I might convince him to pay thirty thousand," is a statement an attorney will make when the client *must* have the property and has authorized him to pay sixty thousand. "My client won't let me settle this case; he insists we go to trial" is generally preceded by the client's begging his lawyer to settle at any cost. Are these lies more acceptable because they're part of the game?

But, try as he might, Eric Stone could not rationalize telling an eight-million-dollar lie — in a court of law and under oath — by likening it to the expected evasions and deceptions in everyday negotiations. If he were going to do it, it was purely because of his fear of what Darlene DuPres could do if pushed to the wall. And also because of his greed.

And now here he was. His answers to Sarah Jenkins's questions would determine which path he would take, possibly for the rest of his career.

"Well, the first thing I recall about this Stillman thing," he was now telling Sarah Jenkins, "is that Darlene mentioned it during one of our meetings. As I remember it, she said one of her patients, a Ben Stillman, had indicated a desire to leave his estate to the clinic. He either didn't have a lawyer or didn't want to use him — I can't remember which — but in any event he asked Darlene to make the arrangements. I guess he thought the clinic's lawyer would make sure it was done right. I didn't see anything wrong with that. Lots of times people ask me to write wills for someone else."

"Even when they're to be the beneficiary?" Sarah asked.

"Sure. It's common, for example, for someone to ask me to do a will for an elderly parent. Maybe the parent's too ill to come to the office. And the child who asks me to do it is the one who gets the money. That's normal."

"Let's talk about that for a minute," Sarah said. "I don't write wills, so I'm in strange waters. Also, I want to press you on some of these points because, sure as hell, others will before this is over. I want you to be prepared. Nothing personal, but I'll be the devil's advocate for a while."

Eric Stone braced himself. "Fire away," he said, trying to sound casual but sensing that Sarah Jenkins could see right through him.

"Okay," she said. "I understand there's nothing suspicious if a person asks a lawyer to write a will for an elderly parent, particularly if the will names all the children and not just the one making the request. But don't you want to ask some hard questions when someone asks you to do a will for a nonrelative, a will that leaves him or her everything?"

"No, not really. I've known Darlene Du-Pres for years. She'd never ask me to do something wrong. If she said that's what Ben Stillman wanted, that was good enough for me." Darlene, sitting on the edge of her chair, gave a slight sigh of relief. "Anyway, my drafting a will doesn't mean a thing until the testator signs it and the witnesses attest it. *That's* where the safeguards come in. If Stillman didn't want the will, he simply wouldn't sign it. And if he *did* sign it but was goofy at the time, either the witnesses wouldn't sign it or it would come out when the witnesses testified in court."

Sarah thought Stone's explanation was adequate, but she decided to press a little further. Give him a little taste of cross-examination; see how he handled the pressure. She put her elbows on the desk, leaned forward, and asked in the same voice she would use to cross-examine a suspicious witness in the courtroom: "But don't you think it would have been a good idea to check with Stillman?" She leaned a little closer to Stone and half-shouted: "Wouldn't a *prudent* lawyer do that? Isn't that what a *good* lawyer would do? Don't you think — ?"

"But I *did* do that! I *did* check with Still-man!" *Shit, why did I say that?* He had promised himself before the meeting that he wouldn't lie about talking to Stillman. He had some room to fudge when discussing the stock certificates or his bill for fees, and he could somehow meet Darlene halfway on these points, but he would preserve *some* self-respect by admitting that he'd never talked with Stillman.

And yet the second Sarah Jenkins put his feet near the fire, he lied! He took the easy way out. He wanted Sarah and, by extension, everyone else, to believe he was a good lawyer. So the minute Sarah implied that a competent lawyer would have talked to Stillman, he said that was just what he had done.

Now he was committed. *Shit!*

Sarah Jenkins leaned back. She had to make a split-second decision. All of her instincts told her that Stone was lying and that he'd never talked to Ben Stillman, but she loved his answer. It made her case, and if Eric Stone, a member of the bar, said he'd talked to Ben Stillman, that was just fine with her. Who was she to say it wasn't so? But she had to button it up. Get him to feel comfortable with the story, and get him to add to it so retreat would be that much more difficult.

"Well, of course you talked with Stillman, Eric. I assumed that all along. I was only curious as to *when* you talked to him and whether it was in person or over the phone."

"Uh, by phone," he replied, not very convincingly. *That's not quite as big a lie,* he thought, *as saying we met in person.*

"And when was that?" Sarah prodded. "Was it before you actually prepared the will?"

"Well, let's see," Stone said, looking at the ceiling as if trying to remember. "I'm not really sure, but if I think about it a while I'll prob — "

"That's okay, Eric," Sarah said. "It's quite natural that you wouldn't remember that. It was more than two months ago and might not even be an important detail." Sarah actually preferred that the conversation be by phone; an office meeting could be disproved by an appointment book or a secretary.

"What *is* important," she continued, "is what was said." Stone didn't volunteer an answer right away. Sarah was afraid he might be wavering and she didn't want to lose him. Time to help him out a bit, throw him a life preserver. "That was a bad question on my part, Eric. Too broad. Let me break it down." She paused. "I assume you told him you were the lawyer who'd been asked to do his will?"

"Oh, sure."

"And that you wanted to confirm that he wanted to leave his estate to the DuPres Clinic?"

"Yeah, right."

And that, Sarah Jenkins said to herself, *is why we can't ask leading questions in court.* It's too easy to get the witness to say what you want to hear. But what a great way to prep a witness. And now that she'd carried Stone this far, she might as well carry him across the goal line. "And during that conversation, Eric, I suppose he told you he was doing it because he was getting excellent treatment at the clinic?" Another question that suggested the answer.

"Uh-huh, definitely."

What the hell, Sarah figured, might as well go for the extra point. "And when you talked with him, he sounded rational and in full control of his faculties?"

Now Eric Stone was beginning to relax. "Rational? Hell, Ben Stillman was as sane and competent as any man I've ever talked to."

"Well," said Sarah, "I don't think you have to go *that* far."

Throughout this entire dialogue, Darlene DuPres had remained quiet just as Sarah had instructed. But inside she was rejoicing. Eric Stone and Sarah Jenkins were doing her bidding. Now all she had to do was get Alice Doakes and Willard into line, and that should be a piece of cake.

30

"Oh, my God! I don't believe it!"

Sam Altman said it over and over again after Leon Schlessinger told him and the others of the DuPres will. His head shook despairingly.

"Believe it, Sam," Schlessinger said impatiently. "It's true. The question is, what should we do about it?"

Howard Rhyne, Pete Golden, and Ed Hirsch were seated around the large conference table with Altman and Schlessinger. They were meeting at the Beth Zion business office at six o'clock on Wednesday evening, only a few hours after the DuPres bomb had been dropped by Sarah Jenkins, who at this very moment was in her office putting words in Eric Stone's mouth.

Rabbi Jacob Weiss, having just finished a religious school class, was entering the room.

"Good evening, gentlemen. Sorry I'm late. What's up?"

Sam Altman shook his head. "You won't believe it."

Schlessinger handed a copy of the DuPres

will to the rabbi. "It seems that our friend Stillman liked to write wills. I'll save you the trouble of reading it. Just before he died he wrote another will, later than ours. It leaves everything to the DuPres Oncology Clinic — whatever the hell that is — up in Evanston."

Rabbi Weiss lowered his eyebrows and nodded his head, registering the news. After a few moments he spoke: "Judging from your long faces, I take it this means — "

"It means," Sam Altman blurted out, "that we don't get a damn thing. We lose the whole eight million dollars. God, I don't believe it."

"Dammit, Sam!" Pete Golden shouted. "That's the umpteenth time you've said you don't believe it. If you don't believe it, then you've got nothing to worry about. So go home and have dinner and let us decide what we're going to do. It's bad enough — "

"Loosen up, Pete." Howard Rhyne, who had been in many meetings where emotions were tested, realized the need for cool thinking. "Sam's the president of this place, and he feels responsible to the whole congregation. It's understandable that he's taking this news a little harder than the rest of us." He looked at Altman, who was chewing on his knuckle. "But, Sam, you've got to pull yourself together. And you talk like we've already lost the money." He looked at Leon Schlessinger. "Is it really that bad, Lee?" he asked.

"No, not necessarily," Schlessinger replied. "While a later will always takes precedence, it must first be proven valid. Even though the DuPres will *looks* valid, there are a couple of areas where it could be vulnerable, and I've already got my staff working on that.

"Specifically," he explained, "suspicion surrounds a will signed in a hospital and leaving everything *to* that hospital, especially when it's done shortly before death. Questions of sanity and undue influence — or even the effects of drugs — inevitably arise. And this particular will smells even worse because it was witnessed by two employees of the hospital."

"How do you know they were employees?" Golden inquired.

"One of them, Willard DuPres, is a doctor there. The clinic bears his name but, according to their lawyer, his wife owns the place. We're checking on that now. It's a critical point. The other witness also works there. That was easy to learn. Maggie Flynn called and asked for her, she came to the phone, Maggie asked if she worked there, and she said yes, she's a nurse. Then Maggie hung up." The lawyer paused to look at his wristwatch. "By the way," he wondered aloud, "Maggie was to meet me here. It's not like her to be late."

"You said there was something critical about who *owns* the clinic?" It was put as a question by Howard Rhyne.

"Yes, it's a very important point, Howie." Lee Schlessinger summarized the law disqualifying beneficiaries from acting as witnesses to a will. "Since the clinic is the beneficiary and Dr. DuPres seems to be only an employee, he probably did nothing wrong by witnessing the will. We'd have a much better case if he were the owner of the place. Even so, he could hardly claim to be disinterested; after all, if he's not the owner, his *wife* is."

Schlessinger checked his watch again. "Where could she be? I had Maggie doing some research on this very point this afternoon, and I wanted her to tell us what she's come up with so far."

As if on cue, the sound of high heels was heard clicking down the tiled hall.

"Sorry," Maggie said as she came rushing into the room, her arms burdened with a huge briefcase, a purse, and two bulky law books that looked as if they were about to slip out of her grasp. Ed Hirsch immediately

373

jumped up to offer her a hand, but she shook her head.

"Be careful, Ed," said Schlessinger. "The more heavy books a woman lawyer carries, the more apt she is to scream 'chauvinist' when a gentleman offers to help her."

Maggie plopped down in the one remaining chair, blew a few wisps of hair out of her eyes, and comically whispered in a husky and sexy voice: "If you really want to prove *you're* a gentleman, Mr. Schlessinger, give me a raise."

"He'd rather carry your books," Pete Golden laughed.

After Maggie had made herself comfortable and had her first sip of the coffee Sam Altman poured for her, Schlessinger got back to business. "Maggie," he said, "I was just explaining about beneficiaries not being witnesses to wills and how you were checking on whether the rule could be extended to employees of beneficiaries.

"In other words," he said, summarizing the question so none of the others could possibly miss the point, "would the rule — the prohibition — apply to Dr. DuPres and his nurse?"

All eyes turned toward Maggie Flynn. They remembered her propensity to give overly detailed explanations of the law, but she surprised them.

"Makes no difference," she said.

Confused silence.

Leon Schlessinger restated the question. "Maggie," he said, speaking slowly, "I asked if Dr. DuPres and his nurse are proper witnesses."

"I understand. But it just doesn't make any difference, at least not to Beth Zion. I wanted to mention this to you before the meeting, but you left the office before I could get to you."

"Well, go ahead and explain what you mean." The senior lawyer was glaring at his young associate, his eyes saying she'd better make it good.

Maggie was up to the task. One of the ironies of the legal profession is that a young, inexperienced lawyer will generally have a better recall of obscure rules of law than a seasoned practitioner. The reason is clear: many seldom-used doctrines are taught in law school but hardly ever applied in everyday practice. What law student hasn't had the Doctrine of Worthier Title, the Rule in Shelley's Case, and the Fourteen Axioms of Equity drummed into his or her head, only to get out into the real world and find the knowledge useless? A lifetime of practice might not provide even one occasion to apply any of these principles. And the further one gets away from law school, the less likely one is to remember these dormant rules, which is why the silver-haired lions of the profession candidly admit that they could no longer pass the dreaded bar examination.

Likewise, the practicing attorney who is all too familiar with the basic rules governing the eligibility of witnesses to wills might, at the same time, be totally in the dark as to the effect of a violation of those rules. And that's understandable: if you knew the rules and never violated them, you would have no reason to know precisely what would happen if you did violate them. But the law student who has just recently completed Wills and Trusts, as Maggie Flynn had done just a few years earlier, knows these things.

As Maggie was beginning her research that afternoon, her memory drifted back to her law school course on wills and the recollection of just such a detail came to her. She checked it out, hoping her memory had played a trick on her, because if she was right it could be disaster for the synagogue. It turned out to be the easiest thing in the world to find, assuming someone looked for it. And damn it, she *was* right. Before getting to the bad news, however, she wanted to clear up a few loose ends.

"First of all," she told the group, "the

clinic's lawyer told us today that Ms. DuPres owns the place and Dr. DuPres is nothing more than a salaried employee. Well, I checked with the secretary of state's office this afternoon and learned he's a heck of a lot more than that. According to their last annual report, he's the president and director — the *sole* director."

Alarms went off in Schlessinger's head. This news could make a big difference. Regardless of what the law said about an employee witnessing a will benefiting his or her employer, his instincts told him a different rule would apply where the employee was actually the president and sole director — and all the shares were in his wife's name.

"And there's more," Maggie was saying. "He actually owns all the stock in the place! He *has* to — by law!"

Leon Schlessinger couldn't believe his ears. Maggie wouldn't say it if she weren't sure, but then how could Sarah Jenkins have said that *Darlene* DuPres owned the stock? It would be insane to lie about something so easy to check. "Maggie," he asked, "how would you know who owned the stock? That wouldn't be shown on the annual report."

"The DuPres Oncology Clinic," she answered, "was incorporated under the Illinois Professional Corporation Act, not the Business Corporation Act, which covers most corporations. That was easy to find out. It's public record."

"So?" Schlessinger was aware of the existence of the Illinois statute permitting corporate professional practices for doctors and lawyers but had never had occasion to study it. He'd left that to the corporate specialists in the firm.

"So the Professional Corporation Act has a very interesting provision." She flipped through a few pages of her yellow legal pad. "I'll read it for you:

> *No corporation organized under this Act may issue any of its capital stock to anyone other than an individual who is duly licensed or otherwise legally authorized to render the same specific professional services or related professional services as those for which the corporation was organized.*

"Since the DuPres Oncology Clinic is incorporated as a *medical* corporation, only licensed physicians can legally own stock in it. And Ms. DuPres isn't a licensed physician. I checked that out with the Department of Education and Registration. Only Dr. DuPres is licensed to practice medicine in Illinois, so he has to be the sole shareholder."

Schlessinger was silently nodding his head, half to approve Maggie's thoroughness and half to acknowledge that her conclusion seemed right. He cleared his throat and addressed another question to his associate. "Did you have a chance to find out what the law would say about Dr. DuPres, as the sole shareholder and director, being a proper witness?"

"I'm sure he isn't, based on my preliminary research. The legal test is whether he has an *interest* in the bequest. Ordinarily, an employee — even if an officer — wouldn't. But there's no one who'd have a greater interest in a corporate bequest than the sole owner and sole director of the corporation. I mean, he *is* the corporation. If he doesn't have an interest, then nobody does. In short, Dr. DuPres blew it when he signed."

The mood in the room would have been much brighter but for the serious expression on Maggie Flynn's face and the dejected tone of her voice. "But, as I said earlier, that really doesn't make any difference to Beth Zion. Here's why: if the DuPres will is valid, then it follows that Beth Zion gets nothing. Right?" She looked up to see the others nodding their heads and then said: "Well, unfortunately, the will is still valid even though Dr. DuPres did witness it."

"Now, wait a minute!" Sam Altman half-shouted. "First you say he blew it, and now you say he can set up his own corporation, own the whole goddamn thing himself, and then get some sick old man to — "

Leon Schlessinger's mind was racing. How the hell could she say the will was valid? Every lawyer knew a witness couldn't have an interest in a will, but Maggie was too smart to make a statement like that unless she had something to back it up. He'd been telling these people for the past half hour that this DuPres thing would go away if it turned out that the doctor was ineligible, and then — *Wait!* There was *something,* but what the hell was it? Something from way back. Something he'd read, or maybe learned in —

" — because he would still be a legally qualified witness," Maggie was saying.

"But Lee was telling us that you can't witness a will if you get something under it," Howard Rhyne pointed out.

"That's not exactly what Mr. Schlessinger said." Maggie knew what he'd said, but she didn't want to point out his error in front of clients. "A person *may* legally witness a will even if he or she is named in it, but then the person can't take anything under it. The will is still valid, but the witness forfeits the inheritance."

Rabbi Weiss wanted to be sure he understood. "Do you mean," he asked, "that once a beneficiary becomes a witness, he ceases to be a beneficiary?"

"Exactly."

"But if that's the case," he said, "then wouldn't the clinic forfeit the money since, as you said, the doctor and the clinic are in fact the same?"

"Yes," Maggie replied, "but it wouldn't do the synagogue any good."

Sam Altman was perplexed. "But if the clinic can't get the money, then won't it go to us?"

"No. Let me back up and explain. You should understand this so you'll be able to answer the questions you'll be getting from the congregation." Maggie glanced toward Leon Schlessinger, receiving his nod to go ahead. "First, I'll quote the exact language from the Probate Act." She reached for one of the books she'd brought with her, opened it to a page she'd marked, and read:

If any beneficial legacy or interest is given in a will to a person attesting its execution . . . , the legacy or interest is void as to that beneficiary . . . , unless the will is otherwise duly attested by a sufficient number of witnesses.

"By the way," she said as she looked around the table, " 'attest' and 'witness' mean the same thing. As I said before, this language permits beneficiaries to witness wills but, once they do so, they lose their right to the inheritance. When this happens, the court simply deletes the bequest to that witness or, in this case, the clinic, but doesn't nullify the entire will. In other words, we're left with the rest of the will."

"But the will leaves everything to the clinic," said Altman. "There is no *rest* of the will."

"Perhaps I can address that," Leon Schlessinger said. As soon as he'd heard the words of the statute, it had all come back to him, and now he felt responsible for having earlier misled his clients. "I confess that I forgot about that particular rule; it doesn't come up except where some lawyer screws up. Since that never happens at Schlessinger, Harris & Wade," he said with a wry grin, "I hope you can forgive my lapse. That's why we keep bright young attorneys like Maggie around. They keep us on our toes.

"Anyway," he continued, "let's assume Dr. DuPres is considered to be the beneficiary because the clinic is. The law would nevertheless accept the will *but only as if it left nothing to the clinic*. Now, Sam, you said a minute ago that that's all the will does. But that's not true. If you'll look at the preamble in the copy I gave you, you'll see that it revokes all prior wills, and that would include ours."

Howard Rhyne, who as a real estate developer was in constant contact with lawyers and legal documents, was the first of the nonlawyers present to catch on. "Oh, Christ, I get it. What you're saying is that the DuPres will is valid insofar as it revokes ours but invalid when it comes to leaving Stillman's money to the clinic. Is that it?"

"That's it," answered Schlessinger.

"So who would get the money?"

"Stillman's heirs, if they could be found."

"But that's crazy!" Pete Golden blurted out. "Ben Stillman writes two wills within a year of his death, one for a synagogue and one for a clinic. A charitable guy. So he clearly didn't have any family he wanted to leave his money to. But now, because of some legal mumbo-jumbo, neither of the two charities gets a cent. And the goddamn relatives — who he tried *twice* to disinherit — sneak in between the cracks and take the candy. Is that really how the law would handle this, Lee?"

"Yeah, it is. But remember, there are other ways we can attack the DuPres will — the *whole* DuPres will. And if we can do that successfully, we're home free. If it comes out that Stillman was somehow duped into signing it or that he didn't sign it at all, then the whole will gets tossed out and we're okay."

"Well," Pete Golden sighed, "it looks like our work is cut out for us. How do we go about it?"

Maggie extended her arm to get Schlessinger's attention. "May I address that, Mr. Schlessinger?" Her employer nodded. "There are several areas I'm exploring for that. But it's important that we move fast. Sarah Jenkins, the clinic's attorney, hasn't done her homework yet. That's obvious. She didn't seem to know this morning that Ms. DuPres couldn't own the stock or that her husband was the president and only director. She went out of her way to say that Dr. DuPres was merely an employee.

"So I think we should immediately subpoena the clinic's records and at the same time try to get statements or depositions from the other employees and maybe even patients. We have to find out what treatment Stillman was getting when he signed, and whether he was on medication. If we give those people time, they'll alter the records and brainwash all the witnesses.

"Also, I'd like to check into Stillman's *mental* health — his competency — at the time he signed. Remember, if he was out of touch, then even if the clinic's people did nothing wrong their will wouldn't be any good. We could interview — "

"I wouldn't waste much time on that last point, Maggie," Schlessinger interrupted. "He was holding down a pretty responsible job, one that required competency, right up until the cancer finally got him. Moreover, just a few days before he died he wrote a very well-thought-out letter of instructions to Phil Ogden. Ogden even told me how impressed he was with the details of those instruc — " Leon Schlessinger stopped in mid-sentence, closing his eyes and furling his eyebrows as if in pain.

Rabbi Weiss was on his feet in an instant. "Lee, are you all right?"

The lawyer raised his hand. "Yes, Jake, I'm fine. Just thought of something, something important. Trying to sort it out in my mind. Give me a second."

The others at the table looked at one another, relieved, and shrugged their shoulders.

Finally Schlessinger opened his eyes and looked around the table with a big grin on his face. "The DuPres will," he announced, "is a fake! Now all we have to do is prove it."

Leon Schlessinger had remembered the letter Stillman sent to Philip Ogden a few days before his death. To Phil, the letter was evidence that Ben Stillman was mentally competent. But Schlessinger now pursued the implication of this letter to another level: If just a few days before his death, Stillman was competent, and at that time he still believed he had left everything to Beth Zion, then he wasn't aware that he had signed the DuPres will.

And if he hadn't known of the DuPres will in November, only two and a half months after he'd supposedly written it, then he'd probably *never* known about it. That could only mean it was a forgery. Or, if Stillman had signed it, he hadn't known he was signing it. Maybe he'd been drugged or tricked. In either case, the *entire* DuPres will would fall. And the Beth Zion will would stand up.

After the meeting, Schlessinger told this to Maggie Flynn at a coffee shop a few blocks from the synagogue.

"When Jenkins first mentioned the DuPres will in Lloyd's chambers this morning, I immediately remembered that letter. I knew there was an inconsistency, but I didn't zero in on its significance until a little while ago.

"As of right now," he went on, "we know more than Sarah Jenkins. She doesn't know about the stock, and she sure doesn't know that in November Stillman still thought the Beth Zion will was good. You were right, she hadn't done her homework. But I don't want her and the other lawyers in the case to know what we've learned — not yet."

"Why not?" Maggie asked. "The sooner she learns she's a loser, the sooner she and the DuPres people will go away."

"But play it out a step further, Maggie. Once she knows, then it won't be long before the others, including Tom Andrews, know. And once *he* figures this thing out, we're in trouble."

"Why?"

"Right now he's prepared to fight the DuPres will tooth and nail. And ours, too. He doesn't want *either* will. But the second he learns that the clinic only forfeits its inheritance and that the rest of the will — including the revocation clause — could be valid, he'll change direction in a flash."

"And do what?"

"And fight to prove that Stillman was mentally competent and that he knew exactly what he was doing when he signed that second will. Then Andrews wouldn't have to attack our will. It would automatically be revoked by the other one. And since the clinic can't take the inheritance, the effect of the DuPres will is to leave everything to Stillman's heirs."

He was shaking his head. "Just imagine the paradox we have here. Ordinarily, the only way the heirs can win in these cases is to show that a will is no good. But here the heirs can win if they can prove the DuPres will *is* good. I haven't seen anything like this in thirty-eight years of practice. Up until now, Andrews had a tough assignment: attack both wills. Not an easy job, especially since ours doesn't have any weak spots. But now he can forget about that. All he has to do is support the DuPres will. And that's a much easier job."

They were silent for a few moments. Then Schlessinger reached for the check. "Okay, Maggie, let's bear down and try to show there was some hanky-panky over at the clinic when that will was being signed."

He grinned for the second time that evening, and added: "With luck, we can keep Andrews on our side until we do it."

It was now exactly one week after Benjamin Stillman's death.

PART VI
THE SECOND WEEK

31

LAWYERS IN SLUGFEST; $8 MILLION LEGACY UPSET BY NEW WILL

BY ELOISE BYRD

Benjamin Stillman, the reclusive millionaire who died 10 days ago, is attracting more attention in his death than he did in his lifetime. War has already been declared in the courtroom of probate judge Verne Lloyd.

As reported in this column last Saturday, Stillman, who for more than 40 years worked at Barnett Brothers brokerage firm, left stocks, bonds, and cash valued at $8 million, and he willed it all to Beth Zion Synagogue. But the folks at Barnett Brothers — especially William Barnett, the firm's president — suspect Stillman stole the money from the firm and have hired local attorney Maxwell Kane to see about getting it back. Courthouse watchers were reserving seats for the expected battle between the brokerage house and the house of worship.

Now two new claimants have come forth, promising to make this the most dramatic probate case in this city's memory. First, flamboyant trial lawyer Sarah Jenkins produced a later will signed by Stillman, this one leaving his entire fortune to the DuPres Oncology Clinic. "This was Mr. Stillman's last will," Jenkins told this reporter, "and I have every confidence that Judge Lloyd will uphold it. The previous will in favor of Beth Zion Synagogue is no longer valid."

Just as Jenkins was dropping her bomb, cannons were fired from still another quarter by attorney Alan Fiori, who claims to represent all the past and present clients of Barnett Brothers, "Stillman stole the money," Fiori told us, "and I can prove he stole it from the people who had accounts at Barnett Brothers. He didn't steal it from the rich guys who own the firm. He stole it from the little guys like you and me."

This column learned that Judge Lloyd summoned all the lawyers in the case to his chambers Wednesday morning for what turned out to be a stormy meeting with accusations flying and tempers flaring. In addition to Jenkins, Fiori, and Kane, Philip Ogden attended as the original lawyer to represent the Stillman estate and attorney Leon Schlessinger and an associate were there on behalf of Beth Zion Synagogue. The cast was rounded out by attorney Thomas Andrews, whom Judge Lloyd appointed earlier to represent the interests of Stillman's heirs. Mysteriously, those heirs have not yet been identified or heard from.

There is already speculation as to which of the six contesting —

The shrill ring of the telephone interrupted Verne Lloyd's third reading of Eloise Byrd's column. He answered the phone and then waited a few seconds before speaking. "I must warn you that the sheriff has a tracing device on this phone, and he should be at your doorstep within the next ten minutes." The judge's voice was calm, but there was nothing calm about the way he slammed down the receiver.

"Bastards!" he muttered as he walked into the kitchen where Clara Lloyd, his wife of nearly forty-five years, was digging through her cupboards. The children and grandchildren would all be over for Thanksgiving dinner next Thursday, and she was making her list of things to pick up at the grocery.

"Sounds like you got another one of those calls," she said over her shoulder.

"That makes five already this morning," he said as he opened the refrigerator, "and so far the Jews are losing four to one. They sure don't want Beth Zion to get the money, and they're not bashful about the way they express their views."

"Did you use that line about the sheriff listening in on the phone?"

"Yeah, but if this keeps up I just might have to do something like that. Christ, one of the reasons I moved over to the probate division was to get away from this kind of thing."

"It just doesn't seem fair — hey, put that doughnut back. You've already had two." She playfully snapped the dish towel at him, and he feigned great injury. "C'mon," she said, "let me get you out of the kitchen where you won't be tempted."

As they walked into the living room, Clara Lloyd took his arm. "Now that you mention it, I don't recall you getting this many calls since the time you let off those boys who vandalized the church."

"Aw, honey, don't start in on me again about *that* one. There was no proof that those kids did it, and anyway the police screwed up the arrest. They didn't read 'em their rights and they didn't let 'em call their parents or a lawyer until after they grilled 'em for a couple of hours."

"But they confessed."

"Hell, *you'd* have confessed by then."

"It's odd, isn't it," she asked as she settled onto the couch, "that the people who called to defend a church are now calling to berate a synagogue? Or maybe it isn't odd. Maybe it's just plain anti-Semitism."

Verne Lloyd wasn't listening. His full attention was once again on the Stillman case. *This thing's getting out of hand. Too many issues, too many claimants, too much public interest, and too many lawyers with loud mouths. I guess I'd better get 'em together Monday to get things back on track.*

On Monday afternoon all the lawyers who had been present the previous Wednesday were once again in Judge Verne Lloyd's chambers in response to calls from the bailiff, Wysocki. Sarah Jenkins and Al Fiori (whose sport coat was even more garish than the one he'd worn on Wednesday) shared the couch, as if it were reserved for the spoilers.

Lloyd had already decided to assume a "cool but stern" attitude for the meeting — cool because he wanted the lawyers to know their conduct couldn't irritate him to the point where he might make procedural errors or impulsive decisions and stern because he didn't want them to forget who was in charge. His first order of business was to remind everyone about statements to the press. "If made at all, they should be guarded and confined to the facts of the case. Opinions, conjecture, and bravado are off limits, as are indirect attempts to influence a judge or jury or sway public opinion."

He then specifically addressed Jenkins and Fiori. "I'm going to let it pass this time, since you weren't in the case when I admonished Mr. Ogden and Mr. Andrews on this issue. Even so," he couldn't resist adding, "I should think you would have been more circumspect with your remarks to Eloise Byrd. May I have your assurances that we won't see or read more of the same in the future?"

Since he was looking at Sarah Jenkins when he finished speaking, she elected to reply first. Misconstruing Lloyd's coolness to mean this wasn't really a big issue with him, she chose the wrong response. "Your point is well taken, Your Honor, but it's hard to refuse to answer a reporter's questions. The public's interested in this kind of case, and they *do* have a right to know our positions. Nevertheless, I'll try to keep your view in mind."

Verne Lloyd managed to restrain himself. Nodding his head slowly and giving the impression that he accepted Sarah's position, he looked toward Al Fiori.

"I guess I'd have to go along with Ms. Jenkins on that one, Judge," Fiori grinned. "Freedom of the press, ya know."

Maybe it was the grin, or maybe it was the "ya know." In any case, Judge Lloyd slowly rose half out of his seat, leaned far out across his desk and, shifting his gaze back and forth between Jenkins and Fiori, whispered fiercely: "How dare you! How dare *both* of you treat so contemptuously the feelings of this court on an issue that is so vital to the proper administration of justice. This is not my view, as you call it, it is the *only* professionally responsible position that can be taken in a case such as this."

Lloyd then came around his desk and approached Jenkins and Fiori, coming so near that they involuntarily shrank back against the couch.

"You!" he spat, pointing his finger at Sarah Jenkins. "You have the temerity to pass off your statements to that reporter as being mere answers to routine questions? And you thought I would buy that? Madam, you insult me!" He whirled around just long enough to grab the Saturday newspaper from his desktop and then turned back to Sarah, who seemed genuinely frightened. "I quote: 'This was Mr. Stillman's last will, and I have every confidence that Judge Lloyd will uphold it. The previous will in favor of Beth Zion Synagogue is no longer valid.'"

He looked Sarah straight in the eye. "You were not merely answering questions or stating basic facts. You were making a statement — a highly *improper* statement, because you predicted what my ruling would be and because you stated flatly that the first will is no longer valid. That is *my* decision to make, Ms. Jenkins, not yours. You were attempting to use the press to help you gain public support for your position, and you tried — not very subtly — to put pressure on me by making it seem that I would be a fool to uphold the first will. And you scared the hell out of every member of the Beth Zion congregation, probably by design to force a premature settlement. I find this conduct, *Ms.* Jenkins, reprehensible."

"Your Honor, I — "

"You needn't respond, Ms. Jenkins," said the judge. "I didn't address a question to you." He turned his attention to Al Fiori, whose visible discomfort showed that he expected a similar lashing. "Now let's all hear, Mr. Fiori, what you had to say to this reporter — this protector of the public's right to know. Ah, here it is: 'Stillman stole the money, and I can prove he stole it from the people who had accounts at Barnett Brothers. He didn't steal it from the rich guys who own the firm. He stole it from the little guys like you and me.' "

Judge Lloyd threw the paper on his desk and addressed his next remark to the room at large. "Isn't this interesting? Here we have one of the most complex cases to come before this court since I have been a probate judge, a case with issues that may not be resolved for years, and the brilliant Alan Fiori has already solved it! He says so, right there in the paper. He specifically states that Mr. Stillman stole the money and that he can prove it. Incredible! And Mr. Stillman has been dead for less than two weeks."

The judge started to walk away, but then turned and stared at Al Fiori: "Your *proof*, Mr. Fiori? Just what *is* your proof? Tell us so we can all save the time and expense of a long trial."

Since Judge Lloyd seemed to be waiting this time for some response, Fiori cleared his throat while trying to think of something to say in his defense. "Well, Judge, isn't it obvious that Mr. Still — "

"Obvious? The only fact that is *obvious*,

399

as far as I can see, is that Mr. Stillman is dead. But you have chosen to condemn him publicly before the earth has even settled on his grave. And also to curry favor with the so-called little people who may end up on your jury."

The judge returned to his desk, feeling good about the way he'd handled the situation. He'd cut those two grandstanders down a peg or two, and that should make the rest of the case a little more manageable.

He folded the Saturday newspaper deliberately and put it in the wastebasket, a signal that that particular subject was closed. Then he rearranged an item or two on his desk and looked up as if nothing of moment had taken place. "When we last met," he said, "we were trying to resolve some procedural questions. Does anyone have anything to say on that or, for that matter, on any other point?"

It was as if someone had opened a valve to release pressure from the room. As soon as the judge changed the subject and brought all the other lawyers back into the conversation, there was a simultaneous release of breath and shuffling of bodies to find relaxed positions. Sarah Jenkins and Al Fiori seized the moment to move an inch or two farther apart on the couch.

Fiori had planned to ask permission to

400

use estate funds to retain auditors to examine Stillman's and Barnett Brothers' records. But now, in light of the beating he'd just taken from the judge, he had second thoughts.

It was Leon Schlessinger who broke the ice. "Your Honor, it seems certain things will necessarily take a good deal of time to complete. For example, I would suppose that Mr. Andrews will need time to try to find the heirs." He looked toward Andrews, who nodded. "And it could take even longer for Mr. Kane and Mr. Fiori to unravel all the financial records, assuming they're really serious about wanting to prove that the money was stolen." Schlessinger said this in a way that told the room a challenge to the synagogue would be both foolish and immoral. "So I think that — "

"Excuse me, Lee." It was Max Kane. "For the record, I haven't yet said that Barnett Brothers believes the money was stolen, nor have I yet filed a claim on behalf of the firm." He was playing the hand as he and Bill Barnett had agreed. "In fact, it's far too early for us to draw any conclusions on that subject, and we certainly wouldn't want to make any accusations against Mr. Stillman prematurely." Al Fiori squirmed, and Sarah Jenkins moved still farther away from him. "We haven't started any audits, but we would look with interest at anything Mr. Fiori finds in his."

"You're absolutely right, Max," Schlessinger said. "I guess I just assumed you were making a claim because of what I read in Eloise Byrd's column. She wrote something about people already reserving seats to watch the war between the brokerage house and the — what did she say? — oh, yes, the 'house of worship.'"

"Amazing, isn't it, what people will read?" Judge Lloyd interjected. "Go ahead with your point, Lee."

"My point, Your Honor, is that even if we can't have any meaningful hearings for some time, we could at least get started with pretrial depositions of anyone who could shed light on the validity of the wills — specifically, the witnesses and the lawyers who did the drafting."

"Your Honor?"

"Yes, Mr. Ogden?"

"I would agree with Mr. Schlessinger, but I think the initial discovery should be directed to *anyone* who may have relevant information."

"Such as?"

"Such as other personnel at the DuPres Clinic. And I think we should also be permitted to examine the clinic's records so we can determine Mr. Stillman's condition at the time he signed the will, what medications were given him, and so forth."

Sarah Jenkins wasn't happy with what she was hearing. Ogden was really suggesting that *her* witnesses and records should be scrutinized by the others before she herself could examine them and, if necessary, shore them up. Then, if anything came up that would hurt her case, she'd be out of the box before she could even bail out with a quick settlement. While she'd wanted to keep a low profile for the rest of this meeting, it was clear that she'd better speak up now.

"I would have to object to such an inquiry taking place too quickly," she said. "I haven't yet had a chance to fully investigate all the facts bearing on our will, and I will need time to do additional research into the law and procedures governing this kind of case. I don't think I can adequately represent my client during discovery until I do these things, and I don't see where a short delay would hurt anyone. Stillman's money isn't going anywhere."

"I assumed from reading the newspaper," said Leon Schlessinger, "that you had *already* fully investigated the case. After all, you said you were confident that the judge would uphold *your* will, and you certainly didn't hedge when you said that Beth Zion's was no longer valid."

Sarah blanched, but before she could reply the judge stepped in. "Please, let's not revisit Ms. Byrd and her column. I agree that we can get started with discovery, but I don't see the need to raid the DuPres Clinic before Ms. Jenkins has a chance to prepare herself. As she pointed out, Mr. Stillman's money is secure." He looked around the room. "Does anyone else have anything to bring up?"

"Your Honor?"

"Yes, Mr. Andrews, what have you got for us?"

Andrews was opening a notebook as he began speaking. "Your Honor, in the short time I've been on this case I've taken some steps to locate Mr. Stillman's family. I admit I haven't done an exhaustive job, but the little I have done convinces me that I'm not going to have much luck unless I broaden the search. I've examined his apartment and found nothing helpful. No address books, correspondence, or albums. Neither his landlady nor his cleaning lady knew of any family, nor did any other tenants in the building. In checking with the utility companies, I learned of two former addresses for Mr. Stillman, but no one there could help either. I'm advised by Mr. Kane that no one at Barnett Brothers has information on Stillman's family, and so far I haven't found anything in any public records — such as marriage licenses — to indicate he had a family. We even called all the Stillmans in the telephone directory. Some who knew about the case said they'd *like* to be related to him, but they weren't as far as they knew. I'll interview some of them further to make sure."

"How would you broaden your search?" Judge Lloyd asked.

"There are several ways, but I'm not recommending most of them. Not yet, anyway. For example, we could go to private investigators or professional tracing firms, but those should be last resorts. I do, however, have a suggestion. A rather unusual one."

"Unusual, Mr. Andrews? There isn't much in this case that *isn't* unusual. Let's hear it."

"Well, Judge, Phil — Mr. Ogden — and I have reason to believe that if Benjamin Stillman has any living relatives, they wouldn't be in the United States." By prearrangement, Phil and Tom had agreed not to divulge any more than they had to about Stillman's background. "If I want to find them or satisfy you that they can't be found, I think I will have to go to Europe. That's where he was born and raised. Otherwise, I'll just be running around in circles over here."

"Europe's a big place," Judge Lloyd observed.

"We have a place and date of birth. Also the family name." When he saw the judge's eyebrows rise, Andrews explained. "He changed it to Stillman after he came to America. I have the documentation on that."

While Lloyd was taking this in, Philip Ogden decided to give Andrews an assist. "Your Honor," he said, "I agree that Tom should begin an inquiry in Europe, in Stillman's hometown, and I think it would be proper to advance estate funds for this purpose. After all, it's his family we're looking for. I can't imagine," he added, looking around the room to the other lawyers, "that anyone would object."

There was no dissent. Regardless of how vigorously lawyers battle over a fund, they are surprisingly cooperative whenever one of them asks to dip into that fund to help finance his or her case. An objection would be remembered when the objector makes a similar request later. The thinking parallels that which dissuades one lawyer from resisting too strenuously another's petition for legal fees: *Next time it may be my turn.*

Judge Lloyd leaned back in his chair, slid his glasses up onto his forehead, and rubbed his eyes, his normal pose when pondering a lawyer's request calling for more than a yes or no ruling. Without taking his hands from his eyes, he asked, "Don't you think it would be appropriate to put this in the form of a written motion, setting forth your reasons and a projection of expenses? And, of course, your destination."

The question was Tom's to answer. "Ordinarily I would put the motion in writing, Your Honor, but I hoped it wouldn't be necessary in this instance. Because of the circumstances."

"What circumstances?" Lloyd asked, bringing his eyes back to the lawyer he'd appointed to represent Stillman's heirs.

"Eloise Byrd, for one. Every piece of paper we file in this case becomes a matter of public record. If she or other reporters write about every step I take and what I propose, the whole world will know it even before you have a chance to rule. We'd all be second-guessed. Worse, all the Monday morning quarterbacks out there would be trying to tell all of us — including you, Judge — what we should be doing. I think it'd be a mistake, but of course I'll do whatever you ask."

The judge was nodding. *Andrews's point is a good one, but should routine procedures be sidestepped just because of busybodies like Eloise Byrd? And if so, isn't it an indictment of our system that people like her can alter the courts' processes?* "I could sign a protective order keeping everything confidential. Would that be a solution?" It was as much a question to himself as to the others in the room.

"I don't think so," Philip Ogden volunteered. "The protective order itself would be public record, and it could set off an angry reaction from the press if they thought you were trying to hide things. I could just see Byrd's next column! If I may," Phil continued, "I have an idea on how this might be handled."

"Go ahead."

"Simply sign an order permitting Tom to conduct whatever search he thinks is necessary and reasonable and authorizing me, as the acting administrator of the estate, to advance or reimburse Tom for these expenses out of estate funds. Naturally, all the expenditures would be subject to your later approval. Such an order wouldn't create undue speculation."

"That makes sense. Any objections?" the judge asked as he looked around the room. Hearing none, he looked to Phil and Tom. "All right, prepare an order for my signature, but show it to the others first. And make sure it reflects that no one had an objection. Now, is there anything else we have to talk about?"

Al Fiori was biting his lip. *It's now or*

never, asshole. Do it now or bag the whole thing. Don't cut and run just because that prick jumped all over you before. "Yes, Your Honor, there is," he said in a voice so high that it betrayed his fear but so loud that it startled even him. "Mr. Kane said that Barnett Brothers hasn't yet decided what course to take, but he *did* say he'd be interested in the results of an audit. On behalf of all the people I represent, the Barnett Brothers customers, and in the interest of justice, it would seem — "

"Save yourself the trouble, Mr. Fiori." Lloyd's voice was quiet but firm. "I will not authorize an advance of estate funds to finance an audit."

"But with all respect, Your Honor, when Tom Andrews asked — "

"That was different. It's one thing to use Mr. Stillman's money to locate his own family. It's quite another to use it to try to incriminate him after his death. Moreover, Mr. Andrews was appointed by the court. You, on the other hand, rushed in here voluntarily saying that you represented many people — 'little people,' I believe you told Ms. Byrd — and that you could already prove that Mr. Stillman stole the money."

Fiori was in a bind, trying to decide whether to push any harder or accept his setback gracefully. The judge saved him that decision.

"I'm inclined to grant your earlier request for class action certification, Mr. Fiori. I suggest, therefore, that you go about the business of identifying your clients. I'm sure Mr. Kane will see to it that Barnett Brothers cooperates with you on that. Then decide with your clients how you will finance the case. That's your collective problem. If you should produce evidence that Mr. Stillman came by his money illicitly, I'll reconsider at that time a petition for reimbursement."

Judge Lloyd concluded the session by announcing that the lawyers should go about preparing themselves, and their clients, for the battles ahead. "Get started with your research and discovery. I'm here to help resolve your conflicts along the way, but do your best to cooperate as much as you can without jeopardizing your clients' interests. I'll set a status call for a few weeks hence. And Mr. Andrews?"

"Yes, Your Honor?"

"Fly coach."

32

Within two weeks after Benjamin Stillman died, six sets of lawyers were already busily devoting themselves to the task of laying claim to his money. All spoke fervently and eloquently on behalf of their clients, even though two, Tom Andrews and Al Fiori, didn't even know who their clients were.

These first stages of litigation are something like a mating dance, each participant strutting around and showing off his feathers, except that with lawyers it's verbiage instead of plumage.

After announcing their positions and casting a few obligatory barbs, the Stillman case warriors set about the tedious road to trial. Friendly witnesses would be interviewed in depth — and then prepped; not-so-friendly witnesses would be deposed under oath — and then attacked. Documents would be examined and analyzed. Above all, endless hours would be spent in the law library studying the statutes, precedents, and rules that would govern the case.

Each player's preparation set him or her

on a different course, and each hoped that course would lead to an eight-million-dollar jackpot. Tom Andrews's route was the longest. He was off to Germany "to find me some Schtillermanns." While he was trying to identify his clients in Europe, Al Fiori was doing the same in America. Sarah Jenkins's task, as she saw it, was to confirm that Darlene and Willard DuPres and Alice Doakes would testify that Stillman had signed the second will voluntarily, that he had known what it said, and that all the lights had been on in his attic. She hadn't yet focused in on her larger problem, the effect of Willard DuPres's witnessing that will.

Maxwell Kane had no specific agenda for the time being, other than to see what the others developed. It made little difference to his client which of the two wills was upheld. And Bill Barnett had agreed, at least for now, not to try to show that Ben Stillman had stolen the money. If that point was established by Al Fiori, then — well, they'd take another look at things.

It was obvious to Leon Schlessinger that he and Philip Ogden should get their heads together as soon as possible. Their interests, with respect to both the wills and the potential claims of Fiori and Kane, were identical. And it would be far better for Ogden, whose "client" was the late Ben Stillman, to carry the laboring oar; it wouldn't subject the people at Beth Zion Synagogue to being labeled money-grubbers.

It was here, in the relative quiet that separated the initial skirmishes from the violence of trial, that the lawyers really became familiar with their cases. It was here, with that familiarity, that the positioning began in earnest.

"Burning the midnight oil, eh, Maggie?"

"Oh, you startled me, Mr. Schlessinger."

"I don't know why an associate in the firm should be startled to see me working after hours. I often do."

"I didn't mean that," she explained as she lowered her feet from the tabletop and tried to slip them into her pumps without looking. "It's just that I was reading and wasn't expecting — "

"Quite all right, Maggie. I have an idea kicking around up here," he said, tapping his skull. "Mind if I try it out on you? I'd like to hear your reaction."

"Not at all," she replied, flattered that he was inviting her comments.

He lowered his tall frame into a chair facing her. As he doodled on a yellow pad on the library table, he proceeded to unfold his plan. If successful, it would produce both the defeat and the cooperation of the DuPres Oncology Clinic. Like most good ideas, it was simple and nearly surefire. It required only one ally: Philip Ogden.

When he'd finished his explanation, Maggie just smiled and shook her head, not to reject the idea but to reflect her embarrassment at not thinking of it herself. After they'd massaged the scheme for a few minutes and satisfied themselves that it was worth a go, Schlessinger slid the phone toward his young associate.

"Go ahead, call him. He may still be at the office. If not, try his home. The three of us for breakfast tomorrow. Don't let him say no."

Saying no was the last thing Philip Ogden would have done. The Stillman estate was his first priority, and when Maggie hinted at a plan that might well shoot down the DuPres will — and that bitch Sarah Jenkins along with it — well, there would be no keeping him away. If he needed an additional incentive, he found it by picturing Maggie Flynn, blue eyes and all, on the other end of the line.

Owing to the publicity surrounding the Stillman case, they chose for their breakfast meeting the coffee shop of a second-rate motel just west of the Loop near the Eisenhower Expressway. Eloise Byrd would have had a field day if she'd known the estate and synagogue lawyers were huddling.

When Phil arrived, Maggie, already seated at a corner table, beckoned to him. She looked even better this morning than when he'd seen her on the two occasions in court — neat, crisp, freshly made up, and wearing an alluring perfume. Her blond hair, which had previously been pulled back into a tight bun, was this morning hanging loose almost to her shoulders, and her tortoiseshell glasses were gone, probably replaced by contact lenses. She was holding a cup of coffee and had the morning *Wall Street Journal* spread out before her.

"Morning," he said, sliding into the chair to her left. "Am I late?"

"No, I'm early. I wanted to be here before the boss."

"The boss?"

"Mr. Schlessinger."

"Oh, it wasn't clear from your call that he'd be here." He was disappointed to learn they'd have company, and he hoped it didn't show.

"Phil," she said, covering his hand with hers and fluttering her eyelashes in mock flirtation, "I really think you're a doll, but I wouldn't invite you to a seedy motel on

415

our first date without a chaperon."

His face reddened at the thought that she might have been reading his mind. "It's eight in the morning. You don't need a chaperon."

He told the waitress he'd wait to order breakfast until the third member of their party arrived, but yes, he'd love a cup of coffee. They occupied the next few minutes with small talk, silently agreeing that lawyer talk should await Schlessinger. They discovered that they'd both gone to the University of Illinois Law School (though Maggie had started after Phil graduated), they'd both written and edited for the *Law Review*, and they were members of the same legal fraternity. Phil was trying to decide if that made them fraternity brothers when Leon Schlessinger joined them.

"Good morning," he said tossing his overcoat with the others on the fourth chair and sitting to Maggie's right. It was then Phil noticed that Maggie had put her coat on the chair opposite hers, thereby insuring that she would wind up in the middle. Accident?

After pleasantries, more small talk, and orders for breakfast, Schlessinger got down to business. "Phil, we wanted to talk to you about a little coup. Interested?"

"I don't know yet. Talk to me."

Schlessinger nodded to Maggie. It was obvious to Phil that the plan she had hinted at the night before — the plan to shoot down the DuPres will — was to be sold by Maggie. So it was no accident that she was in the middle; it was center stage.

"Phil," she said, shifting her chair slightly to face him, "you realize, of course, that we have a common interest in the estate. That interest requires that the first will — the one you drafted in favor of Beth Zion — be upheld. Agreed?"

"Sure, I agree." *Big deal,* Phil thought. *Of course we both want to see my will stand up. I'd get the legal and executor's fees and they'd get the eight million bucks. I hope they didn't get me out of bed to tell me that.*

"And that means," Maggie continued, "that we both want to see the DuPres will thrown out. Right?"

"Yeah, right," he echoed.

"So it only seems logical that we should work together to destroy the DuPres will. Then — "

"Look, Maggie," he interrupted, "you don't have to spell it out for me. When Sarah Jenkins sprang that phony will on us in Judge Lloyd's chambers — the very second she pulled it out of her purse — I knew I had to attack it."

"Certainly you know that, Phil," Maggie

said. "I'm merely stating the basics before making my main point. Please bear with me."

"Sorry. Go ahead."

"Okay, but let me ask you a question first. Just how do you think you're going to throw out the DuPres will?"

"Well, I think it would be next to impossible to show something really bad, like undue influence, forgery, or even drugs — though I wouldn't put anything past that DuPres outfit. And I'm sure Stillman wasn't mentally incompetent. Hell, you could see that from the letter he sent me just before he died. So we'd have to do it by showing that Dr. DuPres was an ineligible witness."

Maggie quickly glanced toward Leon Schlessinger. He winked in return. *Good, he hadn't done his homework.*

"I hate to disappoint you, Phil, but you're riding the wrong horse."

Maggie went on to explain about the true stock ownership, the fact that Willard DuPres was both president and director, and the consequence of his having attested the will. "The result, therefore, is cancellation of the clinic's bequest, a crushing defeat for the DuPreses, but no consolation for Phil Ogden or the Beth Zion Synagogue."

"Do you mean to tell me that the rest of that goddamn will is still valid, even though

418

it doesn't do anything?"

"But it *does* do something," Leon Schlessinger replied. "It provides that all former wills, including the one you prepared, are revoked. It also names Darlene DuPres as executor. And *that* means that the eight million dollars goes to whatever heirs Tom Andrews is able to find and Darlene DuPres manages the money in the meantime."

"Oh, Christ!"

"And Sarah Jenkins, as Darlene's lawyer, gets the legal fees."

"You mean that rotten bitch — excuse me, but I can't forget how miserable she was that first day in Judge Lloyd's chambers. And to think that she'll get rich on —"

Maggie Flynn put her hand on Phil's for the second time, but now she was earnest. "Hey, wait a minute, Phil. It doesn't *have* to be that way. Let's just forget about those signatures on the will; they're not worth wasting time on. Think about getting rid of the will. That would put you back in the driver's seat, and the money would pass to Beth Zion. That would make the three of us happy and leave your friend Sarah Jenkins out in the cold."

Phil regained his composure. "Think we have a decent chance?" he asked.

Maggie had played her part perfectly, and

now it was Schlessinger's turn to perform. He cleared his throat to get Phil's attention. "Phil," he said, "we feel sure that Stillman was duped into signing the DuPres will — or maybe he didn't sign it at all. But, like you, we think we'd have a hell of a time proving it, unless . . ." He let the unfinished sentence hang there to tantalize Phil.

"Unless what?"

"Unless we got Sarah Jenkins to help us."

"Help us?" Phil half-shouted. "You gotta be nuts!"

It was then that Leon Schlessinger laid out his grand but simple plan for getting the DuPres Clinic out of the picture once and for all.

33

Howard Rhyne was genuinely impressed as he was ushered into Maxwell Kane's princely corner office on the top floor of one of the newest office buildings in the Loop. His eyes recorded the beautiful Oriental rug on the glossy parquet floor, the contemporary chrome-and-leather furniture, and the large canvases of colorful abstract art. Instead of a desk, Max Kane was sitting at an oval marble table with nothing on it except a pen set, a phone, and a thin folder that couldn't have held more than a few sheets of paper. It was the kind of office that said its owner didn't need drawers and cabinets to hold things, because he didn't need *things* to do his job. His job was to counsel and advise, and for that he needed only brains and clients, both of which he had in abundance.

"Howard," Kane said as he walked over to his visitor and extended his hand, "my secretary told me you called to say you were stopping by." He motioned toward chairs surrounding a granite coffee table on which Kane's secretary had already placed a coffee carafe, china cups, and a sugar dish, creamer, and spoons of heavy silver.

Kane was impeccably dressed in a well-pressed three-piece suit accented by highly polished shoes, gold watch chain, and bright silk tie, with matching handkerchief peeking from his breast pocket. All of this was in sharp contrast to Howard Rhyne, who had as much success in the world of real estate as Maxwell Kane did in the world of the law. Rhyne conveyed a casual air whether visiting friends socially or negotiating with business tycoons. He generally opted for tweeds or muted plaids, loafers, pastel shirts, and club ties.

"Anything stronger?" Kane asked as he started to pour the coffee.

"No, thanks, Max. Not till five, and I don't think it's five *anywhere* yet."

Kane chuckled as he poured the coffee. "I think I know why you're here, Howard, but I don't know why you're here. That is, I suppose you're here to try to make a deal, but I can't for the life of me imagine what it would be."

"It's blackmail, and you won't like it."

Kane's smile faded as he stirred his coffee. He waited a moment before he spoke. "I probably shouldn't be speaking with you. It's against legal ethics for an attorney to talk to an opposing party whose lawyer isn't present."

"Oh, horseshit. That rule was designed by slick lawyers to protect their dumb clients from other slick lawyers. I'm no dummy, Max, as you know from the times we've beaten our heads together, and I don't need Lee Schlessinger here to protect me. Anyway, *I* called *you,* and that absolves you."

"Does Lee know you're here?"

"He sent me," Rhyne replied with a sheepish grin. "He and the rest of my pals at Beth Zion."

The tall lawyer shook his head, smiling once again. "Okay, let's talk. My curiosity's aroused."

Howard Rhyne wasn't sure how to begin. He made a fuss over his coffee, then finally sighed and looked up. "Max, not knowing a better way, I'm going to put this to you cold turkey." Kane said nothing, but he looked directly into Rhyne's eyes, inviting him to proceed. "I'm asking you — Barnett Brothers — to back off."

"Back off? From what?"

"From pressing a claim against the Stillman estate."

"Now wait a second, Howard. Except for some dizzy newspaper dame, no one ever said that Barnett Brothers even *had* a claim against that estate, or if they had one that they would press it. But if they *do* have a claim, it's for eight million dollars, and it would be up to them, not you, whether they'd go after it."

Rhyne was a good negotiator, appearing more composed than he felt. "Of course, I realize it's up to you and your client, but I wouldn't want you to make the decision without knowing all the facts."

"How could we possibly know the facts yet, Howard? It would take months to unwind Stillman's transactions, and even then we might not know for sure if he stole the money."

"But there's one fact — one very important fact — that might persuade you to forget about filing a claim, regardless of whether you think Stillman robbed your clients."

Maxwell Kane had a hunch he knew what was coming. "Go ahead," he said, forcing Rhyne to say the words.

"Well, we've had several meetings over at Beth Zion about this." *Damn, why in the hell do I have to be the guy to do this. It wasn't my idea in the first place, and I think it stinks to high heaven.* "The fact is, Max, that we'd hate to see you fight for the money because, if you did, then we'd have to fight for it too. And even if we won, the community would see us as a bunch of money-hungry Jews."

"And if you lost you'd still look like a bunch of money-hungry Jews, except you wouldn't have the eight million dollars to lighten your burden."

"Touché." Howard Rhyne pursed his lips, knowing the time had come to play his final card. "I hoped it wouldn't come to this, Max, but I've been asked to convey a message. As of last night, a number of prominent Jewish families in town, most of them not connected with Beth Zion, have come forward to tell us they have business or personal accounts at Barnett Brothers but would take their business elsewhere if the firm fought us for Stillman's money. And I'm joining 'em. There you have it, for better or worse."

Maxwell Kane stared at the other man, shaking his head in a way somewhere between resignation and disgust. "You were right. It *is* blackmail."

"Before you throw me out of here, I've been authorized to say something else. In the event you make no claim, and in the further event that Beth Zion actually gets the money, I can assure you that the entire fund will be placed with Barnett Brothers to be invested. The commissions alone should — how did you put it? — lighten your burden."

"I'm very disappointed in you and your congregation, Howard. Nevertheless, I'll relay your — uh — proposition to Bill Barnett and his partners, as distasteful as it is."

"Oh, cut the bullshit, Max. You'd do the same thing if you were in our shoes. We're not screwing widows and orphans here, we're playing hardball with sophisticated stockbrokers."

Kane rose and began to move around the office, straightening some books, rearranging some knickknacks on the shelves. Finally he turned to speak in a tone that was calm, even friendly. "You know, Howard, these are odd games we play, and the dangerous thing is that we often forget that we're playing."

Rhyne nodded but chose not to speak; he assumed the lawyer had something more to say.

"We knew before today," Kane continued, "that putting up a fight for the money would alienate the Jewish community. And we knew that an inevitable part of the fallout would be the loss of Jewish investors at Barnett Brothers, including some large trusts and pension plans." He was now standing over Rhyne. "That's one reason why we all but decided, even before you came in here and made an ass of yourself, that we'd back off and let everyone else fight for the damn money."

"Damn! Did I go through this torture for nothing?"

"I enjoyed watching you squirm."

Rhyne laughed. "You barristers take the cake. Here I was, asking you not to do something you had already decided not to do, but you resisted me anyway. And then when I threatened to withdraw the accounts — something you already knew without my telling you — you went into this 'I'm so shocked' routine. They must give acting classes in law school."

Kane sat down and reached for the coffee carafe. "That's what I meant when I said we play odd games. I wasn't acting. I actually found myself resisting and shocked, to use your words. It wasn't until I stopped to think about it that I realized your threat really doesn't change a damn thing.

He poured more coffee and took a sip. "But you're right, of course. We lawyers *are* a hypocritical lot. We find ourselves disagreeing when we're not in disagreement; we argue whenever we have the opportunity to do so, even if nothing's in dispute; and we fight because we're paid to, even if there's nothing to fight about or there's nothing to be gained or even if it's not in our client's best interest. Hell of a profession," he said half to himself, "that turns innocent young law students into pit bulls."

34

Moments after Howard Rhyne made the call to set up his meeting with Max Kane, Maggie Flynn also made a call. But unlike Rhyne, Maggie was relishing hers.

It was Leon Schlessinger's idea to make both calls, but in each case he decided the message should come from someone other than himself. The call to Kane, with its threat to cancel accounts, would have more impact and credibility if it came from Rhyne, who could better speak for the members of the congregation and for the Jewish community in general. As for the call Maggie was about to make, well, she was the one who had discovered the point and therefore she'd earned the right to drive it home.

"Yes, this is Sarah Jenkins."

"Hi, it's Maggie Flynn." There was no sound of recognition. "I'm with Schlessinger, Harris & Wade. We met in Judge Lloyd's chambers — twice."

"Oh, yes. Excuse me, I didn't place — "

"It's understandable. I haven't opened my mouth once in there."

"Well, that's standard for the large firms, isn't it? Carry the seniors' briefcases, do their research, and write their letters, but don't dare open your mouth?"

You bitch, Maggie thought, *I'm going to love this.* "Right. The associates get to do all the partners' dirty work, like set up discovery schedules. Which is why I'm calling."

"Jumping the gun, aren't you? Lloyd said we'd defer that until I had a chance to get better acquainted with the case."

"Yes, he did say that, but — "

"And don't you think that *I* should get a chance to talk to my witnesses before *you* start grilling them?"

"But — "

"And review the clinic's records before you go in there with your subpoenas and tear the place apart?"

"May I answer? Please?"

"Go ahead, but hurry. You're wasting your time and I don't want you wasting mine."

Maggie had had enough of this. It was time to make her move. "You're *already* wasting your time, Ms. Jenkins. I'm hoping to keep you from wasting more of it, but that's up to you."

Now Sarah Jenkins was angry. It's a normal negotiating ploy for one lawyer, in the course of a conversation, to tell another that he can't win, that he's wasting his time, or that he's got a weak case. That's all part of the game. But it's high-handed to make a special telephone call to convey such a message. And it's downright insulting for the call to come from an inexperienced second-teamer. *If Leon Schlessinger has something to say to me,* Sarah thought, *the son of a bitch should have the balls to make the call himself.* "You're telling *me* that I'm wasting my time? That I'm going to lose this case?"

Maggie was starting to love this. "I'm telling you that you've *already* lost it. That is, your clients have. It's already out of your hands." She heard silence — not protest — from the other end of the phone. *Must've hit the right button.* "May I explain?"

"Go on," Sarah said, trying not to sound concerned.

"First of all, you made the point that Darlene DuPres owns the clinic stock. But she doesn't."

"Wrong, Ms. Flynn. The stock certificates are in her name and are dated more than a year ago. That's when Dr. DuPres transferred them to her. I saw them myself."

"I'm sure you did," Maggie replied, "but the fact remains that she's not the shareholder. That transfer was void."

"And just why is that?" Sarah was getting

the sinking feeling that this young lawyer knew something and that Darlene DuPres might be working a scam after all. Experience had taught her to listen at times like this — to resist the temptation to argue.

"Because," Maggie replied, "the clinic was set up under the Illinois *Professional* Corporation Act as a medical corporation. It's against the law for anyone other than a licensed physician to hold its stock, and Ms. DuPres is not a licensed physician — I checked. I have the statute right here and can read it to you if you wish."

Silence.

"Moreover, your Dr. DuPres is not just a hired hand around there, as you tried to make us think. He's the president and sole director. I have a certified copy of the annual report and can show it to you."

Hang on! Too early to get shot out of the water. Gotta be a bluff. "Are you trying to tell me that the will is void just because Dr. DuPres attested it? I don't believe that."

Maggie chose her next words very carefully. "Believe it or not, that's up to you," she said. "But when your Dr. DuPres attested that will, the clinic blew its inheritance. Poof. Gone. The law is very clear on this. Shall I read you the statute? I have it right here."

Damn, should've checked that myself. But

431

wait! Something doesn't fit here. Why is she calling to tell me this? If she's right, why not let me spin my wheels and then cut me down later? Nothing to gain by warning me off the case early. Unless —

"No, Maggie," she answered in as friendly a voice as she could find at the moment, "it won't be necessary to read it to me. I'll check it out. But may I ask *you* a question?"

"Of course."

"What do you want from me? I believe you think I have a weak case, but I'll never believe you called me to do me a favor. What do you really want, Maggie?"

"Well, there *is* something."

"I figured. What is it?"

"Where can we talk?" Maggie Flynn asked.

"Something the matter with the phone?"

"Not for this. How about the East Bank Club at four o'clock?"

The East Bank Club, named for its proximity to the Chicago River, was a mile or so northwest of the Loop and less than two blocks from Sarah's office. Known principally as a large and well-equipped physical fitness club, it was also a favorite meeting place for the younger and single crowds.

The two lawyers were sharing a carafe of wine in one of the booths. It was late afternoon and the after-hours crowd hadn't yet arrived.

"This is most unusual, Maggie."

"And this is a most unusual case."

Sarah Jenkins, oblivious to the unfriendly stares from the couple at a nearby table, was lighting her second cigarette since they'd met less than ten minutes earlier. As she exhaled a cloud of blue smoke, she repeated the proposal Maggie Flynn had offered only moments before. "You actually want me to permit you to inspect all the DuPres Clinic records and interview all the clinic personnel in private. You don't want me present, you don't want my clients present, and you don't want the other lawyers in the case present. You don't want Judge Lloyd or the other lawyers to know what you're doing. And you want to do it right away. Is that right?"

"That's right."

"And why, may I ask, should I accommodate you?"

"To save your ass, my dear." Maggie looked directly at the other woman. "Let me explain."

She leaned forward. "Your DuPreses are as crooked as a three-dollar bill. We know it, and we think you know it. For example, if Dr. DuPres *did* transfer the stock to his wife — or try to — a year ago, then why

433

didn't he also make her the president and director? I'll tell you why. Because they didn't change the stock ownership until *after* Stillman died, probably when Eric Stone told them DuPres had screwed up by being a witness. Then they backdated the certificates. But they couldn't backdate the other documents; they were already on file with the secretary of state. In other words, those other documents alone are pretty good evidence that the stock transfer was a fake. The irony is that they went to the trouble of setting up a phony transfer to someone who isn't even allowed to own the stock.

"For another thing, Ben Stillman didn't sign that will. Or if he did, he was somehow duped into it. And we can prove that! Sarah, we're giving you the chance to do the right thing by helping us fill in a few missing pieces. Then you could put some space between yourself and those cutthroats you represent. No reason you should lose your reputation as well as the case."

Sarah nodded her head slightly. "Your concern for my well-being touches me deeply. But since you haven't yet seen the clinic's records or talked to the people there, how can you be so cocksure that Stillman didn't sign the will voluntarily?"

Maggie and Leon Schlessinger had known

the question would come up. In fact, when Schlessinger was rehearsing her for this meeting they'd worked on several different responses. In the end they'd decided to bluff, but Maggie was to disclose one actual fact that could be substantiated and thereby lend credence to the rest of the scenario. *Here goes,* she thought. *Now we find out how good a liar I am.* "Look, Sarah, I'm not about to give away my whole case, but I can tell you part of it. First of all, do you agree that Ben Stillman was rational, that he was of sound mind until the end? You don't question that, do you?"

"Of course not," Sarah quickly replied. "I'll certainly agree he had all his marbles when he signed the DuPres will, and that was only a couple of months before he died. I *have* to agree to that, or I'd be conceding my will was no good."

"And you can't very well claim that he completely lost his sanity within the next couple of months. People don't lose it that fast."

"Not usually. But so what? Where does that take us?"

"Because during those few short months Ben Stillman still believed that he'd left his estate to Beth Zion Synagogue."

"I suppose you have proof of that?"

"You bet we do." *Okay, here it is. Just*

say it like you believe it. "He told that to several people, and we have their names. We've interviewed them, and they'll testify to that." Maggie hurried on to make her point. "And if Stillman thought that, then he couldn't have known about the DuPres will. Which means, as I said earlier, either he *didn't* sign it or he didn't *know* he'd signed it. In either case, that will isn't worth a tinker's damn."

"I'd like to verify what you're telling me." Now it was Sarah's turn to lean forward. "Will you give me the names of your witnesses so I can interview them?"

"Not yet."

Sarah Jenkins laughed. "You're bullshitting me. If you had these witnesses, you'd tell me who they are. It's a bluff. You have no evidence that Stillman believed at the end that he was leaving his money to the synagogue. For all you know, he was fully aware of the later will, and knew full well that he left everything to the DuPres Clinic — just as he wanted."

Hook, line, and sinker! *She took it hook, line, and sinker, just like Schlessinger said she would.* Maggie Flynn smiled, reached for her briefcase, and withdrew an envelope. "Here, Sarah, read this. And if you still have doubts, you can authenticate the signature and date

436

through Martha Yolandis, Mr. Stillman's cleaning lady. She's the one who brought it to Phil Ogden, and he gave us this copy." *Thank God Phil mentioned that letter to Mr. Schlessinger and thank God Mr. Schlessinger realized its significance.*

Sarah finished reading. She recalled how she'd gone after Ogden that first day in Judge Lloyd's chambers, abusing him in front of the judge and other lawyers for his lack of trial experience, actually calling him incompetent. Her personal attack had come back to haunt her, and she felt shaken. However, she was determined not to look it as she refilled her wine glass, brought it to her lips, and looked over the rim at Maggie. "Do you think I'm going to lie down and play dead because of this? So Stillman forgot he signed the second will. Big deal. He was sick, frightened, and confused."

"Aw, climb off it, Sarah. Does this letter look like he was confused? Hell, he writes better and thinks more clearly than half the lawyers in our office. And he worked at a job that required competence — certainly more than is needed to write a will — until only a few days before he wrote this. The people at Barnett Brothers will testify that his mind was as clear as a bell." This last point, based only on something Ed Hirsch had said, was a risky one. But it was worth the risk if it helped convince Sarah that their confidence was based more on preparation than bravado.

Sarah Jenkins was in a tight spot, and she knew it. She believed what Maggie had said about Darlene's not being allowed to own the stock and Willard's being an improper witness. There was no reason to lie about these things, since Sarah could easily check them out. In fact, Maggie had offered to show her the statutes and cases right there. She believed that Maggie could prove that Stillman didn't know he signed the DuPres will. She'd said she had witnesses, and anyway Stillman's letter to Ogden gave credit to that point. And she believed that Stillman's mind was sharp right up to the end. Again, the letter supported that, and Maggie probably *did* have witnesses from Barnett Brothers who would so testify.

Sarah was racking her brain trying to decide if she had a way out of this mess. She finally spoke. "You said you wanted me to let you privately interview the clinic staff and inspect the records. If, as you say, the case is all over, then why go through all the trouble?"

"Because we want to prove to the world that the DuPreses are crooks. And once we prove that — and we *will* prove it, Sarah — we're

438

going to the prosecutors. With what we'll find, Willard and Darlene DuPres will go to jail."

"And you seriously think I should cooperate with you? When it means that my clients could do time?"

"Yes, because they'll go even if you don't cooperate. It will just take us a little longer. But by then Sarah Jenkins will be so wrapped up with them that you'll all be in the shit house together. There goes your reputation, perhaps your license, and certainly all the time you've wasted on this lost cause. And you know what the DuPreses will do the minute that egg shows up on their faces, don't you? They'll point their fingers at you and say, 'She did it, she masterminded the whole thing.' What prosecutor wouldn't gladly give them immunity to get them to testify against you? Hell, Sarah, you're big game. Hotshot trial lawyer, yourself a former prosecutor. That's the stuff headlines are made of, and that's the stuff that'll drive the D.A.'s office to go after you."

"How could I have masterminded it? I never *heard* of the DuPreses until Mrs. DuPres came into my office after Stillman died. Eric Stone drafted the will, not me."

"Eric Stone's a scumbag. We asked around. Every lawyer in town who knows him says he's a jerk who gets fly-by-night clients by promising to cut corners, cheat on taxes, and bypass regulations. Just the kind of shyster a quack clinic would hire to write a phony will. If you want to climb in the sack with *him*, that's up to you. But I'll bet a month's salary that the phony stock deal didn't take place until after *you* got in on the case. I'm not saying you engineered it. Maybe the DuPreses and Stone cooked that up all by themselves, but who'll believe you had nothing to do with it? Do you think Stone will back you up? Or your sleazy clients?"

Sarah stared at her empty wineglass for a full minute, moving it slowly in random patterns to spread its condensation across the formica tabletop. Finally she grabbed her purse, rose, and looked down at Maggie. "You know, you're a snotty, arrogant, punk lawyer from a big silk-stocking firm, the kind I love to kick around the courtroom."

Maggie blanched. The whole plan had fallen apart, just like that. *She saw right through me and called my bluff. Now she's walking out.* "Wait," she said, "Don't leave!"

"Who's leaving? I'm going to the john. I'll be back in a minute and then maybe we'll deal."

Maggie exhaled more air than she thought her lungs could hold. *Hot damn! It's working!*

She wondered if she dared run to the phone while Sarah was away. Phil Ogden and Lee Schlessinger were nervously awaiting the outcome of this meeting, and she was bursting to tell them how well it was going. *No,* she told herself, *be cool.* She had the fish on the line, but not in the boat.

When Sarah returned, she took her seat and spoke with resignation. "Listen, Maggie, no matter what I might think about the DuPreses, they're still my clients and I can't sell them out. If I play it your way, I could be sending them to Stateville on a one-way ticket. And you know that, so I figure you have a fallback offer. What is it?"

Maggie put her elbows on the table and spoke slowly. "We want you to withdraw the DuPres will. Tear the goddamn thing up, flush the pieces down the toilet, and we'll all forget about it. It's better than your clients deserve."

"I don't suppose there's anything in this for me — besides your not dragging my name through the mud."

"Sure there is. You'll have a whole synagogue full of Jews praying for you next Friday night."

35

"For Chrissakes, can't you see what this could mean for you?"

"Yeah, I can see. I can see thousands of hours of work, followed by public disgrace and ending with no money. Thanks, but no thanks."

Al Fiori had expected some resistance, but he hadn't expected such unanimous rejection. Even Paul Kiddle, one of his last choices, was now turning him down. And if the word got out that others were saying no — *damn!*

It had all started a few days earlier when Fiori and Carl Sandquist were having their daily breakfast at the Courthouse Square Café. "Here it is, partner," Fiori said as he pulled several sheets of paper from his attaché case and set them next to his plate. "We can go over the list while we eat."

Sandquist's fork, piercing a sausage link, was suspended halfway between his plate and his mouth. "My God, are there really that many accountants around here? I can't believe that many people want to do such shit work."

442

He made a sound of disgust to describe how he felt about tax and accounting work.

"Of course there are that many accountants around here. D'ya think I copied the yellow pages from somewhere else, for Chrissakes?"

Carl Sandquist ignored the question, concentrating instead on whether to use his fork as a spear or a shovel.

"The fact is," Fiori continued, "I only copied the pages of CPAs. I don't want one who isn't certified. Now this is gonna take some time, so let's get started and see who on the list we know."

"Okay," Sandquist mumbled as he slurped his coffee before swallowing one more mouthful of egg, toast, and sausage. "Gimme a couple of those pages; I can look at 'em while I eat."

Within twenty minutes they had settled on three certified public accountants, each of whom "looked right" and was known to at least one of the partners. Fiori would try to enlist one of these as his expert witness to testify that, after a careful audit, it was his professional opinion that Ben Stillman had stolen his millions from the customers of Barnett Brothers.

Surely, Fiori figured, one of these would accept the assignment. The publicity alone would be attractive, to say nothing of the fee.

While nonexperts are not allowed to charge for their testimony, except for a nominal statutory amount, experts are permitted to charge handsomely for their time in studying the case, doing whatever research is necessary to formulate an opinion, giving depositions, and testifying in court. Many will also spend time consulting with the lawyer to plan the overall case, including the cross-examination of the other lawyer's expert witnesses. The only restriction on the expert's fee is that it can't be contingent — it can't ride on the outcome of the case.

But it wasn't working out that way. The first three CPAs had turned Fiori down. So had the next five. And several after that. He had never heard more horseshit excuses. This one did work for a few Barnett Brother partners and didn't want to go against them. That one had some Jewish clients and didn't want to go against *them.*

Then there was the other reason — money. Fiori sensed that this was the *real* reason. It wasn't that the experts he'd solicited had wanted too much money; it was just that they'd wanted an *assurance* that they'd be paid. And that's where Al Fiori had lost them; he couldn't provide that assurance. He couldn't guarantee that he'd win the case, or even that he'd get a good settlement, and he certainly couldn't afford to finance the audit out of his own pocket.

His dilemma was a common and frustrating one in these situations. A lawyer can take a case on a contingent fee basis even when it isn't a sure winner. The risk of losing is offset by the premium on winning. He gambles on the result. But when he needs an expert witness, it's catch-22: he can't win without the expert, he can't afford the expert except by offering a contingent fee, and he's not allowed to offer the expert a contingent fee. This rule is based on the fiction that an expert witness is one who gives impartial testimony to aid in the pursuit of justice and who shouldn't be tempted to shade his or her testimony to produce a result that could be financially rewarding.

The only problem with that logic is that it really isn't very logical. The plaintiff and defendant are permitted to testify, and *they* certainly have a financial interest in the outcome of the case. Are they therefore presumed to be liars? And what about the lawyers with contingent fees? Is it presumed they will produce phony evidence or otherwise break the rules just because their fees depend on victory? Legal scholars have debated this point for centuries, but those debates did nothing to solve Al Fiori's problem.

"Look, Paul," he was pleading now. "I know it looks like an iffy thing, but it really isn't. Will you at least hear me out?"

The accountant leaned back into a listening posture, a sign that he'd give the lawyer a few more minutes to make his case.

"It'll work this way," Fiori continued quickly. "You keep track of all your time, and I mean *all* of it. I expect it'll take plenty. When we start to show some progress — you know, a few irregularities in what Stillman was doing — we'll petition the judge to get you paid from the estate funds. He already said he'd leave the door open for that."

"But suppose I can't find any irregularities? Then what?"

"Shit, Paul, that ain't gonna happen, and we both know it. No way are you gonna review all the things Stillman was doing for forty years and not find *something* wrong. There's not an accountant in the world who'd agree with everything that another one did, and this guy Stillman wasn't even a CPA. I checked with the state. He was a fuckin' *bookkeeper* and an old one at that. Even if you can't find mistakes in his entries, you're sure to find his procedures — his checks and balances — were screwed up. You'll find *something* to arouse suspicion. And that's all we need to get you paid. Whaddya say?"

Well, Paul Kiddle was thinking, *Fiori was right about one thing. CPAs had the best twenty-twenty hindsight in the world. Rectal vision at its finest.* Kiddle knew that a methodical, microscopic review of what another accountant, even a good one, did in the rush of day-to-day duties could easily produce a thousand questions. Why wasn't that fact verified? Where did that valuation come from? Why was interest calculated that way? Accountancy wasn't the exact science people thought it was. There was plenty of room for discretion, judgment, and downright speculation, and all these things were fodder for the Monday morning quarterback.

"Maybe I could, and then again maybe I couldn't. And maybe the judge would pay me out of the estate, and then again maybe he wouldn't. What I'm trying to say, Al, is how the hell can I be sure? The best thing that could happen is that I get paid for my time, and I don't need your goddamn estate for that; I already got plenty of work in the office that'll pay my time. So why take the risk that the judge'll toss me out on my ass — unless *you* want to guarantee my fees."

"Very funny," Fiori said without smiling. "I would if I could, but we're talking hun--

dreds of thousands of dollars here. *Several* hundreds of thousands of dollars."

As much as the accountant wanted to say no, his reaction to that last comment betrayed him. Fiori noticed the change of expression and knew he still had a chance to land Paul Kiddle as his expert. It all depended on how he fired his next two shots.

"Look, Paul, there're a couple of things I didn't mention. For one, the odds are that this whole thing will settle out, and I *can* promise you that I wouldn't even consider a settlement that didn't include your fees. I can put that in writing."

"What's the other thing you didn't mention?"

So much for that, thought Fiori, knowing he had to resort to his last desperate salvo. "Here's the thing, Paul. No one's gonna be lookin' over your shoulder when you fill out your time sheets."

"Jesus, Al, are you saying that I should deliberately — "

"Oh, hell, no!" Fiori interjected, shoving his arms forward as if he were trying to stop a freight train. "Relax! Let me explain. I'm not saying you should pad your hours. No way. I'm only saying that this is a hell of a big case and there's a lot of money involved. It would be a big responsibility for you, and everyone would know it. You'd be expected to put a lot of time into it — more than you would on a routine audit."

"So what exactly is your point?"

"My point is that every single minute you spend on this case should be compensated. And I mean every single minute you spend even *thinking* about the case. I don't care if it's while you're on the can or while you're humpin' your receptionist out there. We all know how easy it is to forget to charge for a quick phone call. Well, don't forget in this case, and don't forget to charge for the time it took to decide to make the call and for the time you reflected on it afterward. And those little chats with your partners about the case? Well, dammit, they're not chats. They're *conferences,* and you should be paid for every one of 'em."

The message Fiori was delivering, and Kiddle was receiving, was: overcharge the hell out of the case. I'll back you up.

The end result would be that Kiddle would have a contingent fee in disguise. If they lost, he'd get nothing; if they won or managed a good settlement, he'd be paid an amount exceeding his normal fee. This excess was the premium for taking the risk. Presto! They would have sidestepped the rule forbidding a contingent fee.

"All right, Al, I'll talk to my partners and we'll give it a little thought." He then added the standard line, which Fiori was expecting. "But if we *do* decide to help you out, we'll play it perfectly straight with the time. I hope you understand that."

"I do understand, Paul."

What I understand, Al Fiori thought as he rose to leave, *is that you're as big a whore as the rest of us.*

36

As soon as her meeting with Sarah Jenkins was over, Maggie hurried back to Schlessinger, Harris & Wade, where Lee and Phil were waiting. When that session broke up half an hour later and she and Phil left the building, she was still bubbling with excitement. Phil, too, was delighted with the way Maggie had handled her meeting; it was good for his case, but he was also happy for her.

"You did really well this afternoon," Phil said as they walked to Maggie's car.

"You're damn right I did. I handled her a hell of a lot better than all you big hairy-chested men did the other day." She put her hand on his arm. "I didn't mean — "

"Sure you did. And I had it coming. But she took me by surprise that first day. C'mon, Maggie, let's have a beer and you can tell me about it again. And I don't want you to leave out a single word."

Maggie didn't need any encouragement to retell what she considered her first major conquest. It seemed only natural that they should go to the bar at the same motel where their plan had been hatched that morning.

"I said I wouldn't come here with you without a chaperon," she reminded him as they sat at the bar.

"You said you wouldn't come here on our *first* date without a chaperon. But this is our second date."

"It's not a date. I'm only giving a report on my meeting with Sarah." They ordered two beers. "Anyway," she said, smiling coyly, "it doesn't seem as seedy at night as it does in the morning."

"Motels never do."

"You . . . mean, you mean . . . to say," Phil was laughing so hard he could hardly speak. "She was . . . was only getting up to . . . to take a pee?"

"Really! And I thought she was . . . was walking out — thought she saw right . . . through me." Maggie, who was laughing almost as hard, was slapping Phil's shoulder with one hand and holding her chest with the other. "But wait till you . . . hear this. She said, 'What's . . . what's in this for me?' and I said — oh, you're . . . you're gonna love this, Phil — I said, 'You'll have a whole . . . a whole synagogue full of Jews' — I can't stand it — 'a whole synagogue

452

full of Jews praying for you Friday night.'
Could you scream?"

More beers. More storytelling. More laughs. Dinner became the peanuts and pretzels from the bowls on the bar.

Soon their conversation drifted away from the case and became punctuated with not-too-subtle questions and comments about their personal lives — more specifically, their personal availability.

"Shouldn't you call your wife, Phil, and let her know where you are?"

"No wife. Not anymore."

"Oh, I'm sorry, I didn't — "

"Don't be. I'm not." He took another sip of his beer. "And I'm sure she's not, either." Then, after a few awkward moments of silence: "What about you? Don't *you* have to make a call?"

"Uh-uh," she answered faster than she'd intended. "Not really. There's this guy I see now and then, but it's not going anywhere. We're both in the firm and they frown on intra-office romances. Anyway, it's no big deal. We do little more than keep each other company until . . ." She let the point hang in midair.

"Well, you won't be having any trouble," he volunteered, trying a little flattery. "Not with your looks — and brains."

"Oh, c'mon, Phil. I've been looking at *you* since this case started, trying to think of ways to catch your attention and convince you I'm more than a dizzy blond law clerk."

"I'm convinced, I'm convinced."

Then more stories and more laughs and more beers. And closer bar stools. And more touching.

Then it finally came time to go.

While Phil was settling the tab, Maggie, trying to stand up, slid off the bar stool and ended up on the floor — and on her behind.

"Oh, Christ, are you okay? Give me your hand."

"I'm . . . fine," she said, starting to laugh all over again. "Just get me . . . out . . . out of here. Every . . . everybody's staring."

As they reached the parking lot, Phil remembered they had driven to the motel in Maggie's car. "Look," he said, "I don't think you should be driving. I'll drive you home in your car and then pick you up in the morning. All right?"

She leaned against him with her head on his shoulder. "It mosht shertainly ish *not* all right," she said, trying to imitate a burlesque drunk.

"But — "

"If I can't drive, Shtan, then you can't

either. You had ash much to drink ash I did."

"Then I'll call a — "

"Oh, shit, Ogden," she said with perfect enunciation, "we are going back into that motel — that seedy motel — where we are going to get a room in which we — you and I — are going to spend the night." She stood back and looked up into his eyes. "Or are you too sober to take the plunge?"

"No, thash okay," he said, taking her arm and reversing direction toward the registration office. "Whatever you shay."

37

"Remember, Sarah, it's just as dangerous to overestimate your opponent as it is to underestimate him." It was one of the earliest lessons Sarah Jenkins had learned from "Uncle Sid," her first supervisor in the prosecutor's office over twenty years ago, and it was one she'd never forgotten. How many times had she seen a lawyer fail to capitalize on an adversary's mistake because he hadn't anticipated that such a mistake was possible? And how many lawyers believed what their opponents told them because they assumed that the other guys knew what they were talking about, or, worse yet, that they were truthful? "Be ready for their mistakes," Sid had told her, "and don't *ever* believe what they tell you. Above all, *beware of any lawyer who says he's doing you a favor.*" It was that last lesson Sarah had been thinking about since her meeting with Maggie Flynn.

So while Maggie was celebrating with Phil her conquest of Sarah, Sarah was holed up in her law library. Except for a few procedural points she'd checked out earlier, this was her first real research since she'd taken on the Stillman case.

Her first objective was to find out if Maggie was right about Darlene DuPres's not being allowed to hold stock in the clinic. It wouldn't take long to check — just pull out the Professional Corporation Act and read what it says about shareholder eligibility. She quickly confirmed that the young lawyer was absolutely correct. *Goddamn that Eric Stone. Calls himself a corporate lawyer. Asshole!*

If Darlene couldn't own the stock, then the transfer was void and Willard was still the sole shareholder. Would that make him an improper witness? It took Sarah longer to research that point, but within an hour she stumbled onto a few cases that nailed the coffin shut. Maggie Flynn was right: Willard DuPres — as the clinic's president, sole shareholder, and sole director blew it when he witnessed the will. His was *not* a remote interest. The law was clear on that.

C'est la vie, she sighed, tossing her pencil on the library table amid all the open books. Then, as she started to put the law books back on the shelf, she decided to make copies of the exact wording of the relevant cases and statutes. Even though it was already past midnight, it wouldn't take that much longer, and she'd want to show the precise words to Darlene when she broke the bad news in the morning.

It was then that it hit her. As she was re-reading the words of the Probate Act, the same words that Maggie had read to the men at Beth Zion, she finally realized the *consequence* of Willard's witnessing the will. She sat there without moving for several minutes, pondering what she had just learned, then playing it out in her mind.

"That little bitch!" she said aloud as she reached for the phone. "No wonder she wants me to withdraw the goddamn thing! And she said she was doing *me* a favor!" Sarah smiled triumphantly. *Thanks, Uncle Sid.*

"Must be important," said Darlene DuPres as she set her purse on Sarah Jenkins's desk.

"It is."

"Good or bad?"

"Hmm. Good question."

"Okay, Sarah, what the hell's going on? You call me in the middle of the night and tell me to be here by seven-thirty in the morning, and now you want to play twenty questions. What's up?"

"I'm sorry, Darlene, but this whole thing is so screwed up that it's actually fascinating. And after I explain it I'm not sure if you'll think it's good or bad."

"Try me."

It took only a few minutes for Sarah to explain about the corporate stock, the law dealing with interested witnesses to wills, and the effect of having such a witness.

Since Darlene had never really believed deep down in her heart that she could be lucky enough to get Ben Stillman's eight million dollars, she wasn't completely devastated by the news that she wouldn't. Also, the severity of the blow was softened — surprisingly so — by the knowledge that she was by no means out of the picture yet. Indeed, her new role as the spoiler brought a slight smile to her lips, evidence that her malevolence was as strong as her greed.

"You mean that if Willard *did* screw up when he witnessed the will, it's still legal? We don't get the money, but neither does the synagogue? And I'm the executor?"

"And I'm the executor's lawyer."

"But what does it all mean, exactly?"

"In a nutshell, the executor's job is to take control of all the decedent's assets, pay all his debts, and then turn everything over to whoever inherits. In the meantime, you'd be in charge of investing the money, and for that you'd be paid a fee and all your expenses."

Eight million dollars to manage and invest! Darlene had no trouble imagining herself as the darling of the local investment community, the center of attention. Bankers would fawn over her just for the privilege of having her account. "And how long would I be able to play in the sandbox?"

Sarah laughed. "Well, ordinarily it would be for a year or two, but in this case we could be talking about *several* years. Al Fiori will have to litigate his class action, and that alone could take five or six years, maybe longer. He can't even start until his audits are done, and they're going to cover forty years. And after a trial there could be a couple of years of appeals. Barnett Brothers may be doing the same thing." Sarah was relishing this, since she'd be the lawyer paid to fight these cases. It was better than an annuity. Hell, she'd earn more than Darlene.

"And even if we didn't have *those* lawsuits, think of all the fights we'll have just to decide who gets whatever is left."

"But wouldn't that be Stillman's relatives? I mean, since the synagogue's out of — "

"Sure," Sarah interrupted, "but who in the hell *are* they? Tom Andrews is running around Europe trying to dig 'em up now. And we'll challenge every damn one who shows up."

"Why? What do we care who gets the money?"

"We don't. But the tougher we make it for everyone, the longer you'll be playing in your sandbox." Sarah winked at Darlene. "And that's the greenest sand you'll ever see."

Sarah couldn't have been happier about the way Darlene was reacting to this. She'd feared she might have trouble persuading her client to accept her substitute role as executor instead of beneficiary, but Darlene seemed comfortable, even relieved, at the prospect. This made Sarah's next job easier.

"All right, Darlene," she began, "we still have one more hurdle to jump, and it could be a big one."

"What's that?"

"Actually, it's two hurdles — Willard and Alice Doakes. Our Jewish friends at Beth Zion were hoping they could get us to withdraw our will, which would have given them clear sailing. Since we won't, they'll level all their guns at Willard and Alice."

"I'm not sure I — "

"If they can throw out the will — the whole will — they'll get the money. So they'll try to show that Stillman was either goofy or was somehow tricked into signing the will."

"You don't think we would have done anything dishonest, do you?"

461

Sarah bit her tongue on that one. "Look, Darlene, I'm not saying you did anything wrong, but I want you to tell me right now if you did."

"But I didn't."

"Did Ben Stillman know he was signing that will?"

"Yes. That is, that's what Willard and Alice said. I wasn't standing there at the time."

"And that's what Willard told me when I interviewed him. He also told me they saw Stillman sign the will and Stillman saw them witness it. Sound right?"

"If they say so," Darlene replied.

"Well, I haven't interviewed Alice yet, but I assume she'll tell me the same thing Willard did."

"I don't know why not."

"What about drugs or medications, Darlene? Had any been given to Stillman near enough to the time he signed that it'd have an effect on his mind? *Any* effect?"

"You asked me that the first time we met. The answer is still no."

"Fair enough. But we'll go over all of this a thousand times before we go to court."

"I'm sure you'll do whatever's necessary, Sarah. The sand's green for you, too." Darlene returned the wink.

PART VII
THE FIFTH WEEK

38

Immediately after their first meeting, Al Fiori secured a court order authorizing his expert witness, Paul Kiddle, to examine the records necessary to formulate the professional opinion Fiori was looking for: that Benjamin Stillman was a crook. These included Stillman's accounts at banks and investment houses and various records at Barnett Brothers. (The court order specified that information relating to earnings and holdings of the firm, its partners, and its customers would, at least for the time being, be kept confidential.) Kiddle began the task promptly and pursued it diligently, partly because Fiori was prodding him daily but mainly because he wanted to get a jump on it before the end of the year, when his work load, like that of any accountant, would become insufferable.

Now, nearly three weeks later, he was meeting the two partners of Fiori & Sandquist for lunch at a small Chinese restaurant near his office on the west edge of the Loop. The restaurant was curiously named Won

Tu. What it lacked in fine food it more than made up for, to the distress of Mr. Won, in privacy. The waitress had just taken their orders and left a pot of tea.

"Ever notice that they never write down your orders in these places?" Al Fiori asked of no one in particular.

Kiddle nodded, but his attention was riveted on Carl Sandquist, who by now had already poured his tea (spilling part), emptied a packet of sugar into it (spilling part), tested its heat with his pinkie (licking it dry), and begun his rapid slurping.

Fiori sighed and shook his head. He couldn't wait until he could afford to go it alone, mostly because of his eagerness to deliver the "Dear Carl" speech he constantly rewrote in his head. In a recent version, he would break the news at one of their daily breakfast meetings, punctuating it with a grapefruit in Carl's face à la Jimmy Cagney. He abandoned the idea after deciding that Carl would probably like that.

"Well, Paul," he said, breaking the ice, "what've you got for us?"

"Not much. At least not much that you'll like. And I'm not liking it much, either," he added, with a touch of irritation in his voice.

"I gathered as much, judging from the way you sounded on the phone. But, hell, they've got to have tons of records at Barnett Brothers, and you've hardly had a chance to do more than scratch the surface. I'm sure you'll find something."

"I haven't even started to look at the books over there, Al, and I don't think I'll have to."

Al Fiori stared at his expert witness, not sure if he'd heard him correctly. "Whaddya mean, you don't think you'll have to?"

"Because of what I found — or didn't find — at the banks and other brokerage firms." He sipped his tea. "Let me explain."

The two lawyers eyed him closely. They knew they wouldn't be happy with the explanation they were about to hear, and they wanted to be ready to pick it apart.

"You'll recall that Stillman did his investing at about a dozen firms but didn't do any with Barnett Brothers. I decided to start at those other places and also at his banks. Their names were on that court authorization you gave me."

"Yeah, right," said Fiori, "the judge told Phil Ogden to give us the names."

"I still don't see why you'd want to start with them instead of Barnett's," Carl Sandquist commented while wiping tea from his chin with his bare hand. "If you're looking for theft, you won't find it where he invested or banked. Shouldn't you be looking where he worked and handled other people's money?"

"Not necessarily," the accountant said. "By first checking his bank accounts I could see if and when he made any unusual deposits. That would furnish a clue as to *when* he may have stolen money, and that could narrow my search when I got into Barnett's books. Likewise for his investment accounts. If I could pinpoint a sudden surge in his holdings — a surge that couldn't be explained by an increase in the market — it might suggest the time of a theft. Look at it another way; if the value of his holdings was relatively stable for, say, five years, discounting market growth, and there were no unexplained bank deposits during that time, I wouldn't have to waste my time picking through Barnett's records for those five years."

The conversation stopped while the waitress served their orders. Fiori and Kiddle resumed the moment she left, while Sandquist, already chomping on an egg roll, clumsily attacked his chow mein with plastic chopsticks.

"As I was saying," Kiddle continued, "I decided to start with the banks and the other investment houses. The bank where he had his checking account was the easiest, so that was my first stop. I checked the monthly statements for the last seven years. That's all that were available without going to the dead storage vaults. The guy's routine was just that — routine. He made three deposits every month, his two paychecks and social security, and no others. And his pattern of writing checks against those deposits didn't indicate anything suspicious. Utility bills, rent, groceries, that kind of thing."

"He had only one checking account?" asked Fiori.

"As far as we know. My secretary went to most of the other banks in town with a copy of the court order. A few had CDs in his name, but none had a checking account. We can check further but I doubt that it'll be necessary. That's because of what I'm finding at the investment houses."

"Which is what?" Carl Sandquist mumbled through a mouthful of food.

"Bear in mind," the accountant replied, "that I haven't had time to make a complete audit, but I did review Stillman's records at two places so far. I chose them at random. Peabody's was Stillman's broker for roughly a million dollars' worth of the securities he owned when he died. Through their records I learned when he bought them and what he paid. In most instances he sold something in order to make the purchases, and I found out what he paid for those earlier securities and when he acquired *them*. Sometimes he'd sell something and just have Peabody's hold the cash until he decided on another investment, and in a few instances he used the cash to buy a CD. I figured that out by comparing the dates and amounts of the withdrawals with the list of CDs I got earlier from the banks."

Al Fiori was nodding his head, closely following the explanation.

"Anyway," Kiddle continued, "by working backward like that at Peabody's, I could track the value of the portfolio and tell you what it was worth at any given time. And Stillman invested with Peabody's for over twenty years. By the way, if he'd let his brokers hold his securities, as most investors do, my job would've been a lot easier. Then I'd only have to check the broker's copy of his monthly statement showing the current value of the stocks and bonds in his account. But even so it wasn't too complicated because Stillman didn't make all that many trades. He held on to things a long time."

"So what's the bottom line?" Fiori asked impatiently.

"Well, based only on what I found out so far from Peabody's and Fletcher-Day, I'd say that Stillman was not really a hot investor, and he wasn't a thief — at least not over the years I reviewed."

Carl Sandquist was so surprised that he stopped eating long enough to refute Kiddle's statement. "Impossible! He had to be one or the other. Shit, he had eight million bucks. If he wasn't stealing it, then he was sure as hell slick enough to make a killing in the market. Right?"

The accountant was ready for the question, which he answered with one of his own. "What if a man starts with a million dollars and puts it all in the stock market? Over the next ten years the Dow Jones doubles and his stocks are worth somewhere around two million. Would you say he was a shrewd investor? Hell, he could've done better picking a mutual fund with his eyes closed."

"Are you saying that Stillman's net worth only kept pace with the market?" The question was Fiori's.

"Probably a little worse, at least from what I've seen so far. And I've seen enough to believe that I won't find anything that'll change my mind."

"Then you're saying that Stillman had this money all along?"

"Right, which means he wasn't stealing as he went."

"Christ! This doesn't make any sense at all," Fiori said as he rubbed the back of his neck. "If he didn't steal it, where the hell did he get it?"

471

"Like I said, Al, I'm not done yet. I still have eight or ten other firms to review, and I'm not even done with these two. Maybe we'll find that he made one big heist twenty-five years ago, not a series of small ones, and it just grew with the market to be eight million. Wouldn't that be just as good for us — I mean you?"

"Yeah. I suppose. At least it would be easier to prove if he did it that way. Can you imagine what we'd have to go through to prove he took three dollars a day for forty years?"

"Well, I'll tell you this much," Paul Kiddle said. "If Ben Stillman did any stealing it was a hell of a long time ago. And if that's the case, I don't think we'll ever be able to prove it. Records won't be available and neither will witnesses."

As the three of them left the restaurant, Fiori urged Paul Kiddle to dig a little deeper, try a little harder. "Don't start believing that the old guy was honest, Paul, or you'll get careless. Assume that he was a fuckin' crook and you're out to get him."

Kiddle stopped in his tracks. "If you don't like the way I'm doing this," he said, his voice threatening, "then get yourself a new patsy. This whole thing has shakedown written all over it, and it wouldn't bother me one bit to — "

"Hey, relax! I'm only trying to give you a little pep talk. Hell, you're my man, Paul. That's why I picked you."

"Save the bullshit, counselor. You talked to plenty of other CPAs before you got to me, and every one of 'em turned you down. It's all over town. Now I've got to decide if I even want to continue."

As he turned to walk away, he added: "By the way, Carl, you may want to change your tie before seeing any clients this afternoon. Either that or have Won Tu autograph it."

39

As soon as Tom Andrews cleared customs at O'Hare Airport, he hurried through to the public waiting area of the international terminal. It took no time at all to spot Philip Ogden waving his arms and shouting Tom's name. After enthusiastic handshakes and shoulder slaps, they each grabbed one of Tom's bags and headed for the parking garage.

Once in the car, Phil pursued the subject that Tom had only hinted at when he telephoned from Europe two days earlier. "Okay, out with it. What's the big news?"

"Big news? Did I say anything about big news?"

"C'mon, you bastard. You were having a goddamn orgasm on the phone."

"You got great ears, Ogden. Fact is, I *did* have a couple of those over there."

By the time Phil paid the parking fee, Tom had decided he'd stretched things out long enough. He knew it was time to get serious. "Phil," he said in a tone that made it clear the kidding was over, "I'll tell you everything I found over there. I promise.

But first tell me if there've been any developments on this end."

"Fair enough," Phil said as he turned onto the Kennedy Expressway. "I'll give you a quick recap. Fiori hired a CPA to try to find out if Ben Stillman was stealing. Name's Paul Kiddle, and he must be one of Fiori's last choices. I hear half the accountants in town had already turned him down. Anyway, Kiddle's been on the job about three weeks, and from what I hear he's already getting disenchanted."

"Is Fiori paying him out of his own pocket?" Tom asked.

"I doubt it. He probably took the case on the come, just like Fiori. He'll have some gravy built into the fee if they get anything; otherwise he takes it on the chin."

"And Barnett Brothers? Anything from them?"

"Not a sound. My guess is they're waiting to see if Kiddle turns up anything. If he does, then they'll pounce. If not, they play the roles of gentlemen and stay on good terms with all the Jews in town."

"That leaves your good friend Sarah Jenkins. She still taking shots at you?"

"You're gonna love this, Tom. She was bullshitting us all the way. It turns out that all the stock in the DuPres Clinic is owned by Dr. DuPres — not his wife. He's also the president and sole director. Since he's the one who attested the will, the clinic's fucked. There's been no ruling yet, but it looks like they blew the whole inheritance."

"Jesus Christ! That *is* news! That puts you in the driver's seat, doesn't it? If their will's out, yours is in." Tom shifted in his seat to face his friend, sensing something was wrong. "But you don't act very happy about it. What am I missing?"

"Their will isn't out, and mine isn't in."

"But you just said — "

"What I said was that the clinic is screwed. They lost the inheritance." Phil went on to explain how Maggie had figured everything out. "She and Schlessinger invite me to breakfast to break the news, and I react like you did just now. I start to cheer, and then I notice that they look pretty bleak. So I say, 'What'd I miss?' and then they give me the bad news. Except in your case it isn't bad news; it's good news."

"What bad news and good news, for Chrissake? You're talking in circles."

"Even though the clinic can't inherit, the *rest* of the DuPres will is valid. It still revokes prior wills, including the one I drew up. And it still names Darlene DuPres as executor."

"So why should that be good news to me?

I can see why it hurts Beth Zion, but — "
Then he saw it all at once, as if someone had switched on a light. *"Oh, shit!"*

"That's right, pal. You and your Schtillermanns walk away with first prize, and it's worth a cool eight million." Phil turned to look at Tom. "But we can still knock you out of the box if we can show that Stillman was tricked or coerced into signing that will or that someone forged his signature. And I swear to God, Tom, we're going to do it! When we're done, Sarah Jenkins can take her will and shove it right up her ass!"

"Who's 'we'?"

"Schlessinger, Maggie, and me."

They rode in silence for a few minutes. Finally, Tom spoke: "Three against one, huh?"

"Not quite. You'll have Jenkins on your side. She'll fight to protect that second will as long as she thinks her client will be the executor and she'll be the attorney."

"My God, talk about strange bedfellows."

After another minute or two, Tom reached over and put a hand on Phil's shoulder. "You and I still gonna be pals?"

Phil smiled. In the short time they'd known each other, Phil had developed an affection for Tom, that rare kind of affection that binds two men who have fought side by side in the same trench or in the same backfield. He suspected it was mutual. Tom's irascibility, so obvious that first day, had been held in check. Was it some defense mechanism triggered only when he met someone for the first time? Or when he felt he was being judged? No matter. He was a good guy, the best, and Phil wanted this friendship to survive the case.

"You bet we're gonna be friends. I don't want to sound corny, Tom, but you're the second best thing that's happened to me since this whole thing started."

"What's this 'second best' shit?"

"Well, while you were chasing around Germany, I was back here with the vultures. It was only natural — "

"Wait! Let me guess. Maggie Flynn?"

"Right. I'll tell you all about it later."

"Shit, everybody has a chick but me. Even clods like you can find someone, and a cool stud like me — "

"Aw, cram it, Andrews. I'll listen to your hard-luck stories some other time. But right now I want to hear about Germany."

"Okay, counselor, sit back and drive while I talk. And keep both hands on the wheel."

After Phil had heard Tom's story, he began to make some sense out of what his secretary had told him a few days after Benjamin

Stillman's death.

"Carol," he had asked her, "you mentioned having a conversation with Mr. Stillman out in the waiting room while you were typing his will. Do you recall what you talked about?"

"Well, he was sitting there only a few feet away," she'd replied. "He must've realized I was typing his will, and it was like he thought he should explain why he was leaving everything to the synagogue. I'll never forget his words; he had an accent I can't place, but he spoke very clearly. He said: 'What else could I do?' He kept saying it over and over again. *'What else could I do?'* It was so sad."

"Sad? Why was that so sad?"

"He was crying."

40

"Ms. Jenkins. Ms. Flynn. Gentlemen. To what do I owe the pleasure?"

"We're here at my request, Your Honor," Sarah Jenkins announced as she rose and walked over to Judge Verne Lloyd's desk. She handed him a single typed sheet, the top of which bore the official caption of the case. "I hand you a formal renunciation of inheritance, duly executed by the DuPres Oncology Clinic, properly notarized and attested." She then furnished each of the other lawyers in the room with a copy.

As soon as Sarah revealed her intention to have the clinic voluntarily renounce its inheritance, Philip Ogden, Maggie Flynn, and Leon Schlessinger exchanged glances. Their original plan, which Maggie had tried to execute at the East Bank Club, was to persuade Sarah to withdraw the will — the *entire* will. But she'd foxed them! She must have figured things out since that night. What Maggie and Schlessinger hadn't realized at first was that their plan was in jeopardy from the beginning: even if Sarah withdrew the DuPres will, Tom Andrews could petition to have it enforced.

While the renunciation was being read and its ramifications considered, Sarah mentally reviewed the events that had prompted the filing of what amounted to an eight-million-dollar concession. Concessions were not part of her nature, but neither was shame, disgrace, or economic suicide. She knew beyond doubt that the clinic would never be allowed the inheritance after Willard DuPres — *that idiot* — attested Stillman's will. It would be futile to fight it. And what if subsequent facts revealed that Darlene DuPres and Eric Stone had engaged in a little hanky-panky to get Stillman to sign that will, as they had probably done with that inane stock transfer? Who needed that?

Sarah reasoned that if she voluntarily stepped forward to disclaim the inheritance, which the clinic would never get anyway, it would put her in a better light if and when the shit hit the fan. She knew, of course, that the best way to protect herself would be to walk away from the case entirely, say good-bye to the DuPreses, and let them find another lawyer to do their bidding. But that would also have meant saying good-bye to the fees that would come with representing Darlene as the executor of the estate.

No, she'd concluded a few days earlier, *I'll hang in there for the big score.* But she'd also keep the back door open and the motor running for a quick getaway if she needed it. Fortunately, it was easy to persuade Darlene and Willard to let her file the renunciation. Since they had already lost all chance of winning the inheritance, Darlene was happy to settle for the distinction of being executor — and the fees that came with it. As for Willard, he'd be happy to forget the whole damn thing.

"Ms. Jenkins?" Judge Lloyd finally broke the silence.

"Yes, Your Honor?"

"The renunciation is signed by Willard DuPres, M.D. — who, it says here, is the president, sole director, and sole shareholder of the clinic. Don't I recall your telling me that his wife owned and controlled the place?"

"Your recollection is correct, Judge, but my information at the time was not. My clients and I honestly believed that what I told you was true. However, we overlooked a legal technicality." She looked at Maggie Flynn. "Ms. Flynn was good enough to call it to my attention."

Verne Lloyd was nodding his head. "I presume, Ms. Jenkins, that the legal technicality to which you refer is the provision that only physicians can hold stock in a medical corporation? I believe that's in the Illinois Professional Corporation Act."

"Yes, Your Honor."

Every lawyer in the room then realized that Judge Lloyd knew, and evidently had known all along, that Darlene DuPres was a bogus shareholder of the clinic. Sarah Jenkins was seething. *That smug son of a bitch knew from the first day that I was chasing my tail, and he's been laughing at me all along.*

Verne Lloyd had another question for her. "Assuming, Ms. Jenkins, that your will is validly executed, would Ms. DuPres still intend to serve as executor? Or would she renounce that as well?"

"It's my understanding that she would serve, Your Honor."

"Are you satisfied that she *could* serve?"

"Yes, sir. My research isn't finished, but there doesn't seem to be any authority for denying her the right to be executor."

Again the judge nodded. Everyone wondered if he was a step ahead of them on this issue too. He then smiled politely at Sarah. "Thank you for having filed this so promptly after being apprised of the law by Ms. Flynn. It saves us all a good deal of time."

Oh, you rotten bastard! Sarah screamed to herself.

Judge Lloyd held out his arms. "Does anyone else have anything he or she would like to talk about before we break up?"

"I do, Your Honor." It was Tom Andrews.

"And what does our traveling guardian ad litem have for us?"

"I thought you and the others would like to know what I learned in Europe. I intend to file a written report, but since we're all here, perhaps I could cover the highlights." After Tom had told Phil about the trip, they'd agreed a full disclosure of his findings should be made as soon as possible.

Judge Lloyd leaned back in his chair. "Proceed, Mr. Andrews. I'm sure all of us would like to know if you found any Stillmans."

"Schtillermanns."

"I beg your pardon?"

"That's the family name, Judge. *Schtillermann.*"

"I see. Go ahead."

Without referring to notes, Tom Andrews spoke for nearly forty-five minutes. No one but Phil had known the search for heirs "somewhere in Europe" would take Tom into East Germany. His first step, he explained, had been to contact an international law firm in Washington for help in arranging a visa and the necessary travel permits and referring him to an attorney in Dresden who, as it turned out, was worth his considerable weight in gold.

"This lawyer — his name is Dr. Erich Kessler — is something else," Tom said. "Ate like a horse, worked like a dog. Don't know what I'd have done without him, especially since he spoke English fluently." Tom smiled as he reflected on the German lawyer who'd been so helpful to him. He told them how he and Kessler had culled through the public records in Pirna, the town of Stillman's birth, and Dresden, the nearest large city, where more complete records were maintained for the district. The idea was to make a list of all the Schtillermanns in the area.

"Schtillermann is not a common name over there," Tom was saying. "We located fewer than a dozen families with that name, three of them in Pirna. As luck would have it," here he paused for effect, "one of them turned out to be Ben Stillman's brother."

It was a jolt to everyone in the room. They had grown accustomed to the idea that Benjamin Stillman had no relatives, that he'd existed in a vacuum, somehow spontaneously appearing on this planet without ancestors and departing without descendants. Even if there was a living relative, they'd all assumed it would be a thirty-fourth cousin thrice removed who'd never heard of him. And now,

485

just like that, Tom Andrews had produced a *brother*.

"Excuse me for interrupting, Judge," Leon Schlessinger said, "but I wonder if I might ask Mr. Andrews a question."

"I don't see why not."

"Tom, were you able to verify that this individual was in fact a brother of Mr. Stillman's?"

"I'd say yes to that, although Dr. Kessler is trying to button it up a little tighter. For one thing, he produced a birth certificate that named his parents. They were the same names as on the birth certificate we found in Stillman's safe-deposit box. For another, he knew about Stillman's wife and son and even had their names right."

Stillman's *wife?* And *son?* He was a real person after all. He loved. He made babies. He probably even laughed and cried.

"If you didn't know he had a wife and son before you left," the judge asked, "how did *you* know their names?"

"There was a letter in Stillman's box. It wasn't dated but was obviously old. Phil Ogden and I had it translated — it was in German — and we learned it had been written by someone named Frieda. She mentioned in the letter that someone named Hans was with her when she wrote it. We didn't know more than that. But Herr Schtillermann — that is, Ben Stillman's brother — identified Frieda and Hans by name without my saying a word."

Tom then described how they'd located the brother, how reluctant he'd been at first to discuss Stillman with them, and how they'd finally won him over. "It took two or three days before Walter, Herr Schtillermann, opened up to us. He finally agreed to meet us at a small tavern. He was in his late seventies and quite frail. By the way, there had never been any other brothers or sisters, and Walter had no children. That would make him the only heir. Anyway, I don't know if it was the schnapps, but he finally told us the story of his older brother."

Andrews stopped for a moment, wrinkled his brow, and then shook his head. "It was kind of sad, really," he said. "On the one hand, he obviously had strong feelings for the brother he hadn't seen in all those years; once he started talking about him, there was no stopping him. But on the other hand — and this is what was so frustrating for him — he regarded his brother as a traitor."

"A traitor?" Verne Lloyd asked. "Because he left Germany before the war?"

"No, Judge. He was there when the war broke out. But he managed to leave in 1943.

And I learned he was in the German army, but not as a gun-toting soldier. Seems he was kind of a bookkeeper, as he had been in the prewar days."

"Well," Al Fiori volunteered, "we're all aware he knew his way around the books. Right, Max?" He looked at Maxwell Kane, grinning.

No one in the room acknowledged the tactless remark. When Benjamin Stillman was still the faceless, mysterious "decedent," he'd been fair game for each of the contestants. But now, as a man with a past, a family, he was deserving of more respect. Perhaps it was because Tom Andrews now, for the first time, was revealing the personal and private aspects of his just-ended life that a slur against his character seemed especially out of place.

"Please continue, Tom," Judge Lloyd said, looking at Fiori as one might look at a hair in one's soup.

"Apparently, Mr. Stillman's bookkeeping skills were in demand during the Nazi war effort. According to his brother, he was involved with shipments and inventories. In the early days of the war in Europe, he was assigned to the Ruhr Valley — where many of the factories were — to allocate munitions and other supplies to wherever they were needed. Later he was reassigned to other kinds of shipments and inventories."

"What other kinds?" inquired the judge.

"People."

"I beg your pardon?"

"People," repeated Tom Andrews. "I know that sounds flip, Your Honor, but I don't mean it to. It's just that we're getting into an area where the Germans don't like to sound too knowledgeable. So they talk around the subject, dropping clues, just enough so you know what they're saying without their saying it. Kessler was the same way, even though he probably wasn't even born then. Anyway, it was clear that what brother Walter was telling me was that Stillman kept track of the shipments and inventories of people going to the camps.

"I'm talking about the concentration camps. 'Relocation' camps, according to Walter Schtillerman and Dr. Kessler. They were very careful to call them that. But we all knew they were really extermination camps."

"So why did this brother think Mr. Stillman was a traitor?" Judge Lloyd asked, trying to move things along. "It seems to me he was up to his elbows in the Reich's dirty work."

"Because," Tom answered, "he committed a sin for which his family could never forgive him. A sin for which the surviving Schtillermanns still feel shame."

"Killing Jews?"

"No, sir. He *married* a Jew."

Silence. Finally Judge Lloyd spoke. "I suggest we take a ten-minute break."

When the meeting reconvened, Judge Lloyd directed his first comment to Tom Andrews. "Your report is most interesting, and I see where it might begin to explain Mr. Stillman's motive for his bequest to Beth Zion Synagogue. But we are concerned with the validity of wills and the source of Mr. Stillman's money. Do you have anything that will help us with those questions?"

"Yes, Your Honor. I believe this will be very clear by the time I finish."

"Then please proceed."

"Mr. Stillman married in 1930," Tom continued, still without referring to notes, "which would have made him twenty-four at the time. His bride was one Frieda Schoenhauss. I was able to locate a copy of the marriage certificate from the public records. I have a certified copy with me," he added, reaching into his briefcase and extracting a document that he held up for the others to see. "They had one child, a son. His name was Hans, and he was born in 1932." He held up another document. "I have a copy of the birth certificate.

"As I said, the Schoenhausses were Jewish. In fact, according to Walter Schtillermann, they were 'big Jews.' Dr. Kessler interpreted this to mean they were leaders in the Jewish community and probably wealthy. As indeed they were. Incidentally, they were not from the Dresden area at all. They lived in Berlin. Stillman met Frieda through her brother, a classmate of his at Humboldt University in Berlin."

Judge Lloyd held up a hand. "May I interrupt to ask a question, mostly out of curiosity?"

"Uh, surely," Tom replied, momentarily startled that the judge would request his permission to ask a question.

"If our Mr. Stillman studied at Humboldt University, wouldn't that make him more than a bookkeeper? I mean, couldn't a man learn bookkeeping *anywhere?* Why go clear across the country — and to one of the finest universities in the world, from what I recall — just to learn *bookkeeping?*"

"I asked the same question, Your Honor. Walter said Stillman had been an outstanding student in his younger days, his father's pride and joy. He showed an early aptitude for the sciences. His father, at considerable sacrifice to the rest of the family, scraped up the money to send Bergen — that is, Mr.

Stillman — to Berlin to study medicine. It was his father's prayer, according to Walter, that Stillman would be the first physician — in fact, the first university graduate — in the Schtillermann family."

"So what happened?" Maxwell Kane inquired.

"Frieda Schoenhauss is what happened," Tom answered. "Although the Nazis didn't seize power until 1933 and hadn't gotten around to murdering the Jews — " He stopped in mid-sentence and looked guiltily at Leon Schlessinger.

"Quite all right, Tom," said the elderly lawyer. "It *was* murder, and they *were* Jews."

"Well, as I was saying," Tom continued, "even though the Nazis weren't yet in power in 1930, anti-Semitism was rampant. In fact, if I may digress, Dr. Kessler pointed out to me that Hitler wasn't the *cause* of anti-Semitism in Germany; he *reacted* to it, he took advantage of it. To unite the German people behind him, he had to find a cause — something the people could identify with, something popular with the masses. And the cause had to be something that could help create a new national feeling of pride.

"The 'Jewish problem' was ideal. For one thing, by coming out openly against the Jews, Hitler was playing right into the hands of all those who already hated them. For another, the idea of a master race would certainly create pride. What better way to accomplish that than to proclaim that those who didn't meet the genetic standards were inferior, unworthy of living among the rest of the Germans?"

Verne Lloyd cleared his throat. "The university, Mr. Andrews?"

"Yes, Your Honor, excuse me. When Mr. Stillman took up with a young Jewish woman, his father had a fit. As I said, the Jews were already unpopular. Now his son was carrying on with one and saying he planned to marry her. It was more than the old man could bear. It would bring shame and perhaps ostracism to the Schtillermann family. His reaction was to withhold further financial support from his son. He hoped this would bring Stillman to his senses; if it didn't and the marriage took place anyway, at least the father could defend his own honor by saying he'd tried to prevent it. If his son was a recusant, he would be putting as much distance as possible between him and the rest of the family. The marriage did take place, and young Stillman was disowned. His name was never to be spoken in the presence of his father.

"In spite of that, Stillman and his mother

kept in touch. Through her, Walter knew what Stillman was doing from time to time. When family funds were cut off, he dropped out of the university. He wrote his mother that Herr Schoenhauss, Frieda's father, had offered to pay for school but Stillman had refused. His pride wouldn't permit him to accept such a gift. He did, however, accept a job in the Schoenhauss family business."

"As a bookkeeper, I presume," the judge said.

"For starters, but Walter said that over the next few years he was given a more responsible role in the business. They were in jewelry. You know," Tom added as an afterthought, "Herr Schoenhauss must have been an unusual man. Not many Jews in that day and age would have been so understanding of a daughter marrying a non-Jew or as generous toward the husband. Anyway, later in the thirties Hitler began mobilizing for the coming war effort. Stillman was drafted and sent to the Ruhr Valley and later, as I said, assigned to the death camps. Frieda and Hans — their son — stayed with her parents."

"You said earlier you would also tell us the significance of all this," Judge Lloyd said.

"I'm coming to that, Your Honor. At some point Frieda, Hans, and the rest of the

Schoenhauss family were arrested and sent to one of the camps. It appears to have been the same camp where Stillman was working."

"How could you know that?" The question came from Leon Schlessinger.

"Well, I suspected as much when I read this," he pulled out still another sheet of paper from his briefcase. "This is a translation of the undated handwritten letter I mentioned earlier, the one Phil found in Stillman's safe-deposit box. It's signed 'Frieda' and was obviously written at one of the camps. In it she says she was brought there with Hans, her parents, and her brothers. She also writes that one of the guards would take her letter to Stillman. Since the guard knew him and knew where he was, I'd guessed he was at the same camp.

"Then some years later, in 1948, Ben Stillman wrote his mother a letter from the United States. Walter found this letter among her things after she died, and he saved it. When he read it to us, Dr. Kessler persuaded him to make a copy and give it to me." Tom Andrews now extracted the final document from his briefcase. "This, Your Honor, explains much of the Stillman mystery. It's written in German, but I have a translation. May I read from it?"

"Of course."

Dear Mama,

Forgive your son for not writing sooner and for leaving Germany without telling you farewell. I have been in the United States for two years, and I have a job in a good firm that invests money for people.

"I'll skip the next part where he tells her about the United States, his problems with the language, and so on. But the last part is important; I'll read it just as he wrote it."

What made me leave Germany? And why would I come here? Forgive me again, Mama, but I hate Germany for what they did to me and to my Frieda and my little Hans. I had to leave.

I went first to Mexico, a country that was not in the war. It was not enough. I wanted to be in a country — to be part of a country — that was Germany's enemy. That way I, too, would be Germany's enemy.

I escaped from Germany in 1943, soon after I learned that Frieda and Hans had been murdered. How did I know that? Because I was assigned to the same camp. Part of my job was to keep lists of the camp inmates and also the dead. I saw when they were put in the camp: Dachau, one of the worst of them all. Their names were on the list. And my precious Frieda was able to get a letter out to me. Then I saw when they were "eliminated." That was another list. A list which I was required to countersign as an official. I did nothing to try to save them.

But there is something I can do someday. In 1940, when I was on leave and staying with Frieda's family, I had a secret conversation with her father, Herr Schoenhauss. He suspected his fate and his family's fate. He knew that I, as an Aryan, would be safe, and he trusted me because he knew how I loved his daughter and his grandson.

As you know, Mama, he was a rich man. He was a very successful jeweler. He knew by then that it was only a matter of time before he and his family would be arrested. Jews were being arrested and sent away every day. They had waited too long and it was too late to escape. Frieda would not leave without me, and her father would not leave without her.

He knew the Reich would confiscate his jewels. He told me to take his finest, most valuable gems and hide them. He said they would help us get started again when the *madness was over. You see, Mama, even though he knew he and his family would be taken away, not even the wisest Jews could foresee their elimination. Not even* they *thought the Reich could be so terrible.*

When I learned that my Frieda and my Hans were gone forever, I was lost. I had to run away — from the camps, from the other soldiers, from Germany. I escaped with false papers. It was not difficult. My job was to prepare official documents, so I prepared what I needed for safe passage to the Swiss border, put official seals on them, and walked out of Germany. How I got out of Europe is a long story. Later I went to Mexico and finally to America.

I still have Herr Schoenhauss's jewels, except for a few small ones I sold in Switzerland for the money I needed to cross the ocean. I intend to use them to help Jewish people. But how? If I try to sell them or give them away, I will be asked questions. Where did you get them? Did you steal them? The Allies are hunting for German officers who worked in the camps. If I do anything to call attention to myself, I could be arrested. Mama, your son is a coward.

But I will still use these jewels to help the Jewish people somehow. What else can I do?

The letter stunned everyone in the room, but it was the last five words that particularly jolted Philip Ogden. They were the same words his secretary had recalled Ben Stillman's saying to her more than forty years later, through tears, while she was typing his will.

41

Late that afternoon, several hours after Tom Andrews had related the details of Ben Stillman's past, he and Phil met in Phil's office to review where things stood. There was plenty to review.

In the beginning, neither of them had thought he would be in serious opposition to the other. The first will — the one drawn by Phil — was cut-and-dried; no one had thought it *wouldn't* stand up. Consequently, no one had figured that Stillman's heirs — Tom's clients — had any chance at all, even if they could be located. They were, at most, theoretical opponents.

Moreover, the subsequent discovery of the DuPres will and the threats from Al Fiori and Barnett Brothers had made their dispute seem even less significant. To onlookers, it was shaping up as a four-way battle among Maxwell Kane for Barnett Brothers, Fiori for their customers, Leon Schlessinger for Beth Zion Synagogue, and Sarah Jenkins for the DuPres Clinic. Phil and Tom were merely supporting players.

But now everything had changed.

First, the Stillman heirs now appeared to be very much in contention — to Phil and Schlessinger, at least.

Then there had been Al Fiori's call to Phil shortly after lunch. He said he would be filing a formal withdrawal of his class action. If individual class members — customers of Barnett Brothers — wanted to pursue their claims, they would have to do it on their own. "Our case was falling apart even before Andrews told us what happened in Germany," Fiori said. "My expert said he couldn't find evidence of theft; looked to him like Stillman had money all along. Tom's story confirms it."

Less than an hour later Phil had received a call from Maxwell Kane. "I understand Al Fiori phoned you to throw in the towel. He called me, too."

"That was decent of him."

"Probably the first decent thing the prick ever did. Anyway, I'm calling for the same reason."

"But you haven't even filed a claim."

"No, but it's something we had in the back of our minds, depending on how the cards fell."

"And now?"

"And now we're pulling up stakes as far as

this case is concerned. Christ Almighty, with that information Andrews brought back from Germany — the wife, the kid, the death camp, the jewels — shit, we couldn't beat the synagogue if we had eyewitnesses who *saw* Stillman steal the money. Barnett Brothers is going back to selling stocks and bonds. We'll leave the grave digging to others."

"Thanks, Mr. Kane."

"Max. And good luck in your battle with Sarah Jenkins for the executorship."

It was strange, Phil thought as he set down the phone, how lawyers see cases as battles between other lawyers, not battles between their clients.

"You know," Tom said now, fiddling with Phil's letter opener, "if we could convince Jenkins that the DuPres broad can't be executor, then maybe they'd both go away."

"Maybe, but it wouldn't do me any good."

"Why's that?"

"Because even if DuPres can't be the executor, and even if Jenkins isn't her lawyer, I'll still be out in the cold as long as the DuPres will is valid. And it makes no difference that the DuPreses can't inherit. Unless Stillman was tricked or forced into signing the damn thing, it still revokes the first will, and I have no rights to *anything* without the first will."

"So we're back to square one," Tom said.

"You and Schlessinger have to prove that the second will's a phony, and Jenkins and I have to prove it isn't, which would mean my heirs get the money and *she* gets the fees."

"That sums it up."

"Well," Tom said as he stood up to leave, "let's not start fighting till tomorrow. In fact, let's go out to dinner tonight, in memory of our short friendship. I'll buy."

"Sounds good, but I have a date with Maggie. To discuss the case," Phil added with a wink.

"Hey, bring her along. I'd like to introduce you two to some good soul food. Ribs, pork shanks — "

"Gee, I don't — "

"Ham hocks and chitlins, gobs of spicy sauce and gravy, and a side of black-eyed peas. There's a great place in my neighborhood. That is, if you're not afraid to go down there. Whaddya say?"

"Will Maggie be safe with all the brothers around?"

"Asshole. She'll take one look at them dudes and drop you like yesterday's paper. Don't you think she knows about us black guys?" Andrews asked with an exaggerated wink. "I'll pick you both up here at six. Leave your car downtown and I'll bring you back later."

42

"Relax, for Chrissakes! You'd think I was taking you to the Congo."

Tom Andrews looked over at Maggie, who was sharing the front seat of his car, and then to Phil, who was in the rear. "Seriously, damn near as many honkies come to the Railroad Inn as brothers and sisters — at least on weekends. Fact is," he added with a chuckle, "they're ruinin' the joint."

During the drive to the South Side, they agreed that the Stillman case was off limits for the evening. The agreement was breached less than five minutes after they'd made it. "Ironic, isn't it?" Maggie asked of no one in particular. The others thought she was referring to something about Chicago's dazzling nighttime skyline, which came into full view as they turned onto Lake Shore Drive. The Christmas lights on the trees and buildings made it especially beautiful this time of year.

"What's ironic?" Phil asked from the back seat.

"That Stillman spent his whole life thinking

he was a coward. But think of the courage it must have taken for him to forge papers and sneak out of Germany, carrying a fortune in smuggled jewels. Just imagine if he had gotten — "

"Can it, Maggie," Tom interrupted. "We made a deal, remember. Start now and we'll be talking about this damn thing all night."

The Railroad Inn wasn't at all what Phil or Maggie had expected, for which they both felt ashamed. The restaurant — converted from an old railroad depot — was clean, quiet, and comfortable. The unobtrusive music from a four-piece combo moved back and forth between blues and soft jazz. A small dance floor occupied the area in front of the combo, and a long bar ran along the shadows to the rear.

A smiling middle-aged hostess came up to greet them moments after they'd come through the door. "Tommy, honey! How ya doin'?"

"Catherine," Andrews said, giving her a peck on the cheek, "meet some friends of mine."

Introductions were made and then Catherine led the three lawyers off toward a rear corner. "Heard you were coming in, Tommy. Saved a nice, quiet table for you."

505

After drinks were ordered, Tom invited Maggie to dance. "If you had to wait for that clod Ogden, you'd wait all night." They worked their way past the tables and then began to dance slowly to the music.

"You're good," she observed.

"Yeah, we got — "

They both burst out laughing.

"Is all this teasing really all right with you, Tom, or does it bother you just a little?"

"Depends. I like it with pals, like Phil. You too. But if it wasn't someone I felt close to — well, that's a different story."

"Thanks for including me as a pal." They danced for another minute before she spoke again. "Phil's very fond of you, Tom, and he's sick about the way the case is turning out. Not because he doesn't think he — we — can win, but because he can't really bring himself to think of you as the enemy."

"I feel the same way. You know," he added, ignoring their agreement not to discuss the case, "we've actually been opponents all along. As lawyer for the heirs, I'm supposed to contest the will — any will — and we've both known that since the day Lloyd appointed me."

"But that was just judicial protocol," Maggie said. "No one seriously believed the heirs had a chance. It wasn't until we discovered

506

the crazy things that could happen if part of the DuPres will was effective and part wasn't. Now all of a sudden the heirs have a chance, and you've become a bona fide player."

When the music stopped, she looked up. "So you and Phil didn't become genuine opponents until you returned from Germany to learn you'd been promoted out of the chorus line."

They returned to the table where Phil and their drinks were waiting, and where dinner was shortly served.

The conversation thereafter was general, mostly comparing backgrounds, families, law schools, and their first frightening experiences practicing law. But as they were finishing dinner and a large bowl of bare ribs loomed between them, Tom moved the table talk back to the case.

"Funny thing," he said, "but now that I have a client it turns out that he probably wouldn't want me to win."

"Why's that?" Phil asked.

"Well, the more I talked about the possible inheritance, the more uneasy Walter Schtiller-mann seemed to become. 'Please,' he said, 'I do not want publicity. Let the past remain the past.' I got the feeling — and Dr. Kessler did too — that Walter didn't want publicity because he was hiding some dark secret, possibly some kind of war crime, and didn't want to bring attention to himself."

"Does this Walter have any idea how much is at stake? Protecting his ass is one thing, but is it worth eight million dollars?"

"Well, Phil, Walter's a smart cookie. I doubt if he would really want to be the richest guy in the penitentiary. In fact, he was visibly relieved when I told him the chances were slim that he'd actually get anything. Remember, when I was over there I didn't know what the effect of the DuPres will could be, and I had little reason to think that Phil's wouldn't stand up." Tom reflected for a moment or two. "You know, it's not as crazy as it sounds. The guy's a lot like his brother. He lives alone, he has no wife, kids, or siblings, and he's as old as the hills. What does he need it for? And who would he be hurting if he walked away from it?"

Catherine, the hostess, reappeared, pulling a fourth chair over to the table and placing it next to Tom. "How was dinner?" she inquired.

"Delicious," they all agreed.

"How 'bout a round of after-dinner drinks — on the house?" she asked, signaling for a waitress without waiting for an answer. After they ordered, Catherine instructed the server to bring a fourth drink, Kahlua and cream.

Tom's eyebrows rose. "Thought you didn't drink on the job, Catherine."

"It's not for me. There's a friend of mine at the bar who'd like to meet you."

The lawyers' heads turned toward the bar, their eyes settling on a tall, attractive black woman who was closing her purse and rising from the bar stool.

"Hey, all *right!*" said Tom. "Who is she?"

"Here she comes," said Catherine. "I'll introduce you." She stood and offered her chair to the woman. "May I present Alama Dakkar? Alama, meet Maggie Flynn and Philip Ogden, and this is Tom Andrews." They all shook hands as the new member of their party took the empty seat.

As Tom started to make small talk with Alama Dakkar, Maggie nudged Phil with her knee. He looked at her and she winked back. The message was clear: Tom had lucked out with a beautiful — and obviously not bashful — companion for the evening.

Both couples danced while waiting for the after-dinner drinks. Then they talked, laughed, had another round of drinks, and talked and laughed some more. Finally Maggie looked at her wristwatch. "I don't know about you three, but I've got a busy day tomorrow."

"So do I," Phil agreed. "Why don't you

and I leave and — oh, hell, Tom drove. My car is still downtown."

Alama Dakkar spoke up. "No problem. Tom can drive you, and I'll go along for the ride."

Tom Andrews couldn't have been happier. He'd spent the better part of the past hour figuring ways to talk her into leaving with him, and here she was making the suggestion herself.

Fantastic!

PART VIII
THE SIXTH WEEK

43

"I called you in today so we could go over a few things, things we've talked about before and will talk about again."

"Is that necessary?" Willard DuPres asked. "I mean, if we've already gone over it — "

Sarah Jenkins cut him off in mid-sentence. "I know it all seems redundant and even foolish, Dr. DuPres, but it *is* necessary. The more you review the facts, the more your recollections are refreshed — and the more you'll feel comfortable with them. And the more comfortable you are, the better your testimony. You'll be more confident, more credible, and less likely to get tripped up on cross-examination. Trust me. And by the way, Doctor, intelligent witnesses aren't always the best ones; they don't think they have to prepare."

"Not to worry, Sarah." Darlene DuPres's pursed lips and cold eyes betrayed the fact that she and her husband had had words on this very subject since Sarah's call earlier in the day. "It's just that Willard has this *thing* — this aversion to anything about money or lawyers. He'll be okay." She didn't look at him as she gave this assurance. She didn't have to.

"Fine," continued the lawyer. "I'd like to go over the signing and attesting of the will again."

"Wait a second," Willard blurted out. "I'll promise to cooperate, really, but I don't understand what the hell this is all about. We already gave up on the inheritance, which, by the way, is fine with me. So why are we still screwing around with this thing? So what if Darlene *is* the executor? Is that such a big deal?"

"You'd better draw him a picture," Darlene said testily. "Maybe he'll listen to *you.*"

"Executors are well paid. Several hundred thousand dollars would be standard for an estate of this size, even without complications," Sarah explained. "But there are elements in this case that could run the fee a lot higher. The longer an estate is open, the longer the executor controls the assets. That means still higher fees. I wouldn't be surprised if Darlene ends up with maybe two million by the time we're done."

"Okay," Willard DuPres said, "I get the message."

Trying to ignore the sarcasm in his voice, Sarah called for her secretary to refill their coffee mugs, then opened a folder and pulled out some notes — both from their previous meeting and from some legal research she'd been doing. She finally looked up at the doctor. "Now, I'd like to go over the signing of the will again, both by Stillman and by you, Willard."

"What about Alice Doakes?"

"I'll talk to her next." She looked Willard DuPres in the eye. "I assume that you'll be telling me the truth and she'll do the same. So can't I assume that she'll tell me the same thing later that you've been telling me all along?"

Willard DuPres didn't answer.

"All right. Now, in a nutshell, here are the requirements. We have to produce testimony on four points. I'll enumerate them: First, that Stillman signed the will voluntarily, without anyone coercing or unduly influencing him. Next — "

"Sounds like three things," Willard interrupted.

Sarah was getting fed up with him. It wasn't his questions or even his disagreeable attitude. It was his constant reminders that they could lose his cooperation at any time. If that's the case, Sarah thought, we may as well find out now. "Look, Willard," she said, "let's bring this thing to a head once

515

and for all. If you can't truthfully testify to these things, then tell me right now. I've got other things I can be doing."

He didn't answer.

"Yes or no, Willard? Tell me right now. I won't spend another minute on this fucking case until I know I have your cooperation." The strong language was calculated. It was, Sarah had learned over the years, one of the best ways to get a man to listen to her and take her — and her ultimatums — seriously.

"You have it," he answered with a sigh. "I'll say whatever you and Darlene want."

"Uh-uh, Willard. Not good enough. You're not going to testify to what *I* want or what your *wife* wants." She spoke slowly and deliberately. "You are going to testify to the truth, Willard, just as you remember it. The whole truth and nothing but the truth. Right?"

"If you say so."

"Right?" she shouted. Then, changing her course abruptly, she spoke with resignation. "Look, Darlene, it's no use. Let's call it quits." She tossed her notes on the desk.

Darlene DuPres's jaw was pulsating from the grinding of her teeth. Her eyes were fixed on her husband, but he wisely chose not to return her stare. Finally she shifted in her chair and addressed her lawyer: "Sarah, would you mind leaving Willard and me alone for just a few minutes?"

Willard, satisfied that he'd registered his revulsion but knowing that he'd gone as far as he dared, held up his hands. "Hold on. That won't be necessary. I'll behave. Let's get on with it."

Sarah looked at him for a moment, took a deep breath, and resumed speaking. "As I was saying, our testimony has to cover four points: "First, that Stillman signed the will voluntarily, without coercion or the undue influence of anyone else. Second, that he was mentally competent at the time. Third, that he signed in the presence of the two witnesses, you and the nurse. And fourth, that the two witnesses signed in *his* presence and the presence of each other."

Sarah looked up from her notes. "While these four requirements must be met, we have a little leeway. For example, if Stillman was alone when he signed but later *told* you it was his signature, that would be okay. But once we drift away from the strict requirements, we open the door to serious cross-examination. So I'm hoping we can meet them head on."

"That shouldn't be a problem," Willard assured her. "It *was* in August — that's nearly four months ago — but I do recall seeing Mr. Stillman sign the will, and I recall witnessing it in his presence." *God, I hate doing this, but going to jail for perjury couldn't be worse than going home to Darlene if I tell the truth.*

"And," Sarah prodded, "was the nurse there at the time? Did she witness it when you did?"

"Alice and I signed at the same time, yes. I remember that." That much at least was true, the only truth in his entire statement. Willard recapitulated the events for himself. Stillman had signed the will earlier — when alone — along with some other forms Darlene had left for him. Willard and Alice Doakes had done their "witnessing" later in his own office. But what the hell, he rationalized, he just as easily *could* have walked back to where Stillman was to sign it. And Alice surely wouldn't remember. All he'd have to do was remind her that they did it in front of the old man. She'd never remember differently.

Hell, he thought, still trying to ease his conscience, she signed and witnessed hundreds of papers each week, endless mountains of insurance forms, medical records, admission and discharge sheets, disclosure and consent forms, and so on. *I can't remember what I signed yesterday, let alone where I was standing when I signed something last August. And if I can't, Alice can't either.*

518

Sarah asked a few more questions about the signing, mainly to give Willard a chance to get comfortable with the colloquy. But he wasn't comfortable, and he wanted to move into less treacherous waters. "May I ask a question, Sarah?"

"Sure."

"You said earlier that Stillman had to sign the will voluntarily. Is that right?"

"Uh-huh."

"And then you said, as a separate requirement, that he had to be mentally competent. Isn't that the same thing?"

"No, but it's a good question, and you should know about this. A person is mentally competent if he knows generally who is in his family and the nature of his assets. It's a very loose test, actually. A person can be pretty ignorant, in fact, and still have sufficient mental capacity to sign a valid will.

"The other requirement, signing voluntarily, is much different. If you had the awareness and capacity of Albert Einstein, but I held a gun to your head and threatened to pull the trigger if you didn't sign the will I'd just put in front of you, you wouldn't be signing voluntarily. A more common example is where, say, a daughter tells her eighty-year-old father that she'll put him in a nursing home unless he signs a will leaving everything to her. In either case we'd have coercion or duress, and the will wouldn't be worth a damn.

"And then there's something else that could invalidate the will — and that's undue influence."

"What would be an example of that?" the doctor asked.

Sarah thought about it for a moment. "Again, say you're eighty years old and I'm your daughter. If I lie to you and tell you that your other children despise you and say horrible things about you, or that *they* want to throw you into a nursing home and I'm the only one who loves you and is willing to take care of you, and as a result you have your lawyer prepare a will leaving everything to me, it's not worth the paper it's written on. Even though you signed it voluntarily and were perfectly rational, you did it as a direct result of my influence — my *undue* influence — because what I told you wasn't true.

"Actually," she explained, " 'undue influence' is a broad term generally used to include any excessive or unreasonable pressure. It's not limited to outright lies."

"Very interesting," Willard remarked. "But I promise you won't have any problems like that in this case. Mentally Ben Stillman was sound as a dollar — maybe not Albert Einstein but certainly competent. Remember, I'm a doctor who works with older people, and that guy was about as savvy as they come. And as for coercion or undue influence, nobody at my clinic threatened him or lied to him about anything. And he didn't have any mind-impairing medication when he signed." He looked at his wife, who was starting to relax. "Right, Darlene?"

As the meeting broke up and the DuPreses were getting ready to leave, Sarah asked one final question, a question she'd purposely delayed asking until then. "By the way," she said, "there's one other requirement. It's so basic I forgot to mention it."

"What's that?" Darlene asked.

"Mr. Stillman did know, didn't he, that it was his will he was signing?"

44

The formality of legal proceedings varies from case to case and courtroom to courtroom, but it's neither the case nor the courtroom that is the determining factor. It's the presiding judge. Some are insufferably stuffy; others are inexcusably casual. But most, fortunately, are somewhere in the middle and, like Judge Verne Lloyd, are able to oversee the proceedings with dignity and efficiency without stifling the lawyers' ability to present their clients' cases in the most favorable light. The best of them, again like Judge Lloyd, are able to glide back and forth along this continuum, adding a dash of humor here or a pinch of severity there to maintain proper balance in the course of changing moods and tempers.

More than most judges, Verne Lloyd favored holding many court sessions in his chambers. The open courtroom was, of course, preferred for everyday motions and petitions, so they could be handled with dispatch and without needless conversation, or for formal arguments on contested issues, where the more stately setting helps the judge render his or her decisions with the authority they deserve.

But when the purpose of a session was to explore issues and positions, and where prodding and probing could produce ideas or encourage suggestions, Judge Lloyd usually preferred the more inviting ambience of his spacious chambers. Coffee was available, smoking was permitted, and conversation was chattier, even earthy at times. And the sometimes inhibiting presence of courtroom personnel — clerks, bailiffs, and court stenographers — could be dispensed with.

There are three ways in which a court session — a hearing — may come about. The most common is when one of the lawyers wishes to present a request to the court, generally called a motion or petition. The petitioning lawyer sends a notice to the other lawyers in the case telling when he or she will appear and what will be requested from the court. In some instances a court date will be preset, that is, scheduled from a previous session. Finally, the court itself may schedule a session, either through a formal notice or by a call from the judge's secretary, clerk, or bailiff to the attorneys.

On this particular Friday afternoon, in the week following the DuPres Clinic's renunciation of its inheritance and Tom Andrews's report of his European trip, the lawyers remaining in the case were assembled in Judge Lloyd's courtroom for his afternoon call.

"Oyez oyez everyone will please rise this court is now in session the honorable Verne Lloyd presiding." As usual, the instant Rudy Wysocki began droning the words that opened each probate court session, Judge Lloyd, robes flowing, appeared from the door behind his bench.

Like most Friday afternoon calls, this one was short and consisted of uncomplicated matters: the filing of an inventory, a motion to appoint a real estate appraiser, a petition for the approval of attorney's fees. When the rest of the call was completed, the judge looked up to survey the courtroom.

"I see we have the Stillman gang with us again."

Tom Andrews, Philip Ogden, Sarah Jenkins, Leon Schlessinger, and Maggie Flynn approached the bench. Tom spoke first. "Good afternoon, Your Honor. I hate to burden you on a Friday afternoon, but I have an informal request. I could present a formal written motion, but for reasons that will become clear — "

"Should we do this in chambers?" The judge sensed that something sensitive was about to be presented.

"I think that would be a good idea."

"Will you want my reporter?" Lawyers ask for a court stenographer — a court reporter — whenever they want a record of the proceedings that can later be transcribed. This is the case when an important issue is to be argued or decided or a witness is to give testimony. Since a record of the proceedings is generally needed when a later appeal is taken, the request for a court reporter is a veiled threat that the requesting attorney is prepared to take the matter to a higher court. *I'm serious about this,* the lawyer is saying.

"We may, Judge. I'd keep her around."

Judge Lloyd and his stenographer exchanged nods. Then he invited the lawyers into his chambers.

"The cast is dwindling," Verne Lloyd observed as he slipped out of his judicial robes.

Phil reported that Al Fiori and Maxwell Kane had given up any attempt to prove that Stillman had stolen the money.

"That doesn't surprise me, not after hearing about the jewels. By the way, Tom, I presume you have some substantiation to back up Mr. Stillman's brother's story about that."

"Some, but we're getting more. Dr. Kessler, the German lawyer who's been helping me, is getting affidavits. He's now located several people from Berlin who knew the Schoenhauss family and who recall that they were wealthy and dealt in expensive jewelry. As for tying Stillman into their family, I already have a copy of the marriage certificate showing that Bergen Schtillermann married Frieda Schoenhauss; I showed that the last time we were here. And I have proof that Bergen Schtillermann and Ben Stillman were one and the same. Also, Kessler — I spoke with him two days ago — has located people who recall that Stillman worked for his father-in-law and how close he was with the family, especially after the baby was born. It's all fitting together, Judge."

"Looks like it. Just the same, did you give Mr. Kane and Mr. Fiori notice for today?"

"Yes, sir. They haven't officially withdrawn from the case yet, so I let them know I'd be here."

"Well," remarked the judge, "they're not here. Any reason we should wait?" He looked around. "Then go ahead, Tom. What's on your mind?"

Tom Andrews cleared his throat and shifted uncomfortably in his seat. It was the first time in the entire proceeding that he had seemed unsure of himself. And his agitation was apparent to everyone in the room. "Your Honor," he began, "my request today is highly unusual. I wouldn't be making it if I weren't an officer of the court. In fact, I regard myself as a *special* officer of the court in this case." Tom paused before continuing. "I'm not here because someone hired me; I'm here because you appointed me."

"I agree you have an added responsibility to protect me as well as the heirs, but," Judge Lloyd added with a smile, "I hope I don't need it. Now this highly unusual request. What is it?"

"First, I'm asking that Ms. Jenkins and Ms. DuPres reconsider their positions and that they abandon their intent to represent this estate as attorney and executor. Second — "

"Now wait a minute!" Sarah Jenkins was on her feet, and she was loud. "Just what procedure gives you the right — "

"Just *you* wait a minute, Ms. Jenkins," the judge ordered. "Let Mr. Andrews finish. Then we'll hear from you."

"Thank you, Judge. Second," Tom continued, "I'm asking that you appoint Mr. Ogden to serve as executor and attorney for the estate. He's already taken control of the assets, with your permission, and he's off to a good start. Moreover, I'm confident that his fees to do both jobs would be less than would be charged by *two* people." Sarah Jenkins — still on her feet — was livid but remained silent. "But most important, it's now clear that the ultimate beneficiaries of the estate will be either Beth Zion Synagogue or Mr. Stillman's heirs. Mr. Schlessinger represents Beth Zion and I represent the heirs, and both of us would prefer to have the money handled in the meantime by Mr. Ogden, not by Ms. Jenkins and Ms. DuPres."

Phil was dumbstruck. He had had no idea Tom would be doing this. Schlessinger, on the other hand, was coolly nodding his head, showing that Tom had cleared this with him in advance.

"May I *now* be heard, Judge?"

"Yes, ma'am."

Sarah stepped forward and spoke directly to Judge Lloyd. "I don't know what's going on around here or who's been talking to who, but it's clear there's a conspiracy afoot to deny my client, Darlene DuPres, her right to serve as executor of this estate. Forget about me for right now, and let's talk about her. The DuPreses willingly waived their chance to inherit Mr. Stillman's eight million dollars. They did it graciously and without a fight. And now Mr. Andrews uses that gesture as a reason for denying Ms. DuPres the right to be executor.

"May I remind you, Mr. Andrews," she said, shifting her gaze toward Tom, "that it was *Mr. Stillman* who designated her as executor, probably because he saw how well she handled things over at the clinic. Just who are *you* — who are *we* — to deny him that wish?

"As for my being the attorney, that isn't for you to say, either. Or, with all respect, for Judge Lloyd to say. It's up to the executor to hire his or her own attorney. No one, not even a judge, can tell a person who her attorney should be."

Sarah looked back at the judge and lowered her voice. "So, Your Honor, I maintain that Mr. Andrews's request is out of order. And if you believe it is entitled to *any* credence at all, then I'm asking that you bring in your court reporter."

"For what purpose?"

"I want to make a record of this. I want to make a formal objection to the motion — if that's what it is — and I want to object to the manner in which it's being presented. His notice for today didn't say he'd be pulling a stunt like this, so I wasn't given the chance to prepare. I'm sure that wasn't an oversight on his part." She looked once again at Tom. "I'm calling your bluff, Mr. Andrews. Shall we go on the record?

I'm prepared to take this to the appellate court if Judge Lloyd grants your motion. Are you prepared to take it up if he doesn't?"

All eyes shifted to Tom.

"Yes, Ms. Jenkins, I'd like that. I was hoping you'd do the decent thing here, but since you won't — well, there's something I'd like to put on the record, too." He then looked at Judge Lloyd. "May we have a ten-minute break, Your Honor?"

"Good idea. It'll give my reporter a chance to set up — and you two a chance to cool down."

45

The court reporter was setting up her steno-type machine off to the side of Judge Lloyd's desk when the lawyers returned. She had already mounted the machine on the extended legs of the tripod base and was just loading in the thick stack of paper.

Leon Schlessinger watched her with interest. When he began practicing law, court reporters — more men did it in those days, it seemed — worked in shorthand on double column pads. And they invariably used fountain pens, the *real* pens that had to be filled with real ink. He could still remember hearing the scratching of those pens flying across the pads when the proceedings were moving at a fast pace. But those dexterous reporters were inexorably replaced by the more efficient steno-typists who were, in general, even faster.

The presence of a court reporter always added a certain solemnity and caution to the proceedings, Schlessinger reflected. It was a reminder that the words spoken would be recorded, transcribed, and kept forever. No one could later claim, "But that's not what I said."

Judge Lloyd's reporter recorded the official name and number of the case, identified all the lawyers in the room by name, address, and client, and announced that she was ready.

Lloyd spoke first. "Let the record show we are here on the oral motion of Thomas Andrews, guardian ad litem for the unknown heirs. The motion, as I understand it, is to have me appoint Philip Ogden as executor of the estate, with leave to act as his own attorney, regardless of which of the two wills before us is upheld. Is that basically correct, Mr. Andrews?"

"Yes, Your Honor. And even if neither will is upheld."

"Then I'll make another preliminary point or two to clarify the record. A person can be an executor only if he or she is carrying out a will. If there is no will, then the person I appoint is called an administrator. The duties are the same and I make the point, as I say, only to keep the record clear.

"Secondly, I suppose we should know in advance whether Mr. Ogden would accept the appointment if I were to grant the motion. Would you, Mr. Ogden?"

Phil nodded.

"Speak up, Mr. Ogden. My court reporter can't hear you nodding your head."

"Excuse me, Your Honor. Yes, I'd be pleased to act, as either executor or administrator."

"My last point," said the judge, "has to do with procedure. The motion before us is an oral one and was not fully described in the notice Mr. Andrews gave for this hearing. Since this motion would have its greatest impact on Ms. Jenkins and her client, I ask you at this time, Ms. Jenkins, if you'd prefer to have the motion in writing. If so I'll require it, and we can continue this hearing to a later date to give you a chance to study and respond to it."

Sarah would have loved to buy some time to do research and hone her arguments. A ten-minute break was hardly enough. But she'd called Andrews's bluff, and then he'd called *hers*. No, her pride wouldn't let her ask for time now. "That won't be necessary, Your Honor. I'm ready — provided, of course, that if Mr. Andrews or his friends have any more surprises for me, I'd like a chance to reconsider. Would that be okay?"

"Certainly." Judge Lloyd looked around the room and then glanced at his reporter. "Let us proceed."

Sarah Jenkins began speaking. "I would like the record to reflect my objection — my *strenuous* objection — to Mr. Andrews's motion. It seems — "

"Objection!"

"Yes, Mr. Andrews?"

"It's *my* motion, Your Honor. I believe I should have the right to state it, and my reasons for making it, before Ms. Jenkins begins attacking it."

"Fair enough. Do you have a problem with that, Ms. Jenkins?"

"No, sir." Sarah had known all along that Andrews, as the moving party, should be the first to state his position. But experience had taught her that the first person to start talking usually has the advantage. It's easier to take the offensive and to raise those points early that are the most favorable. But Andrews wouldn't let her get away with it and she, having been caught, knew better than to make an issue of it.

"Then *you* may proceed, Mr. Andrews."

"Thank you, Judge." Tom referred briefly to a few notes, then put them away and cleared his throat. "My motion is directed primarily at Darlene DuPres and why I believe she should not be permitted to serve as executor of this estate. I realize my motion seems premature, since the will naming her hasn't yet been approved, but I think it *must* be considered at this time. My reasons for saying this will become clear soon enough."

Every lawsuit has a Magic Moment, a moment when all participants know that something is about to happen. They don't know what, but they know there's *something*. The air becomes electrified. More often than not, the moment just happens. A witness will innocently utter something that no one anticipated but that nevertheless changes everything. But this Magic Moment (and no one doubted that one was in the offing) seemed planned. Tom Andrews, who had seemed so nervous and uncomfortable, was suddenly in command, as if his earlier behavior had been an act calculated to create in Sarah Jenkins a false sense of confidence — to lure her into this unexpected confrontation.

"Even where an executor is designated by a will," Tom continued, "the appointment must still be made by the *court*. Technically, the designation in the will is nothing more than a recommendation to the judge. If the judge doesn't feel the named executor should serve, he won't. Or," and here Tom looked Sarah Jenkins straight in the eye, *"she* won't." He looked back to Judge Lloyd. "I can cite many precedents for this, Your Honor."

"You won't have to, Mr. Andrews. I'm familiar with them. They involve cases where the named executor is unavailable or inexperienced. Have I missed anything?"

"As a matter of fact, Your Honor, you have." Tom paused long enough to be sure everyone was listening to his next sentence. "There is another line of cases holding that an executor will be disapproved — or removed — when he or she has done something that leads the court to believe that his or her moral standards are unacceptable."

Sarah Jenkins, as much as everyone else, felt the presence of the Magic Moment. She was trying as hard as she could to figure out what the hell Andrews was getting at. It was clear it had something to do with Darlene's integrity, but what? Had she ever committed a crime? Had she been charged with fraud? Failure to pay her taxes? *What*, for Chrissake? *What does that son of a bitch know?*

"In such a case," Tom was now saying, "the court should act at the earliest possible moment, which is why I'm here today."

"But," Judge Lloyd said, "what harm could there be in waiting until the will is upheld? We can deal with it then. And if the will isn't approved, well, then we'll never have to concern ourselves with Ms. DuPres's moral standards. In the meantime, she's not handling any of the money; Mr. Ogden — your choice — is."

Tom Andrews would not be deterred. "I can't argue against anything you're saying,

Judge. But there are extenuating circumstances here. The evidence that I intend to offer in support of my motion may not be available at a later time."

Evidence, thought Sarah. *What kind of evidence? What in the hell is going on?*

Judge Lloyd slid his glasses up onto his forehead and gazed out the window. After a few seconds he spun back to look at Tom. "I'll hear you out, Mr. Andrews, mainly because of your representation that your evidence may not be available later. But I'm not promising you a ruling today. For now, let's see what you have."

"Thanks, Judge. Please bear with me for a second." Tom quickly walked over to the door and opened it a few inches. "Okay, Rudy," they could hear him call. He left the door ajar and turned back to face the room. "I have a witness, Judge. It shouldn't take too long."

Witness! Sarah was beside herself. *Who could he —*

Her thoughts were interrupted by the entrance of Rudy Wysocki, who was now holding the door open as Tom's witness entered the room.

For Maggie Flynn, the Magic Moment had arrived. She was sitting next to Phil, and the instant she saw the witness come through the door she gasped, her hand spontaneously reaching out for his. Phil's reaction was slower, but just barely. No one else in the room seemed moved one way or the other.

"Where would you like the witness to sit, Your Honor?"

"There, next to the reporter."

The witness's tall frame slid comfortably into the chair.

"Please swear the witness," the judge said to the reporter.

She moved her machine so that she could rise. "Please stand. Raise your right hand. Do you swear or affirm that the testimony you are about to give in this cause shall be the truth, the whole truth, and nothing but the truth, so help you God?"

"I'll affirm, yes." Such an affirmation has the same legal effect as a sworn oath, but is favored by those who, for their own reasons, prefer not to make an oath to God.

Tom wasn't sure whether to stand or remain seated while questioning the witness. He would certainly stand if they were in a courtroom; most judges would insist on it. But sitting seemed more appropriate in the informality of the chambers. "May I remain seated, Your Honor?"

"Whatever's more comfortable."

"Thank you." He addressed the witness:

"Please state your name."

"Alama Dakkar." The tall woman appeared stately and confident. She was the classic mystery witness, and if she was nervous she didn't show it.

"Where do you live, Miss Dakkar? By the way, it is 'Miss,' isn't it?"

"Yes. I live at 3833 South Pine, with my parents."

"Miss Dakkar, have we ever met — you and I — before today?"

"Yes, we met last week. That was the first time."

"And did I seek you out at that time?"

"No. I sought you out."

"To the best of your knowledge, have you ever met anyone else in this room?"

"Yes."

"Who?"

"Ms. Flynn and Mr. Ogden. I met them the same time I met you."

Sarah Jenkins was on the edge of her chair, knowing only too well that she wasn't going to like whatever it was this witness had to say. The only thing she'd learned so far, and *that* wasn't much, was that the witness had met Ogden, Andrews, and Flynn at the same time. Since she had no idea that Tom and Phil were now close friends or that Phil was dating Maggie, she assumed that the witness had met with the three lawyers in connection with the case.

"Please explain, Miss Dakkar, how it was that you sought me out."

"You were having dinner with Ms. Flynn and Mr. Ogden at the Railroad Inn," the attractive black woman answered, "a restaurant on the South Side. The hostess, Catherine Holmes, is a good friend of mine. She knew you were one of the attorneys in the Stillman case, and she knew I — "

"We'll get to that in a minute," Tom interrupted. "But first, please tell Judge Lloyd how we actually met. I want the record to show that you came forth voluntarily and that *I* didn't approach *you*." He wanted to establish that he hadn't violated the judge's earlier instruction against contacting clinic personnel before Sarah Jenkins had a chance to conduct her own interviews.

"Well, Catherine — Ms. Holmes — called me early that evening and told me you had made a reservation at the inn for dinner. She'd been begging me to talk to you, and she persuaded me to show up at dinner. I did and she arranged the introductions. I joined your table. It was all set up by us, and you had nothing to do with it."

Tom glanced at Judge Lloyd, who nodded his head to indicate that he was satisfied and that Tom should proceed.

"And did we discuss the Stillman case with you? Stated differently, did Ms. Flynn or Mr. Ogden have any idea that you had any interest in this case or that you even knew about it?"

"No, as far as they knew, and as far as *you* knew at that time, I was only joining your table for social reasons."

"That's right, Your Honor," Tom said with a smile. "I honestly thought Ms. Dakkar was smitten with my good looks and couldn't resist coming over to meet me."

Judge Lloyd acknowledged the humor with a smile of his own. "Wishful thinking, Mr. Andrews. But can we move it along? I suspect the witness has more to tell us, and I'd like to hear it."

"Yes, sir," Tom said, becoming serious again. He faced the witness. " 'Alama Dakkar.' That's an unusual name. Tell us about it."

"There's not much to tell. A few years ago I chose to take a Muslim name. It was a sign of a commitment I wanted to make."

"A religious commitment?"

"Religious, cultural, something like that. It's Islamic. I believed that Allah was the sole deity and that Muhammad was His prophet."

"Believed?"

"Well, I'm not so sure now. But I liked

the name and I kept it."

"And do you use it all the time?"

"Except at work. I'm licensed in my given name, so that's the name I use at work."

"And what *is* your given name?"

"Alice Doakes."

The Magic Moment!

46

The Magic Moment! A thunderbolt shot through the room.

"Objection!" Sarah Jenkins was on her feet in a flash, waving a hand toward the witness to keep her from saying another word. "This is an *outrage!* I *demand* that you put an end to this right now, Your Honor. Mr. Andrews and his two friends have somehow managed to get to *my* witness, and they had the temerity to sneak her in here behind my back."

"Your witness, Ms. Jenkins?" Judge Lloyd asked. "It doesn't look that way."

"She's employed by my clients."

"That doesn't make her yours. Have you spoken with her? Have you taken a written statement from her?"

"But, Your Honor — "

"Please sit down, Ms. Jenkins, and permit the witness to finish her testimony. If she tells us something today that's different from what she told you earlier, you can bring it out on cross-examination."

Sarah sat down dejectedly. She had no written statement from Alice Doakes. *Shit!*

She hadn't even interviewed her yet. She'd relied on Willard and Darlene's assurances that she could depend on Alice to corroborate their stories. Now she could do little more than sit back and listen.

Maggie and Phil were still stunned by what they'd heard. Alice Doakes! They'd shared drinks and laughs with Alice Doakes, and they hadn't known it!

Tom Andrews was addressing the witness. "Would you object if I refer to you as Alice Doakes? Alama Dakkar is a beautiful name, but since you witnessed the will as Alice Doakes — incidentally, you *did* witness Mr. Stillman's will, didn't you?"

"I signed my name on it, yes. And it's perfectly all right if you call me Alice Doakes."

"Fine. That will make things easier. And you're employed at the DuPres Oncology Clinic?"

"That's right."

"Now, did you ever have any conversations with Sarah Jenkins — she's the woman sitting over there — about Mr. Stillman's will?" Sarah didn't know it yet, but Tom was doing her a favor by asking that question.

"No. I've never met her."

"How about Dr. DuPres? Did you discuss the will with him?"

"Not really. A few days ago he made a passing comment, something like 'Sorry you're being dragged into this.' He's a very nice man, and I'm sure he regrets — "

"Just answer the questions, Alice," Tom said, holding up his hand. "You can only testify to facts, not opinions. You're not allowed to tell us how you think someone else feels."

"I'm sorry, I didn't know."

"No problem. Now, did you discuss the will with *Mrs*. DuPres — Darlene DuPres?"

"Yes, many times."

"Recently?"

"Uh-huh, yes. Nearly every day since Mr. Stillman died. She seems to be obsessed — excuse me, I guess I can't say that."

"Alice, I want to change the subject slightly. I want to talk about the day you signed the will as a witness. Okay?"

"Okay."

"Did you see Mr. Stillman sign the will?"

"No."

Everyone in the room stirred. After all the preliminary questions, Tom had slipped in the one key question and Alice had given the one-word answer that all but destroyed the DuPres will. Maggie and Phil were on the edge of their chairs. Even Leon Schlessinger was having trouble concealing his emotions.

"Did Mr. Stillman tell you later that he

had signed it and that was his signature?"

"No."

All the lawyers in the room knew that that one-word answer clinched it.

"Then how could you have witnessed his signature?"

Alice Doakes adjusted her position in the chair. "I'm required to sign many papers each day at the clinic. I try to sign them all at one time. Usually I do it in Dr. DuPres's office, where I can smoke and have coffee. On this particular day — it was last August — I recall having a particularly large stack of papers to sign. One of them had three blank spaces for signatures. One was signed by Mr. Stillman, and Dr. DuPres had signed on one of the two blanks marked 'witness.' I signed the other."

"How could you remember the incident so clearly?" Tom asked.

"Well, I probably wouldn't have if nothing else had happened. But later that day Mrs. DuPres made a terrible fuss about Mr. Stillman and the will."

"What kind of fuss?"

"Mr. Stillman discharged himself from the clinic that day. He just got up and walked out. Mrs. DuPres was angry with me for not preventing it. Then later she had a loud argument with Dr. DuPres. I heard her raising cain with him for witnessing Mr. Stillman's will. There was such a commotion about Mr. Stillman and his will that it stands out in my mind."

"Alice, you said Mrs. DuPres was upset about the will. I think you said that she made a terrible fuss and raised cain. Can you describe to us exactly what you saw and heard?"

"Dr. DuPres was with a patient when Mrs. DuPres barged in. Dr. DuPres took her out into the hallway, and she started shouting and cursing at him right there. Then I saw them go into her office, which is next to mine, but she was so loud some of her yelling came through her door anyway."

"Could you be more specific? What did she say, if you recall?"

"She called Dr. DuPres an idiot, and she said he blew the whole thing. Those were her words."

"Did she say anything to you — on that day — about the will?"

"Not *to* me," the witness replied, looking embarrassed, "but I heard her call me a bitch and a dumb shit while she was arguing with her husband."

"Alice, when Mrs. DuPres said that her husband 'blew the whole thing,' did she say what she meant?"

"All I heard was that she said Mr. Stone didn't want anyone at the clinic being a witness."

"Mr. Stone? Do you know who Mr. Stone is?"

"Sure. Eric Stone."

"Do you know him?"

"Yes, I do. He comes around the clinic maybe every week or two, sometimes more."

"To do what?"

"He's the attorney. Mostly he picks up and drops off papers."

"Have you ever seen him at the clinic when he wasn't acting in his professional capacity?"

"Well," and here Alice Doakes seemed embarrassed as she looked down at her folded hands, "I guess I *have* seen him when he wasn't acting very professionally."

Sarah Jenkins knew this type of characterization was not proper testimony, but she elected not to object. She had enough problems without trying to protect Eric Stone. *The asshole deserves whatever he gets.*

"Could you tell us what you mean by that, Alice?"

"Lord! Do I have to?"

Judge Lloyd spoke in a quiet but reassuring voice. "Go ahead, Ms. Doakes. It's all right. Tell us what you know or what you saw,

548

but not what you may have heard from someone else."

"Well, it was the way he and Mrs. DuPres
were always talking to each other when they
didn't think anyone could hear. You know,
lovey-dovey. And I saw them kissing a few
times when the doctor wasn't around. And
they would, you know, touch and feel each
other."

"And how did you see and hear all that?"

"They'd do it in the private office. And
when I'd go in the supply room I couldn't
help but see 'em and hear 'em. The two
rooms are connected with a louvered door.
I wasn't trying to spy or — "

"We know that, Alice," Tom said.

He then stood up and walked over to a
position behind Alice Doakes so he could
see everyone in the room during his next
line of questioning.

"I'd like to ask you a few more questions
about the will, Alice. First, did Mr. Stillman
say anything to you about that will?"

"No, sir. He didn't know anything about
a will."

"Objection!" Sarah Jenkins half-shouted,
already on her feet. "The witness already
said that Mr. Stillman signed the will, so
how could she possibly say now that he didn't
know anything about it? I move the last

answer be stricken from the record."

"May I probe the witness further on this point, Judge?" Andrews asked.

"Go ahead."

"Alice, why do you think Mr. Stillman didn't know he signed a will?"

"Because the signature page wasn't attached to the will until later. When he signed it, it was attached to a medical consent form."

Judge Lloyd was half out of his chair. "Miss Doakes, are you sure — absolutely sure — of this? It's a very serious thing you're telling us."

"Yes, sir. I'm quite sure."

"And how can you be so sure?"

The answer was so simple, so logical, that it was impossible not to believe her.

"Because I looked."

"You looked?" asked the judge. "And can you tell us what you saw?"

"As I said, I probably wouldn't have looked except for all the fuss Mrs. DuPres was making. But then I remembered that when I witnessed that paper earlier in the day, the language on the signature page looked different. I wasn't sure at the time what it was, but there was something unfamiliar about it. So, mostly out of curiosity, I looked to see what it was Mr. Stillman was signing, and I saw that it was an ordinary medical consent form. In fact, I'd prepared it myself that very morning — except that when I prepared it I used a different signature page. I couldn't figure out why it was changed, but I didn't think much of it then, not until later in the day when all the fuss was being made about witnessing a will."

"Go ahead."

"Then, after all the arguing, I went back to Mr. Stillman's file and found the consent form. This time it had the original signature page, the one I'd prepared — but it wasn't signed."

Tom walked over to his briefcase and removed a document, which he showed to Alice Doakes.

"Is this the medical consent form, Alice, the one you've been telling us about?"

She glanced at it. "Yes, sir."

"And you gave it to me the other day?"

"Yes, sir."

"Now, tell us what else you noticed when you looked at it at the end of that day."

"I noticed that the original signature page — the one that wasn't signed — had one staple and an extra set of staple holes in it. See? Right here," she said, pointing to the bottom page.

"Anything else?"

"Yes. The *other* page — the front page —

has two staples in it. See? But no extra holes."

"Which you take to mean what, Alice?"

"That the original signature page was removed before the document was signed, another one was stapled on in its place, then *it* was removed after it was signed, and the original one was replaced."

As Tom handed the consent form to Judge Lloyd for his examination, he looked at his witness. "By the way, Alice, are the medical consent forms always prepared this way, in two pages?"

"No, sir. Usually they're all on one page, signature and all."

"Then why was this one done on two pages?"

"Well, a few days earlier, Mrs. DuPres had told me that any consent forms I did for Mr. Stillman should be double-spaced. She said they would be easier for him to read that way. That meant I would have to go to a second page to make room for the signatures."

"Did you ever tell Mrs. DuPres or her husband what you discovered about the apparent switch of the signature pages on the consent form?"

"Lord, no!"

"All right, Alice, let's return to the past few weeks. Did you have occasion to talk to Mrs. DuPres about the will?"

"Yes, sir."

"And did you tell her that you never saw Stillman sign it? And that he never told you he had signed it?"

"That's right. She asked me about that several times, and each time I told her the same thing, the same thing I just told you. It made her angry."

"Angry?"

"Yes. She keeps insisting that I *saw* Mr. Stillman sign the will. I keep telling her that's not the way it happened, but she won't take no for an answer."

"And how do you know that?"

"Because — well, this is very difficult."

"Go ahead, Alice," Tom said softly. "It's all right. Just go ahead and tell us what happened."

"Well, she told me to lie about it. She said it was only a minor technicality and no one would ever know."

For the second time since the testimony began, Judge Lloyd showed emotion. He was biting his lip and shaking his head.

"Had you given her any reason to think you *would* lie?" Tom asked.

"I don't think so. But last week — it was the day I met you at the Railroad Inn — she really worked on me. She said the clinic turned down Mr. Stillman's money, so it wouldn't make any difference if I lied. They weren't getting the money anyway. But she said it would *still* be better if I said I saw Mr. Stillman sign the will."

"Did she say why?"

"She said it was for my sake. She told me that I could get in big trouble for witnessing the will when I didn't actually see him sign it. She said I broke the law and could be punished." Alice Doakes reached into her purse for a tissue. "She scared me half to death!"

"It's all right now, Alice. You're not in any trouble, and you're doing the right — "

"How was I supposed to know? I knew it was his signature, and I witness signatures like that all day long. I didn't know it was going to end up on a will. How could I tell — "

"Alice, it's *okay*."

Judge Lloyd saw that the witness was close to breaking down. "Do you think we should have a short recess, Mr. Andrews?"

"That won't be necessary, Your Honor. I have no further questions. I would, however, like to make a suggestion."

"Go ahead."

"I suggest that you personally go down to the probate clerk's office as soon as we adjourn. Ask to see the original of the will Ms. Jenkins filed. I think you'll find an extra set of staple holes on the signature page, and they'll match up with one of the staples on this consent form."

Sarah Jenkins had sat quietly throughout the latter part of the interrogation. There were several places where she could have objected, but she knew her case was doomed the moment Alice Doakes said she hadn't seen Stillman sign the will. The other testimony, about someone switching the signature pages and Darlene telling her to lie, was just frosting on Andrews's cake. The same for that business about Darlene and Eric Stone playing grab-ass when Willard wasn't looking. None of this implicated Sarah in any wrongdoing. On the contrary, the witness said she had never even spoken to Sarah. So why should Sarah jump up to protect Darlene? The faster she could disassociate herself from Darlene DuPres, the better.

"Any questions of the witness, Ms. Jenkins?"

"No, Your Honor, I have no questions at this time. But I will have to talk to Mrs. DuPres."

"To ask her about Ms. Doakes's testimony?"

"No, sir. To *tell* her about it. I intend to withdraw from the case."

47

One week later Philip Ogden, Tom Andrews, Leon Schlessinger, and Maggie Flynn were having coffee with Judge Lloyd in his chambers. They had minutes earlier completed the hearing on the first will, the one Phil had drafted, which was approved and admitted to probate.

The day before, Sarah Jenkins had appeared in open court to withdraw the DuPres will. For the record, she'd said there were certain defects in the execution of the document. Judge Lloyd had simply nodded and granted the request. He then leaned forward and spoke softly to her from the bench. "I must advise you, Sarah, that I'm referring this entire matter to the state's attorney's office for a complete investigation — fraud and obstruction of justice, for starters."

"But, Judge Lloyd, I never had a thing to do — "

"Not you, Sarah, your clients. I'm satisfied you did nothing improper — other than believing them." In fact, he suspected that she was less innocent than he let on, but it would be impossible to prove. She was too smart to *tell* her clients to lie or prepare phony stock transfers; they'd figure that out for themselves after she advised them what was needed to win. And the switch of the signature pages had occurred before she was even retained.

"Tell me, Tom," Leon Schlessinger asked, "was it the toughest decision you ever made as a lawyer?"

"Bet your ass." Everyone laughed, including Judge Lloyd. "And I had to worry about the man in the robes over there."

"Why me?"

"If I *didn't* put Alama Dakkar — Alice Doakes — on the stand, and you found out later what happened and that I knew about it, you'd accuse me of covering up a scam. But if I *did* put her on, I ran the risk of you clobbering me for shootin' down my own client. After all, you appointed me to represent the *heirs*. And the second I brought out the evidence that threw out the DuPres will, then the heirs were out too. So I really hurt my own client by doing what I did."

"But you only revealed the truth," Maggie volunteered.

"It's not that easy," the judge said as he refilled his coffee cup. "A lawyer isn't supposed to bring out facts that weaken his client's case." He looked at Tom. "How *did* you resolve it?"

"Well, to begin with, it turned out that there was only one living relative who would stand to inherit, and he didn't even want the money." Tom described Walter Schtillermann's alarm at the prospect of the attention a lawsuit or large inheritance would draw. "He told me and Dr. Kessler, the lawyer in Germany, that he'd sign a formal renunciation of the inheritance. Kessler's drawing it up now, and it should be in my hands in just a few days.

"But remember," Tom added, "Walter couldn't get anything anyway, not after we learned what went on over at the clinic. The DuPres will isn't worth the paper it's written on, so everything goes to Beth Zion under the first will — with or without Walter's renunciation.

"But even if I'd thought Walter wanted it, and could get it, I'd have done the same thing. My heart kept telling me that Ben Stillman wanted that money to benefit the Jewish people, and my nose kept telling me that the DuPres will shouldn't stand in the way."

"Your nose?" asked the judge.

"Yes, sir. Sometimes something smells so bad you just know it's rotten. And when Alama Dakkar told me what had gone on at the clinic, I just knew that bringing it out was the right thing to do. I also checked it out with the chairman of the state bar association's ethics committee. He met with me and polled the other members of the committee by phone. He assured me I would be doing the right thing, especially since I'd been appointed by the court. He said they'd give me a letter after the holidays, but I didn't want to wait for it."

"There's another consideration," Judge Lloyd pointed out. "If you'd thought that Ms. Doakes — Dakkar — would remain firm and stick to the truth, you could have kept quiet. The DuPres will would never have been approved."

"Right," Tom agreed. "But what if Darlene DuPres finally got to her? What if she put more pressure on her? Who knows what the poor girl would have done? She might've chickened out and lied, like DuPres wanted, and then we'd have had a miscarriage of justice. I couldn't take the chance. That's why I told you that day in chambers, Judge, that I wanted to move before I lost my evidence."

Judge Lloyd nodded his understanding and then turned his attention to Leon Schlessinger. "Well, Lee, you must have some very happy clients back at Beth Zion."

"I do indeed, Judge. Now they have to

decide what to do with the money."

"No small chore."

"They'll be doing it very carefully. They're putting together a committee to study alternatives and make recommendations. They did take an informal consensus, however, and I'm proud to say the general feeling is that the congregation should use almost all the money to benefit Jews at large. Once they learned about how Stillman came into his fortune, they decided it would be wrong to use it to renovate the building and pay off the debt. The powers that be tell me they'll use a little to fix up the chapel and name it for Stillman, and then put everything else — not merely the eighty percent Stillman directed — into a trust from which periodic grants will be made to international Jewish causes. They've even decided on a name for it: the Stillman-Schoenhauss Foundation.

"By the way," Lee added, "they'll have Barnett Brothers invest the fund for them. They're giving the account to Ed Hirsch, one of Barnett's bright young men, who's also a member of Beth Zion. I'm sure it'll earn him a partnership in the firm."

Schlessinger rose and walked over to where Maggie was sitting. He put a fatherly hand on her shoulder as he continued speaking to the judge. "You know, Judge, the young

560

people really ran away with this case. Maggie here came up with most of the legal answers that proved to be so important. She's the one who persuaded Sarah Jenkins to file that renunciation and to start doubting her clients. It changed the whole complexion of the case."

Judge Lloyd was reminded once again of how judges, secluded in the courthouse, miss much of the intrigue of a lawsuit. How many cases, he wondered, were won, lost, or changed back in the office library or in bars, restaurants, and country clubs?

Schlessinger turned to face Tom. "And who could not admire the fine work this young man did? If it hadn't been for his decision to go to Germany, and his persistence while there, we'd never have learned of Stillman's background or how he came into the money. And the way he had Alice Doakes come forward — " He stopped in mid-sentence and walked over to shake Andrews's hand. "I'm proud to have worked with you, Tom."

Leon Schlessinger then turned to Phil and extended his hand. "Merry Christmas, counselor," he said. "How does it feel to be executor of an eight-million-dollar estate?"

That night Tom Andrews, Phil Ogden, and Maggie Flynn returned to the Railroad Inn. It seemed a fitting place to celebrate.

Soon after their cocktails were served, Catherine Holmes brought over a Kahlua and cream. "Guess who's coming to dinner?" she asked, sliding another chair over to the table. Alama Dakkar, looking even more beautiful than before, appeared from the shadows to join them. While Tom and Phil registered surprise, Maggie and Alama exchanged knowing smiles.

When the after-dinner drinks were served, it was Phil and Tom's turn to exchange knowing smiles. The drinks were their pre-arranged signal. Holding up his glass, Phil announced, "Well, everyone, here's to the new partnership of Ogden & Andrews."

Tom glared at him in mock anger. "Like hell, you honky bastard. Andrews & Ogden!"

THORNDIKE PRESS hopes you have enjoyed this Large Print book. All our Large Print titles are designed for easy reading, and all our books are made to last. Other Thorndike Large Print books are available at your library, through selected bookstores, or directly from the publisher. For more information about current and upcoming titles, please call or mail your name and address to:

THORNDIKE PRESS
PO Box 159
Thorndike, Maine 04986
800/223-6121
207/948-2962